THE BEST, THE BEA
**READY TO GIVE THEIR HEARTS TO CLAIM THIS
LAND, READY TO RISK THEIR LIVES TO KEEP IT.**

JOHN COOPER BAINES—Bold founder of a vast Texas empire. His new bride promises to give him a second beginning for his dynasty, but an old enemy threatens to rob him of his honor, his fortune, and his future.

DOROTÉA BAINES—Her tempestuous beauty has captured the Hawk's love, but her headstrong determination to fight at his side may claim her life . . . and that of the child she carries.

PORFIRIO RAMOS—A powerful Argentinian whose treachery is surpassed only by his greed. He has stolen another man's land; now he plans to take the Hawk's life . . . and the Hawk's wife.

ANDREW BAINES—Proud inheritor of his father's courage and fighting skill. He faces a danger that will test his manhood.

ADRIANA—The lovely child-woman whose first stirrings of desire belong to the son of the Hawk, but whose hand in marriage belongs to a corrupt and vicious man.

CHRISTOPHE CARRIÈRE—His handsome face disguises a villain's heart. A daring robbery will allow him to steal a silver fortune, and take his revenge on a powerful family that scorned his lowly birth.

A Saga of the Southwest Series
Ask your bookseller for the books you have missed

A Saga of the Southwest
Book VI

Cry
of
the Hawk

Leigh Franklin James

BANTAM BOOKS
TORONTO • NEW YORK • LONDON • SYDNEY • AUCKLAND

CRY OF THE HAWK

*A Bantam Book / published by arrangement with
Book Creations, Inc.*

*Produced by Book Creations, Inc.
Chairman of the Board: Lyle Kenyon Engel.*

Bantam edition / September 1984

ISBN 0-553-24361-6

Published simultaneously in the United States and Canada

Bantam Books are published by Bantam Books, Inc. Its
trademark, consisting of the words ''Bantam Books'' and the
portrayal of a rooster, is Registered in U.S. Patent and Trademark Office and in other countries. Marca Registrada. Bantam Books, Inc., 666 Fifth Avenue, New York, New York
10103.

PRINTED IN THE UNITED STATES OF AMERICA

O   O 9 8 7 6 5 4 3 2 1

*This book is dedicated
to bold and courageous families
whose love and strength
make America great.*

SAGA OF THE SOUTHWEST

Raoul
Maldones
b. 1777

⎯ Carlotta
d. 1821

Andrew
Baines
d. 1807

⎯ Ruth Cooper
Baines
d. 1807

María
b. 1820

Paquita
b. 1816

Adriana
b. 1813

Elsie
b. 1794
d. 1807

Virgi
b. 179
d. 180

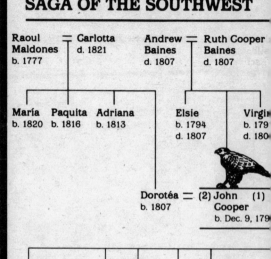

Dorotéa
b. 1807

⎯ (2) John
Cooper
b. Dec. 9, 179

(1)

Andrew
b. December, 1813

Ruth
b. 1818

Coraje
b. December, 182

Charles
b. 1815

Carmen
b. April 29, 1822

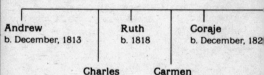

Don Sancho
de Pladero
b. 1758 d. 1825

⎯ Doña
Elena
b. 1767

Tomás
b. 1790

⎯ Conchita
Seragos
b. 1794

Children

FAMILY TREE

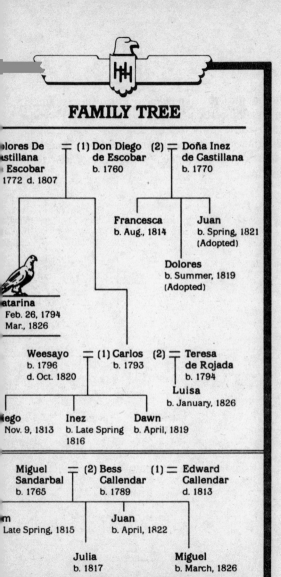

olores De
astillana
a Escobar
1772 d. 1807

= (1) Don Diego
de Escobar
b. 1760

(2) = Doña Inez
de Castillana
b. 1770

Francesca
b. Aug., 1814

Juan
b. Spring, 1821
(Adopted)

Dolores
b. Summer, 1819
(Adopted)

atarina
Feb. 26, 1794
Mar., 1826

Weesayo
b. 1796
d. Oct. 1820

= (1) Carlos
b. 1793

(2) = Teresa
de Rojada
b. 1794

Luisa
b. January, 1826

iego
Nov. 9, 1813

Inez
b. Late Spring
1816

Dawn
b. April, 1819

Miguel
Sandarbal
b. 1765

= (2) Bess
Callendar
b. 1789

(1) = Edward
Callendar
d. 1813

m
Late Spring, 1815

Juan
b. April, 1822

Julia
b. 1817

Miguel
b. March, 1826

The author wishes to acknowledge Lyle Kenyon Engel, Marla Engel, Philip Rich, and Bruce Rosenzweig, whose editorial assistance vastly improved this book. In addition, he wishes to express his gratitude to Fay J. Bergstrom for her tireless work and helpful notes in transcribing the manuscript.

Prologue

There was almost no light in the cell of the *calabozo* in which Raoul Maldones had been incarcerated. There was only a tiny window, almost at the top of a ten-foot plaster wall that was whitewashed, and through the thick bars there would filter the rays of the sun and, paler yet, those of the moon.

He had been seized while breakfasting at his large ranch on the Argentinian *pampas*. Wearing only his *camisa* and trousers and slippers, he had been given no chance to change his clothing or take any with him.

The soldiers, led by a sharp-eyed, thickly mustachioed *capitán* of almost forty, had rudely manacled him, then dragged him out to a waiting *carreta* drawn by two geldings. One of the soldiers had lifted up the gatelike closure at the back of the cart, and two other men with rifle barrels had prodded him to clamber up as best he could—mocking and jeering at his awkwardness and the contortions of his face—while their punitive prods informed him of his disgrace.

For two days and two nights the cart had been drawn on to Buenos Aires, and he had been fed only some maize, brackish water, and, when the *capitán* sought to be compassionate, a few strips of dried beef.

Hardly had he reached the city of Buenos Aires when, still shackled, he had been led before a tribunal in the courthouse, which was next to the *calabozo*. There a white-haired, pompous judge had read the charges against him, brought by the "estimable citizen and patriot, Señor Porfirio Ramos." The charges stated that Raoul Maldones was regarded as a traitor to the provisional government of Argentina and that he had committed crimes against the state, notably allowing his infected cattle to contaminate those of his neighbors—one of them having been Rodrigo Baltenar, the suitor of his lovely daughter Dorotéa, who had instead married John Cooper Baines and was now on her way to the United States with him.

Raoul answered the charges, all lies, as best he could, with growing defiance and anger. But there was no one to defend him, and after the mockery of the trial, which lasted more than an hour, he heard the judge condemn him to life in prison, without hope of remission.

"You may consider yourself fortunate, Maldones," the judge rebuked him, "that your accusers have not asked the fullest penalty for your treason—the garrote or the firing squad, depending on this court's decision. And you may also be thankful that the court in its mercy has allowed your three young daughters to go to live with your friend Heitor Duvaldo, rather than take them into the custody of the state."

And all these long, agonizing weeks in which he could hardly distinguish day from night or calculate time, he had stayed in this cell. Its only furnishings were a wooden stool, a clay pot for necessities—which, at times, the jailer conveniently forgot to remove and cleanse and replace—and a rough cot.

He could only pray that his loyal majordomo, old Fernando, had somehow contrived to get a message to los

Estatos Unidos to his brave *yerno,* because he believed that the man they had called *el Halcón* would come back to Argentina to try to rescue him. It was, indeed, his only hope, and he clung to it.

He had a surly jailer by day and an even more spiteful one at night. The food was execrable, sometimes maize or rice or stale bread and a few badly cooked vegetables. He was not permitted to have a razor, so his beard was long and gray; his face was haggard, and his eyes bloodshot from lack of sleep.

If he dwelled on his miseries, he would be crushed by the enormity of the injustice of what had happened to him. But Raoul Maldones was not characteristically given to self-pity or despondency. He had once spoken with one of his friends who had gloomily predicted that when the *porteño* citizens of Buenos Aires grew in power, they would move against such *hacendados* as the two of them. "Alfonso," Raoul had said, "I know the *porteños* will be our enemies. But once we know about them, we may take steps to strengthen ourselves against their inroads. I cannot live in any other way except positively."

He remembered that conversation now; remembered, too, how Alfonso Bentares had, two years earlier, abandoned the inevitable battle against the wealthy and corrupt government of Buenos Aires and sailed back to Seville.

Raoul's faith in Mother Church strengthened him. He had had in his breeches pocket, the morning of his seizure, a little mother-of-pearl crucifix, which his dead wife had given him on their first wedding anniversary. He was grateful that he had kept it there all that time, for he had meant to put it on the top of his dresser. Because he was imprisoned without communication with any friend or ally, this little crucifix represented to him a power far superior to any that the *porteños* could bring to bear against their enemies. And because he believed in a just and compassionate *Dios,* he resorted constantly to prayer.

"Merciful Señor Dios," he prayed aloud, "hear me, the humblest sinner who kneels before You now and prays for forgiveness for his sins. You know that I am not a traitor to my beloved country. I ask nothing for myself, but do not let my daughters suffer because of what has been done to me. Thank You for giving my eldest such a fine husband, who is taking her to Texas to begin a new life. And thank You for seeing that my three youngest are in the care of my good friend Heitor Duvaldo. If it is Your will that I must end my days here in this cell, at least continue to put out Your mighty hand and look after them."

With this, he crossed himself, and tears fell from his eyes.

He heard footsteps and then the drawing of a bolt. Still kneeling, he turned his head toward the door and saw that the night jailer had opened the partition and thrust in a plate with his supper and a little bowl of brackish water, which was all he was given to quench his thirst. Then the partition was pulled back and the bolt shot into place; the footsteps receded, and he was alone again. It was night now, and the cell was dark, as dark as his hope—and yet, there burned the one vital spark of longing and belief in John Cooper Baines, the one man whose very courage and integrity could take him from this dungeon to freedom.

One

It was not difficult to identify the virile Argentinian *gaucho* Felipe Mintras from among the Texas *vaqueros* surrounding him outside the corral at the *Hacienda del Halcón*—known also as the Double H Ranch. Felipe was tall, nearly as tall as his friend, John Cooper Baines, and at thirty-three was wiry and possessed of enormous vitality. With his high-set cheekbones, sharply aquiline nose, enormous mustache, and skin bronzed by the Argentinian *pampas*—where he had lived before coming to Texas—Felipe stood out from the crowd of men watching him whirl his *bola*—two stone balls attached to rawhide ropes.

Ever since arriving at the Double H Ranch, Felipe had been the center of attention among the *vaqueros* and *trabajadores* alike. He had met John Cooper Baines earlier in the year when the latter had traveled to Argentina to sell cattle and horses to Felipe's employer, Raoul Maldones, a wealthy rancher. After the tragic loss of his beloved first wife, Catarina—who had been killed by a madman bent on revenge—John Cooper had gradually fallen in love with Raoul Maldones's daughter Dorotéa, and they had married. When John Cooper and his young bride returned to the

United States to his own ranch in Texas, he had asked Felipe and his family to accompany him.

Felipe chuckled as he noticed a cackling chicken come quickly out of the hen house, cocking its head this way and that, in search of new provender. "Perhaps you would like a chicken for supper, *amigos*," the tall *gaucho* exclaimed. "Observe this!" He took a few paces forward, whirled his *bola*, which was a smaller version of the ones he had used on the *pampas*, and then sent it whistling through the air. The stones had wrapped around the chicken's legs and body, rendering the bird immobile.

"Take this to Tía Margarita and Rosa Lorcas with my compliments, *amigos*," Felipe said as he doffed his *sombrero* and made a low bow in the direction of the kitchen of the *hacienda*. "Tell them that my beloved wife, Luz, and I have dined like royalty at their table, and this is a small token of our regard for them!"

"Felipe, there's better sport for you to practice your *bola* on than that innocent chicken," John Cooper called as he approached the corral.

The *gaucho* whirled, saw his tall, bearded friend, and slapped his *sombrero* against his thigh as he hurried up to the Texas rancher. "*¿Qué pasa, mi compadre?*" he eagerly demanded. "You speak of sport, and you know that this is a word dear to the heart of every *gaucho*. Lead me to it, and I will be your man!"

But John Cooper's handsome face had sobered, and Felipe Mintras's smile vanished at once. "I see. It is something more serious, then, *¿no es verdad?*"

John Cooper nodded. He held out a letter written by the loyal majordomo of Raoul Maldones. "This is from Fernando. It came just before Dorotéa and I returned from our recent visit to the settlement on the Brazos, Felipe."

Felipe glanced quickly back at the *vaqueros*, Miguel, then murmured, "I can read only a little. Luz has always promised to teach me how to read and write properly, but I confess I am *estúpido* in such things. Tell me what it says, *amigo!*"

Quickly, John Cooper explained the contents of the majordomo's devastating letter: The greedy Porfirio Ramos, a rival *hacendado* in league with the powerful *políticos* in Buenos Aires, had arranged for Dorotéa's father to be unjustly arrested and incarcerated in a prison in Buenos Aires. He had taken over Raoul Maldones's lands and now lived in the very *hacienda* where Dorotéa had been born. Fernando and some of the other faithful Maldones servants had taken flight and were living in the *jacales* of the loyal *gauchos*. John Cooper now read aloud:

> "Señor Baines, if it is at all possible, can you help my master? The other *hacendados* did nothing, in spite of their protests of loyalty to him. Even his old friend Heitor Duvaldo was unable to help, though he is looking after my master's daughters."

When John Cooper finished reading it, he stared fixedly at the *gaucho*, who uttered a furious oath. "*¡Por los cojones del diablo!* I knew I should have killed that stunted offspring of a llama, Porfirio Ramos! He has done this to my *patrón*—he will pay for it!"

"I had hoped you would say that, Felipe. Dorotéa and I must leave for Argentina to see what we can do to help her father. We will need you, *amigo*. You can rally the *gauchos*. It will be a most difficult undertaking—riding into Buenos Aires and taking Raoul Maldones out of that wretched prison into which they have cast him."

"Do you have so little faith in the *gaucho, amigo?*" Felipe bantered, clapping John Cooper on the shoulder. "Look you, the greater the difficulty, the greater the joy in overcoming it—that is the motto by which we live in the *pampas*. And those *porteños*"—here, his lips curled scornfully and his tone dripped with sarcasm—"who think that they are better than we are, it is high time they learned that it would take a hundred of them to equal the brains and the courage of a single *gaucho!* Of course I will go with you, *mi amigo!*"

"Thank you, Felipe."

"And I will leave Luz and my sons here; I know they will be well cared for."

"We will leave at once," John Cooper told him as they walked back to the *hacienda.*

"El Señor Dios is always on the side of the just, *amigo,"* Felipe responded. "I've no doubt that all the *gauchos* have gone back into the thick grass of the *pampas* so that this *cobarde* of a Ramos will not find them. They will know how to outwit him. When we arrive, I know I shall be able to round up at least ten *gauchos* and lead them into Buenos Aires itself in broad daylight, if need be! I have sworn an oath to my *patrón,* the señor Maldones, and if I must die fulfilling it, so be it!"

"There's no need to talk of dying, Felipe. We shall take them by surprise. They won't expect so bold an action. Besides, we will take with us four of our most trusted and courageous *vaqueros,* and they will have plenty of guns and ammunition." He smiled grimly at the *gaucho.* "And some *dinero,* as well—perhaps some of the jailers will be corruptible."

"Now there you speak as if you were born to the *pampas.* It is well known that the hirelings of those lordly *porteños* want *dinero* and *putas,* and the one will buy the other. Yes, by all means, this *dinero* may be as important as the weapons you take with you, Señor Baines," Felipe answered. "And now, *con su permiso,* I'll go tell Luz. We shall take leave of each other very tenderly, of that you may be certain. Indeed"—here he winked at the blond rancher—"it's not a bad idea for a *gaucho* to depart from his family because when he returns, he is the more appreciated.''

"Thank you for your readiness to help," John Cooper solemnly responded. "I owe this to Dorotéa, and I owe it also to your *patrón*."

That evening at supper, at which Tía Margarita and her assistant Rosa Lorcas served, among other dishes, the chicken that Felipe Mintras had so thoughtfully provided, John Cooper revealed his final plans to Don Diego and Doña Inez. He and Dorotéa had discussed the situation as soon as Fernando's letter had arrived, and the lovely young bride was determined to accompany her *esposo* on the rescue mission. Because of her exceptional courage and loyalty to her father and concern for the safety of her three young sisters, John Cooper had no choice but to allow Dorotéa to go along.

Don Diego de Escobar, still frail and weak from the shock of his daughter Catarina's murder, was horrified at the news. "Do you mean that you must go right back to Argentina, *mi yerno?* You have only just come back from there with this beautiful young woman who graces our household, and now you propose to make such a long trip and expose your lovely bride to unknown dangers?''

"Come now, Diego," Doña Inez gently remonstrated, "we must admire John Cooper and Dorotéa for their loyalty to her father. Besides, I have an idea that will make the time of their absence pass quickly."

"And what is that, my dove?" The white-haired former *intendente* of Taos in New Mexico turned to his mature, handsome wife, with an expectant look on his face.

"Why, I have wanted to go to New Orleans for some little time now, and you can escort me. There are such lovely shops and fine restaurants—not that Tía Margarita does not feed us gloriously—but all the same we shall appreciate her cooking the more when we have a change of menu, don't you think?''

"Hm, yes." Don Diego thoughtfully pulled at his white goatee, then nodded. "It is an excellent idea—I am in need of a little vacation after all that has happened. And I want to buy you a lovely present, my beloved Inez. By all means, *mi yerno*, if you have no objection, Doña Inez and I could travel with you as far as New Orleans and see you off in style."

"I'd be proud to have you both," Don Diego's son-in-law by Catarina answered, then turned to his brother-in-law, Carlos de Escobar, who was seated at the table next to his lovely Spanish wife, Teresa. "I'd ask you to go with me to Argentina, Carlos," John Cooper said, "but I know you want to stay here at the ranch with your Teresa."

"That is so, John Cooper," the tall, black-haired son of Don Diego replied as he clutched his wife's hand in both of his. "I want to be with Teresa when she has our child early next year. But I will be with you in Argentina in spirit, *mi cuñado*."

Andrew Baines, John Cooper's eldest son, had been frowning throughout this exchange. "What about me, Pa?" Andrew was nearly thirteen years old, a sturdy young man, eager to prove his courage to his father.

"You'll stay home here and mind your p's and q's, Andrew," was the brusque answer.

"Oh, pshaw, Pa, that's not fair!" the youth protested.

"There's no need for you to come," his father declared. "There's dangerous work ahead. I've already told you that Raoul Maldones has been thrown into prison through the treacherous efforts of Porfirio Ramos, who covets his land and has taken it over now. We have to get Raoul out of Buenos Aires, and that's going to take a heap of doing. There's no place for an untried youth—begging your pardon, Andrew. This mission demands skillful and cunning men, and although you're a son I'm proud of, it's too dangerous a task for you. Don't take offense—I'm not trying to hurt your feelings—but that's the simple truth."

Andrew sulked through the rest of his meal. John Cooper eyed him from time to time, then shrugged at Dorotéa. She nodded sympathetically and tried to cheer her stepson.

"We'll be back soon, I promise you, dear Andrew," the lovely, dark-haired young woman said. "With Felipe Mintras and the *gauchos* behind us, we can't fail."

Andrew responded politely to his new stepmother, but his heart was obviously not in it.

Miguel Sandarbal, *capataz* of the Double H Ranch, had been invited to dine with the family this evening, and John Cooper now turned to him. "Tomorrow morning, Miguel, choose four *vaqueros*. I know our men are reliable and courageous and can follow directions and show enough imagination to do what has to be done when they accompany us to Argentina."

"You can rely on them, *patrón!* May I consider myself as a candidate?"

"No, Miguel, and again I don't mean to offend you any more than I did Andrew. But you're the *capataz* here, and there's plenty of work for you to do on the ranch. We owe my factor a thousand head of cattle by November, at a good price, and we'll need that money to pay for our trip. Besides, with your lovely wife, Bess, and the new child, you'd best be close by to keep her happy."

Miguel sighed heavily and shrugged. "Very well, then. But I'll be with you in spirit, and maybe one day out on the *pampas,* you'll wish that I was along to have that traitorous dog of a Ramos in the sights of my rifle."

"When it comes to that, it's I who must avenge the wrong done to Dorotéa and her father. As her husband, I consider it my duty, Miguel. But now, let's have some wine and propose a toast." John Cooper raised his glass. "To a successful venture and freedom for Raoul Maldones!"

"And happiness to all of us when it's over!"
added Carlos.

Old Stancia, who had been Dorotéa Maldones's nurse
almost since her birth, knelt in the little chapel of the
Hacienda del Halcón. Her wrinkled cheeks were wet with
tears as she clasped her hands and fervently prayed to the
Holy Mother that her young charge, now the beloved
esposa of the *gringo* known as *el Halcón,* would return
safely from Argentina.

When Dorotéa had asked old Stancia to accompany
her and John Cooper to Texas, the nurse had been secretly
overjoyed. She regarded Dorotéa as the most beautiful and
intelligent of Raoul Maldones's four daughters. He had,
with the help of the *dueña* Señora Josefa, reared his daughters without the guidance of a mother. Old Stancia herself
had tried to undertake that role of surrogate mother, and
happily, she felt she had succeeded.

Yet the constant political machinations and never-ending
threat against the Maldones family from Porfirio Ramos
prompted Stancia to pray that she might end her years in
comfort and peace beside the girl whom she had watched
grow from a child into a beautiful and intrepid young bride.

Thus, although Señora Josefa had been horrified at
the idea of Dorotéa's marrying a *gringo* from such a
faraway land, old Stancia had rejoiced. On the occasions
when she had spoken with John Cooper, she had found the
tall blond Texan—and his son Andrew—most congenial
and considerate. She had no doubt that John Cooper truly
and dearly loved her Dorotéa. But now, to have to go back
to rescue the Señor Maldones from the dreadful jail in
Buenos Aires—there would be great dangers. Also, she
knew that Dorotéa was with child. And so she prayed,
rocking back and forth on her knees, weeping softly, as
she implored *el Señor Dios* to intervene for the two of
them and for the unborn child of her darling charge. . . .

Two

Early the following morning, Miguel Sandarbal summoned the *vaqueros* in front of the bunkhouse and said, "I ask now for volunteers to accompany Señor Baines and his lovely young *esposa* back to Argentina on their rescue mission. The Señor Baines, his wife, and the *gaucho* Felipe Mintras plan to journey there at once."

Even before he had finished speaking, there were eager shouts of, "I volunteer, *capataz!*" and "Choose me, Señor Sandarbal!" But the four *vaqueros* who had gone with John Cooper and Andrew on their first trip to Argentina—the one in which the tall Texan had delivered livestock to Raoul Maldones and fallen in love with the beautiful young Dorotéa—crowded forward. Pedro Martínez, who acted as their spokesman, indignantly declared, "You can make no other choice, *señor capataz*, than me, Jaime Portola, Bartoloméo Mendoza, and Enrique Saltanda, for you well know that the four of us accompanied the *patrón*, and we acquitted ourselves ably."

"Yes, that is true," Miguel nodded. "But do you not think that others should have the chance to make the long voyage and see the sights of the *pampas?*"

"Then at least two of us should go, *señor capataz*,"

Pedro Martínez at once responded. "Let straws be drawn, and let the two of the other *vaqueros* who pick short ones accompany two of us. The four of us will decide among ourselves who will go with the two that you select that way."

Miguel considered this to be an excellent solution and directed Bernardo—the tall, young son of Esteban Morales, assistant foreman of the ranch—to prepare the straws from the dry reeds by the Frio River.

"At once, *señor capataz!*" Bernardo brightened, for, at sixteen years old, he was anxious to prove his mettle and was very proud that his father had been named the assistant *capataz*. Someday he would like to be *capataz* himself, though, in truth, he and his parents had also discussed the possibility of Bernardo's entering the ministry, for he was a very bright young man and excelled in his studies at the ranch's school.

In about a quarter of an hour, Bernardo returned with his fistful of reeds from the riverbank and handed them to Miguel Sandarbal. Meanwhile, the four men who had accompanied John Cooper on the first trip to Argentina held a consultation among themselves to decide which two of them would be privileged to accompany the *patrón*. "There is certain to be trouble and much danger," Pedro Martínez said. "So certainly I should be one of the two from among us to go because I can best help the *patrón* when it comes to fighting."

"No, no. We must do what the other *vaqueros* are doing and choose by lots," Jaime Portola loudly declared.

"I have it!" Enrique Saltanda said. "We will test our skill with the *cuchillo*. Here is how: All four of us will throw our knives at a difficult target, and the two men whose throws are closest to the mark shall accompany the señor Baines and his beautiful *esposa*."

"That is an excellent idea," Bartoloméo Mendoza said, nodding his head.

"So be it," Pedro boastfully agreed. "It, of course, means that I shall be one of the two selected. Now get your knives ready and prepare to make the best throw of your lives. Even so, your throws will not best mine."

"We shall see, Pedro. We shall see," Enrique replied. "I will prepare the target. Skill alone will decide who shall accompany *el Halcón.*"

So saying, the tall, heavily mustachioed *vaquero* strode off toward the shed in which Yankee, John Cooper's trained wolf-dog, slept overnight. With a piece of charcoal, the *vaquero* drew concentric circles in the middle of the door, creating a target. At the very center, he made a tiny black circle and filled it in, and then, satisfied with his handiwork, returned to his companions. "Each of us will throw two times from a distance of one hundred feet," he declared. "The two who are closest to that bull's-eye will be those who shall accompany our esteemed *patrón.*"

"I have no objection," Pedro arrogantly declared as he drew his hunting knife from its sheath on his thick, black leather belt, balanced it in his right hand, and made wide sweeps and lunges with it to get the proper heft and feel in preparation for the throw.

Enrique had taken thirty-three paces back to his companions and now stooped to draw a line with the bone handle of his knife. "Let us see your skill first, Pedro, *mi amigo.* One who boasts so much should surely be ready to set a good example!"

"*Seguramente, mi amigo,*" Pedro agreed, smirking. Stationing himself just behind the line, he poised the sharp knife between right thumb and forefinger, his eyes narrowing as he considered the target, then drew back and sent the knife flying toward the shed door. It stuck about four inches to the left and below the bull's-eye, and Enrique jested, "That will do as a try, but it will surely not bring you passage aboard the vessel for Argentina, *mi compañero.*"

"To the devil with your remarks, Enrique! I know that I am the best. And I still have one throw left. Remember that!" Pedro boasted.

"It will be as *el Señor Dios* decides," Bartoloméo said as he came forward.

He took a long time to judge his target and balance the knife in his hand. Then he drew back a step and flung it out, and a simultaneous cheer from Jaime and Enrique greeted his success, for his knife stuck quivering in the very heart of the bull's-eye.

"Your turn, Enrique," Bartoloméo said, turning to his friend. "Either you or Jaime would be a pleasant *compañero* on this voyage."

"It is not yet over." Pedro was glowering.

Enrique's toss was perhaps an inch better than Pedro's first, and Jaime's throw struck the bull's-eye about a quarter of an inch below Bartoloméo's throw.

All eyes turned to Pedro. Because of his boasting and poor throw, much depended upon this toss. But just as he was about to throw, a pretty, seventeen-year-old *criada* came out of the kitchen toward the bunkhouse, carrying a bowl of stew, which Tía Margarita had prepared for the men. She was petite but possessed of ripe breasts and haunches, with a warm olive complexion. Her legs were bare to midcalf, her skirt swirling about her pretty legs, and she wore *zapatillas*, which made a soft smacking sound as she walked.

"*¡Caramba!*" Pedro breathed, then flung his knife, which struck the target a quarter of an inch outside the last circular line and to the left. "It does not count, this *muchacha* distracted me, *amigos!*" he shouted.

"No, we will not accept that as an excuse. It was a fair trial," Bartoloméo said, and was supported in this by his two companions.

Thus Pedro was eliminated from the contest. But seeing that the lovely *criada* was still looking at him with widened, dark, soft brown eyes, he shrugged. He had had his eye on this young newcomer to the Double H Ranch for some time now, and her show of interest in him did much to ease his distress over his poor performance in the knife-throwing contest. *"Bueno, mis compañeros.* While you are fighting in Argentina, I shall be here with this so charming *mujer linda."* Pedro strode forward, retrieved his knife, thrust it back into its sheath, and very gallantly, doffing his sombrero, said to the young *criada, "Por favor,* that bowl is much too heavy for you, *mi linda.* Allow me to carry it."

"But, señor, I do this work every day," the girl protested.

"No longer. Henceforth, I shall be your protector. Come, give it to me. I will take it to the bunkhouse."

His three friends burst out laughing and nudged one another. "At least Pedro will have some compensation," Enrique chuckled. "So now, Bartoloméo and Jaime, you have won fairly. I will not take my second throw, for I feel that *el Señor Dios* has already chosen the two of you. But I will be with you in spirit, *mis amigos."*

Meanwhile, Miguel Sandarbal had asked Bernardo Morales to hold out the fistful of straws and ordered each of the *trabajadores* to come by, one by one, and draw. When all forty of the men had taken their straws, he called, "Now then, those two of you who have the short straws, come forward!"

Two men stepped forward, grinning at each other, hugely pleased at having won the opportunity to go on an adventure about which one day they might regale their children. "Well now, it's you, Paco Rivera, and you, Sancho Vinaldo!" Miguel exclaimed. "You may both stop congratulating yourselves and begin the preparations to leave this afternoon. There is a wagon to be packed, supplies and weapons to be taken along. Also, you are to choose sturdy horses. You embark upon a hard life, *mis compañeros.*"

Paco Rivera, a jovial, swarthy, black-bearded man in his early thirties, smilingly retorted, "But when we return, all the lovely *criadas* will look on us as heroes, and the rewards will be great!"

"A plague on your rewards!" the white-haired *capataz* testily answered. "You volunteered because you are brave men and because it is an honor to stand side by side with *el Halcón.*"

"Of course, *señor capataz.* I was only joking," Paco chuckled.

"Then do not stand here wasting my time. Isn't there enough work to be done? Go back to your tasks!" Miguel fiercely gestured at the crowd about him. "I tell you, if it were not that the *patrón* himself bade me stay home, I should be one of the first to go to Argentina! And do not think that I would not give a good accounting of myself!"

Miguel Sandarbal assigned four *trabajadores* to polish Don Diego's carriage and to make certain that the harness poles and wheels were in good working order. Two strong horses would be attached to the carriage to draw Don Diego and his Doña Inez on the journey to New Orleans, where they would have a much-needed vacation. John Cooper approved of this plan, for he knew that his father-in-law had been grievously saddened by Catarina's death and, since that time, had declined in vitality and health.

After losing the knife-throwing contest to Bartoloméo Mendoza and Jaime Portola, Enrique Saltanda went to Miguel and urged him to let him drive Don Diego's carriage to New Orleans. The *capataz* shrugged and agreed, "*Bueno.* You're a good man, Enrique, and I can't deny you that privilege because someone here on the ranch will have to do that job. But mind you, you're to bring Don

Diego and Doña Inez home safely. I know you bachelors, and if Don Diego tells me that you have disgraced yourself with *mujeres* and *tequila*, heaven help you."

"But, *señor capataz*," Enrique said, a look of genuine dismay on his heavily mustachioed face, "you know I'm not a rascal like that Pedro Martínez. I will take good care of Don Diego and his lady, never fear."

"Just see you remember that," Miguel sternly told him.

At this very moment, Felipe Mintras was saying goodbye to his wife, Luz, and his sons, Guillermo, who was five, and Pablo, who was scarcely four. He squatted down and took both black-haired little boys in his arms and scowled fiercely at them as he said, "And now, *mis hijos*, you will look after your mother, and you will be good, and you'll not cry for me. *Gauchos* do not cry, and you will both be *gauchos*."

Guillermo, who had already learned to speak a few words of English, eagerly nodded and declared, "It is Mama who will cry."

"*Por Dios*, it is expected that a *mujer* will cry now and again—though your mother is a strong, proud woman, the wife of a *gaucho*, and she cries only for good reason. See that neither of you gives her such a reason, or when I return, you will hear from me on the matter."

The two little boys both nodded and hugged him. His face softened. "I will bring you back something from the homeland that we knew. But for now, this is your home, yours and your mother's."

His sons nodded and hugged him again, and then Felipe turned to Luz and took her into his arms. "*Querida*," he murmured into her ear, "say a prayer and light a candle for me on a dark night if there is a storm. Its light will reach me, for you are my light. And I shall bring you a special present when I have brought my old *patrón*, Señor

Maldones, out of that damnable jail in Buenos Aires and shown those accursed *porteños* a thing or two.''

Yankee, the get of a timber wolf and an Irish wolfhound, whom John Cooper had raised and trained, sensed that his master was going away and followed him everywhere. When the blond rancher went out to the Frio River to visit the grave site of his first wife, Catarina, Yankee sat by silently as John Cooper knelt and prayed. Then when the young Texan solemnly crossed himself and rose, heading back to the *hacienda,* Yankee let out a bark, as if to say, ''I know you feel sad, but remember I'm here with you!''

Yankee was also present as John Cooper paid his farewells to Carlos and Teresa, then gave Miguel Sandarbal final instructions about managing the ranch, reminding him of the message from Jim Bowie that had come the previous evening, saying that he and some of his Texas Rangers were going to pay a visit to the Double H Ranch to see about acquiring additional manpower for the Rangers.

Finally, Yankee sat quietly by his master's side as the latter met in the dining room with his children by Catarina— Andrew, Charles, Ruth, Carmen, and little Coraje—and explained in simple terms where he was going and why. Then when John Cooper said he wanted to speak with the older boys privately, the wolf-dog dutifully went off with the younger children, who would be his special charges while their father was away.

Alone with Andrew and Charles now, John Cooper said, ''Boys, Dorotéa and I want you to look after your little brother, Coraje, and your sisters. Bess Sandarbal is going to take care of Coraje while we're away. With any luck, we should be back in six months. In the meantime there'll be plenty for both of you to do. I've told Miguel I want you to get acquainted with the stock, to work with the horses, the cattle, and the sheep. You're my heirs and the ones who will someday share in the inheritance of the Double H Ranch. You're both smart as a whip, practically men. Rely on Miguel to round out the education you'll need to become *patrones* yourselves. It won't do any harm if both of you get a little more book learning. If it hadn't been that my mother had given me plenty of it when I was growing up, I don't think I'd be here today. Well, that's the long and the short of it.''

"You're sure you don't want me to go along with you, Pa?'' Andrew plaintively asked.

The Texan shook his head. "Don't plague me, Andrew. Forget it for once and for all, shake hands with me, and promise that you'll work with Miguel.''

"All right, Pa,'' Andrew slowly said as he held out his hand. John Cooper did not see that his eldest son was crossing the index and median fingers of his left hand behind his back because of the white lie he was telling. "I'll do what you want, Pa,'' Andrew added.

"Good boy!'' John Cooper shook his son's hand heartily, then clapped him on the back. "Well now, I've got to make sure the *vaqueros* have finished all our preparations.''·

"Good-bye, Pa,'' Charles said. He glanced at his older brother. "We'll study, and we'll learn all we can. The time will go fast that way.''

"That's right. I'll be proud of you. I always am.'' John Cooper Baines quickly turned away, deeply moved.

Andrew's face was taut with concentration, for he knew how little time there was left before his father, Dorotéa, and the others would begin the journey to New Orleans, from which the ship would take them to Buenos Aires.

He had never before lied to his father, but this was different. After he had heard that Dorotéa's sisters had found refuge with Heitor Duvaldo, he had been able to think of only one thing: Adriana Maldones was practically an orphan now. He knew that he was in love with her, and he thought that she had already shown him that she liked him very much. They had practically promised to meet again; they had pledged themselves to each other. Well then, this was his fight, too, not only Pa's. If ever he was to marry Adriana—and he knew even now, young as he was, that he wanted to very much—then it was up to him to help her father get free so that she and her sisters could go back to the house in which they had been born.

But how? He would have to hide in the supply wagon or the carriage. And it would have to be done very quickly.

His mind at once made up, he took his rifle and buckled on his knife sheath and cautiously made his way toward the stable. The carriage had been placed just outside the broad door.

He knew that the carriage maker in Taos had made a luggage compartment at the back of the vehicle, which projected out just over the rear wheels. Andrew's heart began to beat faster as he thought of hiding in that compartment. Yes, it would be much safer than hiding in the supply wagon. As Andrew edged carefully around the side of the stable, he saw that only Antonio Lorcas was there, stroking the horses that would be pulling the carriage and talking to them, feeding them lumps of sugar. He took a deep breath, and then stepped out and moved toward the *vaquero*. *"Por favor,* Antonio," he murmured.

The *vaquero* turned, his eyes widening, and then a smile of recognition crossed his pleasant face. "Señor Andrew, it is good to see you—"

"Shh, Antonio, I want to ask a very special favor of you. It means so much to me. I beg of you to do something for me."

"But of course, Señor Andrew, if I can." The *vaquero* was hesitant.

"I want to go with my father back to Argentina, but

Pa doesn't want me to go. But I must—you see, the fact is, I fell in love with Pa's wife's sister Adriana. I want to save her. Please help me—''

"But what am I to do, Señor Andrew? I cannot go against your father's will—'' the *vaquero* began.

"I know, I know. But you didn't hear Pa say I couldn't go. You could say I told you it was a surprise. Please! When we're gone a couple of days and there's no chance of anyone coming after me, you can tell the people at the ranch where I've gone.''

There was such desperation in young Andrew's voice, such anguish in his eyes, that Antonio turned his back on the youth and, reaching out to the nearest horse, stroked its head and said, "I thought I heard voices, but it must have been my imagination.''

There was a soft thud behind him, but he did not move. Andrew had swiftly lifted the lid of the compartment, leaped inside, and pulled it down over himself. The boy was confident that if he hid himself way in the rear of the compartment, there would be enough room for him and his grandparents' luggage. As it chanced, there was a thick blanket there, and he pulled it over himself and lay waiting, his heart pounding wildly.

A few moments later, Antonio, who had hurried back to the bunkhouse, returned to the carriage. The *vaquero* moved quickly to the back of the vehicle, glanced around to make certain that no one was observing him, and, opening the lid of the compartment, hastily dropped into it a packet of dried jerky and a leather canteen of water. "There's food and water here, so you can keep out of sight for a long time. *Vaya con Dios,* young master!''

"God bless you, Antonio,'' came the muffled answer from under the blanket.

Three

Antonio Lorcas did young Andrew Baines still another favor. Anticipating that the luggage of the old *hidalgo* and his lady might be put into the rear compartment of the carriage by another *vaquero*, who might be taken by surprise and perhaps call out the identity of the stowaway, he himself went to the porch of the *hacienda*, where, in neat rows, stood Doña Inez's and Don Diego's valises and boxes. Antonio quickly carried these back to the carriage, set down the pieces, opened the compartment, and murmured, "I am putting the luggage in, Señor Andrew. Do not say a word. You will not be discovered."

"I'll never forget you for this, Antonio."

"Hush, Señor Andrew! Miguel Sandarbal is coming. Move out of the way so I can put the luggage in." With this, he loaded the front of the compartment and closed down the lid just as Miguel affably approached.

"You are industrious today, Antonio."

"As always, *mi capataz*," Antonio smilingly responded, inclining his head in a mark of respect to the foreman of the Double H Ranch. "I wish I might go along to Argentina and fight beside *el Halcón*."

Miguel put his hand on Antonio's shoulder. "Everyone

24

knows of your courage and loyalty. No one here will forget what you did for poor Señora Catarina after she was shot by that madman. Few horsemen could have followed the trail of her murderer as you did, thus allowing you to tell our *patrón*, Señor John Cooper, where the murderer was hiding out so that he could hunt him down and obtain vengeance." Gloomily, he shook his head. Then, brightening somewhat, he said, "Well now, our coachman will be along, and so all is in readiness. My Bess has prepared beef stew and plum tart. Come and share them with me, Antonio." He kissed his fingers in rapt anticipation of these culinary treats.

"Muchas gracias, mi capataz," Antonio respectfully replied, "but my Rosa will have something for me from the *hacienda*'s kitchen." He sighed with relief to realize that the stowaway would not be discovered until well into the journey.

Meanwhile, Andrew found that he could breathe rather easily. The chinks in the sides of the luggage compartment permitted enough air to come in, but if he planned to remain hidden all day long, there would be certain relief he would need to obtain—and so he knocked out a small knothole in the floor at the back of the compartment. As for the rest, when the others were sleeping late at night, he could emerge from his hiding place and ease himself.

Now that he was settled in, Andrew cursed himself for being so impulsive as not to have foreseen that there were no extra horses. The driver of the carriage would eventually return to the Double H Ranch with Don Diego and Doña Inez, while the four *vaqueros* accompanying John Cooper and his Dorotéa would take their horses aboard the ship bound for the *pampas*. How would he himself travel once he made his presence known?

The time had come for the departure. John Cooper had chosen a gelded four-year-old palomino, spirited and powerful, from old Fuerzo's get. For Dorotéa, the tall rancher had chosen a mare similar to the one he had brought to Argentina to sell to Raoul Maldones and that the Argentinian rancher had given his daughter as an engagement present. This new mare Dorotéa had named Rauda, the Spanish word for "fleet." Remembering that Dorotéa was carrying his child, John Cooper had insisted that she ride sidesaddle on the long journey to New Orleans. And when she had remonstrated, he had said almost fiercely, "In this I shall have my way. I want nothing to harm our child. Yes, I know it is very early, but all the same there will be enough danger to think about when we reach Argentina."

The four *vaqueros* who had won the right to accompany John Cooper, his wife, and Felipe Mintras had mounted their geldings. In his saddlebags, Felipe carried some provisions for himself, for a *gaucho* instinctively prepares for the days ahead and does not count on fortune to provide food and water if he is on a mission. Enrique Saltanda climbed to the driver's seat and took the reins of the two sturdy horses attached to the carriage. The supply wagon was pulled by another team of horses, driven by one of the *vaqueros,* whose own horse was tied to the wagon.

When Andrew Baines heard his father call, *"¡Adelante, hombres!"* and felt the wheels begin to turn, he breathed a sigh of relief. Thus far, he had escaped detection.

Since he had ridden with his father to New Orleans on two occasions, he knew approximately how long the journey would take, although they would take more time because of Don Diego's imperiled health. Turning onto his side, Andrew shoved the blanket under him as a kind of mattress and prepared himself for a long journey.

In the supply wagon, besides food staples, John Cooper brought a cache of weapons: rifles, two braces of pistols, and ample powder and balls and flintlocks. In New Orleans, he would visit a gunsmith and purchase an extra dozen newer, more improved rifles. These could be distributed among the *gauchos* whom Felipe Mintras would recruit to aid Raoul Maldones.

John Cooper rode at the head of the column, with Dorotéa beside him in her sidesaddle. The brown mare responded instantly to her touch, and she reached forward to stroke its neck and to murmur an endearment to it. Then she looked at her husband and made a saucy little moue, which John Cooper took to say, "I would much prefer to ride astride this mare, for I could outdistance you if you would only give me the chance. But of course, like all men, you think I am a mere woman. You will see how much of a tigress I can be when it comes to defending my father and fighting for his freedom!"

And the Texan smiled back at his beautiful young wife and nodded, then blew her a kiss, which made her blush. She felt the most ardent love and admiration for John Cooper. Compassionate and sensitive, Dorotéa had understood his loneliness after Catarina's tragic death, and she had vowed to be all things to him, to drive away his grief and give him a new life. That was why now she smiled proudly, knowing that within her belly was their first child.

The weather was oppressively hot, and at sunset the sun was a flaming ball. Don Diego and Doña Inez were chatting, and she was happy to see that a little color had come back into her husband's cheeks. She smiled and caressed the back of his neck as she sighed silently, not wanting him to know that she was more and more concerned over his poor health. Well, this vacation was imperative for both of them, but most of all for him.

In his hiding place, Andrew Baines felt the intense heat of the September sun, and the lack of air and the cramped space made him even more uncomfortable. In addition to this, he was jolted at times when the carriage went into a pothole along the trail. But all the same, it was an exhilarating adventure, and he contented himself with thinking of Adriana, with conjuring up her lovely, sensuous features and trying to remember the words she had spoken to him at their last meeting at her father's *hacienda*.

There was no doubt that she cared for him; that alone would be inspiration enough to fight for her and win her. And why not, after all? He was very nearly a man, and here on the frontier youthful marriages were almost inevitably the custom. It seemed to him to be the most natural and wonderful thing in the world to think of marrying Adriana in the next few years—and growing old with her with many long years of contentment between them. Lulled by these happy thoughts, he closed his eyes and fell asleep.

When Andrew wakened, he heard nothing but the faint chirping of crickets and, very cautiously, tested the lid above him. His palm pressed upward, the lid lifted, and he saw the blurry outline of a hazy quarter-moon high in the sky. He gulped in breaths of air and then warily glanced around. All was darkness. The campfires were put out, and everyone had gone to sleep.

He eased himself out of the compartment, stifling the urge to groan as his cramped muscles were stretched. He put his hand to his belt to feel the reassuring pressure of the knife in its sheath.

It was past midnight, and he felt refreshed from his sleep. He grinned boyishly to himself, for now he was certain that his father would not send him home. The worst that would happen would be an angry scolding—or, if his father were really furious, he would order Andrew to remain in New Orleans with Don Diego and Doña Inez.

Andrew cocked his head, listening for sounds, but only the crickets were heard. After he took a swig from his canteen and a few bites of jerky, he hurried into a clump of bushes to ease himself and silently crept back to the compartment, crawled back into it, and pulled down the lid. He was not eager to return to his hiding place, but risking detection by remaining outside the compartment would be foolish. Drawing the blanket over him and rolling onto his side, he was soon fast asleep.

On the second day of the journey, Don Diego seemed more animated and garrulous, which Doña Inez knew was always an excellent sign. He commented on the scenery, then turned to Doña Inez and said with a wistful smile, *"Querida,* everything comes so late for us. This trip of ours, this vacation, it should have been taken years ago. You must forgive me, *mi corazón."*

"But there's nothing to forgive, Diego dear," she smilingly responded as she kissed his grizzled cheek. "Truly, the good God has been merciful to us and smiled upon us. In the midst of misfortune, when you were exiled by the king of Spain to Taos in New Mexico, we found each other, Diego dear. We saw Carlos and Catarina, your beloved children by your first wife, my sister, grow and become adults. We were blessed when we had our *own* daughter, Francesca, and when we adopted the two little Texas orphans, Dolores and Juan. And we were further blessed when John Cooper Baines entered our lives and brought us all from Taos to Texas to live. Now it remains only for us to be happy and to enjoy each other and our family during these mellow years. It is heartening that John Cooper has someone to live and work for, and that your son, Carlos, is happy with his Teresa."

"Yes, yes, of course you are right, dear Inez," he amicably nodded. "We have many blessings, indeed. But I still wish I had taken you to New Orleans some years back."

"We will make up for the time lost, then. You are going to dance with me, flatter me, and behave like a true *caballero* when we reach there, I have decided. Now close your eyes and try to take a little nap, though I know the road here is bumpy."

"It is strange, but I hardly feel it. Perhaps it is because we have so much to look forward to, Inez."

"Of course that is it, my darling. Now rest. Save your strength for New Orleans, for I warn you, I shall be very demanding of you. When a wife goes to visit a colorful city, she expects her husband to squire her about and to see to it that she has a good time," Doña Inez teased.

He smiled gently and nodded, then closed his eyes and leaned back. She watched him, sighing inwardly with relief. Decidedly, he seemed much better today.

All the same, John Cooper and the *vaqueros* camped at sundown, after they had come some twenty miles since departing after a leisurely breakfast that morning. They had made excellent time, but John Cooper knew that he must not endanger Don Diego's health by hastening the journey, even though every hour counted in seeking to rescue Dorotéa's father.

John Cooper and Felipe Mintras huddled before the campfire after the others had had their supper. Dorotéa had gone to the bed that her bearded husband had made for her out of a sleeping bag and a blanket placed on a bed of thick buffalo grass.

John Cooper put his hand on Felipe's shoulder. "How many *gauchos* do you think will follow you to Buenos Aires, Felipe?"

"There were some thirty of us, *Halcón*," the *gaucho* declared, "who were bound to our *caudillo*, the señor Raoul Maldones. I am certain that I can locate at least ten of them who will come with me."

"That's good—a strong force. We'll provide their weapons, in addition to their spears and knives and *bolas*. Felipe. I plan to buy plenty of rifles, pistols, and ammunition," John Cooper declared.

"Good idea, *amigo*. The *porteños* have their own

army, and their soldiers carry Belgian rifles, cumbersome things, but useful if there are many targets."

"I know what you mean." John Cooper held his own treasured weapon, "Long Girl," between his hands. "But I wouldn't trade fifty Belgian rifles for 'Long Girl,' Felipe." The tall rancher stretched his long legs in front of him. "Well, we'd better get some sleep. We've had good weather so far, and I'd like to make time. An early start is the best way to do it."

Both men stood, stretched, then scattered the ashes of the campfire and covered them with dirt. Felipe turned to face the blond Texan. "I spent some time with your Don Diego, *Halcón*. He has learned, even though it is late in his life, that it is most important to be free and proud and self-sufficient. The same is true for Señor Raoul, which is why we *gauchos* are loyal to him. We *gauchos* trust only those who shoot with us, ride with us, eat with us. We view with suspicion those who talk about great deeds when they have never ventured outside their houses—like the *porteños!* Well, *buenas noches, mi amigo.*"

"And to you, as well, Felipe." John Cooper clapped him on the back and then went back to where Dorotéa lay sleeping. Tenderly, he bent over her and stroked her hair, then kissed her forehead and her ear. She murmured in her sleep and smiled. He lay down beside her, closed his eyes, and was soon fast asleep.

Not fifty feet away, John Cooper's son was stirring, wakened by hunger. He had always had a hearty appetite, and his meager rations of jerky and water did not entirely satisfy him. On this second night, he looked longingly at the supply wagon. He would have given a great deal for a piece of venison and some cornbread, but it was too risky. Someone might hear him rummaging around for food.

Instead he walked into the woods, hoping to find some berries or wild fruit. Straining his eyes, he crouched and thought he saw a clump of wild grapes. But at that same moment, there was an angry snort and a squeal, and to his horror, he saw an old *jabalí* surging out of a clump of *manzanilla* and coming toward him.

There was no time for anything except defending himself. Drawing his hunting knife from its sheath, he lunged to one side as the creature charged by. It had spearlike tusks and little beady eyes. It gave off a stench, like a skunk's, that Andrew figured would waken the camp if the *jabalí*'s snorts didn't. The animal had been slightly grazed by a hunter's ball sometime before, and it had convalesced, but it had been starved during that period. Hence it behaved as though it were mad.

Now the animal wheeled, having seen that its charge carried it beyond its young adversary. Halting a moment, releasing a coughing bark, the *jabalí* again charged with all its power, tusks gleaming in the faint light of the quarter-moon overhead. Andrew braced himself, the knife clutched in his right hand like a dagger, and as the *jabalí* came upon him, Andrew lunged to the left and drove the knife up to the hilt into the creature's side. There was a frenzied bellow of agony as the bristly beast rolled over, kicking, trying to jab at Andrew with its tusks, but by now the boy had drawn out the bloodied knife and stabbed again and again until at last a chance lunge found the *jabalí*'s heart. There was a final convulsive kick and a hideous squeal, and then the animal rolled onto its back and lay still.

But in that last lunge, the *jabalí*'s tusk had caught Andrew's right wrist and made a slight gash. He saw his own blood drip upon the earth.

The noise had wakened the camp, and it was John Cooper who came first, along with Felipe Mintras.

"What the devil—Andrew! What the hell are you doing here?" his father bellowed at him.

"I—I'm sorry, Pa. I—I just had to come along."

"So you disobeyed me!"

But this time, instead of lowering his eyes, Andrew stared levelly at his father: "Yes, Pa, I did, but I have reasons. I'm worried about Adriana. Look, Pa, you'd feel the same way about Dorotéa, wouldn't you? Well, maybe I'm not old enough to feel the same things you do, but I've got feelings just the same—and I love Adriana. I want to help her and her father. That's why I stowed away. By now Antonio Lorcas has told everybody at the ranch where I've gone—I asked him to do that, Pa. If you don't like it, you can beat the hell out of me and send me back home, but I want you to know how I feel."

John Cooper, his hands on his hips, stood staring at his son. Then he looked down at the ground where the dead *jabalí* lay. "You did that with your hunting knife? That took guts, Andrew." The powerful man paused, looking at his son. "Well, you're here now, and I'll bet you've figured out that we don't have any extra horses to send you back—or, by the eternal, I would have, so help me! All right, then, you'll come along with us. But you'll take orders from me from now on, and if you're up to any more tricks, I *will* whale the hell out of you. Is that understood?"

"Yes. Thanks, Pa. Thanks a lot."

John Cooper noticed that his son's wrist was bleeding. "Let's get that wrist of yours tied up—I've got to play nursemaid besides looking after this expedition, it seems," he said, shaking his head and scowling. But when he saw the ghost of a smile on Andrew's lips, he burst out laughing, came to his son, and embraced him. "You're a sly dog, but I guess if I were your age and felt the way you do about Adriana, I'd have done the same thing. I'll bet you're hungry."

"I am, Pa. All I had was some water and jerky. In fact, I was in the brush here trying to find something to eat."

"Well, once we get your wrist attended to, we'll raid

the supply wagon together. Come to think of it, I could stand a little more dinner.'' John Cooper burst into hearty laughter as he led his son and Felipe Mintras along to the supply wagon.

Four

It was a warm, sunny day, this first of October in the year of 1826, and New Orleans had recovered from a scorching summer, with its attendant plague of the dreaded yellow fever. Citizens had died by the hundreds during the blistering heat, despite all the panaceas contrived by the physicians. But this evening, there was a refreshingly cool breeze from the Gulf, and in a squalid little waterfront tavern a hundred yards from the huge levee, two men sat at a table in the back, each nursing a mug of buttered rum.

One of the men was stocky, about forty, his dark-brown hair already receding from his temples and showing a hint of bald patches along the scalp. He wore a black cravat, a matching waistcoat, and white cotton trousers. His face was seamed and lined, while his dull, watery-brown eyes made him look older than he really was. Yet tonight his face was unusually animated as he raised his mug and toasted the man across the table.

That man was in direct contrast to him: nearly six feet

tall, wiry, with the poise of a ballet dancer or a fencing master. He had jet-black hair with a distinguished patch of gray exactly at the center just above his forehead, bushy eyebrows, and a trim little beard. He wore a white linen waistcoat and trousers and elegantly tooled leather shoes, while on his long, tapering right forefinger was a gold ring in which was set an enormous black onyx.

He lifted his mug and clinked it against that of his companion, took a modest sip, and set it down. Then he took from his waistcoat pocket a silk kerchief steeped in cologne and dabbed at his nostrils and temples. *"Mordieu,* Alexander, this is the first relief we've had in many a month. I sometimes ask myself why I tolerate this intensely hot climate."

"Because it suits you, like hell suits the devil—and because you have the money to buy the luxuries that New Orleans offers," was the almost bitter answer.

Christophe Carrière chuckled mirthlessly, dabbed at his nostrils and temples again, then put the kerchief back into his pocket. "Yes, you're right, in a way. But, like you, I have the same frustrations—only on a larger scale."

"After today, I won't give a damn," was his companion's answer. Alexander DuPlessis stared down at the table, moodily rubbing his mug back and forth along the scarred, unpolished surface. "Imagine the injustice! Here I work for the same damnable bank for over fifteen years, and today the president named that fop Étienne Valcours as vice-president! He passed me up, I tell you, M'sieu Carrière. I, who have brought the bank such good business; I, who have been commended by its stock-holders—to be ignominiously shoved aside in favor of a Creole dandy who knows absolutely nothing about the banking business and who came to it only two years ago."

"Obviously, Alexander, he has good connections and a better background than you."

"Yes, unfortunately that's all too true," the older

man morosely declared. "But damnation, I'll have my revenge. That's why I asked you to meet me here."

"And that's why I'm here, Alexander," was the suave answer.

Christophe Carrière was thirty-one years old. Fairly well-off and very handsome, still a bachelor, he was as much an outcast as his companion—for a reason that had haunted him since his childhood.

His father, Henri Carrière, had been one of Napoleon's most highly regarded seamen, in command of the fighting frigate *L'Espoir* during Napoleon's campaign to strike against Egypt. But during the first two days of August of 1798, Lord Nelson's English fleet attacked the French and destroyed almost all of Napoleon's ships. Henri Carrière, however, managed to flee. Taking advantage of a favorable wind, he outdistanced two pursuers and evaded them, until he was safely out in the Atlantic and on his way to Cuba. Once there, he procured additional crew members to man his ship, gunpowder, and cannonballs, and embarked on a career as a privateer.

In a short time, Carrière was feared as one of the most dangerous pirates along the coast between the Gulf and the young American colonies as far north as the Carolinas. His wife, a charming girl from an aristocratic French family, fell into despair at her husband's outlawry and killed herself. She left her son, five-year-old Christophe, at the mercy of his brigand father. Henri Carrière made his base in Florida, and there he brought Christophe and a pretty doxy whom he had found in Havana and whom he married so that his son might have a mother.

Christophe's stepmother, Elena Reyes Carrière, engaged a private tutor for the little boy and saw to it that he had a decent education. By the year 1809, Christophe's father had purchased a pleasant house on the outskirts of New Orleans, and there young Christophe and his stepmother lived comfortably. The boy saw his father only several times a year, when Carrière took a little time out from his profitable life of piracy. But five years later, Henri Carrière's piracy came to an end. He was captured by the crew of an American frigate, brought ashore at Charleston, there given a swift trial, and hanged in the public square.

The news of this reached New Orleans, and at the age of nineteen, Christophe Carrière found himself a virtual outcast as the aristocratic Creoles of the city snubbed and insulted him because of his father's ignominious and traitorous life. The handsome young Christophe was determined that one day he would make his peers pay for the contempt with which they treated him. In the meantime, being devilishly handsome and virile, he plunged himself into a series of liaisons with beautiful and unscrupulous young women, increasing his notoriety among the Creoles of the city.

After his widowed stepmother ran off to St. Louis with a wealthy trader, young Carrière decided to do some traveling himself. He invested the small legacy that his father had deposited in a New Orleans bank for him, and financed a party of traders bound for Santa Fe. Carrière accompanied these men and passed through Taos and Santa Fe, visiting the great fair at Chihuahua, delighted to see the profits that accrued to him from the sale of his trade goods.

In 1823 he returned to New Orleans and fell madly in love with an exquisite dark-haired beauty of seventeen, Madeleine de Courvent. But when he had approached her father to ask for her hand in marriage, Joseph de Courvent, head of a shipping company on Chartres Street, indignantly told him that he would rather burn in hell than accept Christophe Carrière as his son-in-law, and, further, that he had forbidden Madeleine ever to see Christophe again.

That was why, on this October evening, Carrière listened with growing interest to the complaints of Alexander DuPlessis, for well he could understand what rejection meant, what being passed over in favor of someone else could do to the spirit of a man who believed that he should be judged on his own merits and not by what had happened in the past, particularly when he had in no way been responsible for it.

DuPlessis was beckoning to the tavern keeper to send over the serving girl. She was a buxom wench of about twenty, barefooted, with a long, red-and-white striped skirt, which did not quite hide her firm, rounded, tawny-sheened calves and clung almost salaciously to the curves of her haunches. "Another mug of rum, girl," he demanded. Then, turning back to his companion, he went on, his tone conspiratorial, "I've news that should be of real importance to you, M'sieu Carrière. What would you say if I told you that in the vaults of La Banque de la Nouvelle Orléans, along with sacks of gold coins and fabulous jewels, there are something like thirty bars of pure silver?"

Christophe Carrière sharply glanced around to make certain that no one could overhear their conversation and hunched forward over the table, closer to his companion. He took another swallow from his mug of rum and then muttered, "That's an incredible fortune."

"A fortune that could make the most despised man in this or any other city in the world fawned upon even by his betters, I'm certain," DuPlessis retorted.

A crafty look came into the sparkling dark eyes of Carrière. "You're right. If I could lay my hands on all that wealth, I could have power, any woman I wanted, and indeed I could almost rule New Orleans."

"You could do exactly that, M'sieu Carrière," DuPlessis said, his expression brightening.

"So you propose that I avail myself of what is in the vault of the very bank that has thwarted your ambition of becoming a leading officer, is that it?" Carrière mockingly demanded.

"Why not? You know men who are bold enough for such an enterprise."

"Yes, though it would be quite an undertaking," the Creole mused. "It would require a wagon and at least a couple of men to handle the weight of the silver and other valuables. And time would be of the essence. It would have to be done at night."

"Of course, of course! Whatever you say!" Alexander DuPlessis excitedly broke in. "You have the skill, the means of bringing off such a coup, M'sieu Carrière."

"You tempt me, Alexander. That untouched fortune beckons to me. Indeed, it fairly cries out to change ownership. But let us consider the subject further. We must create some diversions that will take the full attention of the city's night watchmen. And while they are distracted, the men I shall have chosen will be extracting the fortune from your bank into my warehouses."

"Then you'll do it?" DuPlessis excitedly gasped, his eyes bright with anticipation.

"Let me think about it. What would be your share, do you think?"

"Well, I don't know—but certainly you wouldn't have known about the fortune if I hadn't told you."

"Yes, that's true enough," Carrière observed. "Perhaps a third."

"Well, that will do. Mind you, there's such a fortune there, one shouldn't be niggardly," DuPlessis said in a hesitant tone. Then he lifted his mug and swallowed down the rest of the rum, not seeing how the handsome Creole opposite him gave him a quick look of withering contempt.

Carrière leisurely rose, took out a small purse, and laid two coins down on the table. He turned to the bank employee. "I'll reflect over what you've told me tonight, Alexander. And I'll let you know what I've decided. Do you know who owns this fortune?"

"Of course. The gold and jewels belong to some of

the most prominent citizens of our community. As for the bars of silver, they are assigned to the name of John Cooper Baines, who owns the Double H Ranch near the Frio River in Texas."

The Creole stroked his pointed beard for a moment, then nodded. "I don't know this John Cooper Baines, but it certainly would be delightful to get back at some of these despicable aristocrats who have insulted me in the past. Well, as I said, I will let you know what I decide. And now I will bid you good night." Turning on his heel, the tall Creole strode out of the tavern.

Alone at the table, DuPlessis turned and called once again to the serving girl, "Hurry with that mug of rum, girl! I have a great thirst, and I want to drink a toast to my good luck!"

Five

The afternoon following his father's discovery of him after the fight with the wild boar, young Andrew Baines dismounted from the carriage, where he was now riding with his grandparents, and ran up to Felipe Mintras on his gelding. The boy sought to reinstate himself in John Cooper's favor.

"Lend me your *bola*, Felipe," Andrew pleaded. "I

want to kill some game to show my father I can earn my keep on this journey.''

"With the greatest good will of all! Here is my *bola*, and may good fortune attend you!''

Disengaging the Argentinian weapon from the saddle horn, the *gaucho* handed it to Andrew.

John Cooper had pretended not to notice this exchange, but he smiled to himself, for in Andrew he saw something of himself. His deep-rooted determination to come along on a journey that he had been forbidden to undertake was like John Cooper's own passion for justice and the right to defend it. He was intensely proud of his son.

Taking a deep breath, Andrew now ran well ahead of his father, who had dismounted along with the other riders in order to begin making camp for the night. There was a patch of swampland far off to the left, some five hundred yards away, and Andrew began to sprint. He moved just beyond a large clump of live-oak trees, which gave way to a long tangled stretch of mesquite. A small, young deer suddenly darted out of the mesquite bushes and raced toward the west. Andrew whirled the *bola* over his head and shot it out. John Cooper saw it flying through the air and uttered a shout of acclamation as the *bola* wrapped around the legs of the deer and tripped it so that it lay motionless on the grassy plain.

Andrew hurried up to the quarry, took his hunting knife, and swiftly cut the deer's throat. Then, untangling the *bola*, lifting up the deer, and carrying it around his shoulders, he waited, grinning, for his father and Felipe to come up to him.

"That was an excellent throw, Señor Andrew,'' Felipe jovially declared. "I myself could not have made a better one. You have mastered the *bola*. A pity that Porfirio Ramos was not the target. But perhaps destiny has reserved him for me, as is my prayer.''

That evening, as the travelers ate their supper and

Andrew cleaned his deer and cooked venison over a fire, the boy suggested to his father that Felipe be given a share of the meat. "There's too much for me to eat, Pa, and Felipe deserves some because he let me use his *bola*."

"That's a good thought, Andy," John Cooper said as he ate, like the others in his party, a rich soup made from dried vegetables and the meat from the boar Andrew had killed. Enough food had been packed for this journey so that John Cooper and the other men would not have to take time out for hunting expeditions, and the fact that Andrew had managed to kill two animals with such dispatch made the rancher very proud. John Cooper now clapped his tall son on the back. "I'm almost ready to admit I was wrong when I decided not to take you with me. But whoa now, boy"—as he saw a glow of joyous hope light Andrew's eyes—"you're still on tolerance. And you're going to take strict orders every step of the way, I'll see to that."

Despite John Cooper's admonishment, Andrew shot his father a covertly grateful look. Now he felt complete acceptance.

It was mid-October when they sighted the sprawling city of New Orleans, the stucco buildings covered with brick, and, in the distance, the great levee to which ships from many nations came. The sky was bright with the warm sun, and John Cooper considered it a good omen. Throughout this journey, there had been no untoward incidents, and they had made excellent time.

"A few miles more, and we'll come to the home of Fabien Mallard," John Cooper cheerfully announced as he rode his palomino up to the carriage and leaned in his saddle to speak to Don Diego and Doña Inez. "They'll treat you royally, and my factor's wife, Hortense, is the most gracious of women—so very much like you, Doña Inez!"

"You are a born flatterer, John Cooper," Don Diego's

wife declared, smiling with pleasure at the compliment.
"But from what you have told Diego and me about the
Mallards, we are most eager to meet them. And he has
done very well for you and the business of the ranch, *¿no
es verdad?*"

"Indeed he has, for he's a man of good judgment,
and a friend as well. A combination like that is very rare
these days. Sometimes if a man is engaged in commerce,
he loses the human touch, but not Fabien Mallard. Well,
now, we'd best move a little more quickly—I'm looking
forward to a fine dinner and a good bed," John Cooper
said.

He rode back to where Dorotéa waited for him at the
head of the column, then swung his arm to tell the others
to follow him onward.

As twilight descended on New Orleans, John Cooper's
entourage approached the first house on the corner of
Greenley Street, just above Chartres, and the tall Texan
reined in his horse and turned to call, "Here's Fabien
Mallard's house. I hope we aren't imposing upon his
hospitality by not having let him know in advance that we
were coming tonight, but I'm sure he'll put us up, at least
for the night."

Indeed, the sound of John Cooper's voice had brought
the factor out of the salon of his house, where he had been
conversing with his wife, Hortense. He uttered a cry of joy
and strode forward to extend his hand to John Cooper,
who had dismounted. "What a pleasant surprise, M'sieu
Baines! And Madame Baines! I certainly didn't expect to
see you quite so soon again in New Orleans!" he exclaimed.

"We didn't expect to be here either, M'sieu Mallard!
But you see, no sooner had we gotten home than I had a
letter from Dorotéa's father's majordomo in Argentina,
telling us that a very powerful enemy of her father had
arranged to have the Maldones property confiscated and to
throw her father in a Buenos Aires jail. Dorotéa and I are

going back there, together with my son, our friend and fine *gaucho,* Felipe Mintras, and our four *vaqueros.''*

The factor nodded a greeting to Andrew, Felipe, and the other men, then turned back to John Cooper. "Of course all of you will be my guests tonight. As before, your *vaqueros* can stay in the carriage house, and there is room in my stables for your horses. Now do come in. Come, Madame Baines. Hortense will be delighted to see you."

John Cooper gallantly helped his wife down from her mount. "I have Don Diego and Doña Inez with me in the carriage, M'sieu Mallard," he said.

"Ah, that is wonderful! I have always wanted to meet this father-in-law of yours and his lady—I feel as if I know them from all the wonderful things you've told me about them," the factor smilingly declared. He went to the carriage just as Enrique Saltanda had clambered down and was about to open the door to help out the old *hidalgo* and his wife. "Allow me, my good man. What a privilege this is for me!" he said.

The *vaquero* stepped out of the way, somewhat taken aback by the exuberant friendship of this stranger, who was elegantly dressed with a flowery cravat, new yellow waistcoat and matching trousers, and elegantly polished shoes. He glanced down at himself self-consciously, observing his own dusty boots, riding breeches, and jacket. John Cooper observed this and chuckled to himself.

"Welcome to New Orleans, Don Diego, and you also, Doña Inez. I am Fabien Mallard, and it will be a great pleasure for me, as well as for my lovely wife, Hortense, to be your hosts this evening. Allow me to help you down, Doña Inez." Fabien Mallard offered his hand.

"Thank you, Señor Mallard. You are most kind." Doña Inez turned back to her husband with a radiant smile. "Come, Diego, with such a warm welcome, our little vacation begins beautifully."

Don Diego carefully stepped down from the carriage, then shook hands with the factor. By now Hortense Mallard had come out of the elegant house, with its second-floor balcony decorated with a wrought-iron fleur-de-lis design. She had recently celebrated her fortieth birthday, and she was still extremely beautiful, with her oval-shaped face and her eloquent, large, widely spaced dark-brown eyes. She wore her dark-brown hair with a fringe of curls along her high-arching forehead, drawn back to the top of the back of her head in an oval-shaped bun in which she wore a silver comb set at each end with a huge pearl.

"This is my beloved wife, Hortense." Fabien Mallard proudly made the introductions to Don Diego and Doña Inez. Then Hortense Mallard greeted Dorotéa, John Cooper, and Felipe Mintras, even inquiring about the *gaucho*'s wife, whom she had met when that group had traveled from Argentina two months before. Then the Baines entourage was ushered indoors, while the *vaqueros* took the horses to the stables and then proceeded to the carriage house, where the men would have their own dinner.

The Mallards' Jamaican cook, Ernesto, provided a magnificent supper, and Don Diego and Doña Inez enjoyed themselves thoroughly. For the old *hidalgo*, the beautifully set table, the rich food, the fine wine, and, above all else, the animated and colorful conversation proved to be a stimulant that contributed to his increasing vitality. Fabien and Hortense, observing what pleasure the supper was giving Don Diego, purposely directed the conversation to him in order to give him every opportunity to feel not only welcome but also a valued participant.

And at the conclusion of supper, his voice was hoarse with emotion as he thanked his hosts. "You have given such pleasure to a stranger, Señor Mallard, Señora Mallard. You cannot know what pleasure you have given to me tonight. I feel as if we were old friends. For myself and for my adored wife, Doña Inez, let me extend our grateful thanks.''

"It is our pleasure, Don Diego. And let me add that you and your lovely wife must be our guests for as long as you stay in New Orleans. Now, my majordomo, Antoine, will go with you to your rooms. Since they are in the back of the first floor, near the patio, it will be very quiet there, so you may have a long and restful sleep after your journey.''

The grave, stately mulatto majordomo appeared now and, bowing to both Don Diego and Doña Inez, escorted them to their rooms. Meanwhile, Hortense came forward and took Dorotéa's hand in hers. "You're such a beautiful girl, and I can see how happy you are with M'sieu Baines,'' she murmured.

"More than words can say, Señora Mallard,'' Dorotéa whispered back, her cheeks flaming as she saw her bearded husband, talking with Fabien Mallard, glance quickly at her and smile and nod. *"El Señor Dios* has answered all my prayers.''

"I shall pray also in the chapel, dear Madame Baines,'' the factor's wife murmured, "that you and M'sieu Baines bring your father back safely. Do you not think he would enjoy coming to this new world of ours and living away from tyranny?''

"I think the change would be difficult for him. He loves the *pampas* so, but the first thing is to free him from that prison. And thank you for your prayers, Señora Mallard. Thank you, too, for being so kind to my dear husband. You also have a husband who`is kind and good and who adores you, as I can already see.''

Hortense impulsively hugged John Cooper's beautiful young wife. "And now, let the two men talk business for a bit, as men must. Come with me. I should like to give you a little gift. My mother gave me two crucifixes, one when I took communion for the first time and the second on her deathbed. I wish you to have the first because it is blessed and because perhaps it will bring you good fortune when you return to liberate your father.''

"How thoughtful, how kind!" Dorotéa could not help the tears that sprang to her eyes. Hortense Mallard put her arm around the young woman's shoulders and led her off.

Six

John Cooper could hardly sleep, though his gracious host, Fabien Mallard, had provided Dorotéa and him an airy, quiet bedchamber, graced by a sumptuous four-poster, canopied bed. His beautiful young wife and he had made passionate love after they had retired, and in her embrace, the rancher could sense Dorotéa's mingled emotions of the most ardent trust and the most poignant anxiety. Her love for her father ennobled her in his eyes, and this, too, was part of his own nature. Family devotion was an unspoken part of John Cooper's creed: To find that Dorotéa was as firm a believer in this only further justified his having wed her on such short acquaintance. Dorotéa had an inherent loyalty and the capability of feeling an unselfish passion for what she believed in. Now it would be justice for her father, just as he himself had fought for justice for his father-in-law in Taos and punished those who had be-smirched Don Diego's name.

Long after Dorotéa had fallen asleep, he lay on his side toward her, his hands stroking her hair, as he pondered what was in store for them both. That there would be danger, he took for granted; but he would see to it that he protected her to the very utmost. For now their lives were totally intertwined, not only because of this communal cause to which they were both dedicated at great risk, but because she bore within her their first child.

And so, at dawn, he was already awake, dressed, and waiting for breakfast. He would go down to the levee to arrange for a ship to take them to Argentina. Fabien Mallard, had, the night before, already told him that he would not have trouble finding an appropriate vessel.

John Cooper quickly ate a breakfast of freshly baked biscuits, shrimp, and a cup of black coffee with chicory as its base—all superbly prepared by Ernesto—then set off for the docks. But first he went over to the carriage house to see the *vaqueros* and Felipe Mintras. Climbing the stairs, he found Felipe waiting for him in the large, second-story room.

"Señor Baines," the *gaucho* said to him, "are we to sail back to the *pampas* today?"

"That's exactly what I'm going to find out now, Felipe. I'm going down to the wharf. Why don't you come with me? If we're lucky, we can be on our way to rescue your *patrón* by early this afternoon."

"I am eager to settle accounts with that dog of a Porfirio Ramos," the *gaucho* retorted, his eyes narrowing and his lips tight with anger. "I am ready to go with you now, Señor Baines."

There was the sound of someone coming up the stairs, and in a moment, John Cooper's tall son strode into the carriage-house quarters on the second floor.

"I wanted to catch up with you, Pa, so I ate quickly. *Buenos días*, Felipe!"

"And to you too, young señor! Well, a good walk early in the morning when it is not too warm is a fine way to start the day. Come now, let's be off!" the *gaucho* urged.

Half an hour later, John Cooper, his son, and the *gaucho* walked down the levee in search of the ship that would take them back to Argentina. The Texan suddenly stopped in his tracks, pointed far ahead, and excitedly exclaimed, "By the eternal, it's the *Miromar*, the same ship we went on to get to meet you, Felipe, and your *patrón*. I'll never forget that three-masted frigate or its captain. I'll bet that Fabien Mallard knew it would be here—he looked like the cat that swallowed the canary when I asked him about a ship. Let's see when they're going to sail!"

A few minutes later, John Cooper ascended the gangplank with long strides and headed for the quarterdeck. He saw a tall, sparse-bearded man in his midfifties, his back to him, and exuberantly exclaimed, "Captain Blake, this is better luck than I bargained for!"

Silas Blake turned to confront his visitor, his face softening with a warm smile of recognition as he came forward to extend his hand. "Well now, Mr. Baines! I'm returning to Argentina, but I'm wondering what you're doing here. Last I knew you were still in Argentina."

"Yes, Captain Blake, and while I was there, I met and married a wonderful young woman, Dorotéa Maldones. We sailed back from Argentina together on the *Sea Witch*. When we got back, we found a letter from Dorotéa's father's majordomo. A neighbor, who was in league with the *porteños*, has had her father put into jail in Buenos Aires. We're going back to rescue him."

"I could have suspected as much, Mr. Baines," Silas Blake dryly answered. "You'll remember those three men from the Buenos Aires government who shipped aboard with me that time you went out there. They're in full command now, and the political situation is getting messier and messier. There's a struggle for power down there in Buenos Aires, Mr. Baines, and I've got my cannoneer checking his guns, just in case we have any trouble."

"How is it that you're here again?" John Cooper pursued.

"I went back up to Boston for a load of whale oil, some grain, manufactured cotton goods, and some dried beef. That beef is bound for one of the South American ports long before we reach Buenos Aires."

"When are you sailing?" was John Cooper's next anxious question.

"This afternoon about three, Mr. Baines."

"It couldn't be better! Can you find room for my son and me, my wife and four *vaqueros*, as well as a *gaucho?*"

"I can accommodate all of you. There are only a few passengers aboard ship this time, all of whom will be disembarking before we reach Buenos Aires. I can book your passage very easily, without your seeing the purser. Let's sit down at this table, and I'll draw up the contract at once," the New England sea captain said.

"I'll sign your contract, Captain Blake, and then Andy and I and Felipe here will go back and round up the others. By the way, we're bringing our horses."

"That will present no difficulties, Mr. Baines. I've ample room in my hold."

"Good. Here's our payment in gold, Captain Blake. I couldn't be happier that the first available ship has you as captain. It's my hope that you can take us to Buenos Aires swiftly, danger or no danger."

"Well, we'll have to allow for the winds, as I'm sure you know by now. With any luck, I might get you to Buenos Aires in four weeks."

"That's fine, Captain. Now we'd better go ashore.

We just arrived in New Orleans yesterday evening, and there's been no time to purchase weapons. I want to get what weapons I can and plenty of gunpowder and ball. So I'll leave you now.''

"Very well. Figure on two-thirty in the afternoon for our leave-taking, which ought to give you time to get to a gunsmith," Silas Blake said.

The tall Texan shook hands with the New Englander, and then he, Felipe, and Andrew left the frigate and boarded a calash, John Cooper directing the driver to take them to the gunsmith shop near Jackson Square.

There was a grizzled old man, nearly bald, with enormous spectacles, presiding over the shop, and when John Cooper entered and declared his needs—a dozen Lancaster rifles—the old man chuckled and nodded. "I've what you want, sir. But I warn you, they're expensive. Twenty dollars each and in gold, if you please."

"I can handle that. And, of course, plenty of gunpowder and ball for all of them," John Cooper replied.

"That's understood. Will you be wanting anything else?"

"Just the dozen Lancasters, and let's say six braces of your best pistols, as well as supplies necessary to their firing and plenty of ammunition." He took out his leather pouch, opened it, and laid down a dozen twenty-dollar gold pieces. "This is a starter to show you my good intentions. I'll be back before two o'clock to pick it all up and pay you any balance; and I'll have my men come with me. I'd appreciate it if you could have everything ready."

"For an order like this, I'll do it myself." The two men shook hands.

John Cooper took Andrew by the elbow and led him out of the shop, followed by Felipe. "You know," he said to them, "it wouldn't do any harm to have some good throwing knives, knives strong enough to cut vines and foliage if we have to go through the jungle or the thick grass of the *pampas*. Maybe a dozen of those would be a good idea. There's a shop down the street. Let's see what they've got to offer."

Andrew accompanied his father and Felipe to a little shop at the end of the street and noticed that in the window there was a display of knives, sheaths, daggers, and stilettos. Inside the shop, a tall, gaunt man with wispy gray hair and the scars of smallpox affably greeted them. "Good day to you, gentlemen; how may I serve you?"

"I need about a dozen knives, suitable for throwing, with good heft and balance, but sturdy enough to hit the target if it's a long throw. Also, I might want to cut through thick grass or vines."

"Well, sir, I can show you a fine Spanish dagger, with narrow handle and a sturdy blade, tapering to a fine, sharp point. It can be used for stabbing, throwing, or cutting. And, of course, you'll want a good grindstone with you to keep it sharp at all times."

The gaunt man bent to the counter, took up a case of purple velvet, and unfolded it. John Cooper's eyes widened as he saw six superbly shaped knives, not unlike the one James Bowie used. Picking up one of the daggers, he examined it, took it by the handle, and balanced it as if to throw.

"I like it," he said at once. "Do you have a dozen for sale?"

"I do. Ten dollars each, in gold, and well worth it. For that, I'll throw in some pumice and a little grindstone."

"That's a bargain. I'll pay for them now and take them with me," John Cooper declared.

The purchase made, he, Felipe, and Andrew walked back to Mallard's house and were met by the factor himself, who had seen them from the second-story window and come down the stairs and into the street to greet them. "You had luck, M'sieu Baines?" he eagerly asked, the amused expression returning to his face.

"The very best, as you probably know."

"Yes, M'sieu Baines. I knew your Captain Blake was returning to Argentina today. I arranged to buy a portion of his cargo. But I wanted you to have the pleasure of learning this for yourself."

"We're sailing this afternoon, so we'll take leave of you, M'sieu Mallard, with great thanks to you and your lovely wife and to that superb cook of yours, Ernesto, for all your hospitality. We'll leave Don Diego and Doña Inez in your keeping. I hope it isn't an imposition.".

"By no means!" the factor said as he ushered John Cooper, Felipe, and Andrew back into the house. "They are a fascinating couple. Don Diego has many anecdotes—he has been regaling Hortense and me at breakfast. Indeed, it will be our pleasure to have them stay with us as long as they wish."

Enrique clambered into the driver's seat of the carriage as Don Diego and Doña Inez entered it to accompany John Cooper, Dorotéa, Andrew, Felipe, and the four *vaqueros* on their way to the harbor to board the *Miromar*. John Cooper and his lovely young wife rode their palominos while Andrew rode a horse his father had bought for him from Fabien Mallard. Felipe and the four chosen *vaqueros* rode their horses alongside the carriage, in which the factor and his Hortense were also seated, for they wished to bid John Cooper and his group bon voyage and success in their daring venture.

The carriage stopped en route to the wharf at the gunsmith's shop. Felipe again accompanied John Cooper into the shop, and glancing at the rifles and pistols, which had been packed and readied for transport, he turned to the rancher, smiled wryly, and said, *"¡Por todos los santos, mi amigo,* we have a veritable arsenal here! These weapons should even the odds against those accursed *porteños!"*

"That's exactly what I have in mind, Felipe. What I

intend to do as soon as we board ship is pack these guns, along with the ammunition and our knives, in some crates, in among our clothes and riding gear. That way we won't get stopped by any nosy *porteños* in Buenos Aires.''

John Cooper paid the balance of the money due on the rifles and the pistols, thanked the gunsmith, and he and the *gaucho* carefully laid the weapons into the very same carriage box where Andrew had hidden as a stowaway.

"Well then, let's be off," the Texas rancher said as he mounted his palomino and gestured to the *vaqueros* and Felipe Mintras to follow. "I don't want to cut the time too fine."

They arrived at the dock where the *Miromar* lay at anchor. The time had come for parting. Don Diego, his eyes moist, stood beside Doña Inez as he turned to his son-in-law and held out his hand. *"Vaya con Dios, mi hijo."* In his love for the younger man, the old *hidalgo* honored John Cooper by the term that meant "son," rather than *yerno:* "son-in-law." He straightened, his head high. "I will pray for you, and so will Doña Inez. For you and your sweet Dorotéa. Hurry back to us, my son."

"Don Diego, be sure that we shall return. And thank you for your prayers; we shall need them very much," John Cooper softly replied. Dorotéa stepped forward now and embraced Don Diego and then Doña Inez. "I am so grateful for the welcome you have given me, a stranger," she murmured to Doña Inez.

"You are no stranger, my darling. You have brought youth and warmth and happiness and love to the *Hacienda del Halcón*. Now may you return safely to preside over it for many long years of happiness," was Doña Inez's answer.

Fabien and Hortense said their farewells, and then the two couples went back to the carriage, where Enrique sat waiting to return them to the Mallard house.

At last the gangplank was drawn up, and Captain

Blake on his quarterdeck gave the order to rig full sail and take the wind with the tide. The white-haired *hidalgo* and his handsome wife sat watching until the three-masted frigate passed slowly and majestically along the line of docks and out toward the Gulf.

Seven

—◆—————————————————————◆—

Behind the long, rectangular, one-story wooden building of La Banque de la Nouvelle Orléans was a narrow alleyway. In the alleyway was a wagon with four men in it, dressed in dark clothing and boots to blend into the black night—dirty, unkempt men in their late twenties and early thirties—with tall, debonair Christophe Carrière in the driver's seat. In the wagon were several kegs of gunpowder, to which long fuses had been attached.

Carrière got down, patted the roan gelding that drew the wagon, and turned to the four men. ''Our friend in the bank is going to open the back door on my signal. In the wagon you have gunnysacks that you will use. I'll need two of you in here to load the booty. You, Dalzell, and you, Gros Ventre, you'll take the kegs of gunpowder and plant them down the street from the bank, where I've told you. Get them out of sight, but where they'll make a real noise and do some damage, understand? I want the night watchmen far enough away investigating the explosion that they won't trouble us inside the bank.''

Dalzell, a lanky, almost toothless towheaded man in his late twenties, tapped his forehead to signify that he had understood. The man called Gros Ventre, stocky and heavily set and, though only thirty, with a heavy paunch from which he derived his name, growled, "The fuses will take about ten minutes, M'sieu Carrière. When are we to start them?''

"I'll tell you when." The elegant Creole took a gold watch out of his waistcoat pocket and consulted it. "I've given you watches, though they're not quite so fancy as this one. At a quarter to twelve, you'll start lighting the fuses. By that time, you, Pascal, and you, Jimson, should have loaded most of what we're after. Is everybody clear as to what he has to do?''

"That we are, M'sieu Carrière," replied Georges Pascal, a man of twenty-eight, tall and lean, with a purple scar on his left cheek near his chin, secured no doubt in a knife fight.

Dan Jimson, who was to help carry the ingots from the bank, was thirty-two, with a black patch over his right eye socket; he had lost the eye in a tavern brawl over a slut's favors in Natchez. All four men were expert killers, and none of them was known to the New Orleans civil guard.

Christophe Carrière again consulted his pocket watch and scowled. He turned to his accomplices. It was time to begin. "Dalzell, Gros Ventre, remove the gunnysacks from the back of the wagon and leave them here by the door. Then take the wagon and plant the gunpowder at the locations I've decided on, and then you, Dalzell, will stay behind to light the fuses exactly fifteen minutes from now. Gros Ventre will drive the wagon back here so that we can start loading the ingots and what other bounty the bank has so thoughtfully provided for us. Now be on your way, *vite!*''

As the two men nodded and drove off, the Creole said, "Pascal, Jimson, pay close attention. M'sieu DuPlessis is inside. After all the other employees had left for the day, he hid in the vault. Now for the signal.''

Carrière knocked three times at the narrow side door of the bank. Then, counting off sixty seconds to himself, he knocked three times again, and then two quick knocks. A moment later, the door was slowly opened, and Carrière beckoned to his two aides, carrying the gunnysacks, to enter.

"A pleasant evening to you, *mon ami,*" Carrière lightly said to Alexander DuPlessis, who was sweating profusely from fear. "I'd no idea it was so warm inside. You really must remember to change your shirt and cravat by midday in this city.''

"Hurry, for God's sake! Don't let anyone see us!'' the bank official panted, feverishly glancing outside the alley to make certain that no one was in sight. "We don't want the civil guard on us.''

"Patience, *mon ami,*" the Creole counseled. "I want them no more than you do. That's precisely why, in about—'' again he consulted his watch "—twelve minutes, we should begin to listen for some explosions. These will divert the civil guard while we load our treasure aboard the wagon.''

"The contents of the vault are even more abundant than I had thought, M'sieu Carrière,'' DuPlessis babbled, mopping his sweating forehead with an already damp handkerchief. "Besides the ingots, gold, coins, and jewels, there are safety-deposit boxes filled with bank notes. And forgive me for prying, but that young lady in whom you once had an amatory interest—''

"What about her?'' Christophe Carrière's face turned sullen.

"Well now," DuPlessis wheedled, "her father has a large box with at least forty thousand dollars in federal notes and a fortune in jewels."

"Ah! I mustn't forget to include that in our take. Come along, Alexander. Lead me to all this treasure. Be quick, Pascal, Jimson!"

They went down the narrow flight of steps to the vault.

"There are the ingots belonging to John Cooper Baines, M'sieu Carrière," DuPlessis excitedly declared as he pointed to a huge, reinforced shelf at the base of the left wall of the vault. A curtain had been tacked over the shelf to hide its contents, but he crouched now and tore it away to reveal the gleaming bars of pure silver.

Jimson and Pascal swore under their breath, and Carrière whistled softly and shook his head. "Your count is very bad, Alexander," he chided. "I count close to sixty, and you told me there were only thirty."

"That's true, that's true, I, uh—I—had miscalculated in my haste," the banker hurriedly stammered. Then, brightening, his eyes greedy, he turned to the Creole. "But then, you see, that should increase my share considerably, should it not?"

"We'll discuss that later. Enough talk. Jimson, Pascal, put the ingots into the gunnysacks. Don't load them too heavily. There's time enough to dispose of them once we meet at the warehouse and make our future plans. I'll take a gunnysack myself and rummage in these boxes with you, Alexander. This is really child's play. Does your president think this bank is sacrosanct that he has no better security?"

DuPlessis shrugged. "There has never been a robbery here, that's all," he said. "Which reminds me, it would be a good idea to leave some marks on the back door. It can be said that you forced your entry. In that way I shan't be implicated."

"Not a bad idea. That's easily done with a crowbar.

There's one in the wagon. We'll give the door a few dents once Gros Ventre and Dalzell come back. You spoke of the box of my would-be fiancée's father, M'sieu Joseph de Courvent. Let me see it.''

''It's over here on the opposite wall, M'sieu Carrière.'' DuPlessis helpfully put out his hand to take the Creole by the elbow and lead him, but the latter shook him off with a frown. ''Do not touch me again, Alexander. This box, you say? Ah, you are right—there is certainly a fortune in jewels here, and the bank notes . . .'' His eyes glowing, he swiftly transferred the contents of the box into a gunnysack, then rose and, at random, chose another box. In this one, he found more jewels and about ten thousand dollars in bank notes. At this point, Pascal called out to him, ''M'sieu Carrière, there's a little receipt here with the ingots—you want to look at it?''

''Of course. Give it to me!'' Carrière went over to the two ruffians who were busy thrusting the silver bars into the gunnysacks. He took the note from Pascal, read it, and chuckled. ''This is the duplicate of a receipt that was given to one John Cooper Baines about a year ago, in the amount of $196,875 in silver at current market value. I am on my way to collecting a huge fortune. With money like this, I can rule New Orleans. I'm grateful to you, Alexander.''

''I thought you might be. We must talk about what my share will be worth from this enterprise,'' the sweating banker said.

Carrière ignored the other man, turning instead to the shelf nearby. He drew out another box made of inlaid wood and with a metal handle. '' 'This belongs to Fabien Mallard,' '' he read aloud. ''I have heard that name—he's one of the most respectable factors in all New Orleans and the most honest one. Your bank has many excellent customers, I'll give you that, Alexander.''

''Please, please hurry!'' the bank official whined, once again mopping his sweaty forehead.

"I think you'd best go on ahead to the warehouse. That way, you won't be implicated just in the event that some of the stupid civil guard should blunder into here." A muffled sound came to Christophe Carrière's ears, and he grinned with satisfaction. "Ah, there goes the first explosion. My men carried out their orders properly." He drew out his pocket watch and nodded in confirmation. "Exactly right. And there will be others soon. But go on ahead, Alexander. With luck, we should be there in half an hour."

"I'm going, I'm going, M'sieu Carrière," DuPlessis babbled, "and for God's sake, don't forget to leave some marks on the back door."

"I don't like to be reminded like a schoolboy. Get hold of your nerves. When you get to the warehouse, you'll find a bottle of excellent Madeira in the office. Take a stiff glass of it, sit down, and rest until I get there."

With a frantic nod, the frightened bank official scurried out of the vault and closed the back door behind him, then disappeared down the alley.

Carrière shrugged, then turned to Pascal and Jimson. "A man with nerves doesn't belong in our profession, eh, gentlemen?"

"That's right," Pascal grunted. "We've packed all the bars, M'sieu Carrière."

"Good. Take a look outside right now, Jimson, and see if Gros Ventre has come back."

"Right, boss," Jimson assented. He hurried up the steps of the vault, then down the narrow corridor to the back door, through which Alexander DuPlessis had departed. Opening it, Jimson glanced outside. Gros Ventre was already in the driver's seat, with the reins in his lap. Jimson made a sign to him, then went back into the vault.

"Gros Ventre's there, boss."

"Excellent! All right, I'm just about finished. There. A very fine haul, plenty for all of us. Now let's load up the wagon and get over to the warehouse. I hope Dalzell won't take too long coming back. Pascal, after the wagon's loaded, take the crowbar from the back of the wagon and hammer on the door to make it look as if we forced it.''

"Yes, boss."

"You're a good man, Pascal. You'll get a bonus for tonight's work.'' The Creole took a last look around and chuckled to himself. Fully two-thirds of the boxes had been emptied into the gunnysacks, and he now slung the last one over his shoulder. It was heavy, but it was a pleasant weight. The silver ingots would complete his plans for turning the tables on all those who dared to denigrate him because of his father's disgrace. Money could buy a beautiful wife, an estate, a great name. History had recorded many such instances.

He ascended the steps of the vault and went outside. Dalzell had come back and clambered into the driver's seat alongside Gros Ventre. Pascal and Jimson were arranging the gunnysacks, and now Christophe Carrière swung his into the wagon. Pascal had taken the crowbar and was beginning to strike heavy blows against the wood, making large, jagged dents.

"That's enough! Leave it slightly open to suggest to the stupid civil guard that someone broke in. And now, to the warehouse, messieurs!"

Don Diego had been emotionally exhausted from seeing his son-in-law and grandson off on the *Miromar*. He had guessed what perils John Cooper might encounter but had tried nonetheless to be jovial in his farewell until that last poignant moment when John Cooper and Andrew ascended the gangplank for their rescue mission. What little Don Diego knew of South America had been garnered in the distant past, when he had been at the court of Madrid. There had been much talk of the savage *indios*, headhunters, and cannibals. And these things, drawn back out of the clouded memory of the past, had secretly terrified him when he thought that John Cooper, Andrew, and lovely, courageous young Dorotéa might be beset by great danger.

Upon returning to the Mallard house, he had immediately gone to his room and went down on his knees to pray. Doña Inez had come to get him, concerned over the length of his prayers, and had instructed him to go to bed and rest. Happily, the long *siesta* had revived him. He dressed and now looked forward to an evening out. He embarrassedly admitted to a ravenous hunger, although in the same breath and in front of Hortense Mallard, who smiled tenderly at him, for she was very fond of this old *hidalgo*, he stammered, "I do hope that your fine cook, Ernesto, will not hear that I am looking forward to a dinner away from his kitchen. But it has been years since my Inez and I had a supper away from our own *hacienda*."

"There's no need to apologize, dear Don Diego," Hortense graciously replied. "We, too, revere Ernesto for his genius but confess to enjoying a leisurely meal with wine and fine service at one of the better New Orleans restaurants."

Fabien Mallard's coachman, Pierre Durey, drove the two couples in the elegant black carriage to the restaurant and then remained near at hand in a little square where the carriages of other patrons were waiting.

The restaurant's proprietor, Robert Metrier, and his wife, Emily, effusively greeted the Mallards, Don Diego, and Doña Inez. "You've come late, and we have had few guests. Thus, we can devote all our lavish care and love for good food and wine to your pleasure!"

The wife brought a plate of shrimp cooked in white wine and herbs, and her husband, sensing that this was a special occasion, produced a bottle of rare vintage white Bordeaux. There followed a fish stew, which Don Diego pronounced the best he had ever tasted, a light salad, and a majestic entrée. This was a *canard à l'orange*, with almonds, browned in butter, resting on a bed of wild rice. Accompanying this were dishes of tiny peas cooked with pearl onions, okra, and sweet yams in a wine sauce, over which Don Diego again smacked his lips and ecstatically praised the smiling Emily.

For dessert, Emily Metrier had concocted a plum tart with clotted cream, plus strong Creole coffee with a dollop of rum and more whipped cream to fortify it.

Doña Inez smiled happily as her elderly husband, enjoying himself hugely, began to relate many anecdotes of the court of Madrid and his early days in Taos. Robert Metrier and his wife came out of the kitchen to listen, his arm around her shoulders, and Fabien and Hortense eyed each other tenderly, then linked their fingers under the tablecloth. It was, indeed, a most intimate and romantic interlude.

Fabien insisted on paying the reckoning, and Don Diego left a generous *pourboire* for the cook herself.

They rose at last from the table, and Fabien walked toward the door while Doña Inez took her husband's arm and murmured, "We shall sleep late tomorrow, for you have had far too much to eat and drink. But I am happy to see how much you enjoyed it, *mi corazón*."

Just as they reached the door, there was a sudden explosion. Emily Metrier uttered a cry and crouched down as one of the shutters came flying toward her. Fabien Mallard threw up his arm and groaned in pain, as he felt a sharp piece of wood sting the fleshy part of his right arm. But Don Diego, standing to one side of the factor, seemed to receive the full force of the blast. The front door of the restaurant was blown back against him, felling him to the ground.

Doña Inez uttered a cry of horror and bent down over him. "Oh, Diego, my Diego, please, open your eyes and speak to me—are you badly hurt?"

"What happened?" Hortense gasped, pale and shaken. Fortunately, she had emerged unscathed.

The restaurant proprietor, after first seeing that his wife was not hurt, hurried forward to do what he could. "M'sieu de Escobar seems to be stunned. I don't see any blood— What a calamity! What could have happened? I have no enemies—"

"The civil guard will soon be here, do not worry," Fabien said after putting his arm around Hortense and making certain that she was not hurt. "I have a slight wound, but I fear my friend here may be seriously hurt. Madame Metrier, call for my carriage, please. We'll take him right to our house and call the doctor. Please, m'sieu," he said, turning to the proprietor, "help me with him. Take his feet, and I'll take his shoulders, and we'll carry him gently out to the carriage."

And so the little party made its way back to the Mallard house, Don Diego unconscious, and breathing heavily. The second honeymoon of the aged *hidalgo* and his beloved wife had received a distressing setback.

Eight

The warehouse to which Gros Ventre drove was about half a mile southeast from the levee. It was an old stone building that had stood vacant for some time. Because of its distance from the wharves, the property was not especially desirable. Thus it had become an ideal place of operations for the Creole dandy.

Alexander DuPlessis was already in the warehouse, nervously pacing back and forth. He stopped every few minutes to consult his own watch, and then again, interminably, to mop his forehead with his soaked handkerchief. When he saw the narrow door at the side open and the tall figure of his aristocratic partner enter, he uttered a cry of relief. "Praise the good God that you've come at last! I've been worried—I've heard noises—"

"Calm yourself, Alexander. It went off very easily." Then, turning to his four henchmen, he directed, "Leave the ingots in the wagon. Just unload the contents of the boxes."

"Why, boss?" Jimson grumbled.

"They'll have to remain hidden until the hue and cry die down, Jimson. If I were to attempt to turn that silver into immediate cash, there would be too many questions.

Never fear, they'll be hidden safely, and all of you will get a fair share. Besides, just from what's in the gunnysacks, every one of you will be rich for life. Spill the contents here on this big table so we can see what we really collected!"

The four men went out to the wagon to bring back the gunnysacks of jewels, gold, silver, and bank notes, and DuPlessis began to rub his hands, a greedy look on his sweaty face. "I really tipped you off to something big, didn't I, M'sieu Carrière? I should have a bigger share of this venture. If it hadn't been for me, you'd never have gotten into the bank, and you'd never have known about the silver or the rest of the things."

"I'll grant you that. Wait until we see what comes in. Then we'll talk sensibly. You're much too nervous. If I were you, I'd get a good night's sleep, go back to the bank, and try to act as if nothing had happened."

"I—yes—you're right. But it's going to be hard—I mean—my nerves—I almost feel sick. Are you sure no one saw us?"

"I don't know about 'us,' *mon ami*," the Creole mocked him, "because I don't know if anyone saw you when you scampered off to the warehouse in safety. But I can assure you that no one saw the five of us. Ah, here come the men now. On the table here, let's take a quick look and make an inventory!"

The four men came inside and emptied the contents of the gunnysacks onto the wide table. DuPlessis watched covetously, his eyes glittering. He gasped incredulously as his eyes fell upon necklaces; sapphire, turquois, and emerald rings; even diamonds and gold and silver coins; and bundles of bank notes, all of large denominations. "But I'm sure that what you have here, M'sieu Carrière, surpasses the value of the ingots! Ah, it was a lucky day for me when I saw those bars of silver and decided to tell you how we could both get our revenge!" he greedily exulted.

The tall Creole glanced at him, his face bland. But inwardly he loathed this fawning sycophant. Anyone could have an idea: It took genius to carry it out successfully.

"I'd like mine now, boss," Dalzell spoke up, and Gros Ventre grunted, echoing the sentiment. "I'd just as soon leave this city before the sun comes up in the morning, if it's all the same with you. Might be hot around here, once the civil guard gets done looking over the damage and finding out what's lost at the bank."

"I've no objection." Carrière patronizingly nodded as he adjusted his cravat. "Let's see what we have here, then divide it six ways. That's fair, is it not?"

Both Dalzell and Gros Ventre nodded, smiling at each other. Meanwhile, DuPlessis was outraged that he was being considered for only a one-sixth share. He was about to protest but then had another idea. He sidled toward one side of the table, to Carrière's right, and as the latter took out a leather cigar case and carefully chose a fine Havana panatela, the bank official swiftly pocketed a gold ring with an enormous star sapphire.

Pascal and Jimson noticed this and scowled, and Pascal was about to speak when Carrière held up his cigar and almost imperceptibly shook his head. Then, in a pleasant tone, he declared, "Of course, without an appraiser of fine jewels to set an accurate value on these baubles, we'll have to estimate their worth. However I'd say we've taken at least three hundred thousand dollars in bank notes and coins. The amount for the jewels would be at least double that—making it about nine hundred thousand—"

"Perhaps more!" DuPlessis breathlessly interrupted.

"Well then, let's say a million."

"But the ingots in the wagon, M'sieu Carrière, don't forget those. Aren't you declaring them into the inventory?" DuPlessis pursued.

"I told you before, Alexander, it'll be a long while

before we can cash in those ingots for money. It's much safer that way."

"Boss, why not figure a sixth of what was on that receipt you found in the vault with the ingots, add it to a sixth of the amount for the jewels and cash, and divide it that way and give us our share?" Dalzell spoke up again.

"Very well. Put the rough figure of our haul tonight at one million, two hundred thousand dollars. Then divide it by six—"

DuPlessis broke in. "I make it out to be two hundred thousand dollars to a man."

"Bravo, Alexander!" The tall Creole turned to the sweating banker and made a mockingly low bow in his direction. "Now, here is what I propose. Since we are not going to cash the ingots right away, you men take your shares from among the cash and jewels on the table. My share will be the ingots alone, which works out more or less to the two-hundred-thousand dollar amount per man we've agreed upon. I will worry about cashing them and realizing my profits in due time." He lit the cigar and took a puff, considered the glowing tip and delicately flicked off the ash with a fingernail, and said to Dalzell, "All right, Dalzell, you and Gros Ventre count out that amount for each of you. Take equal amounts of cash and jewels. I'll look on to see that the jewels you select are of equal value."

"Now that's what I call divvying up the swag straight off, no fancy tricks! I like working for a man of your jib," Dalzell chuckled as he advanced to the table and, his hands trembling slightly, began to pick up sheafs of bank notes, furling through them to determine the denomination, and then setting aside one sheaf for himself and one for Gros Ventre, who came to stand beside him. Then he created two equal stacks of coins, following that by giving both to himself and Gros Ventre several small diamonds, some emerald rings, and two sapphire necklaces.

Carrière watched with an indulgent smile as he enjoyed his cigar. When the two men had finished, he stepped forward and negligently remarked, "I don't want you boys to cheat yourselves. You've done well with the jewels, Dalzell, but you may have miscounted the notes. Let me double-check them for you and make certain that you've made no error."

"Sure, boss, sure! I ain't all that good at figures, and I'll tell you this. I've never seen this much money in all my life before," Dalzell breathed.

"And you're not likely to again." Swiftly, his lean fingers furling through the bank notes, Carrière counted, his lips moving silently. "I compliment you, Dalzell. I really didn't think you knew that much about figures. You're accurate within a dollar or two. Very well, and now for Gros Ventre's share—" He went through the same procedure, then nodded. "You gentlemen are free to leave. I'd prefer that you didn't tell me where you're going. Keep out of sight, and don't spend a great deal of that money suddenly in any one place because, wherever you are, it might draw the suspicion of the authorities."

"Don't worry about that," Dalzell chuckled. Then, touching his forehead, he and Gros Ventre hurried out of the warehouse.

DuPlessis turned to look after them and then came toward the tall Creole. "I think that was too fast. I really think that I should get more than a sixth."

"Consider how much two hundred thousand dollars is, Alexander. It will buy you a superb house, get you any woman you want, allow you to indulge in gambling or fine horses or wines, or whatever your penchant is. You can move across country, go even to the very end of these United States where you won't be found. Why should you be so greedy?"

"You know perfectly well! I deserve more than those

fellows. I told you, if it hadn't been for me, you wouldn't have known anything about what was in this bank."

"Well, I'll concede that much," Carrière sighed. "You really feel you should have more of a share, then?"

"Of course, I do!" the banker stubbornly insisted.

"*C'est bien,* Alexander. I shall give you something that will content you until eternity. I promise it." In the same moment as he finished his remark, Carrière drew a sharp stiletto from the inside pocket of his waistcoat and thrust it home to the hilt in Alexander DuPlessis's heart. The banker's eyes bulged with horrified surprise, then his face twisted in agony, and he slumped to the floor and lay with his arms sprawled out to each side.

Carrière coolly removed his stiletto and wiped the blade on the dead man's trousers. He turned to his remaining two men.

"You both saw him take that star sapphire ring, didn't you? We'd have trouble with a man like that. He was robbing you of your share. And our shares now increase by approximately sixty-five thousand each."

"What about his body?" Jimson asked.

"Wrap him in the tarpaulin in the wagon and drop him into the river. There are alligators enough who enjoy scavenging, and tonight they'll dine very well. Help me with him!"

In a few minutes, the lifeless body was wrapped in the tarpaulin, and hemp ropes were tied around it to keep the cloth in place. The two men looked to their leader now for instructions.

Carrière took another puff at his cigar. "And now, I'm willing to give each of you a substantial bonus for one final little errand tonight."

"What's that, boss?" Pascal eagerly demanded.

"I plan to hide the ingots. My father, peace to his memory, bought a small plantation about fifteen miles upriver. It's abandoned, and anyone around there avoids it like the plague. The slaves even have a superstition that it's haunted. We'll take the wagon there with the ingots and bury them underground. I'll give you your share plus the bonus I promised, after which we can go our separate ways.''

"I'm with you, boss," Pascal volunteered, and Jimson nodded that he shared his confederate's opinion.

"Good! Now first, put the jewels and cash back in the gunnysacks and put them into the wagon. When we complete our errand, we'll divide the loot up. Now, also lift M'sieu DuPlessis's body into the wagon. We'll throw him in the river near the plantation, rather than here near the levee, for it might attract some attention. We'll take the road just skirting the swamps to avoid any of the civil guard. I've planned this well, gentlemen, and I know they won't be in that section of town for at least another two hours, and besides, they're probably all at the locations where Dalzell and Gros Ventre left their little presents of gunpowder to welcome the new day.''

The two ruffians laughed, and after they had seen to the jewels and cash, they lifted the tarpaulin-wrapped body into the wagon, then got into the driver's seat as Carrière, putting a hand on the side of the wagon, nimbly leaped into it and seated himself beside the body of the banker. He chuckled softly, taking from his pocket the sapphire ring, which he had removed from Alexander's body while his subordinates fetched the tarpaulin. "Let's be off. I'll direct you. We will not travel too quickly—we must not rouse the slightest suspicion.''

The night was still, and as they took a narrow alleyway out toward the levee and northeastward, Carrière looked back to see men moving here and there far to his left. It was the civil guard investigating the explosions.

Carrière lit another cigar and languidly sank back against the side of the wagon, his feet resting on the tarpaulin with its grisly contents. He closed his eyes and, with a smile, reflected on what he had achieved this night—and what he still had in mind to do. When at last he was able to convert all of this booty into a foreign bank account that could not be traced, he would begin to exact his own revenge for the snobbery to which he had been so long subjected in New Orleans.

It was nearly four in the morning when the wagon reached what seemed to be a forest of gnarled cypress and live-oak trees, the ground thick with plantain grass, weeds, and brambles. Through the trees, the outline of an old frame house could vaguely be seen, with a cupola and portico, once whitewashed but now dingy and faded with the years. The shutters were broken, and the gate, whose picket fence was covered by ivy and moss, yawned wide, its hinges broken.

"Here's the place, gentlemen." Carrière leaped down from the wagon, his eyes bright with anticipation. "No one would ever think of looking here for the ingots."

"My gawd, boss," Pascal grumbled, "I see why they call this place haunted. How long is it since anybody lived here?"

"Seventeen years, Pascal," the tall Creole explained. "My father had hopes of settling down, living in retired luxury, but it wasn't to be. No matter. It will make a perfect hiding place. I have two shovels in the wagon. Now then, you see the porch?"

Both men glumly nodded, eyeing each other somewhat warily, then their aristocratic leader, who said, "Take the shovels and dig a deep hole on each side of the porch. Then divide the silver bars into the holes, and in that way, we'll lessen the risk of anyone's finding them. When that's done, we'll divide what's left in the gunnysacks and a little more for all your trouble."

"Sounds fair enough, boss," Pascal assented, reaching for one of the shovels. He strode to the left side of the porch. Jimson took his shovel to the right side. Carrière, meanwhile, lit still another cigar and watched them with narrowed eyes and a mocking little smile on his lips.

The horse that had drawn the wagon was weary now from all its exertions of the night and early morning and it stood passively, its head bowed, not even caring to try to graze on the rank grass and weeds before it. It was a quiet night, with only the slow murmur of the river downstream and, from afar, the twittering of a night bird and the soft hoot of a screech owl. To this now was added the *thuck-thuck-thuck* of shovels thrusting deeply into soft loam and the softer thud of the dirt being tossed to one side.

"Make them wide and deep, gentlemen. Then you'll smooth them over after we've put the ingots in."

"As you say, boss," Pascal genially remarked, pausing to stretch and ease the crick in his back. "Hell, I'm really aching."

"Think of how well you'll feel after it's all over," was Carrière's instant rejoinder as he took a puff of his cigar and, looking up at the half-moon waning in the sky, blew two wreaths of smoke upward toward it.

Twenty minutes later, Jimson called out, "See if this is deep enough, Mr. Carrière!"

"Very well." He walked slowly toward them. Both holes were ample—wide and deep, a good six feet or more.

Carrière casually unbuttoned his waistcoat, then suddenly drew out of his vest a small pearl-handled pistol and pulled the trigger. Jimson stiffened, his eyes bulging with surprise, as a tiny blue hole appeared in the center of his forehead. Then he toppled back, not far from the hole he had just dug.

"What the hell are you doing? Now wait a minute! You son of a bitch!" Pascal cried. Lifting his shovel on high, brandishing it like a club, he ran toward Carrière. But the Creole had plunged his left hand into the other pocket of the vest, drawn out the twin of the small, pearl-handled pistol, and pulled the trigger. Pascal stopped as if struck by lightning, the shovel dropping from his fingers as a tiny blue hole appeared just under his left eye. He took another step, unseeing, then pitched forward almost at Christophe Carrière's feet.

"Most accurate." The Creole thrust the little guns back into his pockets and then walked over toward Jimson's corpse. He gripped the man's collar, dragged him toward one of the holes, and shoved him down into it. He then dropped Pascal's inert body into the same hole. The men had been obedient but stupid. They had got what they deserved.

Carrière filled in the grave, smoothed and patted it, and then, going over toward a thick clump of bushes, he gathered some leaves and branches and spread them over the surface of the grave, so that there would be no sign of a freshly dug hole.

Swiftly and purposefully, he turned to the wagon and began to lift the silver ingots. Dalzell and Gros Ventre would never learn what had happened to their associates. With all that money, they would care even less.

An hour later, all the ingots were buried in the second hole and covered with leaves and broken branches. Carrière took a long last look around, lighting a fresh cigar. One day, a few years from now, he might restore the place—assuredly, he could afford it. But for now he was going to the wharf to find a ship that would take him to Amsterdam. There were excellent banks in that city, and he had always wanted to see the Low Countries. From there, he would travel to Paris for a well-earned vacation. After that, he would gather news of New Orleans, and if there was no danger, return wealthier than he had ever dreamed he could be.

In the wagon lay the large gunnysack into which had been transferred the rest of the bank notes and jewels. The other gunnysacks he threw into the gently flowing river after weighting them with rocks.

Then, ascending to the driver's seat and taking up the reins, he cajoled the horse, "Come on, now, you've had plenty of time to rest, for I've been doing all the work."

The horse raised its head, responding to the touch of the reins and the familiar voice. It plodded along the trail back toward New Orleans. Christophe Carrière watched the first red and purple hues of the dawn. The sun would rise to a brighter future than he had thought he would ever have. And it was only the beginning.

Nine

On the day after John Cooper Baines and his party had boarded the *Miromar* for Argentina, an exhausted courier, Ferdinand de Lloradier, galloped through the gateway of the *Hacienda del Halcón*. He was a *caballero* from Taos, and he had been sent by Doña Elena de Pladero to seek out her old friend Don Diego de Escobar.

Don Diego's son, Carlos, eating noon dinner with his beloved wife, Teresa, was told of the arrival. He excused himself and went out to meet the *caballero*.

"You've ridden a long way, *amigo*," Carlos genially

told the slim, mustachioed, black-haired rider. "You say that you come from Doña Elena de Pladero?"

"I do, Señor de Escobar. There are a nobleman and his entourage in Taos who have come from Madrid to see your father. The political situation is much more sensible in Madrid now, and the junta has made a full investigation of charges made against Don Diego when he was at the court. The investigation has resulted in the complete exoneration of your father."

"*Gran Dios*, what memories and what years that brings back to mind!" Carlos said thoughtfully. "I was just a child then—and my mother was dying, peace to her memory—" Here he crossed himself, and the *caballero* imitated him. "It was more than nineteen years ago. My father had been summoned to a private audience with His Most Catholic Majesty Charles IV and charged with treason. Queen María Louisa and Prime Minister Godoy banished my father and confiscated his lands. Although the king was too weak to stop them, he also knew well that my father had so loyally served him and his father before him. So King Charles appointed my father as *intendente* in the province of Taos." Carlos paused, thinking of those days. "But come now, I'm failing my hospitality! You've ridden all this long way, and you look hungry and thirsty and tired. Come to the kitchen, and old Tía Margarita will prepare you something very good to eat. Then you shall rest. Later today we shall talk again. Our *capataz*, Miguel Sandarbal, will replace your horse."

"You're much too kind, Señor de Escobar!"

"Not at all. Besides, you're bringing news that will enchant my father. I know that he has felt bitter over his rejection by the throne that he so loyally and arduously served."

The handsome Carlos de Escobar led the *caballero* to the kitchen, where Tía Margarita, as was her wont, fussed over the guest. After the courier had eaten and drunk two glasses of wine, Carlos took him to meet Teresa, quickly relating the message that had come from Doña Elena de Pladero.

"But that is wonderful news!" Carlos's lovely wife exclaimed. "Don Diego will at last feel himself freed of the anguish of banishment from his homeland. The court occupied so much of his early life that it will be a great blessing in his mellow years to know the court officially recognizes that he was never really guilty."

"Your sentiments do you great credit, Señora de Escobar," the *caballero* said, graciously inclining his head. "However, Doña Elena and her son, Tomás, think this newly arrived nobleman may have some hidden motive. She told me to tell you that she is not quite certain whether to trust him. Naturally, since her late husband was a dear friend of Don Diego, she is looking out for Don Diego's best interests."

"I understand," Carlos replied. "It was kind of you to make the journey all the way from Taos to bring us this message. If you have the inclination, Señor de Lloradier, I might ask you how things fare in Taos since I was there last. Is the *alcalde*, Cienguerda, treating the *indios* properly? Are there any signs that he still tyrannizes the impoverished residents of the pueblo?"

The *caballero* shook his head. "I'm happy to tell you, Señor de Escobar, that Alonzo Cienguarda seems to be a different man. He is more tolerant now of the *indios*— there have been no outrageous taxes against them nor any raiding by his soldiers. Of course, it was you and your friends, the Jicarilla Apache, who put an end to Cienguarda's tyrannies."

Carlos grimly smiled. "Yes. Well, now I should like to go to Taos on another errand. I want to visit this Spanish nobleman who comes with news of my father's exoneration."

"You're going to leave me, Carlos?" Teresa asked, wide-eyed.

Carlos turned to her with a tender smile. "With the greatest reluctance, *mi corazón*. I will be back as soon as I can. I promise you that. Indeed, I will invite this nobleman to visit us, so that my father, when he returns from New Orleans, can hear for himself the news he brings him. I feel confident, despite Doña Elena's apprehensions, that this nobleman has no hidden motives and is bringing great and glorious news indeed."

"Very well. There is enough for me to do here with the school and looking after the children . . . and waiting for the arrival of our own child, my dear one." Teresa suddenly had another idea. "Perhaps you'll allow me to tell your father, when he comes back from New Orleans, something of this news about the Spanish noble?"

"Yes, let him enjoy the anticipation of his visit." Carlos sighed sadly. "Perhaps it will distract him from his grief over Catarina. Well then, Señor de Lloradier, let me take you on a little tour of the Double H Ranch. We have a thriving community here, and it is so much different from Taos, where affairs are still as they were when Taos was ruled by Spain, before Mexico declared its independence."

"I envy you," the *caballero* said, sighing. "Life in Taos is extremely dull, though I'll admit that living in Taos kept me from the dangers of the upheaval that took place in my native Spain during the reign of Napoleon. Well now, I'm anxious to see your ranch. It seems so vast—horses, cattle, and sheep, and I saw the steeple of a church—"

"Yes, and there is a school. Also, we breed dogs—we have Irish wolfhounds that mated with timber wolves, and the strain is being continued. The result makes for an excellent watchdog, often valuable in the event of surprise attacks by enemies," Carlos explained.

Ferdinand de Lloradier bowed to Teresa de Escobar.

"It is an honor for me to have met you, Señora de Escobar. Thank you for your hospitality and your good wishes. I am happy that I brought this news for your *esposo.*"

"You are welcome here for as long as you wish to stay, Señor de Lloradier," Teresa responded.

The handsome *caballero* went with Carlos to the corral, where the latter selected a black gelding. "While you're here, Señor de Lloradier, you'll ride this horse, and it shall be yours when we go back to Taos. Indeed, I rather welcome this opportunity to be outdoors, to camp under the stars, and to be alone with my thoughts."

By the end of the day, the courier had seen the entire ranch, its remarkable preparations for defense, the *trabajadores* and their families, the livestock, and outbuildings, and as he rode back with Carlos to the huge ranch house, he exclaimed, "Compared with what I do in Taos, you have here a world of activity and courage. I'm tempted to join you."

"Do so, then, *mi amigo,*" Carlos enthusiastically proffered. "You will shake off the dusty traditions of old Spain and the indecision of the new, independent Mexico, which proclaims itself a republic and yet is dominated by that ruthless Santa Anna—and instead you will gain friends— and who knows, perhaps even a *mujer.*"

Ferdinand de Lloradier's eyes brightened, and he chuckled. "I confess what you have just said is almost enough to tempt me, *mi amigo.* Let us start out for Taos tomorrow. The sooner we go, the sooner we shall return to this wonderful place."

"That is fine with me. I confess I'm eager to see Taos and visit the *padre* who has done so much for *los indios,* as well as to visit my blood brothers high in the stronghold of the Jicarilla Mountains. But now, let's go back and enjoy the good supper that Tía Margarita and Rosa Lorcas have prepared for us."

And so, early the next morning, after kissing his wife and each of his children a tender farewell as they slept in their beds, Carlos de Escobar tiptoed out of his quarters and to the corral, where Miguel Sandarbal awaited him. Ferdinand de Lloradier was there also, his black gelding already saddled, his saddlebags laden with provisions. Miguel had suggested they take an extra two horses, which would carry ample provisions to see them through their long journey to Taos.

After saying good-bye to Miguel, the two men rode out through the gate above which rose the imposing sign of the *Hacienda del Halcón*. Etched into the wood was John Cooper Baines's double H brand, and as Carlos looked back, he knew this was a brand to be proud of, a brand destined to be renowned in the great Southwest.

Pastanari, son of the Jicarilla *jefe* Descontarti, had, at twenty-five years of age, become chief of his tribe, following the death of Kinotatay. He was the youngest chief the Jicarilla Apache had ever had, yet he had displayed unfailing courage in battle and had proved himself time and again as a worthy brave. Even the older braves did not resent his youth, for they knew that Pastanari believed that maintaining an army of fighting warriors was the best possible defense against the enemies of the Jicarilla. Thus their stronghold high in the Jicarilla Mountains of New Mexico was strong and secure, and Pastanari's people lived in peace.

On this mid-October day, young Pastanari turned to his handsome, soft-spoken wife, Numasari, who was sitting outside their wickiup, weaving one of the little baskets for which the Jicarilla Apache were renowned at the trading fairs in Taos and all the way to Chihuahua in Mexico. Pastanari said, "My wife, in due time, I must go to Taos to speak with the one who is now leader of the Pueblo *indios*. I go on a happy mission, to arrange the marriage of the Pueblo girl, Epanone, daughter of the deceased Rocaldi and his wife. It will be a happy event, and there will also be a celebration for us here in the stronghold tonight when she weds our own fine young brave, Lortaldo, He Who Hunts Without Fear. Out of respect to Lortaldo's parents, Epanone asked to be wed by our customs. But she also wants to take Lortaldo to her old village outside Taos and be wed again in the style of the *indios* of the pueblo. I think it is a good thing.''

"And I do also, Pastanari," his young wife noddingly assented as she put her hand on his shoulder and rubbed her cheek against his. "I would wed you a thousand times over, if it were within our customs, my beloved." She closed her eyes and put her arms around him and murmured, "I am so content with you, my husband. I think that the Great Spirit must love us both to give us such happiness when we are both so young, to give you such honor, which you deserve. And I am sure that your father, whose name we cannot speak, looks down upon you from the heavens and is proud of his son Pastanari."

Greatly moved, the young Apache leader put his arms around his wife and held her close for a moment, then abruptly rose. "I must go now to the elders to help prepare Epanone for the wedding ceremony tonight."

Pastanari smiled tenderly at his wife, then went out to talk to the elders. For the ceremony, he was dressed in tribal costume, with its beaded shoulder bands and with his hair plaited and enclosed in beaded tubes of bark and shell. And the colors of the Jicarilla would be visible to all, so they would know that he was *jefe*. They would be the colors of green and brown now, for it was harvest time.

It was a lovely, serene evening over the mountain stronghold. Only a gentle wind blew, an augury that the spirit gods approved of this union between the orphaned Epanone and the stalwart Jicarilla brave Lortaldo. And because Epanone was an orphan, Pastanari, as chief, would stand for her and proclaim that she had been adopted by the tribe.

Just before sunset, the shaman of the Jicarilla, Marsimaya, tall, with gray hair, sturdy and wiry, with kindly face and soft voice, had instructed Epanone in the responses she would make when she stood before him with her husband-to-be, Lortaldo.

Epanone's hair was gathered at the back of her neck and covered with a rawhide hair form, and she was known as "White-Painted Woman," wearing leggings, a jacket, and a skirt of white goatskin. There were amulets of beads, in the colors of the Jicarilla tribe, about her neck, wrists, and ankles.

Pastanari came toward the young couple and, smiling benevolently, gestured that they should follow him toward the wickiup of the shaman. When they stood before it, Marsimaya emerged, his face painted with the tribal markings of the foreteller of ceremonies, with a long wand in his right hand. Moving it in an arc, he beckoned for them both to kneel.

Epanone and Lortaldo sank down on their knees before Marsimaya, and then, as he laid the wand before them, he took the young warrior's right hand and Epanone's left. Drawing a sharp knife from his belt, he made a small incision on the first joint of the index finger of both hands, thrust the two cut places together, then swiftly bound the fingers with twisted thong.

Their faces were radiant as they looked up at him, and he intoned the ceremonial of the Jicarilla that binds squaw to mate till death: "There is no rain and no snow for you, for one is shelter to the other. There is no night for you, for one is light to the other. For you, the cold has ended always, for one is protection for the other. Thus it will be from now on. There will never be loneliness for you both—now and forever."

This said, they bowed their heads and closed their

eyes, and Marsimaya sprinkled flower pollen on them.
Picking up his wand, the shaman made a circle over them
and proclaimed, "The two I see before me in the circle of
our marriage rites are now one and the same person."

Then there was the wedding feast, and after this,
Pastanari approached the young couple, extending both
hands with his palms upward, and said, "Go to your
secret wickiup."

The father and mother of Lortaldo had brought forth
two mustangs, the one white, the other black. Epanone
joyously mounted the white mustang, her husband the
black, and they rode off to their wickiup. In ten days, they
would return, and then, as Epanone had requested, the
marriage ceremony would be repeated in the pueblo village
near Taos.

In their secret wickiup, hidden from all the villagers
of the stronghold, Lortaldo and Epanone communed. The
orphan girl now had a mighty tribe sponsoring her, and she
could feel that at last she belonged. What was more,
Lortaldo was not merely an Apache warrior but also a
young man of articulate and sensitive understanding and
ambitions.

On their first night together, after they had gently
made love, he said, "Epanone, I wish to do things for my
people, using what skills I have acquired to help the sick
and the old, to drive away pain, and to help humans as I
have helped animals."

"Tell me about your helping animals, Lortaldo,"
Epanone said.

"When I was a boy of fifteen, I had been told to hunt
so that I could prove my right to be a warrior. I came upon
a deer that stared at me with eyes that were mournful and
full of great pain. Its leg was broken. I cast away my bow
and arrows, and I came to it and gentled it. I spoke to it,
and it seemed to understand me. I broke off a piece of fir
branch, and I made a splint and bound it around the deer's

leg with a rawhide thong I had. I felt the leg go back into place, and the poor deer uttered a cry of agony, but then it licked my hand after the splint had been set into place. I brought it back to our stronghold and made a pet of it. I fed it corn and goat's milk until it was strong again. When it could run again, I put a leash about its neck and took it down to the ledge where I had found it, and freed it. It turned back to look at me, and its eyes were no longer full of anguish or suffering. It bounded away, and I felt as if I had counted more coup than if I had been a warrior.''

"Truly, Lortaldo?" she breathed.

The handsome young brave nodded. "There are those among our tribe who fear the *wasichu* and believe that he will destroy us all. But I do not think of this. I think only that he has knowledge that we do not have. If I could learn some of it, if I could go to the schools with some of the *wasichu,* perhaps I might learn more so that when some of my people are ill, I might free them of pain. This is what I wish more than anything else in the world, Epanone.''

"Lortaldo, you are good and kind, and as your squaw, I will do all I can to help you realize your hope. You will be a shaman among the whites, just as you wish to be now among your own people. I, Epanone, squaw of Lortaldo, of the Jicarilla, do pledge you this on this our wedding night!''

After ten blissful days in their secret wickiup, Epanone and her brave Lortaldo returned to the Jicarilla stronghold.

The people of the tribe greeted the young couple and nodded knowingly at the glowing expressions on the faces of the young man and woman. Pastanari and the shaman, Marsimaya, came out of their wickiups, also to welcome Epanone and Lortaldo home.

The young *jefe* strode up to them. "You have lived for ten days in the wickiup, in accordance with Apache law, and your wedding ceremony was that of the Jicarilla.

Do you still wish to travel to Taos and to the pueblo, there to repeat the ceremony of Epanone's people?''

Epanone took her husband's hand and squeezed it. Lortaldo turned to her, gave her an ardent look, then turned back to Pastanari. "It is our wish, yes."

"So be it," the *jefe* assented. "Go now to your own lodge, and on the morrow before the sun has reached its zenith, I will accompany you to Taos."

Epanone, Lortaldo, and the young *jefe* of the Jicarilla rode silently and slowly toward Taos. Far above them towered the mountains of the Sangre de Cristo range, the peaks snowcapped, silent, and eternal. The air was cool, and as they rode the trail, they could see below them the shrouding rows of pine, fir, and spruce, of tall oak and sturdy birch, of mountain flowers in profusion, in a kind of suspended bowl of life in which they alone moved forward.

As was the custom, Pastanari had brought with him the sparsest of provisions—two pouches filled with corn, one with jerky, and two large leather flasks of water. They took three days and two nights to reach the outskirts of Taos and to ride into the pueblo. Taos had once been the dream of old Madrid for wealth and unlimited power but had now been forgotten. Instead of mining silver and gold, brass and copper, the residents of Taos herded sheep, went to the fairs as far south as Chihuahua, and seemed content to drowse within their own limited boundaries. Pastanari, in his tribal dress with the mark of chief, was recognized by the villagers, who summoned their new *cacique*, or spokesman, Palvarde. The two *jefes* met in a clearing of the village to hold a council.

Pastanari quickly explained that Epanone and Lortaldo had already been wed by the Jicarilla law, but that it was Epanone's wish, as a native of the pueblo, to marry in the tradition of her own people. Palvarde nodded solemnly, "It is good that the young people have respect for the old ways. It would be very easy for them to die out—as our *alcalde* would undoubtedly wish.''

"I know of your *alcalde*, Palvarde,'' Pastanari agreed. "I know also of *los Hermanos Penitentes*—the penitent brothers, who watch over the pueblo and punish any who would do you harm. It is fortunate that they are still powerful in Taos—otherwise this *alcalde* of yours would surely carry out his wish.''

"It is a hard time for the *indios* of this region, *mi jefe*,'' Palvarde said. "But we are fortunate to have the help of *el Halcón*, who has given our people much silver with which to buy food and clothing and tools to make the artifacts we sell at the trading fairs. Yes, we are fortunate indeed to have *el Halcón*, along with his *cuñado*, Carlos de Escobar, the good priest of Taos, and your own people, Pastanari, to help make the people of the pueblo grow stronger. And now our people will make a joyous festival of the marriage between Epanone and your warrior, Lortaldo. I will tell my people, and tomorrow we shall have the ceremony. But in the meantime, I must instruct both Epanone and Lortaldo in what we do when two young people join their lives under the sky of the Great Spirit. They begin a kind of courtship, as if they had never met before, and the one must accept the other. Then they come before me to seek the union of themselves into one, in a way just as you of the Apache do. We have much in common, Pastanari.''

"I am happy to have made this journey to the pueblo, Palvarde,'' the young Jicarilla chief responded. "I renew my pledge that my people will aid you if ever there is trouble between you and the *wasichu*.''

"That will make my people rejoice. The spirits of honesty that you and we both prize can be upheld, especially as a lesson to our children, who will lead our villagers in the years ahead. I am glad that you have come.''

As spokesman and chief elder, Palvarde took a sharp knife and bade one of the older men of the council to hold a clay bowl between them as he cut Pastanari's wrist and then his own, pressed the wounds together, and had another elder bind their wrists with a leather thong until the flow of blood had ceased. "Now we are blood brothers, and I pledge that my people will always be the friends of the Jicarilla, and that we, too, will do all we can to fight against your enemies," Palvarde intoned.

Then, summoning Epanone and Lortaldo to stand before him, he declared, "When one of the pueblo is to marry, it must be by command by those who govern. Since it is known that you have already wed in a ceremony on which my blood brother Pastanari can testify, we may ease our customs, but still, Epanone, since it was your wish that you be married according to pueblo law, you must agree to do those things that are unique to our way of life."

"Willingly, mighty *cacique*," Epanone said, bowing her head.

Palvarde turned to Lortaldo and said, "You must spin and weave a mantle and place it before this woman. When she covers herself with it, she becomes your wife. Now, since I know that Apache men do not spin, what I order you to do is to go to the *jacal* of old Estufemia, who is the best spinner and weaver of the villagers. She will set the loom for you, and then you must sit before it and work as she bids you, even if it takes all through the night. Thus you will have earned the right to put the mantle before this woman who is to be your squaw."

Lortaldo smiled and nodded in understanding and said respectfully, "I will do whatever the *cacique* orders of me."

This answer pleased Palvarde, who raised his right hand in benediction, then made a sweeping sign across his chest and to his left hip. "It is ordained that you shall have this woman as your squaw. Epanone, you shall have this brave as your husband. Let it be so said that the pueblo consents to the wedding! Now, Lortaldo, there is one thing more. Tomorrow at noon, I shall send Epanone to the well. She will carry with her a clay jug with our tribal markings. You will be there, and when you see her coming, you will go to her and take away the jug. This will show to all the village that you wish to marry her. And then, at sundown, you will present the mantle to her. This is how it will be. Remember it well."

"I vow that I shall do all that is asked of me," the Jicarilla warrior declared. He hurried off with an elder to the weaver's *jacal*, and calling out to her, he asked permission to enter. When this was granted, he knelt before her and explained his mission. She nodded, led him to the crude spinning wheel, and took white threads and began to show him how it was that a mantle was made.

The next noon Epanone took the ceremonial water jug and walked slowly toward the well. Lortaldo, who had worked throughout the night and had little sleep, awaited her. As she neared the well, he came forward and very gently murmured, "My beloved, let me take the jug to show all these villagers of your native pueblo that I wish no other squaw in all this world, now or ever!"

A chorused shout went up from the villagers as they watched the ritual, and the young couple walked back toward the *jacal* of the *cacique*, who made a sweeping sign with his right arm to signify that the gods were pleased over the observance of this ancient tradition. And then, at sundown, Lortaldo proudly stood in the clearing circle where the council of the Pueblo *indios* was held, and as Palvarde and Pastanari watched side by side, he laid the mantle before Epanone and bent his head, outstretched his arms, and waited.

A hush came over the villagers as they watched Epanone contemplate the white mantle, and then they murmured and smiled and nodded to one another as she stooped to pick it up and to place it around her shoulders. Then she held out her hands to her husband, who embraced her.

"Now the two of you are one, truly in the way of our ancestors," Palvarde intoned. Raising his arms to the sky, he chanted, "Let the gods of the sun, the moon, the wind, the sea, the mountains, the fire, the grass, and all living things that are good upon this earth behold that Epanone and Lortaldo have become one, from this moment forth."

There was a great feast. Epanone and Lortaldo sat in the center of the circle, and the *cacique* served them with his own hands. And, after the feast, the *cacique* led them both to a newly built *jacal* on the very outskirts of the pueblo, so that they might be alone on this first night after their wedding in the town of Taos.

Pastanari walked back with Palvarde to the latter's hut, where they smoked a ceremonial pipe. The *cacique* said meditatively, "This was a great day for us in the village, Pastanari. It has done the children and the old ones good to see how the old ways withstand what the *wasichu* have sought to do to us. We have honor and dignity now in this village, and I know that the father and mother of Epanone, in the sky with the Great Spirit, rejoice to see their daughter united with so fine a young man of your tribe. Now, my brother, let us smoke a last pipe of peace and then seek the darkness of sleep and dreams that promise much for both our tribes."

Ten

Two days after Carlos and the *caballero* had left for Taos to meet the nobleman who had come from Madrid to clear the name of Carlos's father, Bess Sandarbal asked her husband to accompany her to the mission house where Sister Eufemia presided. She and her eight Dominican nuns had found their sanctuary at the Double H Ranch, and the *trabajadores* had built the mission house for their arrival earlier in the year, after a long pilgrimage from a small Mexican village.

Sister Eufemia and Carlos's wife, Teresa, were chatting with the eight nuns in the downstairs meeting room of the mission house when Bess and Miguel entered the building. Miguel felt uncomfortable in the presence of all these ladies, and he helplessly twisted his *sombrero* in his hands.

"Greetings to you, Señor and Señora Sandarbal!" Sister Eufemia exclaimed. "We were just having a little discussion about school lessons and what we may do this fall and winter."

"Why, that's exactly why my husband and I have come to see you," Bess said brightly. "I'm sure you'll need more room for the pupils."

"Undoubtedly," the mother superior gravely nodded.

90

"If there will be settlers moving here from Eugene Fair's settlement on the Brazos, as we have heard, plus still other newcomers to this area, we shall certainly need almost twice as much space. Thanks to you and to Señora de Escobar, we can give a varied curriculum—English, Spanish, geography, history, mathematics, and reading, of course. And we have exercises in penmanship." She sighed at this and shook her head. "It is not one of the finest attributes of these otherwise bright young children."

"It's because, Sister Eufemia," Miguel said in defense of the children of the *trabajadores*, "here on the Double H Ranch, we try to teach them when they are very young how to ride horseback, avoid dangers, recognize such natural enemies as snakes and wild boars—and perhaps they therefore think more of these things, which are exciting, than of classroom exercises."

"That is a very good point, Señor Sandarbal," Sister Eufemia agreed. "We know how difficult it is to have children concentrate on classroom lessons. But perhaps a happy combination of your survival lessons and our curriculum will achieve what is really vital for these bright young minds."

"Yes, I quite agree," Bess Sandarbal said. "But the reason I brought my husband here, Sister Eufemia, is to see how much space you think you will need, once the new families settle down with us."

"I should think that another classroom exactly the size of what we now have would be extremely useful," Sister Eufemia said. "Each child could be dealt with individually so that he or she would certainly learn more and have an incentive for doing so."

"Yes, I'm in complete accord," Teresa now spoke out. "Señor Sandarbal," she said, turning to the white-haired *capataz*, "how long do you think it would take to build another schoolhouse with an adjoining door so the two schoolhouses would connect?"

"If I set the *trabajadores* to work on it at once, I'm sure that within a month it could be ready," Miguel vouchsafed.

"Then you'll do it, dear Miguel." Bess turned to her husband, her eyes sparkling.

When she looked at him like that, Miguel could refuse her nothing. "Why," he boasted, seeing that Sister Eufemia was looking at him with a smile on her stern face, "I shall try to do better than a month, *querida!* If you will excuse me, I shall go give orders to my men so that the good work may be started up at once."

"Thank you, Señor Sandarbal," Sister Eufemia gently remarked. "My sisters and I will say prayers for you in chapel tonight."

"Thank you, Sister. Well now, I'll be off. I'll see you this evening, *querida.*" This last to Bess as, backing out of the room, he finally opened the door and fled into the daylight with a sigh of relief. Miguel had only come to the mission house in the first place at the insistence of his lovely, blond-haired wife, who wanted him to make his own contribution to the discussion of the schoolhouse, since he and his men would be building it. But still he was unaccustomed to dealing with ladies.

Before he could get very far away, however, Teresa called after him, "Señor Sandarbal, when you talk to the *trabajadores* about building an addition to the school, I think that one section should be for the very little children and the other for the older ones. The new addition should be for the youngest children."

"Very well, Señora de Escobar, I'll see to it," Miguel hastily called back, rolling his eyes and muttering under his breath. He could only hope that once the workers began their toil, these charming ladies did not suddenly come to him and completely change their minds.

In a few minutes, Miguel had summoned half a dozen of the best carpenters among the *trabajadores* and given them specific instructions. "Now let's make the ladies happy because all of you men know that when our women are happy, we are happy in turn. It's a philosophy I've learned to live with, and I'm sure that by now most of you will agree with it."

Two days after Miguel Sandarbal had set the *trabajadores* to work on the foundation of the addition to the schoolhouse, the scout James Bowie—who was already becoming renowned throughout Texas as a defender of the American settlers there—rode in with two of his friends and halted his horse as he watched the workers cut the planking.

"I tell you, boys," the scout said to his companions, "this is the busiest place in all Texas. You can see for yourselves that this ranch is already like a small city, bigger even than most of the settlements along the Brazos."

Miguel, seeing him, hurried over to greet him. *"Buenos días,* Señor Bowie! It's good to see you again! But I'm afraid you won't find *el Halcón* or the Señor Carlos, either—or, for that matter, not even his father, Don Diego. The fact is, Señor Bowie, no sooner had John Cooper and his wife returned from their last visit with you than a letter came from the Señora Dorotéa's majordomo in Argentina, saying that her father had been thrown into jail in Buenos Aires by the *porteños*. It was a political movement, but *el Halcón*, his wife, as well as Felipe Mintras, the *gaucho* who returned with them, and some of our best men, went back to Argentina to try to rescue her father."

Jim Bowie uttered a long whistle and shook his head.

"Don Diego went to stay in New Orleans, and Carlos is in Taos. But John Cooper told me to expect you and your men, Señor Bowie," Miguel put in cheerfully.

"Well, good to see you, Miguel," Bowie said. "Let me introduce you to my friends. Toby, Manuel, this is

Miguel Sandarbal, the best foreman either east or west of the Mississippi!''

''Come now, Señor Bowie, you flatter me beyond my due,'' the white-haired *capataz* said, flushing with embarrassed pride.

''Not a bit! If I had a ranch of my own right now, I'd try to hire you away from here—though I'll bet you'd never go.''

''That's true, Señor Bowie. I owe my loyalty to Don Diego, and I like *el Halcón* as a man and a friend. There's no need to talk of hiring me away—no matter what kind of money you'd offer.''

''Good man! Loyalty's a rare virtue, and we'll need plenty of it in Texas,'' the scout declared. ''I'm lucky to have my own good men, eight of them—including Manuel and Toby here—who have signed up with me as part of this Texas Rangers company I'm trying to found.''

''You'll need more than that, Señor Bowie, if you're going to patrol all of Texas,'' Miguel said, shaking his head.

''You're right there. It's bad enough with the renegade Indians and the warring tribes, but now that the Mexican government is showing disfavor even to Stephen Austin, and Santa Anna's on the rampage, we'll need a great many more Texas Rangers before we're done. That's one of the reasons I came back here again so soon.''

''To enlist some of our *vaqueros* as Texas Rangers, *¿no es verdad?* Señor Baines also told me about this. He was sorry that he could not be here to help, but he has given me the authority to work with you. All our *vaqueros* are brave and strong and would gladly fight to keep Texas safe!''

''Well, that's good news indeed! I'm glad to have your help. I'll need more than bravery and strength, though, Miguel. I'd prefer men without families. There's plenty of danger in this job, and a man who doesn't have a wife and

children is obviously going to do less worrying about what
might happen to him when he's trying to dodge a bullet or
an arrow.''

The *capataz* scratched his chin and nodded. "I can
understand that, of course, Señor Bowie. We have in all
about sixty *trabajadores*. I'd say about a dozen to fifteen
of them are not yet married, and another ten or twelve
have given their word to some *muchachita linda*.''

"Well, that means about two dozen men,'' Bowie
said, "give or take a few. If I could get five or six out of
that lot to join up with me, then I'd have a good talking
point when I go visiting around this part of the country to
try to build my ranks.''

"I'll be glad to talk to them, Señor Bowie,'' Miguel
volunteered.

"Thanks, Miguel, but when I wrote to John Cooper
about this, I mentioned the idea of running a contest to see
which ones among those unattached *vaqueros* of yours
could be auxiliaries. In other words, they wouldn't have to
give up working at the Double H Ranch right now, but we
could call them into action if we needed them.'' Bowie now
explained the contests he had in mind, riding and shooting
with pistols and rifles, but said that Miguel should take
care of all the specifics.

"That I will do. And with all those men competing,
they would try to do their very best so as to shine in the
eyes of their *compañeros*. Yes, Señor Bowie, it's a fine
idea.''

"Now, Miguel, I wish you'd just plain call me Jim
instead of Señor Bowie.'' The scout chuckled and gave
Miguel a friendly pat on the shoulder. "Keep in mind that
a good Texas Ranger must be able to shoot, use a knife,
camp out, forage for food and water, ride long hours, and
yet still be fresh in the saddle when he has to cover ground
in a hell of a hurry. Of course, a Texas Ranger has to love
this part of the country, want to protect it, and hope that

one day it'll be part of the United States, separate and independent from Mexico.''

''I should like to see that myself, Señor—I mean, Jim.''

Bowie patted him on the shoulder again. ''Also, Miguel, a Texas Ranger has to be a man of honor who thinks of the whole outfit, not just himself. Now, of course, I could talk to your *vaqueros*, but I think it ought to come from you. You're the *capataz*, and they respect you.''

Miguel chuckled self-effacingly and twisted his *sombrero* between his strong, callused fingers. ''That's kind of you to say so. I like to think that my *trabajadores* are loyal and respect me, and I'd never ask them to do anything I couldn't do myself. Let me call these *vaqueros* who have no families and who may well wish to join your company.''

''We'll go riding around the ranch while you're doing that, Miguel,'' Bowie said, gesturing to his two friends to remount their horses. ''You've strengthened the ranch's defenses again, I see. It's going to be a solid bastion of defense if ever there's an attack from the *soldados*.''

''I'm praying there won't be, all the same,'' Miguel said, crossing himself. ''Yet, I agree, it never hurts to strengthen oneself against a possible enemy.'' Then, taking his leave of the three scouts, he hurried to the bunkhouse to call out the *vaqueros*.

Half an hour later, the white-haired *capataz* had the men lined up in two rows before him. These comprised all who were not yet married, even including those who had given their word to some pretty *criada*.

In all, there were twenty-seven men, and of these, fifteen volunteered to take part in the contests. There would be, of course, a display of horsemanship, which would narrow the field of competitors considerably. Then there would be target shooting, the invariable test of a man's skill out on the frontier. His ability to draw quickly and to kill, or at least badly disable his enemy, could well mean the difference between his life and death.

"*Amigos,*" Miguel concluded, "remember now, those of you who show the most skill at the contests won't leave our *hacienda* right away. You will be held in reserve for the time when you will be needed. Until then, of course, you will continue to report to me, your *capataz,* and I will assign to you those tasks that are required of you, so long as you are in the employ of the *Hacienda del Halcón.*"

A tall, lanky, black-haired young man in his mid-twenties spoke up, his eyes bright with anticipation. "When do you think we might leave to become regulars in this outfit, *señor capataz?*"

"Oh, I see. You do not like Tía Margarita's cooking, and you are unhappy with me, and you find yourself overworked and weary long before the sun sets, is that it?" Miguel sarcastically countered, amid the laughter of the other men. "Alvarado Jimínez, you are the newest of the *vaqueros* here, and you are still on tolerance, don't forget it. So far, you haven't displeased me. But I have my eye on you, Alvarado Jimínez, and I will say only this: If you should be one of the winners of these contests, I will give you leave to go with Señor Jim Bowie and his two friends before the sun sets today."

There was much good-natured chaffing and bantering among Alvarado Jimínez's companions, and the young Mexican hung his head and looked sheepish. But Miguel Sandarbal held up a hand for silence, and his fierce look told Alvarado that he would brook no more nonsense. "*¡Silencio, por favor!*" he bellowed. "First, each one of you is going to perform an exercise on horseback. Señor Jim Bowie and his two friends, who are already Texas Rangers, will watch you try to win the honor of becoming one of them."

There was an excited murmur among the two ranks of *vaqueros* as Miguel cleared his throat and put on his most

serious mien. "You'll recall that after the Comanche and
the Comanchero attacked us, several of their lances were
found on the battlefield. I had them put into the toolhouse
north of the school. Alvarado, *amigo*, make yourself useful and bring two of them."

"*¡Pronto, mi capataz!*" The young Mexican saluted
and hurried off to the shed. Meanwhile, Jim Bowie and his
scouts rode up, ready to watch the contest.

Alvarado returned in a few moments with two painted
lances, colorful feathers glued to the ends of the barbed
shafts. They were fearsome, the points murderously sharp,
flat, and double-edged, not unlike a broad arrowhead.

"Here we are!" Miguel enthusiastically announced.
"This old *sombrero* will be your target. You will ride,
hugging your horse with your knees. In your hand you will
have the spear. As you near the *sombrero* at full gallop,
you are to impale it with the spear and lift it up in the air
for all to see! I, Señor Bowie, and his two *amigos* will act
as judges." Miguel turned to the scout and chuckled.
"This will separate the *vaqueros grandes* from the ordinary
sheepherders and cowhands, Señor Jim."

Meanwhile, the *vaqueros* hurried to the stable and
returned a few minutes later with their mounts. Miguel
took the old, faded *sombrero* and tossed it on a strip of flat
ground in a clearing. "Now, you will start back at the
hacienda itself, which I estimate to be about three hundred
yards away. Alvarado, unless you are winded from going
to the shed to fetch those spears, you may be first!"

"I'm not winded, *señor capataz*, and I think I can do
it!" the young Mexican bragged.

Alvarado was riding a piebald gelding, stocky in the
withers, but possessed of great stamina. Alvarado himself
was an excellent horseman, willing and enthusiastic. He
trotted the gelding back to the starting line, then leaned
forward in his saddle, having taken one of the lances
in his right hand. Squinting at the *sombrero* on the

ground, he now urged his gelding on, clenching his knees together with a loud cry. The gelding broke into a gallop and headed for the *sombrero*.

Miguel watched intently, his eyes glowing.

Alvarado rose in the saddle, aimed the lance, and lunged it downward at the old *sombrero*. Then, in almost the same movement, he tilted the lance up and rode back toward Miguel and the others with the *sombrero*. He held the lance high, the *sombrero* impaled on the tip, for all to see.

Loud huzzahs welcomed this extraordinary feat, and Jim Bowie slapped his thigh and exclaimed, "I've never seen a better trick! *¡Muy bueno, caballero! ¡Gran vaquero!*" Then, turning to his two friends, Toby and Manuel, he said, "There's a man who'd be a valuable ally for us, boys! If he can shoot as well as he can ride and handle the lance, we'll sign him up this very day, or my name's not Jim Bowie."

In order not to waste time, the second man in line had taken the other lance, mounted his gelding, a roan, and ridden back to the starting line, while Alvarado, basking in the praise from his companions, tossed the *sombrero* onto the ground, dismounted, and handed the lance to Miguel, who in turn gave it to a third rider who would enter the contest.

The second *vaquero*, Santiago Estanza, ruined his timing because of his eagerness. He missed the *sombrero* with his lance by some four inches. There was a shout of dismay from his friends who watched, and he scowled angrily, for he surely would be placed low on the lists now.

One by one, the *vaqueros* and *trabajadores* galloped toward the *sombrero*. When the competition was over, Miguel announced, "*Amigos,* we have four who stand high in this first trial. Alvarado Jimínez, Jorge Simarnal,

Roberto Porterez, and Julio Mortado. Now we shall see how well you handle your other weapons.''

As Miguel was preparing for the rifle and pistol test, the Texans who had settled on the Double H Ranch many years earlier came toward the *capataz*. They were Malcolm Pauley, Jack Williams, Edward Molson, his cousin Ben Forrester, and Henry Ames.

Edward Molson called out, ''We've been watching your maneuvers, Miguel! What's it all about?''

''Why, Señor Molson, Señor Jim Bowie and his two friends are here, recruiting for a patrol group that he will call the Texas Rangers.''

''Well, boys,'' Molson said, turning to his four friends, ''this is what John Cooper talked to us about before he left.''

Ben Forrester solemnly nodded. ''And I also discussed it with Carlos. If we qualify, he's all for us going in order to help bring about law and order in this part of the country.''

Overhearing all this, Jim Bowie now came toward the two cousins, held out his hand, and introduced himself, then shook hands with Malcolm Pauley, Jack Williams, and Henry Ames. He briefly explained what the Rangers' duties would be, and Molson enthusiastically declared, ''I want to enter the competition right now. I'd like to go with the Rangers. How about you, Ben?''

''I'd go if Mr. Bowie'll have me,'' Ben replied. ''We've had a great time here, but we'd be willing to move wherever the Texas Rangers make their headquarters.''

Henry Ames, towheaded, now thirty-two, looked around at the more than a dozen *vaqueros* who had entered the contest to see if they would qualify to join the Texas Rangers. He now spoke up, with a fierceness to his voice that made Edward Molson turn to look at him with surprise. ''I'll pull up stakes, too, if Mr. Bowie will have me.''

''You really don't have to qualify, Mr. Ames,'' Bowie

said, once again extending his hand, which Ames energetically shook. "I've heard all about how many years ago you and your friends escaped the Battle of Medina. That was one of the first of the battles between the Texans and the Mexicans; it won't be the last, I'm sorry to say. Anyway, I'd be proud to have you sign up. I can't promise you anything permanent right now, but I'd certainly like to have you go around with us on patrol. As for pay, well, I can't promise you much in that regard either. We don't really have a Texas government yet—not that it isn't being worked on."

"I'll make my living from the soil, the way I did near San Antonio and the way I've done here," Henry Ames said. "You know, all of us have been talking with John Cooper about resettling—of course, we're very grateful to him, Don Diego, Carlos, and Miguel—there's nothing we wouldn't do for them. All the same, we feel we can be of more use as Texas Rangers. John Cooper suggested we move to that Austin settlement started by Eugene Fair near the Brazos."

"That's not a bad idea at that," Bowie gravely answered. "The fact is that we can use a good deal of protection around that community. They've fewer people on hand who really know how to put up a good defense against attack than the Double H Ranch here. Plus, there are folks living there who'd be mighty glad to move here. That way there'd be an even exchange in people."

"Then we could move there, Mr. Bowie?" Henry Ames pursued.

"By the eternal, yes you can, you and your friends," the scout said.

"Thanks, Mr. Bowie. We'll talk to you after this contest is over," Edward Molson smilingly said. "I'll admit"—this with a relieved chuckle—"that I'm happy you're going to cut out the qualifying test for us. It might just happen that we're a little rusty and we might not score so high as some of these young *trabajadores*."

"Now don't go acting modest on me, Mr. Molson." Jim Bowie grinned. "No, sir, you've shown what you can do in the Battle of Medina; you don't have to pass any tests."

"That's fine news!" Molson said. "The decent thing to do is wait until either Don Diego or Carlos gets back and tell him that we've decided to go ahead with the plans as we discussed earlier with John Cooper and Carlos."

All this while, Miguel and the young *vaquero* Antonio Lorcas had prepared the first target for the rifle competition. There was an old, scarred hitching post east of the corral, and the white-haired *capataz* cut an H with his hunting knife some three inches below the top. The initial itself was no larger than an inch vertically and another inch horizontally. Straightening, he turned and declared, "*Amigos*, we'll shoot from three hundred feet. Each *vaquero* will have two shots. Antonio and I will count the hits that come closest to the horizontal link. *¿Comprenden?*"

"That's quite a difficult target you've got there, Miguel." Bowie chuckled. "I'll tell you this—any man who can hit that target even once is good enough to be a Texas Ranger."

Now the *vaquero* Antonio Lorcas set down a box of rifle balls and a flask of gunpowder to the left of the firing line and squatted down to watch the contest.

The four *vaqueros* who had shown to best advantage in the test of horsemanship also acquitted themselves quite well in rifle shooting. Of the four, Roberto Porterez was the very best. Julio Mortado put one ball about a half inch to the right of the center of the horizontal line, and after it was all over, Miguel declared that Roberto had come first and Julio second. Not that the other *trabajadores* did not shoot well, for not one of them missed the hitching post, though most of them shot above the target or veered to the right, not allowing for trajectory and wind.

Now it was time for the competition of pistol marksmanship, and Miguel nodded to Antonio, who had brought out from the shed a flat, rectangular piece of pinewood, the surface of which had been planed down. The young *vaquero* stood this against the hitching post that had been used as the rifle target and, at another nod from the *capataz*, took a piece of charcoal and carefully drew the outline of a man. He showed excellent artistry, and the outline was fully as tall as an average *vaquero*.

Miguel turned to the competitors and declared, "And now, *mis compañeros,* you will pretend that this is a *soldado* or an *indio* who wants to kill you. Each of you will fire two shots from a distance of one hundred and fifty feet. Each man will use his own pistols."

After Antonio had paced off the requisite distance and then with the heel of his boot drawn the firing line, Alvarado Jiménez stationed himself facing the target and, his left hand holding a gun at his side, slowly raised his right hand and aimed his pistol at the outline of the man drawn in charcoal.

Once he had leveled the weapon, he fired, and Miguel exclaimed, "That shot would have hit your *soldado* right through his heart. Well done, *amigo!* And now your second shot!"

Jiménez's second shot was fired almost instantly, the young *vaquero* using the gun in his left hand this time. The ball buried itself in the soft pinewood slightly to the right and about an inch below the ball that Miguel had first announced as being fatal to the imaginary enemy.

The other three *vaqueros* who had scored so well in the horsemanship competition—Jorge Simarnal, Roberto Porterez and Julio Mortado—also acquitted themselves quite well. After about half an hour, the competition was over, and two other *vaqueros* had scored equally well with Alvarado.

Jim Bowie now stepped forward, the excitement of watching the competition making his eyes glitter. "Miguel, my good friend, let me show you a different kind of trick shooting. If someone has a bandanna, I'd be much obliged if he'd blindfold me."

"By all means, Señor Jim," Miguel chuckled.

There was a murmur among the *vaqueros*, for Jim Bowie's reputation with knives or guns was legendary.

Miguel tied the bandanna over Bowie's eyes. Hardly had he finished when the scout leveled both pistols and fired simultaneously at the plank outlined with the life-sized form. Miguel uttered an incredulous cry. "I do not believe what I see! Both balls have struck the heart of the enemy! That is the most beautiful shooting I have ever witnessed, *¡es verdad!*"

"It's just a matter of concentration. But don't forget, *amigos*," Jim Bowie genially addressed his absorbed audience, "that your enemy isn't going to stand still and let you use him as a target. He's going to try every trick of his own to kill you before you do it to him. Now good luck to all of you and thanks for making it a very enjoyable time for my friends and me! My men and I must head back to the Brazos now, but one day soon I'll be calling on those who qualified to enlist as Texas Ranger regulars. It may still be a while till we're organized, but just as soon as we are, you'll draw your first pay!"

Eleven

In a little *posada* not far from the Plaza de la Victoria
in Buenos Aires, Argentina, two men sat facing each
other. One was Porfirio Ramos, a stout, gray-haired man
with a waxed mustache, heavy jowls, and bulbous nose.
He was elegantly dressed in a white linen suit with ruffled
shirt and neatly tied cravat. His companion was a swarthy,
stocky man with unkempt black hair and beard. Squinting
through narrowly spaced, beady little black eyes, Ramos
said in a supercilious tone, "Now, Villardebo, what's this
news you have to tell me?"

"I apologize for troubling you, Señor Ramos," the
younger man fawningly blurted out, "but I think you'll
forgive my disturbing you. I know what it must be like
when one is a busy, important man and—"

"Get to the point, Villardebo!" Ramos growled, his
eyes slitted in a look of contemptuous distaste. "If any one
of my colleagues from the government should see me in
this wretched place, my reputation would be ruined, and
they would think me no better than the filthy, lice-ridden
gauchos of the *pampas*—may they all perish in the lowest
confines of hell itself!"

"But I'm coming to the point, Señor Ramos," the

stocky man fearfully exclaimed. "I have heard you talk about the *gringo* who once came to our country to bring palominos and bulls to Señor Maldones—"

"Do not grace that traitor Maldones with the title of 'señor,' Villardebo," Porfirio Ramos angrily broke in, hammering his fat fist on the table till the glasses clattered. "He is in the *calabozo* where he belongs—and I'll have him sent to a firing squad before I'm done with him. What news could you have? He's been languishing in the cell ever since my friends in the government authorized me to have him arrested and jailed for making treasonous statements against the government. What could he have done from there?"

"It's not what he did, Señor Ramos," the other man protested. "I started to tell you about the *gringo* who once came to the Maldones *hacienda*—"

"Yes, yes, I know all that. Get on with it, man!" Ramos made a grimace as he looked around him. It was indeed not the sort of place that he frequented, and his proximity to the impoverished and ragged patrons greatly irked him.

"I will, I will, *momentito*, Señor Ramos!" Villardebo whined. "You know that I work in the customs house, and that I am on the docks most of the time. Well now, I was in this very *posada* when I saw a *gaucho* come in and ask for a *capitán* of one of those ships that goes to los Estados Unidos. He said he had a message from someone that he wished delivered. Naturally, I thought nothing about it at the time."

"What has this to do with me or that traitor Maldones?" Ramos angrily broke in. He took a sip of his rum, then reversed the glass and poured the contents onto the floor. "Faugh! This is vile stuff! If your information isn't worth my while . . ."

"But wait, *por favor*, Señor Ramos," the stocky man pleaded, almost frantic now with fear. "Last night, I came here again by myself, as is my custom, and I saw the same *gaucho* come into the *posada*. He was looking for the *capitán* of the ship that had returned and was lying at anchor outside our harbor. And I heard him ask the captain, 'Were you able to get the message to *el Halcón?*' and the captain said, 'It has been done, for when I reached Florida, I entrusted the message to a friend of mine who commands a ship that goes to New Orleans. The letter is surely there by now.' And then, I remembered what you had said about the *gringo* and the name that was given him, and I told myself that this *gaucho* must have sent a message seeking the help of the *gringo* to come save Maldones from the *calabozo*.''

Porfirio Ramos chuckled, nodded, and then leaned over and clapped the stocky man on the back with his pudgy hand. ''You've shown rare intelligence, Villardebo. I shall speak to your *jefe* tomorrow and see if your wages can't be raised and you given a position more in keeping with your intelligence.''

''¡*Muchas gracias,* Señor Ramos!''

''*De nada*. Yes, of course—'' Ramos's beady little black eyes squinted as he leaned back, stroking his chin, deep in thought. After a long pause, he mused, ''Let us see now—if the letter was safely delivered, then I am sure that accursed *gringo* who married Dorotéa, the lovely señorita to whom my friend and ally Rodrigo Baltenar was betrothed, will assuredly return to Argentina to try to save Raoul Maldones from the firing squad.'' He paused again, closed his eyes, and made further mental calculations, then leaned forward across the table again and hoarsely muttered, ''If *el Halcón* was able to board a ship bound for our country, he should be here within the next few weeks. I will see to it that he never reaches the *pampas*—for he would surely go there first and try to find Maldones's closest friend, the Señor Heitor Duvaldo, because Duvaldo is caring for Maldones's other daughters.''

"So my news was useful, Señor Ramos?" Villardebo said, his expression brightening.

"It was worth a good deal, yes. Tomorrow morning, I shall go to Humberto Calciega, who is the port authority, and have him issue an edict that all foreign ships arriving in our harbor must be detained for twenty-four hours. In this way, we shall be able to search each ship and see if this interfering *gringo* is aboard." Ramos uttered a sinister little laugh. "If he is, it's a simple matter to have an accident. There are sharks where ships must anchor, and if the *americano* should by some accident fall overboard, what a pity it would be that he could not be present to watch the execution of his *suegro*."

Pedro Villardebo echoed the *porteño*'s laugh, but feebly, for he feared the ruthless power of this important man.

Porfirio Ramos abruptly rose, tossed a few coins onto the table, and then, with a contemptuous shrug, opened his leather pouch again and tossed five or six coins onto the floor. Villardebo uttered a cry and dropped down onto his knees to retrieve them as Ramos uttered another mocking laugh, then strode out of the *posada*.

"*¡Buenas tardes,* Señor Ramos!" Humberto Calciega rose from his desk. He was a tall, gaunt-faced man with thinning black hair, which he abstractedly brushed to one side with a languid hand. "I am honored by your presence. How may I serve you?"

"It's very simple, Señor Calciega. You are in charge of the port here. You enforce the tariff, and you impose the restrictions upon all ships entering our harbor, do you not?"

"That is true, Señor Ramos."

"Very well, then. Listen carefully. I have the information that there will be an attempt to rescue Raoul Maldones, a condemned traitor, who is exactly where he belongs, under lock and key in our *calabozo*. The oldest daughter of this Maldones married a *gringo*. I am certain that one of Maldones's servants asked for the help of the *americano*, to come to Buenos Aires and free the traitor from our *calabozo!*''

"That is terrible! We must not let that happen!" the port official sputtered.

"We must take precautions against these madmen. This is why, Señor Calciega, you must immediately issue an edict that each foreign ship entering our harbor is to remain at anchor for twenty-four hours. Your men will visit each ship and demand to see the manifest—but most importantly, they must find the *americano* whose name is John Cooper Baines. We shall have to dispose of him before he causes trouble."

"Thank you for this information, Señor Ramos," the port official said as he began to write on a piece of paper. "I have made a note of it, and I shall put your wishes into effect at once."

"Good! Now, as soon as your men find the *gringo*, send word to me. I shall do the rest."

"Of course. You will find me loyal and devoted to our cause—I, too, have no use for these awkward, ignorant, filthy *gauchos*, who rally behind this Raoul Maldones. It would be better for us if they were all lost in the jungle, with the headhunters shrinking their heads into trophies," Humberto Calciega said fawningly.

"I must be on my way," Ramos said, looking at his watch. "It is really a pleasure to converse with you, Señor Calciega. I salute you." With this, Porfirio Ramos strode out of the office.

The *Miromar* came within sight of the city of Buenos Aires on November 12, 1826. Captain Silas Blake tendered his telescope to John Cooper Baines, who peered through the glass and saw the towers of the churches of La

Merced and San Domingo and of the lordly cathedral. In the very center of this square of the Plaza de la Victoria, there was the long, many-arched rectangular building of the fortress. In the distance he could make out the innumerable white-stuccoed houses.

"Mr. Baines," Captain Blake said, "we'll have to anchor about a quarter of a mile away from the harbor."

"Can't we go directly southward to where you landed me before, Captain Blake?" John Cooper asked.

"I'm afraid not. Take a look at the customhouse—there, to the left—and you will see a flag with a signal. It tells me that we must wait here until we have been formally authorized to proceed on our journey. Very shortly a dinghy with customs officials will meet us. I'm sure this is partly because of the unsettled state of the Argentinian government and the continued dispute with Brazil over which country governs Uruguay."

"I hope there won't be too much of a delay—I want to get to the *pampas* and to the house of Señor Duvaldo as quickly as I can," the tall Texan declared.

"I sympathize with your dilemma, Mr. Baines, and I admire your courage. But for God's sake, be very careful. I don't trust these *porteños*, and still less the officials who work in customs and have anything to do with the port. They are corrupt."

"Do you think anyone knows that I'm coming back to try to save Señor Maldones?" John Cooper asked.

"Surely no one that I know of, but it's probable. Experience has taught me to prepare for any emergency," the New England ship's captain said grimly. "Do you remember from your last voyage those men who warned you not to become too friendly with Raoul Maldones?"

"I do, indeed."

"I'm sure they reported your name to the high officials of the government of Buenos Aires."

"Well, I can only pray that the customs officials

don't become suspicious as to why I'm here," John Cooper chuckled.

"If the inspectors see your name on the passenger manifest, there may be trouble."

"You have to give them the manifest?"

"If they ask for it. Otherwise, I'll lose my license to trade in this port. And they might even imprison me. But what would most likely happen, Mr. Baines, is that they'd confiscate my ship and nobody in America would ever find out what happened to me."

"Well, I wouldn't want to be the cause of that, Captain. I'll do whatever you tell me to."

"Look there!" The New England sea captain had taken the telescope back from the tall Texan and now, training it on the port, exclaimed, "There's a dinghy coming this way. That'll be the port officials. Yes, they're going to make a search, all right. I'll have to declare my cargo, but I'll hope they don't pay any attention to the list of passengers."

"I'm not asking you to deny that I'm actually on board, Captain Blake," John Cooper soberly interposed, "but whatever you can do to help us so we can go on our way and get the business done, I'd appreciate."

"I'll do everything I can. You may as well go to your cabin, Mr. Baines. The Argentinians are not used to *rubios,* their name for men with fair skin and blond hair. And if they should see you, they might become suspicious and possibly report you to the commandant of the port, a man by the name of Humberto Calciega, whose rancor I have no wish to arouse, if only for your sake."

About half an hour later, a dinghy, rowed by four surly-looking, blue-jacketed sailors, drew up alongside the *Miromar.* Humberto Calciega himself and his second in command, a plump, fat-jowled, black-bearded man in his midforties, clambered up the rope ladder that Captain Blake always left suspended.

"Señor capitán," Calciega said after pompously clearing his throat, "there is a new maritime law in Argentina. You are required to stay at anchor here for twenty-four hours until we have thoroughly cleared you. Allow me to see the ship's manifest."

"Of course."

Captain Blake turned to his second mate, an affable Portuguese named Jaime Alveiro, and ordered, "Jaime, bring me the manifest from my cabin, *por favor.*"

"At once, *señor capitán!*" The second mate saluted and hastened off to the cabin, returning a few moments later with the manifest.

Humberto Calciega rudely grabbed it from the second mate's hand. *"Momentito, señor capitán.* I do this simply to be sure that you have not attempted to alter anything that was set down at the time of your departure. I will see for myself, *¿comprende?"*

The short, fat man beside him sidled against him now and whispered something in Calciega's ear, and the latter nodded. "Oh, yes, Señor Capitán Blake, my assistant, Jorge Mayoralla, has just reminded me that if you have passengers aboard, we must both identify them from your manifest. Will you be so good, therefore, as to summon them on deck here, *¡pronto!"*

Captain Silas Blake fumed at the arrogance of the port official and his subordinate. But there was no recourse. Shrugging, he said softly, "I shall have it done at once."

"Muchas gracias, Señor Capitán Blake," Calciega said with a hypocritical smile that made his gaunt face all the more repulsive. "You are very sensible."

Captain Blake beckoned now to the boatswain, a New Englander like himself, from Gloucester, lanky, nearly bald, with two front teeth missing and a gold earring. He politely requested, "Bo'sun Carruthers, ask our passengers to come on deck for inspection."

"Right away, Captain Blake!" The boatswain saluted and went down to the cabin of John Cooper Baines.

The latter was in the process of telling Dorotéa that their delay was due to a request from the port official, when there was a knock on the door. He frowned, kissed her, and then opened the door. "Begging your pardon, Mr. Baines, sir. Captain says would you please come up on deck, you and your wife and son, and the men with you. Seems like these fellows from the port want to look you all over and check the manifest to make sure you're all accounted for."

"Of course. Tell him we'll be up directly."

"Very good, Mr. Baines." The boatswain again saluted and returned to the quarterdeck.

"There's no other way, *mi corazón*," John Cooper told Dorotéa. "Bring Andrew, and I'll go get Felipe and the *vaqueros*."

In a few minutes, the tall Texan, Dorotéa, Andrew, Felipe, and the four *vaqueros* from the Double H Ranch climbed the stairs to the quarterdeck.

Humberto Calciega and Jorge Mayoralla stood with their arms folded across their chests, eyeing the newcomers. The port official turned to whisper to his subordinate, "It's the *gringo* Señor Ramos told me about, Jorge. He'll want to know that directly. Now we must give them no reason to be on their guard, *¿comprendes?*"

"*Sí*, Señor Calciega!" the fat man replied.

"Please come forward. You are Señor John Cooper Baines from Texas, as this manifest says?" Humberto Calciega called out.

"I am, señor. And this is my wife, Dorotéa, and this is my son Andrew. This is Felipe Mintras and four workers from my *hacienda* in Texas: Paco Rivera, Sancho Vinaldo, Jaime Portola, and Bartoloméo Mendoza."

"I thank you for your information, Señor Baines," the port official sarcastically responded with a mocking little bow. Then, turning to the dourly silent captain of the *Miromar,* he pursued, "Your manifest states that your ship carries a cargo of whale oil, grain, cotton goods, dried beef, and farming tools. Is that all of it?"

"Except for the personal effects of my passengers, yes, señor," Captain Silas Blake promptly answered.

"I see." Calciega nursed his chin and frowned. The manifest was, of course, in order, as he knew it would be, but he had to contain his exultance. He had found out exactly what Porfirio Ramos wanted to know, that the *suegro* of the *traidor* Raoul Maldones was aboard this vessel. All that was necessary now was to hurry back to port and send a courier to Ramos's villa. After that, the matter would be entirely out of his hands. Calciega handed the manifest back to Captain Blake and said curtly, "You understand that you must remain at anchor until tomorrow afternoon. We shall send the signal by flag when you may unload at the docks."

"Of course I'll comply with your laws," Captain Blake as sarcastically responded.

"Most wise, *señor capitán,*" the port official drawled. "I think that concludes our business with you, Señor Capitán Blake." He turned on his heel, the fat little man hurrying after him to the rope ladder and back down to the dinghy. The sailors plied their oars as the dinghy pulled away.

Captain Blake looked thoughtful, watching it recede in the distance. Then he turned to John Cooper. "So far everything seems to be legal and proper. All the same, I'm going to have Tom Barton, my gunner, prime the cannon, just in case we have a fight on our hands tomorrow. Calciega didn't seem to take particular interest in your name on the manifest. Let's hope that's a good sign. But it's just wise to be prepared for anything in these waters these days, Mr. Baines."

"Amen to that, Captain Blake."

"In the meantime, we'll be at our ease here. I'll put two men on guard duty tonight. Once Tom Barton gets the cannon primed, we can swing into action in a jiffy. I just hope that we won't have to. Now I'm going to have the cook prepare us a fine supper. I think we've earned it after this long journey."

Porfirio Ramos gleefully rubbed his hands and chuckled as he sat beside Humberto Calciega in the latter's office. "I'm in your debt, Señor Calciega," he jocosely declared. "The American John Cooper Baines. And the lovely Dorotéa too, you say?"

"She is really delightful, Señor Ramos." Calciega smirked, a grimace that made his gaunt face still more evil.

"She can be made a widow very quickly. And you say that the cargo includes whale oil? That, too, is a stroke of luck."

"Then you—" the port official began, glancing apprehensively at the mustachioed Ramos.

The *porteño*'s voice was suddenly cold. "I will tell you nothing of my plans. You are not to be involved in this. You have given me information that will be useful, and I shan't forget it when I come in to even greater power."

Twelve

The day had been unusually placid; the night, still and warm. The Atlantic was gentle, and the soft lapping of the little waves against the sides of the frigate *Miromar* made a restful sound. It was two in the morning, and there was a pale, sickly quarter-moon in the sky, hidden at times by great fleecy clouds.

In the darkness, five men clambered into a dinghy. There was no breeze this night, so they rowed out toward the anchored frigate. Nearly every light on the *Miromar* was extinguished, except the ship's lantern, which hung midway up one of the three towering masts. Captain Blake had posted two guards for the night, Jason Bentley and Edward Trask, both men in their early thirties. They had served aboard whaling ships out of New Bedford and had signed up with Captain Blake four years earlier.

One of the five men in the dinghy, the leader of this clandestine venture, sat in the stern. He was Augustín Quirada, a tall man, perhaps forty, wearing a white shirt and black breeches and boots, and he was Porfirio Ramos's personally picked lieutenant. As he drew his oar through the dark, placid water, he instructed his fellows, "The *gringos* will have posted guards, perhaps two or three. We

116

must kill them without a sound so the passengers and the *capitán* aren't aroused, *¿comprenden?"*

The other four men nodded.

"Our *caudillo* has told me that there are hogsheads of whale oil aboard. You, Chirasca, and you, Ignones"—he looked at the men facing him—"you'll pour out some of the whale oil in the ship's hold and ignite it. The entire ship will soon go up in flames; you must depart quickly and get back into the dinghy, so we can row back to shore safely."

"Sí, mi jefe," Chirasca answered in a guttural tone.

"Also, Chirasca, you and Gasparo will kill the guards. Pinamba, with his blowgun, will back you up. If the *gringo* and his friends should try to swim to shore to escape the flames," Quirada added with a grim smile, "the *tiburón* is sure to make a meal of them. Now row swiftly. We shall be back to shore, our job well done, within the hour!"

His four companions nodded, and Quirada chuckled to himself as the dinghy approached the starboard side of the *Miromar*. The clouds hid the moon, and there was an intense darkness over the water. The only sound was the soft lapping of the tiny rippling waves as they caressed the sides of the frigate.

Quirada made a gesture, and Gasparo, followed by Chirasca, climbed the rope ladder that was hanging from the *Miromar*'s deck. The rope was wet, soaking the soles of Gasparo's boots. As he hoisted himself over the ship's railing, his foot slipped, and he came down hard on the deck.

The two guards, Jason Bentley and Edward Trask, had been dozing, but the noise on deck wakened Edward, who stumbled to his feet, scratching his head and scowling at the unexpected disturbance. Guiltily, he glanced around and saw that Jason was asleep. He shrugged and moved in the direction of the noise.

Pinamba, who had followed Gasparo and Chirasca up the rope ladder, took the blowgun, fitted a poison-dipped dart to it, and, drawing in a deep breath, sent the dart flying. It hit Edward Trask in the right cheek, and the initial sensation was that of a mild bee sting. Startled, Edward clapped his hand to his cheek, plucked the dart away, and stared at it. He opened his mouth to cry out as he saw the dark shadowy figures on deck, but blackness seized him, and he pitched forward, rolled over, and lay staring at the dark, cloudy sky.

Jason had wakened when he heard the thud of his companion's body on the deck. He scrambled to his feet and hurried in the direction of the sound. This time, Chirasca awaited him. He had a bow, and the arrow was already nocked. Before Jason could cry out, the arrow struck him in the throat. He clapped both hands to it, trying to wrench it out, gave a gurgling cry, and then fell backwards, convulsing in death.

"¡Bueno!" exulted Quirada, who had followed his men on deck. "Now for setting the fire. Chirasca, Ignones, the hold will be under the hatchway in the center of the deck."

There was silence on the *Miromar*. Ignones climbed into the hold with a tinderbox while Chirasca kept the heavy hatchway door open for him. Then Ignones beckoned to Chirasca, who followed him down the narrow stairs while the other men stood guard.

About a hundred feet from the foot of the stairway, the horses' stalls were located, and a soft whinny and nickering made the two men instantly stiffen. They crouched and reached for the sharp knives thrust through sheaths in their belts. Satisfied that the sound had not wakened the sleeping crew or passengers aboard and that the horses were not alarmed, the two men set to work at once. The barrels of oil were rolled together, at the opposite end of the hold from the horses, and some of their contents was spilled onto the floor. Chirasca noticed a keg that brought a wide smile to his grimy face. The keg was labeled gunpowder, and this would make a wonderful explosion when the flames reached it. Ignones opened his tinderbox and struck his flint until a piece of soft, dry moss, brought along for this purpose, was ignited. He touched the flaming moss to the whale oil, thrust his tinderbox back into his breeches pocket, and hurried up the stairway, followed by Chirasca.

They collected their companions from their stations where they stood guard and hurried down the rope ladder and into the dinghy. As they rowed away, Quirada eagerly demanded, "Did you succeed?"

"Sí, mi jefe," Ignones grunted. "And we found a keg of gunpowder in the hold. The ship is really going to explode."

"Excellent! Now hurry. We've done very well indeed. What the fire and explosion won't do, los tiburones will," Quirada chuckled. "Señor Ramos will be very pleased with this night's work, mis compañeros!"

All of them were pulling at their oars with all their might. Quirada laughed as suddenly he saw flames erupt on the Miromar, contrasting brightly against the dark night. "¡Muerte a los gringos!" he hissed, then crossed himself. "All traitors from los Estados Unidos who try to harm our beloved Argentina, may they perish in this same way!"

"Amen to that, Señor Quirada," Chirasca muttered, and crossed himself also.

The dinghy had covered more than half the distance back to shore when there were two muffled, almost simultaneous, explosions. The sky was brightly lit up for a brief moment, and then the men in the dinghy could see the red and yellow dancing flames that licked the deck and soon had it, as well as one of the masts, ignited. One of the sails burned, its remnants falling, a flaming shroud, off the rail and into the water to be completely extinguished.

*   *   *

John Cooper Baines sprang out of his bunk when he heard the deafening explosions, and almost at once the acrid smell of smoke drifted through his nostrils. Bending to Dorotéa, he urged her, *"Querida*, wake up, wake up! Something terrible has happened!"

She woke almost instantly, got out of her bunk, and demanded, "What must I do, *mi corazón?"*

"Get on deck. I'll go get Andrew and the *vaqueros* and see if we can get the horses off the ship. It sounded like an explosion. The ship may be sinking. Damnation— there are the two crates of arms and supplies we'll have to get out of the hold, too!" He bolted from the cabin.

Captain Silas Blake, too, had been wakened. At once he gave orders, knocking on the doors of his first mate's and second mate's cabins. Both men, dragging on their breeches, ran to the quarters of the sailors to alert them. Some of them, including the boatswain, had already wakened and were bestirring themselves to see what could be done. The ship's engineer, a dour Scotsman, Clinton MacGregor, raced down to the hold to inspect the damage. John Cooper by now had wakened Andrew and the four *vaqueros*, and they also rushed to the hold, to free the horses. The Scotsman cried out, "My God Almighty, the fire's spreading —it's the whale oil—the ship won't last long with such a blaze! We'd best prepare to lower the boats!"

There were four rowboats and a small dinghy, and Captain Blake was on his quarterdeck, cupping his hands and bawling out orders. Six seamen had formed a bucket brigade, taking water from the ocean, trying to douse the fire. But it was too late; already, the *Miromar* had started to list slightly to starboard, and Captain Blake realized at once that there was no hope, except to abandon ship.

"Prepare to lower those boats," the captain called. "Don't overload them. See that the passengers are first off. Then the crew."

Meanwhile, John Cooper and Andrew had taken ropes and rushed to the horses' stalls. The four *vaqueros* looped the ropes around the necks of the eight horses, made them fast, and let the slack end dangle.

John Cooper shouted to make himself heard over the roar of the flames and the whinnying of the horses. "I think it's best you men—and you, too, Andrew—swim for it. First we'll get the horses out of here; then you all follow."

John Cooper released the ropes that held fast the door to the cargo area on the side of the ship. The door slid open, revealing the water below. John Cooper slapped the horses' rumps; panicked, they made for the opening. Then the Texan watched as his son and the four *vaqueros* followed the horses and also disappeared into the dark waters.

Who could have set this explosion? he wondered. *The customs officials? I don't see how. They never got into the hold. Well, no time to worry about that now!* John Cooper ran up the stairs to the quarterdeck, where the captain now told him how he and his crew had found the two dead guards, one killed by an arrow, the other by a poison dart. There was no doubt these guards had been killed by the men who set fire to the ship.

Felipe was helping the boatswain and the ship's engineer, who were preparing to lower two rowboats. The two others were too badly damaged to be of any use. Captain Blake and the first mate would attend to the lowering of the dinghy. John Cooper found his wife on the deck. She wanted to stay with him, but he insisted that she get into one of the rowboats. "*Querida,* think of the child! You'll go in the boat, and you'll be safe! There may not be room for all of us. Hurry now, get in! That's an order from your husband!"

Dorotéa sighed, then kissed him quickly and said, "Very well, I'll go if you insist!"

Captain Blake himself helped the lovely young woman

into the rowboat and gave orders to lower it. John Cooper watched the vessel lowered into the water, with five seamen to row it, and he and the captain hurried back down to the hold, which was almost entirely ablaze by now.

Felipe had preceded them and had seized the two crates containing weapons, ammunition, and other supplies. They were as yet untouched by the flames, and he lugged them to the door of the hold and pushed them into the water. The crates were partially submerged but, thank the Lord, still floating. John Cooper breathed a sigh of relief and was grateful to the man who had insisted that the crates be double-coated with pitch and lined with waterproof canvas. Without weapons, their chances of rescuing his father-in-law would be still more difficult.

He and his men returned to the deck, where the captain was overseeing the last of the evacuation.

"The *Miromar* is going down fast," Captain Blake said to the Texan. "Are all the men out of the hold?"

John Cooper nodded. "Andrew and the *vaqueros* have already gone with the horses. Felipe and I can also swim for it."

"I don't like it. I don't like it at all! I won't go down with a sinking ship, I'll tell you that, and you won't, either. You and Felipe come along into the dinghy with me!"

The ship had begun to tilt even more dangerously toward starboard, and now the water level seemed nearer than ever. John Cooper could see in the lurid reflection of the flames upon the placid water the heads of the horses and of the men—he also made out his son. "All right, Captain Blake. Felipe! Let's get into the dinghy!" he called.

Six crewmen would go along in the dinghy. Several other seamen had leaped into the water, being agile swimmers, confident of their ability to swim the quarter of a mile to shore since there was not enough room in the remaining rowboats and dinghy for them all. Now this last lifeboat was lowered, and the captain and remaining crew and John Cooper climbed down the rope ladder and boarded. The six crewmen began to row just as there was another muffled explosion from inside the doomed ship. It listed even more, till the starboard end was almost completely tilted into the water.

Suddenly, there was a wild scream from the darkness: "A shark—oh, my God—it's got me—*madre mía—el Señor Dios* protect—*aiii!*" and then there was silence, save for the feeble thrashing of the sailor's body as he was dragged under by a great blue shark.

John Cooper thought of Andrew in the water, shuddered, and crossed himself.

The sea captain grimly shook his head and looked out on the waters. "I pray there's not a school of sharks around, because the blood of one man will draw the rest of those hideous killers."

There was another shriek, again the splashing and thrashing of a man's body trying to fight off the deadly jaws of a shark that dragged him down to his death, and again the flickering, infernal sight of the flames of the ship playing on the dark water.

Two of John Cooper's *vaqueros*, Paco Rivera and Sancho Vinaldo, had been far outdistanced by the horses and other men in the swim for shore. The *vaqueros* heard the screams of the sailors attacked by the shark and, as they swam, drew their knives. "Let's stay close, *mi compañero*," Paco said to Sancho, "so we can protect each other in case a shark comes by."

Hardly had he spoken, when a shark struck him at the thigh. "*Compañero*—it's here—defend yourself—*aiii!*" he cried out. But even as he was pulled down, he struck blindly with his knife, and the shark's blood mingled with his.

Sancho Vinaldo filled his lungs and dived, trying to save his friend. Through the dark water, he vaguely saw the outline of Paco's body writhing in the shark's jaws as the shark twisted its wounded body and submerged, dragging Paco to a suffocating, drowning death. Coming to the surface, desperately trying to swim away from the hideous scene, Sancho screamed as a shark took him on the shoulder and another struck him on the leg. It was all over, and he gave himself up to merciful death.

Far from the scene of carnage, the dinghy progressed toward the shore. John Cooper saw one of the floating crates with the ammunition and supplies and cried out, "Can we get that crate, Captain Blake? It's got rifles, pistols, ammunition, our saddles—we'll need them!"

"I think we can get it. Gonzales, you're good at that. Use your grappling hook and see if you can get to the crate and tow it behind the dinghy. You, Elston, and you, Martinson, help him all you can!"

"Where's the other one?" John Cooper asked aloud, staring this way and that. Then, in the light from the burning ship, he saw the crate was floating out to sea, taken by a sudden current. "What damnable luck! Still, if we can salvage this one crate, we'll still have arms against our enemies!"

"And you've plenty of them, judging by what's happened tonight, Mr. Baines," Captain Blake muttered, angrily shaking his head. "Remember those three government officials who warned you not to befriend the man whose daughter you married."

"Yes, and their friend, Porfirio Ramos, is the first person I'd suspect," the tall Texan said.

The men had put their backs into the rowing, and now the dinghy and two rowboats reached the shore. Because it was sandy for the last hundred yards, many sailors waded, in chest-high water, to the shore. John Cooper sighed with relief when he saw one of the seamen hand Dorotéa out of the rowboat. She called and waved to him. "John Cooper, thank God you're all right! I'm safe! And so is Andrew!"

"Thank God for that!" John Cooper cried. He eased himself into the water to join his wife. She ran to him, as did Andrew, and John Cooper held them to him for a long moment. Then he surveyed the scene on shore and saw in the pale-light of the false dawn the sailors huddling on the beach. The horses that had swum to shore were in the care of two of the *vaqueros*.

"My God, what happened to Paco Rivera and Sancho Vinaldo?" John Cooper called.

One of the *vaqueros* shook his head and crossed himself. "It was the *tiburón*, Señor Baines. We could do nothing to help them."

"How dreadful—such brave men to come all this way and to die like that," Dorotéa began to sob.

John Cooper put his arm around her, then turned to Captain Blake. "You and I have lost good men, Captain. God rest their souls. I promise you that when this is all over and we're back in the United States, I will make sure their families are well provided for." He closed his eyes tight to fight back the tears. "Well now, I'm grateful to your men for rescuing that crate of ours. We'd best open it and distribute the weapons and ammunition. The way things are going, we'd better have our pistols and rifles ready for action."

"A good idea, Mr. Baines. Martinson, Gonzales, open the crate," the captain ordered.

Andrew, still soaked to the skin, and Felipe went over to help and, in about twenty minutes, had unloaded the weapons, ammunition, saddles and reins, some rope, a few canteens, and some clothing. The rifles and pistols were all primed and loaded, the horses were saddled, and the bags of extra powder and ball were roped to the sides of two horses. To be sure, they had lost half of their supplies in the other crate, but there were still enough weapons, ammunition, and riding gear for everyone, what with the tragic deaths of the two *vaqueros*. Their absence also left two extra horses.

When all was in readiness, John Cooper turned back to Captain Blake and said, "Well, I guess now we'll head for the *pampas*, to the home of Heitor Duvaldo."

"You mean to say that after everything you—not to mention the horses—have been through tonight, you intend to ride into the *pampas?*"

"It's the only thing we can do," John Cooper said grimly. "We have enemies in Buenos Aires, and I'd just as soon put them well behind us for the moment."

Captain Blake nodded. "I see your point."

John Cooper now took out his pouch and handed the New Englander a few gold pieces. "Please distribute this among your seamen, especially those who helped me retrieve that crate of weapons. God bless you and thank you for your help."

"I'm only sorry I brought you to such a place under such circumstances, Mr. Baines," the captain said. "We'll have to go into the city of Buenos Aires now and take our chances on getting a ship back to Boston. Is there anything I can do to help you while I'm in the city?"

"Yes. I'd be grateful if you can find out anything about where they've jailed Raoul Maldones and any other news about this *porteño* movement against the *gauchos* and the *hacendados* out on the *pampas*. Here are a few more gold pieces. If you find out anything that's important, you can pay some courier to ride out to the *pampas*, to the home of Heitor Duvaldo. I'm sure he's well known."

"I'll do what I can, Mr. Baines. I've got a bone to pick with those no-good dirty rats who killed my seamen and fired my ship. Do you see those torches? Some people are coming down from the town now. They may be soldiers, so you'd best be on your way."

"We will. Thank you again and good luck to you and your men. All right, *querida*, you get onto Rauda, and you, Andrew, take the brown gelding. I'll ride my palomino and rope the extra horses behind me.''

Dawn was breaking over the city of Buenos Aires. The civil guard had sent six soldiers commanded by a *teniente*, and they were coming toward Captain Blake and his seamen, who stood there waiting on the beach. The *Miromar* had disappeared, and only a few burning timbers remained as evidence of what had once been a proud three-masted frigate.

Meanwhile, John Cooper's party rode away and did not look behind them. They had no food or water, but John Cooper Baines had learned long ago how to forage for them. They would rest as much as they could by day and travel at night. In the event that Porfirio Ramos had been behind this attempt on his life, John Cooper told himself, it was best not to give him a second chance. But there would be time enough once they arrived at Heitor Duvaldo's *estancia* to form a plan of action that would save Raoul Maldones from prison—and perhaps execution— and nullify the greedy, powerful Ramos.

Thirteen

As he rode, John Cooper Baines repeatedly glanced over his shoulder, but there were no soldiers in pursuit. After about an hour, he held up his hand. "I think we can rest a bit now and give our horses a chance to do the same."

Dorotéa rode up beside him, and his heart swelled to see how intensely eager she looked, how young, yet poised and mature. It was obvious that she had not been pampered, even though Raoul Maldones had provided her with every known luxury. Her fierce independence had appealed to John Cooper even when he had first met her.

"As I mentioned before, I propose that we head directly for Heitor Duvaldo's *hacienda*," he said as Felipe, the two surviving *vaqueros,* and Andrew rode up alongside him at the left. "As I recall, it's beyond the town of Lobos."

"That's right, *mi corazón*," Dorotéa prompted. "And I agree, it's a good idea to go first to Heitor's house. With my father in prison and Porfirio Ramos having seized his estate, we don't dare go to my father's house until we've learned whatever we can from Heitor."

"We think alike, *mi* Dorotéa," John Cooper said.

"Now, before we stop to rest, I would like to ride a little farther until we're off this trail. It seems to be well traveled, and I'm sure the soldiers are familiar with it. We should head inland, toward the southwest. Perhaps we can find a little farm where we can sleep for a few hours and have some food."

"That is a good idea, *Señor Halcón*," Felipe gravely said.

"We're going to need help, Felipe," John Cooper pursued. "Do you think it will be difficult for you to get word to your *gauchos*?"

"As I have told you, they have gone into hiding in the *pampas*. But for an ally of Señor Maldones, the *gauchos* will come out of hiding. No one finds the *gauchos*, you see, unless they wish to be found. But all of us are loyal to Señor Maldones."

"I'm only sorry we lost the other crate of weapons, Felipe. Your *gauchos* could have used those guns."

"Many of us have old muskets that are still useful, plus the *bolas* and *cuchillos*," the wiry *gaucho* pointed out. "When the time comes for us to save the señor Maldones, we shall not stop until we have brought him back to his *estancia*."

"With spirit like that, Felipe, you convince me that we will succeed in freeing your *patrón*," the tall Texan said with a smile. "How many days do you think it will take us to reach Heitor Duvaldo's *hacienda*?"

"Three days, Señor Baines," Felipe answered. "But I could ride for hours without tiring."

Suddenly, the *vaquero* Bartoloméo Mendoza pointed to the right. "Look there, *patrón! ¡Soldados!*"

John Cooper turned in his saddle and muttered a stifled cry of exasperation. He could see four horsemen in gray cloth uniforms, with shakos, brandishing sabers, while at their head rode a resplendently uniformed young black-bearded *teniente,* whose epaulets and braid atop his shako designated his rank in the Argentinian army.

"We'll have to fight our way through," he told the *vaqueros.* Then, turning to his wife, he ordered, "Dorotéa, *querida,* get off your horse and lead it off to one side; they shouldn't fire on a woman!"

"This is my fight more than yours," Dorotéa indignantly retorted.

"Maybe they just want to know who we are, Pa!" Andrew hopefully suggested.

"I wouldn't count on it, Andy," his father grimly said as he slid "Long Girl" out of the sling. "Now please stay back, son, and no argument." The boy did as he was told, while his father, reining in his palomino, waited to see what the riders intended.

The young officer spurred his horse forward. Raising his saber, he called out in Spanish in an arrogant tone, "You will halt, dismount, and will show your papers!"

"We are *americanos!*" John Cooper called, keeping his rifle at waist level and ready to shoot if need be. "We want no fight with you."

"If you are the *gringo* who is the friend of the *traidor* Raoul Maldones, then you are under arrest, *señor americano!*" The young lieutenant drew out a pistol, cocked it, aimed it at John Cooper Baines, and pulled the trigger. The ball whistled harmlessly by, and in the same moment, the tall Texan lifted his Lancaster to his shoulder and squeezed the trigger. The lieutenant jerked in his saddle as if struck by an invisible hand, falling backward over the horse's rump, then sprawled face down on the ground. The four soldiers behind him drew their pistols and, brandishing their sabers, came at John Cooper and his five companions.

A burly *sargento* bellowed, *"Gringo* assassin, you will die for this. Surrender now, or we will kill you and the *mujer,* too!"

At this, Dorotéa leveled her pistol and fired, and the sergeant, with an astonished cry, clapped at his shoulder and toppled from his horse, falling to the ground. But, defiantly courageous, he cocked his pistol at John Cooper's lovely young wife and fired. His aim, because of his posture on the ground and the pain of his wound, was faulty, and the ball went high over her head. At the same time, Felipe Mintras raised his rifle and fired at the sergeant, killing him.

The three privates had by now reached the six riders, and one of them, a pockmarked stripling in his early twenties, slashed his saber at Jaime Portola, before he could even fire his rifle. The young *vaquero*'s arm was gashed, and with a lurid oath, he leaped from his horse, caught the Argentinian soldier by the throat with both hands, and fell on the ground with him, rolling over and over. The soldier's eyes bulged, his face turned livid as he tried to gouge his fingernails against the pitiless grip of the *vaquero*, and then he sank back, lifeless.

Meanwhile, Bartoloméo Mendoza had fired his rifle at another private but had missed. The private, leveling a pistol, now fired at close range and grazed the cheek of the *vaquero* before the latter, drawing his knife from its sheath, turned in his saddle and hurled the weapon, which buried itself to the hilt in the private's throat. The latter's galloping pinto carried the soldier on until at last he slumped in the saddle and rolled onto the ground, kicking convulsively for a few moments in his final agonies.

Then the last soldier, a tall, slim youth who did not seem much older than Andrew Baines, recklessly charged the wheeling riders, firing his pistol and killing Felipe Mintras's horse, which sank down on its front legs, then rolled over as the *gaucho* nimbly leaped away from it. But the *gaucho*, who hadn't had time to reload his rifle, had drawn his *bola* free and, whirling the *pampas* lasso through the air, wrapped it around the chest of the courageous young private. Running up to the private, Felipe grabbed hold of one end of the *bola* and pulled the soldier from his saddle with a violent jerk, as the latter's horse pranced about, whinnying in terror.

Then, drawing his *cuchillo,* Felipe knelt over the private and, his left hand against the latter's throat, growled, "Now, you young dog, tell us why you came to kill us! We have done nothing. Worst of all, you threatened the life of the *esposa* of my *amigo!*"

"Don't! Don't kill me! I surrender!" the private panted in Spanish. "We had our orders! We were told that we were to search for the *americano* and arrest all who rode with him—"

"By whose orders?" Felipe put his knife to the throat of the young soldier, pricking the flesh so that a tiny pearl of blood oozed from the swarthy skin.

"Por piedad, amigo, do not kill me. I will tell you! It was on the order of the señor Ramos—"

"I thought as much," Felipe growled as he straightened to his feet. "Get up, imbecile! Mount your horse and ride back to Buenos Aires, and be grateful that I am not given to killing children like you!" With this, he unwrapped the *bola* from the shuddering body of the young soldier, who scrambled to his feet, his eyes huge with fright as they fixed upon the face of John Cooper Baines.

"Let him walk back," the tall Texan quickly countermanded. "We'll take his horse. It will replace your horse, Felipe. And we'll have a good start before he can get back to Buenos Aires and bring more soldiers after us."

The private was trembling as he stumbled to his feet, seeing how the two *vaqueros* and Felipe looked at him, their hands gripping their knives, and then looking back at the bearded blond *gringo,* who unwaveringly stared at him. John Cooper now said in Spanish, "When you get back to the city, tell Ramos that we'll find a way of paying him back for trying to kill us, *¿comprende?"*

The young soldier nodded. *"Gracias. Muchas gracias. I did not wish to kill anyone. I was ordered—"* Now that the young soldier found speech, he babbled in his relief at knowing that he was not to die.

"¡Vaya!" Felipe gestured with his knife.

With a frantic nod, the private turned and began to run back toward Buenos Aires.

"There," Felipe said, turning to John Cooper, "now we know for sure who ordered the blowing up of that fine ship."

John Cooper nodded, then dismounted. "Bartoloméo, you're bleeding—and you, too, Jaime! We'll stop to treat the wounds before riding on."

Then he turned to Dorotéa and helped her down from her horse. He took her into his arms and, heedless of the others who watched, held her in a long and passionate kiss. When it was ended, he murmured, "You are truly the mate of *el Halcón*. I apologize, Dorotéa. You are as good as any *soldado*—no, far better!"

After treating the wounds of Bartoloméo and Jaime and resting a bit longer, John Cooper said to Felipe, "We'd best leave this road—Ramos and his men will expect us to follow it."

"That makes good sense, *mi compañero*," the *gaucho* emphatically nodded. "Let us leave this trail and cut through that little forest of *ombú* trees, in the direction of Lobos. There is a wide, fordable stream about fifteen miles from here. The horses will have no trouble taking us across, and we can throw our pursuers off our trail."

John Cooper smiled. "Did you know, Felipe, that I grew up with *los indios* and learned to track and to scout? We'll walk upstream for a while and try to leave the stream on a rock shelf so no one will see the hoofprints of our horses; then we'll head toward Heitor's *hacienda*."

"You think like a *gaucho*, *mi amigo*," Felipe chuckled.

"I will say this. We begin excitingly, do we not? But Ramos, I am certain, is not done with us. Not until we are all in the same *calabozo* with my respected *patrón*."

"That day will never come," John Cooper replied. "But now, let's ride—unless Dorotéa needs to rest longer."

Dorotéa had overheard the conversation and now mounted Rauda and trotted to her husband. "Do you think I am made of porcelain, *mi corazón?* I am not tired. If you are thinking of resting for my sake because I am a woman, there may be more danger because of your gallantry than if you accepted me as one of your *compañeros*."

Once again, John Cooper was struck with admiration for this loyal, brave young woman. "Again I must apologize to you, *mi amorcita*," he murmured for only her to hear. "It's not gallantry—it's because I love you, and I don't want to lose you."

"I warn you, John Cooper, you are closer to losing me by treating me as a helpless, pampered child than as someone who will fight beside you," was her heated answer.

He grinned at her. He felt as if they had been married for far longer than a short few months.

They mounted up and were on their way again. The stream was just as Felipe had remembered, wide and long, most likely out of some tributary of the great La Plata River. It was good, clear water, and John Cooper filled his canteen, as did the others. They rode upstream for a while, then crossed the stream, rode about half a mile farther south, switchbacked toward the north, and finally rode off toward the west. The hoofprints would be confusing even to an expert tracker. Even if the young soldier had reached Buenos Aires on foot by now—and that was highly doubtful— they would have a significant head start on any pursuer.

About an hour later, they came upon a little hamlet, comprising a few *jacales*, penned horses, and a flock of chickens cackling noisily at the mounted newcomers. A white-haired man limped out of the largest hut and greeted them, doffing his *sombrero* and bowing to them as if they were royalty. John Cooper greeted him in Spanish and asked to purchase some food for his party.

"You may have whatever we can give you, señor," the old man responded. "You do not speak like a *porteño*."

"I cannot, since I am a *gringo americano*," John Cooper chuckled.

The old man's face brightened. "Then you are more than welcome, you and yours, *señor gringo*." He shuddered and nodded in the direction of Buenos Aires. "We have already found what it is to live under the ways of the *porteños*. They believe that because they are in the big city, they are better than those who live in small villages or on the *pampas*. They have no understanding of our lives here. For the few handfuls of food we take from the good earth, the *porteños* take much tax—and they would take more, except that they know that we would die and then be of no use to them. Come now, I will have my wife prepare you some *almuerzo*. We have some rice and beans and a little goat meat—we killed the kid yesterday—"

"I would not take your meat from you, *viejo*," John Cooper compassionately responded. "But we shall be grateful for the rest, and if you will allow us to put our horses into the pen while we rest here—"

"But of course. While you take care of that, I will tell Rosa to prepare food for all of you," the old man said as he hobbled back to the hut.

After they had left their horses in the rickety pen with the scrub pintos that belonged to the crippled *alcalde* of the tiny hamlet, John Cooper, Dorotéa, Andrew, Felipe, and the two *vaqueros* entered the large *jacal* and gratefully ate the meager food that was offered with such goodwill.

"I am Tomás Banquetas, *su servidor, señor*," the old man genially introduced himself, then also introduced his elderly wife, Rosa. "We have been married forty years. I swear that I would rather have her as a *mujer* than any of those fancy *criadas* with whom the cruel *porteños* amuse themselves."

"That is a very good thing, *mi amigo*." John Cooper smiled at the old woman as he spoke to her husband. "We shall not stay here long, for I do not wish the *soldados* to come to your village and punish you and Rosa for giving us food and hospitality."

"I don't think they can punish us any more than they have already done," Tomás Banquetas replied. He shrugged philosophically. "Between taxes and stealing our young men for their army—the *porteños* have taken almost everything we have. There are only about two dozen of us, where once there were fifty or sixty in this village. And one of these days those families who are tired of starving so they may pay the taxes of the government will leave here." He shrugged again. "If Rosa and I were younger, we would follow them. There is no purpose to being an *alcalde* in a village that is only filled with ghosts and unhappy memories."

"Perhaps they will not always have their way, *viejo*," Felipe said, scowling. "You see, I am a *gaucho*; the *pampas* has always been my home. I am free and bow to no man, even a king. I will fight and give up my very life if it will cause the *porteños* to lose their power to molest good, decent people like your wife and yourself." Then, turning to John Cooper, Felipe murmured, "Perhaps we'd best ride on, *Halcón*. We should not stay too long in one spot."

"Fine, Felipe." John Cooper got to his feet. "*Señor alcalde*, do not trouble yourself to rise. We thank you for the food and your welcome. Our prayers will be with you."

"It was a pleasure," the old man said, "to have you share food with Rosa and me. I am only sorry that it was not of the best—"

John Cooper put his hand on Tomás Banquetas's shoulder and smiled. "It was as good as any food I have tasted, because it was given in friendship to a stranger. *Gracias.*"

Rosa came out of the *jacal* with a sack of rice and some potatoes, which she shyly handed to Dorotéa. Dorotéa thanked Rosa graciously and pressed a gold coin into her palm.

And so they rode on, and Felipe led the way toward the southwest, doubling back whenever they crossed small streams, to confuse any pursuers. After two hours of riding, the *gaucho* pointed to what looked like a forest glade, with tall trees shading the sun. "It will be cooler here, and we can sleep for some hours. The horses will be concealed, and no one can see us if they ride by."

"Do you see the waist-high grass that surrounds that side of the little forest? We'll rest there, *querida*," John Cooper now murmured to Dorotéa. "I know you are tired, but you have shown as much strength as any man. I love you very much."

"To hear that, my beloved *esposo*, gives me new strength," Dorotéa replied as she turned to him with a radiant smile. All the same, he could see the circles of fatigue under her eyes.

They slept, and it was dark when they wakened. Felipe Mintras made a fire with his tinderbox and, using a little water from his canteen, cooked the rice and potatoes.

Then they left their little camp and rode slowly through the night, with Felipe in the lead. From afar they could hear night birds and occasionally the roar of a puma. John Cooper had "Long Girl" primed and loaded, and Felipe did the same with his rifle and pistols.

They rode until nearly dawn, then slept again. They had passed through several more tiny hamlets, but now they came to a slightly larger settlement. From their vantage point through the trees John Cooper could see peasant women carrying jugs of water from a well, and others tending a fire to cook the morning meal.

"We can buy some food there perhaps," he said to the *gaucho*.

"Yes, these are friendly people. My cousin, Domingo Vardez, came from this village. There are perhaps a hundred who live here. They farm a little and the last I knew, were very lucky that the *porteños* had not levied crippling taxes against them. But if a man like Ramos is allowed to live much longer, he will have tax collectors throughout the whole province, and everyone will be fleeced almost to starvation. It is an abomination!" He said this last with a ferocious scowl and touched his *cuchillo*. John Cooper understood what he was thinking.

Fourteen

By dawn of the third day, skirting the town of Lobos, John Cooper and his companions saw the outline of the villa of Heitor Duvaldo toward the west. "Everything seems to be peaceful here," John Cooper said to the *gaucho*. "Thanks to you, Felipe, I think we've shaken off whatever pursuers we might have had."

"*Es verdad,*" the *gaucho* replied. "I see no *soldados* anywhere. We are in luck, *mi compañero!*"

"Let's ride in," John Cooper said, "but all of you, keep your guns ready in case there is any treachery."

"I can hardly wait," Andrew murmured under his breath, and his father turned in his saddle to cast him a quizzical look. Then he grinned. "I know what you are thinking, Andy. Adriana, am I right?"

The sturdy young son of John Cooper Baines turned crimson as he nodded and mumbled, "That's right, Pa."

"Good for you, Andy! I wish I were your age again. No, *querida*"—this time he turned to his right to smile at Dorotéa, who had given him an indignant moue in having overheard this last sally to his son—"I didn't mean that I am at all dissatisfied with my life. All I'm saying is that I envy Andy because he's just beginning his life and already he's very much in love with Adriana."

"Pa, I'm not exactly a baby, you know!" his son vehemently protested, and both his father and Dorotéa laughed heartily.

"She's a fine girl—far older than her years, Andrew." Dorotéa's delicious Spanish accent in pronouncing Andrew's name in his own tongue made the boy grin and nod his head. "I think it would be wonderful to unite our two families yet again in marriage."

Waving his right hand, John Cooper directed his companions to ride toward the courtyard of the *hacienda* of Heitor Duvaldo. An old woman with a jug of water had seen the riders and, with a gasp, hurried back into the house. A moment later, Heitor himself emerged, several years older than Raoul Maldones, portly, dignified, his forehead high arching, his eyes large, expressive, and dark brown. His black hair was gray streaked, as was his short, pointed beard.

"*¡Caramba!* It is the *gringo!*" he exclaimed, his eyes widening in surprise. "I swear I did not know if I would see you again! Dorotéa! *¡Bienvenida, mis amigos!*"

John Cooper had dismounted and now helped his

young wife to climb down from Rauda. Andrew as quickly dismounted, his heart pounding, for he was longing to see young Adriana.

Heitor's expression became grim. "You have come to aid poor Raoul, of course. I had not anticipated that Señor Ramos would confiscate the estate of my dear friend. But he has great power in Buenos Aires, and others in the government turn a blind eye to his excesses. I have felt so helpless, unable to aid my friend."

"You did Raoul a great service, Señor Duvaldo," John Cooper said, "when you took Adriana, María, and Paquita into your house."

"But Señora Josefa is a most able *dueña* and has assumed all the responsibility for their care," the *hacendado*'s older friend modestly added. "Come in. I will have one of my *trabajadores* take your horses to our stable. How good it is to see you, Señor Baines!"

At this moment, Duvaldo's fourteen- and sixteen-year-old sons, Benito and Enrique, came out of the *hacienda* and, seeing the tall blond Texan, hurried to him with warm greetings. "Señor Baines! ¡*Bienvenida!* We did not think we would see you again! And Señora Baines—"

John Cooper and Dorotéa greeted them in turn with warm smiles.

"I am neglecting my duties as a host," Heitor said. "I am sure that you, Dorotéa, are very anxious to see your sisters. These two men, Señor Baines, are your *trabajadores* from Texas?"

"*Sí*, Señor Duvaldo. We call them *vaqueros,* and of course you know Felipe. We can count on him to help us free Raoul from his imprisonment."

Heitor's face darkened, and he glanced around quickly. "*Por amor de Dios,* Señor Baines, do not speak so loud of such things," he cautioned as he gestured them into his *hacienda*. "Try to understand me, señor. To involve myself as you are now would be suicidal. I have two young sons who might well be imprisoned and shot if I became involved with your plan. Call me a coward if you like—"

"I make no such judgment on a man, Señor Duvaldo," John Cooper interrupted. "You were kind enough to my father-in-law's three daughters. We shall discuss this inside the house."

"Agreed!"

As they walked down the hallway of the *hacienda*, Raoul Maldones's daughters—Adriana, now thirteen; ten-year-old Paquita; and the youngest, María—hurried out of their rooms, uttering cries of joy at the sight of their eldest sister, Dorotéa. Andrew gulped, seeing Adriana appear in a blue cotton dress, her hair drawn up in a knot, with little curls at the back of her neck. John Cooper glanced at his son and smiled knowingly. He thoroughly approved of Andrew's young romanticism, and he murmured to Dorotéa, "Let Andy have a minute alone with Adriana."

Dorotéa took her husband's hand to follow their genial host. He led them to their rooms, where they had time to freshen up before meeting in the dining room for a light meal. Dorotéa's youngest sisters also followed, clinging to the young woman's hands, excitedly asking her questions about her new life and saying how happy they were to be together again.

Meanwhile Andrew and Adriana stood in the hallway, holding hands and eyeing each other for some time. Adriana blushed, as did Andrew. She whispered, "You've come back. I dreamed about you, Señor Andy!"

The smitten youth thought that he had never heard his name more exquisitely intoned, and he gulped again and said, "I wasn't supposed to come with my father, but I stowed away because I wanted to see you."

"How sweet! You are truly a *caballero*, Señor Andy," she whispered. "And now we must join the others and be very good. Señora Josefa is coming, and she expects perfect behavior."

Andrew escorted Adriana into the dining room and took his place at the table, across from Adriana. The *dueña* followed, frowning, then burst into tears at the sight of Dorotéa, to whom she hastened at once, flinging her arms around the young woman, embracing her and sobbing, "¡Mi corazón, que lástima! Thank goodness you are here! It has been a nightmare! Your poor father!"

As they ate their meal, Heitor spoke from his place at the head of the table. "I will tell you what has happened. Shortly after you left, Porfirio Ramos had Raoul arrested, taken in irons to Buenos Aires—"

"What horror!" Dorotéa indignantly cried. "My father is no criminal!"

"This we all know, dear Dorotéa," Heitor soothingly responded. "But the fact remains that he was imprisoned. And Porfirio Ramos appeared at the trial to condemn him as a traitor to the *porteño* cause. The tribunal condemned him to life in prison. But rumors have reached me that Señor Ramos intends to have your father executed for treason."

"The beast! The coward!" Dorotéa vehemently declared, rising from her place at the table. "He skulks like a jackal, to profit where he can. Señor Duvaldo, as you know, we intend to free my father from prison. But as *mi esposo* also told you, you and your sons needn't get involved. Felipe will rally some of the *gauchos* who loyally served my father. With their help and that of my dear husband, we can stop Ramos from coming into the power of a dictator."

"I can do your father more good," Heitor said, "by pretending to take no side at all and to go along with Señor Ramos's wishes."

"That makes sense," John Cooper decided. "It's a matter of adapting yourself to the enemy, and when the right time comes, striking out for your own freedom."

"Precisely, Señor Baines," Heitor agreed. "By pretending to be neutral, I am ignored—and thus I can serve you better. The tribunal made it very definite that Raoul Maldones was to be in prison for life, that there would be no appeal, even to our good *presidente*. Besides, he is kept busy in the dispute with Brazil over Uruguay, and we are not doing too well. This is why the *porteños* are gaining such strength everywhere. Now I am sure you will want to rest." He clapped his hands, and the tall, poised, light-brown-skinned majordomo appeared. "Tomaso, will you escort my guests back to their rooms? Señor Baines and his charming wife have already been to their suite. Señor Andrew may have the room across the hallway, while the *vaqueros* and Felipe may share a large room."

"Understood, *patrón*." The majordomo bowed, then approached John Cooper and Dorotéa. "If you will follow me . . ."

The *hacendado* inclined his head and smiled at Dorotéa, who nodded her thanks with an equally warm smile and then disappeared down the hallway.

Andrew would have liked to stay back to talk to Adriana, who had blown him a surreptitious kiss, but this was not the time. Rather reluctantly, he followed the *majordomo* to the room selected for him.

The gracious *mestiza* maids brought fresh bowls filled with hot water to the guests and, before leaving, bade them a pleasant *siesta*. John Cooper closed the door and turned to his lovely wife. "The nightmare is over for the time being, *mi corazón*. Now let us rest." He led her to the bed, and she linked her arm around his neck and gave him a passionate kiss, then whispered, "I pray *el Señor Dios* to give us a long life. I wish only to die in your arms when I'm an old woman, *querido*. Yes, we'll sleep like little children, innocent and believing that there is only good and justice in this world."

Thus they stretched out on the enormous bed and were soon fast asleep.

For Andrew, however, sleep did not come easily. Tired though he was, he could think only of Adriana. All the way from New Orleans, ever since he had stowed away in the wagon, he had seen her face in his mind. Since their reunion, he knew that he was more in love with her than ever. The slim, brown-haired girl with her heart-shaped face, the adorable dimples in her cheeks, and the cleft of her chin seemed to be to him the most exquisite female in all this world.

He promised himself that he would have a chance to talk with her at supper that night, to tell her what was in his heart. Of course, it would have to be done without Pa's knowing—he didn't want to be laughed at—though he didn't think Pa would. All the same, when a fellow went courting, he didn't want anyone else around, especially his own father.

Supper was served at ten o'clock that evening. Andrew was seated across the table from Adriana, who in her turn was seated beside the frowning, officiously attentive Señora Josefa. He had tried at first to smile at Adriana and to mouth some silent words that he hoped that she could understand, but the *dueña* had shaken her head at him, her brows knitting in disapproval. Andrew, greatly discomfited, sighed silently and occupied himself with what was a marvelous repast.

After the meal, Señora Josefa had María, the youngest child, bid the adults good night and took her off to bed. Adriana and Paquita followed.

"Children are at times a distraction," Heitor chuckled with an indulgent smile, "and must be protected physically and emotionally. That is why I waited for them to be excused before telling you some distressing news."

"What is it, señor?" John Cooper asked.

"It involves Rodrigo Baltenar, the man to whom your dear Dorotéa was once betrothed."

"That weakling, that milksop! He would do nothing to help my father!" Dorotéa scornfully replied.

"Go on, señor," John Cooper said.

"This man Baltenar is a very close friend and ally of Porfirio Ramos," Heitor continued. "After your father's lands were seized, Porfirio Ramos took most of the acreage for himself. Ramos was living in the *hacienda* itself—and perhaps still is—but I also know that he has given the *hacienda* and a thousand acres of the Maldones land to Baltenar. Señorita Adriana has consented to marry Baltenar in exchange for an agreement that her father's *estancia* would be given to her at Baltenar's death. Thus the Maldones property would be kept in the family's hands even though Ramos has succeeded in having it confiscated."

"But she's—oh, no!" Andrew Baines burst out and then clapped his hand over his mouth as he colored hotly, seeing Heitor turn to stare at him with widened eyes.

"Would such an agreement be honored?" John Cooper demanded.

"A woman is not usually allowed to own property like a man, Señor Baines," his host replied. "But since Ramos believes that he needs Baltenar's cooperation, he has agreed to this contract. Thus it becomes law because the *porteños* have the upper hand. You must not fault the lovely Señorita Adriana for agreeing to this union. She did it to protect her father and—though I am reluctant to mention so heinous a possibility—in the event I am unable to continue providing for them, her sisters Paquita and María will not starve."

"No!" Dorotéa broke out, "I will not have Adriana sacrificing herself to that weakling. If she should wed that fool, it would not be long before that detestable monster of a Ramos would force her to be his *querida*. John Cooper, *mi corazón*, surely you won't let this happen? You know how Andrew feels about Adriana, and she would be splendid for him."

Andrew blushed furiously. His heart went out to Adriana, and he was praying that he would have a few moments alone with her later, without the interference of her frowning *dueña*.

John Cooper observed his son's reaction to the news and felt a pang of compassion. He knew that Andrew was really in love. If it were within his power, he would see to it that such a charming young girl did not have to marry Rodrigo Baltenar. He remembered what a dislike he had instantly taken to the man on their first meeting, and perhaps, reviewing his own sentiments at the moment, he realized that part of his dislike had been because he was attracted to lovely young Dorotéa, to whom Baltenar had been formally betrothed. Hence, all the more he could appreciate his son's anxiety upon learning the news.

He leaned over to whisper to Dorotéa, who nodded, and then he said earnestly, "I promise to do everything I can to make sure that Raoul Maldones is freed and that Adriana does not have to marry Baltenar. Those who are responsible for all these things will be punished for their greed and treachery."

It was well after midnight, and Andrew Baines lay on his bed, wearing only his drawers, for it was hot weather in Argentina now, the reverse of what it would have been back in the United States. He had not had a chance to speak to Adriana alone, and now he could not sleep, for his mind was filled with thoughts of her. If only he could do something to prevent her from marrying that fool Rodrigo Baltenar!

Suddenly, he sat up, his eyes widening, his senses tingling. Had he imagined it, or was there a soft knock at the door? He waited, holding his breath, and then there was another knock. Quickly, he sprang out of bed, drew on a robe, hurried to the door, and opened it. It was

Adriana, in her night shift and robe, her feet bare, glancing frantically down the hallway, fearful of being discovered.

"Adriana! Oh, Adriana, come in! Don't let anyone see you. You don't know how I've wanted to talk to you! And now, after what I've heard—" he began.

She put a finger to his lips and shook her head, looked again down the hall, and then crept in and closed the door, shoving home the bolt. "I know what you're thinking, dear Andrew," she murmured. "You mustn't judge me too harshly. I had to do it. You understand, don't you? How was I to know that you and your father would come back here so soon? My only thought was that if the *porteños* took us away from Heitor Duvaldo's, all of us would be orphans and poor and perhaps even put into prison because we were the children of a traitor!" Her eyes sparkled with anger, and her bosom rose and fell with emotion.

Andrew was transfixed, trembling with desire for her, anguished because of her anguish, and yet helpless because he himself could do so little. "But I love you—"

"Do you really, *querido?*" she softly murmured, putting a hand to his cheek.

"Oh, my God, Adriana, of course, I love you! I won't let you marry this man!"

"But I must. Señor Baltenar has agreed that when he dies, I am to inherit the *estancia* of my father. Señor Ramos laughed and said to Señor Baltenar, 'You may die because the young and spirited Señorita Adriana may kill you with her love, but I assure you that the *gringo* and all his men can do nothing to you, now that you're under my protection.' Oh, I wanted to kill him, to spit in his face, for saying such a wicked, filthy thing!"

"My Adriana—" Andrew had taken her in his arms, his throat choked with emotion, and she suddenly laced her arms around his shoulders and kissed him passionately on the mouth. He nearly fainted with ecstasy and desire and anguish, but he knew that he must do nothing to offend this sweet young girl who professed her love for him. "Adriana, my pa said tonight that he, Dorotéa, Felipe, some of the *gauchos* loyal to your father, and our two *vaqueros* will go to your father's ranch tomorrow. Maybe they can stop your marrying Baltenar. I want you for myself. I'm too young yet to marry you now, Adriana, or I'd do it tonight!"

"You are sweet, *mi corazón*," she murmured huskily, and her eyes filled with tears as she put her hand to his cheek and then kissed him again.

Andrew moaned in his ecstasy, for to be held by this lovely girl and to be told that she loved him and to feel her lips against his was the very apex of delight and fulfillment— and yet, the frustrating anguish of knowing that she had pledged herself to a man even older than his father tortured him. He gently moved away from her embrace. "You'd better go now. I don't want Señora Josefa to find you here."

"You're right, this is very wicked of me, and I have compromised you and myself." Then with a sly look at him that made his blood boil, she whispered, "Sometimes I've heard it said that when a girl goes to a man's room and it is found out, she must marry him at once, or else her honor is spoiled forever. In a way I wish that would happen. Say a prayer for us, dear Andrew. I feel so much happier now that I know your father is here, and I know the *gauchos* will come to my father's help! Good night, and sleep well."

"I will dream of you. I love you so, Adriana!" he said hoarsely.

She gave him a last kiss, and turning quickly, she drew the bolt, opened the door very slowly, and glanced down the hallway. Then it closed behind her, and Andrew stood transfigured, trembling with joy. How he loved her, and how he would pray that they could marry and live happily, just the way Pa and Dorotéa were right now!

Fifteen

They met again at breakfast in Heitor Duvaldo's lavishly furnished dining room. At their host's invitation, the two Texan *vaqueros* and Felipe joined them.

As they were finishing their coffee, Heitor turned to John Cooper and said, "I have a pleasant surprise for you, Señor Baines. This morning I was wakened by my majordomo, who told me that Oudobras, the *gaucho* from the Maldones *estancia*, has come to us with many of his *gaucho* friends. As you know, Oudobras was Raoul's *capataz*."

"I remember him well! He and his men will make a valuable addition to our little army when we leave today to pay a visit to the Maldones *estancia*," the tall Texan smilingly answered, glancing at Dorotéa, who enthusiastically nodded her agreement with this sentiment.

"You must take every precaution," Heitor said in a grave tone. "There is no treachery of which this man Ramos is not capable. Like a viper, he gives no warning before he strikes."

"We'll be most careful." John Cooper rose from the table and gave his arm to Dorotéa. "The time has come for us to take our first step forward on Raoul Maldones's behalf.''

Felipe and the two *vaqueros* followed and went out to the stable for their horses. Standing there awaiting them was a tall, haughty-faced *gaucho*, with a hawklike nose and thick, bushy black beard. Near him stood ten other *gauchos*, armed with *bolas* and *cuchillos*, and holding the reins of their horses.

''How good it is to see you again, Oudobras!'' John Cooper exclaimed as he strode forward and offered his hand, which the tall *gaucho* energetically shook, grinning and nodding to his fellows.

All the *gauchos* doffed their wide-brimmed hats and inclined their heads in respect to Dorotéa. Their loyalty to the *patrón* had not in the least wavered.

Now Felipe also came up to the group and shook Oudobras's hand. ''Here are our men, *Señor Halcón*,'' Felipe exclaimed. ''We did not have to look very hard for them.''

An assenting murmur rose from the *gauchos*, and Oudobras vehemently declared, his eyes flashing, ''We swore an oath of the *pampas* to be loyal to Señor Maldones. We are his until death—and, if you command us, Señor Baines, we follow you to Porfirio Ramos and Rodrigo Baltenar!''

There were tears in Dorotéa's eyes as she stepped forward, but when she spoke, it was with a firm, clear voice. *''Hombres*, my father treated you fairly, saw that your families did not starve when there was no game or provender. Yet, if Ramos is allowed to keep my father in prison in Buenos Aires and to hold his land, you will have to live on the *pampas*, without help or friends among the *hacendados*. Ramos will turn them all against you, he will make you outlaws, and your freedom will be restricted. You see here Felipe Mintras.'' She gestured in the direction of the *gaucho*. ''He returned to Argentina because he cannot believe that my father may face a firing squad because a greedy *porteño* covets his land and hates those who work upon it and build for the future. Men of the *pampas*, I promise to fight beside you.''

At this, there was a loud cry of ''Huzzah!'' and ''*¡Muy bueno,* Señora Baines!'' Oudobras said, ''Word just came to me last night that Ramos himself—knowing of your arrival in our country—has hurried to your father's *hacienda* from Buenos Aires and is there this very day. We do not fear him or his *soldados*. We *gauchos* have already spoken among ourselves, señora, and we will stand with you to the death!''

''*Gracias, gracias por vida, la vida de mi padre,*'' Dorotéa said, her voice breaking into a sob at the end.

John Cooper put his arm around her shoulders and then declared, ''Men of the *pampas*, let us ride now to the *estancia* where once Oudobras was *capataz*. If God so wills, he will be *capataz* again, and all of you will be welcome there, and I promise you that I will do all within my power to make that possible!''

There were cheers again, and Heitor, who had come from the house to join them, called out, ''*¡Vaya con Dios, mis compañeros!* May good fortune attend you!''

They rode off, John Cooper and Dorotéa at the head of the column, Felipe, Bartoloméo Mendoza, Jaime Portola, and Oudobras and his friends following behind on horseback, all armed and ready. Although Andrew pleaded to go along, his father insisted he remain behind at the Duvaldo house. In truth, Andrew was not displeased, since now he would have more time with Adriana.

John Cooper estimated that it would take about two days to reach the Maldones *estancia*. He asked Felipe for the best route, and the *gaucho* replied, ''It is best to go in from the west, *Halcón*. If we go the other way, the guards will see us first—I am sure they will be posted. From the west, we shall be able to come close without being seen at first.''

It was midafternoon of the next day when they came upon Raoul Maldones's *hacienda*. John Cooper sighed, remembering his first visit here, observing the wide porch with its colorful cloth canopy, and the French chaise longue and upholstered couch; Raoul Maldones had believed in bringing civilized comfort to this primitive area. And now, he thought to himself, the usurper, Porfirio Ramos, had seen to it that he and Rodrigo Baltenar would enjoy these comforts, seized out of envy and hatred and the blind drive for power that characterized all the *porteños* of this era.

Suddenly, there came a sharp, "*¡Alto, hombre!*" and he saw a thick-mustachioed squat man carrying an old Belgian rifle and dressed in green *camiso*, breeches, and dusty black boots come forward and level his rifle at Felipe.

"We come in peace," John Cooper called out in Spanish. "We mean no one any harm.''

"So you say," the surly guard growled. "Off your horses, *¡pronto!* Whom do you seek here? This is now the property of Señor Porfirio Ramos and Señor Rodrigo Baltenar."

"Ramos is here?" John Cooper demanded.

"*Sí*, though it is no concern of yours, *hombre*," the guard instantly retorted.

"Tell him that the *gringo americano* is here. Señor John Cooper Baines. Tell him that I wish to talk with him," the tall Texan demanded.

"I will do that. But I do not think he will see you. All of you, dismount. Domingo! Salazar! Estufio! *¡Aquí!*" the guard turned to cry out.

Three other soldiers, similarly dressed and carrying rifles, emerged now from behind a large thicket of bushes not far from the corral and advanced slowly, their rifles at waist level. They suspiciously stared at the newcomers on horseback.

John Cooper's party dismounted and stood holding their horses' reins while the guard, who had summoned his three friends, conferred with them in whispers, which did not quite reach the ears of the visitors.

"You will wait here," the guard finally announced. *"Mis amigos* will see that you try no foolish tricks, *¿comprenden?* I will ask Señor Ramos if he wishes to see you." The guard spat, showing his contempt for the *gringo*. Then he strode toward the porch of the *hacienda*, knocked at the door, was admitted, and disappeared.

Felipe murmured to John Cooper, "Ramos was expecting you, *Halcón.*"

John Cooper nodded. "At least now we can meet face to face, lay our cards out on the table."

Oudobras and his *gauchos* stood muttering among themselves, their hands on their *cuchillos*. The sun beat down, as oppressive as in Texas. A silence had fallen over the clearing now, but John Cooper knew that there were others watching from ambush, and he murmured to Felipe Mintras, "We must seem very peaceful, and that is why I have lowered 'Long Girl' to the ground. We come in peace, and we will talk."

"I do not care much for talk, *amigo,*" the *gaucho* shrugged. "For me, if I am given the chance to slip my *cuchillo* between the ribs of that fat pig of a *porteño,* I will be glad that I came back to my *pampas*. Because then I can go back to Luz and my children and tell them that I've paid my debt to my *patrón.*"

The surly guard now emerged and hastened up to John Cooper. "My *jefe, su excelencia* Porfirio Ramos, says that he will see you. Put down your weapons and come with me."

"I wish to go with my *esposo, hombre,*" Dorotéa suddenly exclaimed, stepping forward and confronting the mustachioed guard. So saying, she unfastened the leather belt at her waist and dropped it, with the holstered pistols, and held her arms at her sides.

The guard shrugged. "I do not care. A *mujer* can do him no harm. But remember, Señor Baines, *mis compañeros* are watching you. If you are foolish, your *mujer* will be shot."

"If that happens, you will not live to see the sunset, *amigo*," John Cooper said smilingly, but the bite in his tone made the guard glance at him warily, and a shadow of apprehension appeared in his dark eyes.

John Cooper beckoned to Felipe and murmured, "If Dorotéa and I do not return in half an hour, come in after us. Kill those who oppose you." The *gaucho* nodded, put his hand to his heart, and murmured back, "Agreed, *Halcón*."

"Come with me, then," the guard said, marching toward the *hacienda*.

They climbed the steps of the porch, and the guard opened the door and stood vigilantly by as John Cooper and Dorotéa entered. In the huge, elegantly furnished salon, Porfirio Ramos was seated on the couch, and near him was Rodrigo Baltenar. Each had a goblet in his hand, and there was a bottle of Chilean wine on the dark wooden coffee table before them.

"Welcome to Argentina, *gringo*," Ramos insolently drawled. "I have come to the belief that you have more lives than a cat."

"You assumed I was dead, Señor Ramos?" John Cooper said in a casual, equally insolent tone.

The *porteño* glowered, his face coloring with anger. "What do you want here, *gringo*?"

"I am simply wondering how it is that you have found my father-in-law a traitor," was John Cooper's answer.

Ramos rose, downed his wine, and hurled the glass into the fireplace, where it shattered. He uttered a hollow laugh. "I do not need to explain to you, *gringo*. An *americano* would not understand our struggle for independence. It is not your affair, Señor Baines. You have been lucky thus far, and I counsel you to go back to your own country. You would be well advised to take the next ship out of Argentina."

"Thanks for the advice, señor, but I don't plan to take it. I ask you, man to man, to release Raoul Maldones. I know that he has the welfare of Argentina in his heart and soul, perhaps even more than you. You see, Señor Ramos, he wasn't greedy for land or power."

"How dare you speak like that to me, you insolent *perro americano!*" Ramos flared. "You are an enemy—"

"And that is why you tried to have not only me killed, but also Dorotéa, and everyone else on the *Miromar*," John Cooper interrupted.

Ramos made an ironic bow in Dorotéa's direction. "Oh, I would never harm you, and certainly even less the lovely señora. But the law is the law, Señor Baines, and you can do nothing about it. There is even the possibility that Raoul Maldones will be brought before a firing squad for his treason. Since my friend Rodrigo here is affianced to Señorita Adriana, I will naturally do what I can to spare that charming *muchachita* the grief of knowing that her father was executed like a common criminal—but I can promise nothing. I am not alone the law in Buenos Aires."

"But you have shaped it to your own wishes," John Cooper retorted. "You have land enough for a dozen men, and still you seek more. What will you gain by all this? Do you expect to imprison or execute all those who refuse to bow down to you, Señor Ramos?"

"I will not answer such an insulting question, *gringo,*" Ramos sneered. "Take your *esposa* and go home. You will be allowed to take nothing else back—except perhaps your life. And that you might forfeit if you persist in defying the laws of our country. I have had enough of this discussion. I have no wish to make war upon you personally, but my men grow restless."

Dorotéa could no longer contain herself, hearing Ramos talk so, seeing all her family's lovely possessions being used by these two vile men. All this while, Rodrigo Baltenar had remained seated on the couch, a sickly smile on his dissolute face. She confronted him now, pointing an accusing forefinger at him. "You were once affianced to me, Rodrigo! I am glad I found out what you are, and I despise you now. My father counted on you as his loyal aide. Instead, you consort with this man, who is more a traitor than ever my father could be!"

"*Momentito*, Señora Dorotéa—" Baltenar began, rising to his feet, his face flushing with anger at her insulting denunciation. "You do not understand. Your father was too sentimental, too weak, and he had only to agree to change his politics. He might well have been honored in Buenos Aires. But no, obstinately, stupidly—"

"Enough! I will hear no more insults about my father. You do not even begin to know the meaning of the word loyalty, Rodrigo Baltenar!"

"How beautiful you are when you are angry, Dorotéa!" he insinuatingly murmured, a suggestive, lecherous smile on his face. "A pity you chose a *gringo*. But I shall content myself with the charming Adriana. She is still very young, but she will learn—"

John Cooper was going to stop this exchange, but when he moved, Ramos slid a pistol from inside his waistcoat and held it loosely in his hand as a warning to the tall Texan not to interfere.

Dorotéa cried out in her furious exasperation. "I will not permit my sister Adriana to marry a jackal like you, coward, traitor! I would rather die than see her married to you, Rodrigo Baltenar!"

Baltenar uttered a cry of frenzied anger. His right hand plunged to a holstered pistol at his side, but before he could aim it at Dorotéa, Ramos leveled his own pistol and swiftly pulled the trigger. Baltenar uttered a strangled cry of horrified surprise, trying to turn his head toward Ramos, and then crumpled to the floor, dead from a bullet in his heart.

"You see, Señora Dorotéa," Ramos sniggered, "there is still chivalry in me, and you have greatly misjudged me." He looked disdainfully down at Baltenar's inert body, chuckled, then added, "The poor fool forgot himself. Actually, he has done me a service: I now reclaim the thousand acres and this house, which I awarded him for his valor in allying himself with our faction in Buenos Aires."

"You are a monster, Porfirio Ramos," Dorotéa said in a shaking voice. She turned to John Cooper. "I wish to leave."

"We'll go now, *querida.*" He put his arm around her shoulders as she burst into tears, burying her face against his chest, and he stared at the sneering Ramos. "Understand this: I'm going to challenge your right to keep a decent man in prison, Señor Ramos."

The powerful *porteño* spread his arms wide in a gesture of complete indifference. "Consult with those above me in power. You will get the same answer. There is nothing you can do to save him." Ramos, his hands on his hips, tilted back his head and burst into mocking laughter.

Sixteen

John Cooper and Dorotéa strode out of the *hacienda* to rejoin Felipe, Oudobras and his men, and the Texan's two faithful *vaqueros*. The guards watched them tensely, awaiting orders from their *caudillo* to arrest the couple. They had all heard the pistol shot but did not know who, if anyone, had been wounded or killed.

Felipe stared questioningly at the tall Texan, who said quietly, "Rodrigo Baltenar was there. He insulted Dorotéa, and when she gave him back more than he bargained for, he drew a pistol on her—"

"I should have gone with you, I knew I should have—" Felipe angrily began.

"No, no!" John Cooper shook his head. "Listen! It was Ramos who killed him with a pistol before Baltenar could fire at my wife. And then he said that he was grateful to me for provoking the incident, because now he could take back the thousand acres of her father's land that he had given that weak-kneed toady."

"*¡Diablo!*" the *gaucho* swore. "And he has done nothing? He has let you go?"

"With a warning that if I try to free your *patrón*, I may lose my own life or certainly wind up in prison with

158

him," John Cooper answered, a wry expression on his face. "But we're going to ride directly to Buenos Aires before Ramos can get there, and we'll do what has to be done before anyone can stop us. We've already got our own weapons and plenty of ammunition. There's no time like the present."

"I agree," the *gaucho* said, nodding. He turned to Oudobras. "At least we have one less enemy, with Baltenar killed."

"He was a skulking cur, not a man," the hawk-nosed *capataz* grimly replied. "But the man Ramos, he is still to be reckoned with."

"That is why we ride now, before he has a chance to get to Buenos Aires before us. To the horses, *mis amigos!*" Felipe called.

John Cooper's party mounted up, wheeled their horses, and galloped off, leaving Ramos's guards in a cloud of dust.

A half hour passed before Porfirio Ramos appeared on the porch and barked an order to the surly guard who had first accosted John Cooper. "Have the men saddle their horses, take their weapons. That accursed *gringo* must think me very *estúpido* to let him get away."

"*Sí, comprendo, patrón,*" the guard chuckled. He had been wondering how long it would take before his *patrón* came out of the house to issue these orders.

"You, Pedropillo," Ramos shouted, "tell the men to take the shortcut to the waterfall that is ten miles from here. If we take the southwesterly trail, we will get to the falls well ahead of the *gringo* and his *amigos* and have a very warm welcome awaiting them."

Pedropillo saluted, then hurried out to the corral to summon the riders who had accompanied Ramos from Buenos Aires. There were ten of them in all, swarthy, mustachioed, mostly outlaws who had been granted clemency by the *porteño* government in exchange for their fealty to Porfirio Ramos. They would kill at his orders—he had only to point out what enemy he wished to dispose of to know that it would be done expertly and quickly.

John Cooper was riding in the lead, Dorotéa alongside of him. Felipe rode up to join them.

"There is a forest glade about six miles ahead of us, *Halcón*," the *gaucho* observed. "And to the left of it there is a waterfall, about one hundred fifty feet high. Nature has made a little lake at the top of the high slope and a freshet spring—so that the water is in constant movement. It is not exactly spectacular, but it is an unusual sight after our stretches of *pampas*."

"I'd like to see it."

Felipe glanced back over his shoulder. "I see no pursuers. All the same, I have told Oudobras and his men to have their guns and knives ready. I would not be surprised at anything that might happen."

These words stirred a presentiment in John Cooper's mind. Feeling uneasy, he turned to Dorotéa and said in a low voice, *"Mi corazón,* I wish I had not agreed to let you come with us on this mission."

"I would not have had it any other way, *querido!"* she defiantly told him. Then her expression softened. "You are thinking that Ramos will ambush us."

"Exactly. You know yourself that he let us go too easily. Yet we must confront Ramos and have done with him sooner or later, one way or another."

Now they entered swamplike terrain. Felipe drew his horse alongside John Cooper and said, "We'll soon be at the waterfall, *Halcón*. I've heard and seen nothing, but I feel danger."

"You and I are kindred spirits, *mi amigo,"* John Cooper replied. "We shall face Ramos."

"Yes!" the *gaucho* hissed, his eyes glittering with anticipation. "But he is mine, *Halcón*. I wish to see him whine and grovel for mercy at the end of my *cuchillo,* to take his life slowly and let him know why I am doing it.''

"Ride ahead a little, Felipe, and see if you can find any signs of Ramos's men."

"*Sí, Halcón.*" Felipe grinned.

By now, dusk had begun to fall over the forests. Here and there where the oozing mud of the swamp could be seen off to the right, John Cooper saw the slithering forms of snakes sinking out of sight into the muddy water. As he glanced up, he stifled a cry of surprise, for a huge snake dangled somnolent from an overhead branch of a giant *ombú* tree. John Cooper directed his palomino off to the left and out of range of it, then glanced back. He could see the baleful eyes fix on him and the tongue flicker out. It was a deadly anaconda, coiled in the tree awaiting its prey.

More and more, John Cooper felt a growing uneasiness. He turned now to Felipe, who had just ridden up after his brief scouting foray. "I see no one, *Halcón,* but there is much foliage, and it is a likely spot for an ambush. As soon as we reach the falls, we should all dismount and hide ourselves. If there are men waiting for us, we will not be easy targets.''

The stillness was almost intolerable now. Darkness engulfed them, and the density of this forest with its underlying swamp demanded everyone's keen concentration. Felipe had told John Cooper that there lurked many areas of quicksand, which could drag a man down to his death. There was also a narrow trail that *gauchos* had blazed long ago, and this they followed, drawing ever closer to the waterfall.

The three-quarter moon gave them light. Felipe leaned toward John Cooper and whispered, "Another quarter mile, *Halcón,* and we'll be at the waterfall. Off to the right, where the trail breaks, is a clearing, and just a little ahead of it, all the tangled bushes and the trees behind which we can take refuge if we are attacked.''

"Pass the word to Oudobras and the others so we'll all be ready," John Cooper whispered.

The *gaucho* spurred his horse and rode off toward the tall, haughty-faced *capataz*, and whispered to him. Oudobras nodded and gave a signal to the men who followed him.

John Cooper could hear the soft plash of the waterfall, and instantly he slipped down from the saddle of his palomino, patted the horse on the rump, and gestured to Dorotéa to climb down into his arms. Both of them hastened to the tangle of bushes off to the right and took positions. He saw that Dorotéa had seized her rifle from its sling on Rauda's saddle and was making certain that it was primed and loaded and that the brace of pistols was securely belted around her slim waist. "Can you see clearly over there where the waterfall is, John Cooper?" she asked.

"Yes. There's just enough moonlight. I don't see any movement in the trees or the bushes above us there—"

But hardly had he uttered the last word when there was the sound of a rifle and the flash of gunpowder in the priming pan. The shot had come from a spot on a slope about a hundred and fifty feet above them, at the edge of the waterfall where, behind a rock, Pedropillo had sighted his gun and fired at Felipe. Ramos's aide missed his target, and the ball harmlessly spent itself against a tree well behind John Cooper and Dorotéa. But John Cooper, having seen the flash, triggered a shot with unerring aim. Pedropillo pitched forward into the waterfall, tumbling over and splashing into the deep pool at its base, floating there, face up.

"We've drawn first blood!" John Cooper exulted. "Now we know their position. But it's going to be difficult to draw them out. We're going to have to be pinned down here until they play their hand."

There was a volley of shots from both sides of the waterfall as Ramos's men, hiding behind the boulders, fired down on the *gauchos*. One of the *gauchos*, a young man in his midtwenties, nearest to Oudobras, uttered a strangled cry, stumbled, and then sprawled on the ground, with his arms flung out. Oudobras swore under his breath and, crouching low behind a small bush, drew both his pistols out of his belt and fired them up at the rocks. There was a *spang* as one of the balls ricocheted against the jagged rock at the left of the waterfall, but the second ball drew a yowl of pain from the right side. A burly, thickly bearded outlaw dropped his rifle and crouched down low, clapping his hand over a wound in his right arm and swearing violently under his breath.

The attackers' force now numbered eleven men, counting Porfirio Ramos himself, who was exhorting his men to kill as many of the enemy as they could, but to spare John Cooper and his wife—Ramos wanted to deal with them at his leisure.

A silence ensued after the first volley. Ramos made an impatient gesture toward two of his men, indicating that they should crawl along the ground and down the slope, then out toward John Cooper's men. "We'll cover you with rifle fire!" he hissed.

The two bearded outlaws, in their midthirties, had no doubts that they would win for their *patrón,* for they had the *gringo* and his men in a trap from which there was no escape. But at this moment, the moon fully rose and came from behind a cloud. There was greater illumination, an advantage for anyone to make use of.

One of the outlaws, whose name was Sanchez, whispered to his crony, "Cortubas, you go to the right, and I'll take the left. We can kill many *gauchos* silently, with our knives."

"You go first, Sanchez!" declared Cortubas, a stocky, pockmarked man with squinting, narrowly set eyes.

"Very well," Sanchez growled. "But do not wait too long."

Cortubas crept off cautiously, pausing to glance back to see that Sanchez was keeping his part of the bargain.

His *cuchillo* gripped by the handle between his teeth, Sanchez moved down the slope toward the clearing, taking advantage of the rocks and the stubbly growth of floral plants while Cortubas, convinced now that his friend was acting in good faith, moved out of hiding and came slowly toward the other side. The sound of a broken twig in the silence gave Sanchez away, and suddenly there was the *whirr* of a *bola* cast by one of Oudobras's *gauchos*. The stone balls stunned Sanchez as they fell against the back of his skull. He cried out with pain, clapping a hand to his head and trying to disengage the *pampas* lasso. A slim young *gaucho* named Matinkas crawled toward him through bushes and, finding himself only a few feet away from the outlaw, lifted his *facón* and savagely dug the sharp blade into the outlaw's back. There was a shriek of agony, and Sanchez collapsed, dead. But from the top of the waterfall there was the sound of a rifle shot, and Matinkas uttered a gurgling cry as the ball pierced his throat, and he sprawled lifeless across the dead body of the outlaw.

Felipe had heard the struggle. He turned from his hiding place not far from John Cooper and Dorotéa and saw Cortubas crawling toward the clearing. Felipe swiftly lifted his rifle and triggered it. Cortubas slumped with a convulsive kick as the ball pierced his brain, and he lay dead, as the moon disappeared behind another cloud.

But Felipe's shot had enraged Ramos's band, and all of them now fired their rifles and pistols in a furious volley. They saw few targets, but a pistol ball wounded Oudobras slightly in the right arm as he was reloading his pistol, and a rifle ball killed Fallone, another young *gaucho* loyal to the former *capataz*. Still, the odds of battle were now in John Cooper's favor; there were eight outlaws left in Ramos's band with their *porteño* leader, while there were seven *gauchos*, the two *vaqueros*, Oudobras, Felipe, John Cooper, and Dorotéa.

"Are you cowards to hold back against that accursed *gringo?*" Ramos called to his men in a voice choked with hate and frustration. "Fire again! You have plenty of ammunition! Remember this, if you should see the *mujer*, do not any of you dare to fire at her. When I kill the *gringo*, she'll be mine, my *puta*, my slave!"

One of Ramos's men, a *mestizo*, now straightened from behind the rock at the left of the waterfall, wanting to look down to the clearing below to find a target. Promptly, John Cooper fired, and Dorotéa did the same almost simultaneously. The *mestizo* dropped his rifle, took two steps backward, then pitched forward and lay draped over the rock, his head bowed as if in prayer, John Cooper's bullet having found his temple, Dorotéa's bullet having found his heart. John Cooper and his wife nodded at each other.

Oudobras, having hastily tied a strip of cloth around his wound, was determined to storm the enemy position. He whispered to three *gauchos*, "Go toward the left, all of you. Find our enemies and kill them!"

Now Porfirio Ramos was crouching down behind a rock at the left of the waterfall. He leveled a Belgian rifle toward the thicket behind which two of the *gauchos* hid. He fired once, but the trajectory of the ball was higher than he had calculated, and it went whistling overhead. John Cooper immediately fired "Long Girl," but, in haste and in the darkness, the bullet made an angry *ping* as it ricocheted off a rock a foot below Ramos's head. He instantly ducked, with a vile oath, and began to reload his rifle, while gesturing to his henchmen to fire volleys down at the defenders.

Meanwhile, Oudobras's three *gauchos*, drawing their *facones* and uncoiling their *bolas*—holding these in their right hands with the sharp knives in their left—crawled forward. The night was hideous with the reverberations of gunfire as the seven surviving outlaws of the Ramos band kept up a constant fire of pistols and rifles. A rifle ball, by a chance shot, took one of Oudobras's men in the forehead and killed him, but the tall, haughty former *capataz* put his finger to his lips to indicate to his men that they should make no sound to indicate that loss. Oudobras made the sign of the cross over him, took his *facón* and *bola*, and waited for the success of the two remaining men who were crawling up the slope.

The outlaws were so intent upon firing down toward the clearing that they did not see the two *gauchos* until one of them hoisted himself over the slope and, with a savage cry, hurled himself on a stocky outlaw who was in the act of reloading his pistol. The outlaw turned, uttered a strangled cry as the *facón* plunged deep into his heart. Drawing out the blade, the young *gaucho* sprang at another outlaw, succeeded only in wounding him before a third outlaw killed him with a pistol shot.

The other *gaucho* took advantage of the confusion of this close-range fighting and sprang over the top of the slope, whirling his *bola* and casting it out toward a fourth outlaw, who was conferring with Porfirio Ramos. The heavy stones at the end of the *bola* coiled around the man's neck, and the *gaucho*, running forward, jerked one end of the *bola*, dragging the outlaw down, and buried his knife in his back. Then he drew out his blade and lunged at Ramos. But the *porteño* fired his second pistol, shooting the *gaucho* in the belly. He doubled over and sprawled backward as the moon, emerging from another cloud, sent its rays down on his contorted face.

The wounded outlaw, Roualdo, stanched the flow of blood with a bandanna as best he could. "I don't know how many they have left, Señor Ramos, but we might be pinned up here for hours."

"I know that, you idiot!" Ramos savagely hissed.

"That damned *gringo* is a better shot than any of you *hijos de putas!*"

"Señor Ramos, let me take Ignacio and charge down the slope on horseback. The *gringo* and his men will rise to meet us as they see us coming, and you will be able to fire at them. This will prove at least to you, Señor Ramos, that we are not *cobardes!*"

"Very well. But if you should die, it will not be on my conscience," Ramos sneered.

"I will go tell Ignacio." The outlaw turned on his heel and strode over to one of his friends, a man of forty, with a sightless eye that had no patch, knife scars on his cheeks, and a squat, stocky body. "Ignacio, you and I are going to charge the *gringo* and his men," the lean outlaw declared.

"Very well. It seems as good a plan as any. Myself, I have no stomach for long hours of firing at ghosts and waiting to be killed."

The two men got their horses, primed and loaded their rifles, and made certain that the pistols strapped around their waists were loaded and ready to be fired. Ignacio said to Roualdo, "You go from the right side, and I from the left. That way, there will be two distractions for them."

"Agreed!"

All this while, there had been a lull in the fighting. Silence again had fallen over the waterfall and the clearing, and John Cooper turned to Dorotéa and whispered, "I don't like this quiet. They must be planning something, and we'd best be ready."

Roualdo and Ignacio had mounted, while Porfirio Ramos watched them, then loaded his rifle, gesturing to the three other survivors of his band to gather around him so they could pour concentrated fire down upon the clearing.

Ignacio spurred his horse down the slope and, guiding it with his knees, lifted his rifle and fired at the dark outline of a man whom he saw vaguely outlined near an *ombú* tree. The ball grazed a *gaucho*'s left arm, and he, stepping out of the thicket, swung his *bola*, and threw it, hitting Ignacio's waist, causing him to fall off his horse. But in that moment, the man next to Porfirio Ramos sighted his rifle and pulled the trigger, and the *gaucho* fell over Ignacio's stunned, half-conscious body, dead from a bullet in the head.

Ignacio writhed and tried to push the dead weight of the *gaucho*'s corpse from his body, and just as he succeeded, as he drew a hunting knife from its sheath, Oudobras, who had crawled toward the thicket, sprang upon him and buried his *facón* in Ignacio's chest.

A volley of gunshots that came from the waterfall whistled harmlessly by, just as Roualdo rode down from the other side of the slope. Dorotéa was first to spy him and fired but missed. His wiry black mustang carried him on at a gallop as, guiding his mount with his knees just as Ignacio had done, the outlaw fired his rifle in his right hand, and then the pistol in his left, wounding one of Oudobras's men, but not seriously. John Cooper turned, saw the rider, squinted along the sight, and pulled the trigger of "Long Girl." Roualdo uttered a gurgling shriek, flung up his hands, dropping pistol and rifle, and toppled off his horse to roll over and over on the ground, dead.

Once again, the three men clustered around the *porteño*, firing their rifles and pistols in a concentrated volley, wounding another *gaucho*. But John Cooper had already reloaded his rifle and, aiming up at the rocks, pulled the trigger. The outlaw next to Porfirio Ramos fell backward, dropping his pistol and rifle, kicked convulsively, uttered a low moan, and died.

"Señor Ramos, they are too much for us," one of the two remaining outlaws panted as he crouched beside the *porteño* leader. "We are fighting ghosts."

"You dogs, you *cobardes!* That *gringo* must die, and

the woman must be mine!'' Ramos said in a hoarse, savage voice that shook with rage. ''If you are afraid of him, I myself will take care of him. I have a plan.'' With this, cupping his hands, Ramos called down, ''Señor Baines, can you hear me?''

''I hear you, Porfirio Ramos! Are you ready to surrender?'' the tall Texan called back.

''Yes, yes, I surrender. I am coming down now.''

''I do not trust you, Porfirio Ramos. You would sell your own mother to the devil if you could profit from it,'' John Cooper scornfully called back.

Ramos's face turned livid. ''I swear I alone will face you. I will send my men away—you will watch them go. But you must give me your word that your men will not fire on me when I come down!''

''Have your men ride away, then,'' John Cooper called back. Meanwhile, because he was not yet certain of the sincerity of his enemy's proposal, he had been busy reloading ''Long Girl.''

Ramos turned to his two men. ''Ride back to the Maldones ranch. After I have finished with the *gringo*, I'll join you there with the woman.''

A few moments later, the men rode off. John Cooper saw them and shouted, ''Are those all?''

''I swear to you on my mother's grave!'' the *porteño* called.

''The devil can swear by God, but it's not binding! Come down here, and our men will be covering you. Oudobras!'' he called to the *capataz*.

''I hear you, Señor Baines!''

''Go slowly up there with two of your men, well armed, and if you see anyone, shoot to kill and ask no questions!'' John Cooper commanded.

''It will be done, Señor Baines!''

Porfirio Ramos was already clambering down, unstrapping the holstered belt at his waist and flinging it down. He came forward, seemingly unarmed, but he had a knife, hidden in its sheath fixed against his left side.

Oudobras and his men had reached the top of the slope, and the *capataz* called down, "There is no one here, Señor Baines!"

"Good! So you've told the truth, Ramos," John Cooper said. "Now come closer, arms raised. I want to see you facing me."

"I come at your order, Señor Baines," the *porteño* mockingly responded with an inclination of his head. As he raised his arms, he surreptitiously drew the sharp stiletto out of its sheath, concealing it in his hand.

Dorotéa had now risen, lowering her rifle, her face taut and her eyes cold and narrowed as she contemplated the man who had been responsible for her father's sufferings. She did not see the knife.

Ramos came closer, then wheeling to Dorotéa's right, suddenly seized her with his left hand by the back of the neck and held his sharp stiletto against her throat.

Felipe and Oudobras simultaneously uttered a cry of rage, and Oudobras shouted, "*¡Cobarde!* Is this how you give your word?"

"Now then, Señor Baines, the tables, as you see, are turned," Ramos jeered. "If any one of your men makes the slightest movement toward me, I will kill your lovely *esposa.*"

"Damn you, Ramos! All right, then, what do you want?" John Cooper's voice was hoarse with fury.

"A horse. I shall keep your charming wife as my hostage. I want you to go back to your country where you belong. When you are aboard a ship, Señor Baines, I will have *soldados* put your wife aboard the next ship for los Estados Unidos. Is that very clear?"

John Cooper clenched his left fist but realized that he could do nothing without endangering Dorotéa. He could not bring up the long rifle and shoot Ramos before the

latter would be able to drive his knife into the soft neck of
the young woman.

"So, Señor Baines, you'll get me a fresh horse. The
Señora Baines will ride with me. And you'd best do it
quickly because I rather tire of this little game."

"If you harm her, Ramos, I'll kill you with my bare
hands," John Cooper said between his teeth.

Felipe stared, openmouthed. He gripped his coiled
bola in his right hand, and Dorotéa stared at him, her dark
eyes eloquently trying to communicate with him.

"Suppose you drop your rifle, Señor Baines. I've
already seen what damage it can do at long range—but
then, I'll admit that my men were not first-rate fighting
men, and they did not have the hatred for you that infuses
me. I do not welcome interference with my plans for
power, Señor Baines, and particularly not from an accursed *yanqui*. It appears to me that you have enough
trouble in your own young, barbarous country to stay there
and not to meddle in something that absolutely does not
concern you. But then, we are wasting time." Porfirio
Ramos looked around him. "Where are the horses, Señor
Baines?"

"Why, we *gauchos* do not have to tether them to
trees the way you stupid *porteños* do," Felipe spoke up
with an insolent tone and a mocking smirk on his weather-
beaten face. "We let them free, and when we need them,
we whistle. They are obedient, they love us as we love
them, and they come swiftly to our signal."

"Well then, whistle, and see that you have a horse
for us," Ramos sneered as he continued to grip Dorotéa by
her neck with his left hand while prodding the sharp tip of
the knife against her throat. "I grow weary of this farce,
and I tell you that I have no compunction in letting this
charming *mujer* feel the point of my knife to quicken your
compliance with my request." With this, his lips curled in

a sadistic grin, and he pressed a little harder with the point of the knife. Dorotéa winced but made no outcry.

John Cooper stared at the *porteño*. "I will not be responsible for what happens to you, Señor Ramos, if you try that again," he said in a choked voice.

But Dorotéa was looking again at Felipe, and the *gaucho* made a covert sign with his left hand.

"*¡Dios*, it hurts me so—I cannot bear this—*por favor, por piedad*, let me go, Señor Ramos!" Dorotéa suddenly sobbingly cried.

Startled by her unexpected capitulation, Ramos slackened the grip on her neck and, in the same instant, Dorotéa swiftly flung herself forward on her stomach on the ground. Ramos uttered a savage oath and was about to stoop to grip her hair and drag her up, when Felipe, swinging his *bola* around and around, sent it flying toward the *porteño*.

The heavy stones wrapped around the fat neck of the mustachioed man, and he dropped his knife, uttering a strangled cry. He plunged both hands to the deadly lasso that was strangling him. Felipe ran forward and, with a savage yank, jerked on the *bola*. The *porteño*'s eyes bulged, then went glassy, his hands dropping feebly, as he pitched forward and lay sprawled at the *gaucho*'s feet.

Instantly, Felipe crouched down, drawing his *facón*, and rolled the inert body over, and then a gloating smile curved his thin lips. "His neck is broken, *Halcón*." He glanced at his knife, then sheathed it.

"Thank you, Felipe. I won't forget what you've done," John Cooper fervently vowed. Then, very tenderly, crouching down, he lifted his young wife by the shoulders as gently as he could. "*Mi corazón*, are you hurt?"

"No, *mi esposo*. And you may be sure that no harm has been done to the child. I know how to fall so that I do not hurt myself. I am fine."

Her coolness made John Cooper tilt back his head and, to relieve his agonized tension, burst into hearty laughter. Then he embraced her. "There is no woman in the world like you, *mi corazón*. You are not a dove, but a hawk like myself, and we are fitting mates."

He turned to Felipe and Oudobras, his own two *vaqueros*, Bartoloméo and Jaime, and the three remaining *gauchos*. They had lost seven men in all, but there were still eight left, plus Dorotéa. "We will bury our comrades who gave up their lives," John Cooper said. "Then we will ride to Buenos Aires. We shall free Raoul Maldones!"

Seventeen

The hot September weather had not dampened the enthusiasm of the settlers of the Brazos River community in Texas, which Eugene Fair had begun from a land grant given to Stephen Austin by the Mexican government. It was true that news from Mexico, brought in by an occasional courier, gave the residents of this sprawling, growing settlement some anxiety, for it appeared that the Mexican authorities had begun to regret their liberal terms to the *tejanos*. The residents of the new settlement, however, believed that their strength and unity would prevail over any enemies.

Much of their optimism could be attributed to the energetic outlook of the famous scout Jim Bowie, who had told the settlers of his plan to establish an itinerant force of armed men to be known as the Texas Rangers. It was also comforting that the capital of Mexico, Mexico City, was many hundreds of miles to the south—it would be a long while before an order could be given for Mexican troops to attack a peaceful Texas community. All the same, the rapid ascendancy of Santa Anna to total power was always a threat. And it was this, most of all, that farsighted men like Jim Bowie feared.

As a preventive measure, Stephen Austin had intended to strengthen Texas by opening other areas to settlement and a year earlier had wangled a second contract from the Mexican government, which provided for the settlement of five hundred additional families within the bounds of the first Texas colony.

Eugene Fair had conferred with Austin about a possible attack, and the latter had said to him, "Eugene, we must convince the Mexican government that we are in earnest about recruiting settlers who plan to marry and raise families here. Once the authorities see that we are fulfilling the letter of the law, they will be less suspicious of us. You will have to screen carefully all men who apply for permission to live in our commune on the Brazos, and I would welcome a tour of inspection by Mexican officials, so they can be convinced that we have no intention of attacking Mexico."

Three months before, eighteen men had arrived in the settlement on the Brazos and had applied to Eugene Fair for the privilege of settling in the community. Their applications indicated that they wished to marry and fulfill all the obligatory rules of the settlement. Fair had informed them that their applications would be approved if they could be married by the first of October. One of them, a tall, affable, towheaded Missourian of twenty-seven, Kenneth Dearing, had been appointed spokesman for the bachelor applicants and had told Eugene Fair, "The fellows have delegated me to get wives for them. I have written to a marriage contractor who advertises in a St. Louis newspaper, and he wrote back that he was prepared to furnish as many as sixty girls.''

"Now that's a really enterprising idea, Mr. Dearing,'' Fair chuckled. "Just be warned, you've got until October to be hitched up, or else we'll have to reject all your applications.''

"I know that, Mr. Fair. I sent off a special courier to St. Louis to the matchmaker and told him to ship out the girls.'' Kenneth Dearing grinned. "I like the idea of settling down here. I reckon there's a chance for all of us to build something for the rest of our lives and make this country bigger and stronger.''

"That's exactly what Stephen Austin and I had in mind when we applied to Mexico for permission to settle people in the Texas area, Mr. Dearing,'' Fair responded. "As an act of good faith, I'll do you a favor. I know a young priest about three days' journey from here, Jorge Pastronaz of the Double H Ranch. I'll just send him a letter and ask him to come here and marry all of you off to your girls.''

"That's mighty nice of you, Mr. Fair,'' Kenneth eagerly replied. "We'll have a real big wedding party. You can be sure of that.''

Eugene Fair rose from the desk and clapped the towheaded young Missourian on the back. "You know, we always welcome the chance to have a party, for whatever reason, but a big group wedding will really set things off. We'll have a barbecue, dancing, and singing, and it'll be right friendly for everyone!''

Shortly after Eugene Fair's courier had arrived at the Double H Ranch to ask Padre Jorge Pastronaz to officiate at the wedding of eighteen bachelors to the mail-order brides, two young nuns, Sisters Mercedes and Rosalie, had gone to Sister Eufemia in the study of the ranch's mission house.

"Sister Eufemia," Sister Rosalie said, humbly inclining her head, "Sister Mercedes and I would like your permission to leave here and take up our work at the Austin settlement on the Brazos."

"You are dissatisfied here, my sisters?" the older Dominican mother superior asked, arching her eyebrows in surprise.

"Not at all, Mother. But we think we can be of greater service there. We have heard that many new residents have been accepted in the community. There are already many young children but no real school, such as we have here. We would feel more fulfilled if we could participate in the new community," Sister Rosalie earnestly replied.

"I have no objections," Sister Eufemia said.

Thus Padre Pastronaz and Sisters Rosalie and Mercedes left the Double H Ranch the next morning and arrived at Eugene Fair's settlement three days later, in a wagon filled with supplies that Tía Margarita had provided. She had sent along several cured hams with cloves, melons and berries, jars of preserves, and relishes. Yankee had pursued a young deer a few days before Padre Pastronaz and the two nuns were to depart, and Miguel Sandarbal had followed the wolf-dog with his rifle and killed the deer. Tía Margarita had promptly cured it with plenty of salt, and this, too, was sent along as a contribution to the wedding feast.

The community on the Brazos joyously welcomed the arrival of the young priest and the two sisters. Padre Pastronaz told the enthusiastic crowd that the sisters planned to remain in the settlement and create a mission school. And after the priest and nuns had enjoyed an ample supper, they visited the community's meetinghouse and prayed to *el Señor Dios* for peace.

At the very end of September, to the great delight of the bachelors—and particularly Kenneth Dearing—one of the community's scouts rode back from his afternoon patrol with the news that two wagons were heading for the settlement.

"Here come the wives!" Julius Tenser jubilantly shouted. He had come from Bavaria a decade before. Genial, nearly forty, he had been trained in his homeland as a gunsmith, and he had already set up a little shop in the community. When he had heard that Kenneth Dearing was sending away to a St. Louis marriage broker, Julius had begged the towheaded young man to include his name. "I ask only for a good woman who will love me just a little, even if I am getting old and am not the most handsome fellow she has ever seen," he had told young Dearing.

Now, with all the others, spruced up, clean-shaven, and wearing their Sunday best, he waited nervously for the two wagons to enter the community.

Young Simon Brown, who was already happily married with two young sons, had been appointed along with old Minnie Hornsteder by Eugene Fair to greet all the women. Fair, who had to leave on business in San Antonio, knew that Minnie possessed an earthy sense of humor and a practical, shrewd nature that made her an excellent judge of character on the frontier. Simon, as chief scout of the community, also was a good judge of people.

Two lean, weather-beaten men on horseback rode on ahead to announce the news that everyone anticipated: "Here come your brides, gentlemen!" The men dismounted, and Simon went up to the nearest rider, held out his hand, and introduced himself.

"Glad to meet you, Mr. Brown. I'm Don Kenton, out of St. Louis, and this here's my partner, Clem Rogers. Clem and I and six of our pals rode along as escorts, and we're hoping you can put us up to stand as witnesses—

mebbe feed us, too, and a mite of likker would come in mighty handy.''

''You needn't worry about food and drink, any of you,'' Minnie piped up with a robust laugh, slapping her thigh. ''This is going to be the biggest shindig this community ever had, and everybody's welcome. Well now, Simon boy, line the bachelors up. Say, I want to know how you're gonna pair them off with one another so's everybody's gonna be happy.''

''What I figured was,'' Simon tentatively began, ''to let the girls line up on one side and the bachelors on the other, and see who goes to whom!''

''That's not too bad an idea. Somebody might need a little urging or pushing, and I can take care of that,'' Minnie said, laughing again. ''And you better get the *padre* right now, because we don't want to see any courtin' until the folks have exchanged their vows and said they'll take one another for better or worse, you understand that, Simon?''

''Oh, yes.'' Simon blushed at Minnie's teasing.

Four other scouts now rode ahead of the wagons and dismounted, and some of the older boys hurried forward to take their horses. In each wagon, a middle-aged man rode, a rifle lying across his lap and a brace of pistols strapped to his waist. The driver in the foremost wagon dismounted and came forward to Simon Brown. ''Where's this fellow Dearing, who started it all?''

''I'm Simon Brown, and there's Mr. Dearing. Ken, someone wants to meet you!'' the young scout called.

The freckle-faced, towheaded young man hurried over, his face blank, for he did not recognize the driver. ''I'm Davidson, and I'm in charge of this group,'' the older man flatly declared. ''I believe, Mr. Dearing, you needed eighteen brides, that right?''

''Yes, sir, that's about it. You see, we've got the line of bachelors already there over on the other side of your wagons, standing ready to meet the girls," Kenneth answered.

"Well now, and you'll be one of them, I bet. The price agreed was twenty-five dollars and expenses for each gal, right?"

"Yes, Mr. Davidson."

"We figger about eleven bucks a gal will cover food and necessaries."

"All right, that's thirty-six dollars a person. That would make eighteen times thirty-six, if I'm not mistaken."

"You are, but only a mite, Mr. Brown," Mr. Davidson allowed. "You see, we brought along two others, just in case you found yourself needing two more wives in a hurry. Or maybe, if some of these gen'l'men take exception to the lot I've brought, there are two others to choose from. Of course, I'd hate to take them back." He said this last with a dubious glance at Simon Brown.

The young scout was already figuring the total charge in his head. "Then it comes, as I reckon it, to seven hundred twenty dollars, Mr. Davidson." He was already looking toward the wagons, from which the women were beginning to dismount.

In line, Julius Tenser sighed deeply, for he had already seen a woman who had taken his fancy right off: She was tall, with jet-black hair, and a proud look on her face, despite the rather tattered and dirty homespun dress she wore. She looked around as if she were a queen finding herself in the surroundings of peasant hovels. All his life, he had dreamed of an autocratic beauty, like perhaps a German baroness, to whom he could never have aspired before. But here on the frontier, this young woman, regardless of her station, epitomized his ideal of a proper mate. In his eagerness, he could not wait, but hurried over to Simon. "Herr Brown," he burst out, "please, I've waited so long, and there's exactly the one I want. You see that tall one, with the black hair? See how she walks, as if she were afraid of getting her slippers dirty—''

"Well now, Julius, I don't see any reason why you shouldn't have that one, if your heart's set on her," Simon chuckled. "Tell you what, you go right up to her and introduce yourself. If the two of you hit it off, we'll wed you this evening."

"*Schönen Dank,* Herr Brown!" Julius gasped as he hurried forward to the tall young woman.

Simon and Kenneth, who had collected the monies due from the other seventeen bachelors, paid Mr. Davidson. Then Simon turned to the seventeen men, each eagerly waiting to make the acquaintance of the woman who had caught his eye. "Men, we're going to have all the girls line up. Mr. Davidson here brought two extra, but perhaps somebody else will come forward and decide that it's high time he got hitched."

There was a ripple of amused and friendly laughter from the friendly spectators, and Minnie, cupping her hands to her mouth, bawled, "Now then, you men, act decent, mind you! These ladies came a long way, and they've a right to look you over, just as you have them. I don't want anybody to act out of line, or he'll get the back of my hand."

This time there was even more laughter. Meanwhile, Julius had hurried up to the tall, black-haired young woman and, seizing her hand, awkwardly stammered, "Excuse me, please don't be offended. I know you must think I am *verrucht*—but, when I saw you get down from the wagon, I told myself that you are indeed the Frau I have been dreaming of all these years, *wirklich!*"

The young woman, who was two inches taller than the plump, middle-aged German, looked at him disdainfully and then deigned to give him a thin-lipped smile. "Is that so? Well, you're not exactly a prize specimen, but I guess you're as good as any man here. My name's Mary Caskins.''

"And I, I am Julius Tenser, *Liebchen*," he gasped, almost overcome with delight at this realization of his secret dream. "I have some money, and I have a nice house—I helped build it myself, I will have you know, Fräulein Caskins. I work hard. I make and repair guns, you see—that is what I was taught in the old country—but now I am an American—and I have waited so long to have someone who will care for me, just a little—I will make you very happy, I swear to you on my honor!''

"But you don't know a thing about me, Mr.—Mr.—" she hesitated, frowning at him.

"It is Julius Tenser, *Liebchen*. You may call me Julius. And later, when we are married, I will call you Mary. It is a lovely name, *ein schöner Name*, truly!" He had now taken her hand in both of his and added, "Come with me now, and we will stand in line, so that you will know that I would choose no one else. I do not care if the rest of them are considered the most beautiful in all the world. You are the one I want. Truly that is so!''

Mary Caskins was twenty-seven. She had run away from a Pittsburgh home when she was only thirteen, for her drunken father delighted in applying his belt to both his wife and daughter. A friendly peddler had taken Mary with him, in return for her amorous favors, and had treated her reasonably well. She had left him two years later to work for a farmer and his elderly wife in Ohio. She spent five years with them, until the farmer's wife died and he intimated that he expected Mary to take her place without benefit of clergy. She had moved on to a small Indiana farm, spent a year there, then another in Sedalia, until finally she had come to St. Louis, where she had found a situation as a barmaid in a tavern. She had had several lovers, none of whom had wished to marry her, until finally she saw the advertisement in the St. Louis paper, seeking unattached females who would be willing to go to Texas and marry settlers in a community authorized by the Mexican government.

Mary let herself be led back to the line of the seventeen men—for Kenneth Dearing had now taken his place there to await the selection of the young women. Her eyes quickly scanned the other men. Kenneth was handsome and young, and he gave her a boyish smile, but Julius Tenser saw this and earnestly pleaded, "I told you, I know I am not a great catch, but I will be a good husband to you, I will make you happy, I will work hard and do whatever you wish, if you'll only say yes to me. *Bitte, Liebchen!*"

There was such anguish, such yearning in his voice and in the almost poignantly adoring look in his soft brown eyes that Mary Caskins, despite her cynicism and hardness, which had been her defense through these long years, was touched. "I guess you'll be all right," she grudgingly granted. "I'll try to make you a good wife, too, but I've lots of faults."

"*Liebchen*, everyone has faults." Julius was near tears in his gratitude for her acceptance. "But you will tell me what you do not like about me, and I swear to you that I will correct my faults. I promise this with all my heart and soul."

She could not help liking this man who looked at her with such adoration. She knew that he meant every word he said. Unbending, she put her hands on his shoulders and gave him a soft kiss on the cheek. "There now, I guess you might say we're just about engaged. I'll marry you, Julius."

He uttered a rapturous sigh, gulped, blushed, and then stood as tall as he could, still holding her hand in both of his. His chest swelled, his eyes sparkled, and his face was radiant with joy.

Now Simon turned to Minnie and asked, "Suppose

two or three fellows go for the same girl, what then, Minnie?''

Clapping him on the back, she said, ''Look here now, sonny, these men are so starved for female companionship, there'll be a little rivalry to start with—that's only natural. But you just watch, there won't be much fighting. Take my word for it. I've lived a lot longer than you have, sonny, and I know how men act around women when they haven't seen any for a long time. Just like a new rooster in a hen yard.''

Cupping his hands, Simon called out, ''Let's make it nice and orderly, fellows. See which girl you really like, talk to her a little, and if she's agreeable, pair off. We'll have the wedding tonight, in the church. And then there'll be a real feast. All you can eat and drink!''

Kenneth Dearing scanned the row of women. He whistled softly under his breath, and his eyes widened as his gaze fixed on a pretty, brown-haired girl of about nineteen with the bluest eyes he had ever seen and dimples on each side of her soft, rosy mouth. He uttered a long sigh and went quickly forward. But the man next to him, Abe Jenkens, a lanky, forty-five-year-old farmer, was making steps toward the very same girl, a grin on his homely face. And he was first to speak. ''Say now, missy, I'd like to marry you tonight, if you've no objection.''

Kenneth scowled, for Abe Jenkens was an honest, dependable man. All the same, he didn't intend to be bilked out of this delightfully charming young woman.

''You do have a choice, ma'am,'' he said politely as he doffed his hat and held it against his heart. ''Abe's a good man here, but in a way he's not really a bachelor, you see. He's a widower twice over—and me, I've never even had a girl, much less married one.''

Abe gave him an annoyed, peevish look. ''Now see here, Ken Dearing, you're a mite high-handed, if you want my opinion.''

"Why not let the young lady make her choice? That would be fair," Kenneth promptly interposed, with a pleading look at the girl. She smiled again, and now the dimples were even more in evidence, and Kenneth had by this time completely lost his heart. He was ready to fight a duel to win her, if need be. But she solved matters very capably by saying, in a soft, sweet voice, "Why, I think that is fair. And I've learned your names, because you"—nodding toward Abe Jenkens—"are Abe, and you"—turning to smile at Kenneth Dearing—"are Ken Dearing, isn't that right?"

"Yes, ma'am!" they simultaneously chorused, then looked at each other, scowling as they foresaw that one of them was certain to be disappointed.

"Well, my name is Madge Freeman, and I come from Tennessee. I'm very good at housework, and I can cook." Here she blushed deliciously, and Kenneth knew that, come what may, he had to marry her.

And then she added, her starry blue eyes very wide indeed, "But my mother always said to me, 'Madge, when you marry, you pick a fella about your own age or maybe just a few years more, 'cause you want to grow up with him and your children.' I don't want to hurt your feelings any, Abe, because you seem like a very nice man, and I'm sure you were kind to your wives, but you're lots older than I am. It would sort of be like marrying my father, if you take my meaning."

"Humph!" Abe Jenkens snapped, his face turning red. "If it's a young whippersnapper you want, of course I can't stand up to Ken Dearing here. And, if that's the way you feel, missy, I don't think you and me could get along as man and wife." He moved away and, squinting, began to contemplate the other women. The two extra women who had been brought along in case they were needed waited off to one side. They were sisters, nearly thirty, Ella and Doris Samuelson. They wore homespun dresses, which they themselves had made. They were neat and modest but not as young or as beautiful as some others. Abe Jenkens stared at Ella, who was a year younger than Doris, boldly went up to her, took her hand, and said, "Now you, missy, seem like a nice woman with common sense. Do you think you and me could get along? I'm a farmer here, I grow lots of fine vegetables, and I'm a God-fearing man with no bad habits. I don't drink liquor— well, I might on my wedding night—but you take my meaning. I've got good habits."

"Why, I think that's a good recommendation," Ella Samuelson said, giving him a grateful smile and letting him take her hand.

Meanwhile, the other men hurried forward, having an idea already of whom they wished to choose as their future mates. After an hour, the eighteen men in line had all been paired off. The two remaining young women glanced mournfully at each other and philosophically shrugged.

"Now don't you fret, gals," Minnie Hornsteder called. "There'll be more settlers coming in next week, and I'll bet a dollar to a doughnut that a few will be single fellers looking for gals just like you. You gals can put up with me till then. I'll tell you all you want to know about this settlement. You just bide your time, gals. Your wedding might be no later than next week. Mark my words."

And so, with great joviality and enthusiasm, the men and their brides repaired to the meetinghouse, where Jorge Pastronaz interviewed each couple to ascertain their determination to share a life together. The two newly arrived nuns, Sisters Rosalie and Mercedes, were also kept busy, greeting the couples, conversing with them, and learning what their hopes for the future were. Then Padre Pastronaz gave a short sermon, indicating the blessedness of matrimony, its aspirations and obligations, and performed the ceremony that united them.

"Well now," the marriage broker muttered to Simon,

"from what I hear about your grant from the Mexes, you just got these folks hitched in the nick of time."

"That's true, Mr. Davidson. And we're much obliged to you for bringing the women."

"Well now, Mr. Brown, I'm just going to have me a high old time tonight at the barbecue and the dancing. Shucks, I might even dance with one of those two gals left over, because I've been a widower myself for the last five years."

Simon chuckled, shaking his head. "In that case, Mr. Davidson, why don't you take first pick of all these charming young ladies who apply to find husbands?"

"Well, Mr. Brown, you might say I've always hankered to make my own choice and not to be forced into anything. My philosophy is, if it's going to happen, it'll happen."

"I understand. Just the same, we're very proud that eighteen more families are officially started here in the community," Simon exuberantly declared. "That sort of calls for a drink."

"I'm with you all the way, Mr. Brown," Mr. Davidson enthusiastically said.

After the formality of the marriage ceremony, the newlywed couples emerged from the meetinghouse amid the congratulations of the congregated settlers. Minnie Hornsteder again cupped her hands to her mouth and bawled, "Come and git it, 'cause the weddin' victuals is ready!"

To punctuate this summons, several of the younger men had taken pans and were beating on them with sticks of wood to make a joyous knell, and everyone thronged to a large clearing about two hundred yards south of the entry gate to the settlement, where the married women had already set up spits and were roasting mutton and beef while others were busy portioning out ears of corn, sweet yams, okra, and peas. On one huge table was a stack of clay bowls, and everyone was invited to take a bowl and help himself. Some of the men had brought out jugs of corn liquor, while their wives drank fruit punches and lemonade. However, when they were not looking, the men sneaked over to these drinks and spiked them with some of the whiskey.

In the center of the clearing, four men who were excellent musicians—and extremely fond of square dancing—took up their violins, guitar, and harmonica and played "Turkey in the Straw" and "Yankee Doodle." The musicians then welcomed requests from the spectators and readily obliged.

The newly married men saw to it that their wives' bowls were filled to the brim with good food. The settlers sat on unfinished, rough wooden benches, enjoying their food and listening to the music.

The moon was out, the evening was balmy, and the good cheer and conviviality of one of the first important settlements in Texas were vibrant on this memorable night. Simon Brown put his arm around the waist of his wife, Naomi, while she held their little twin boys in her arms. He murmured, "Honey, God's been real good to us, and I love you an awful lot. I just hope it's always going to be as peaceful as this for the rest of our lives here."

"So do I, my darling." She gave him a look of ineffable love.

"I hope we get lots more settlers, because then this place will be so strong that nobody would be able to attack it."

"I hope you're right, Simon dear."

It was well after midnight when the feast broke up, and the newly married husbands took their wives to the cabins and little houses they had already built. Julius Tenser could hardly believe his good fortune and held onto Mary's hand as if she might vanish into thin air. During the feast, he had waited on her hand and foot. She was touched by this plump little man's devotion, and she warmed to him. When they reached the porch of the house that he and other men had built, she turned to him and said, "Julius honey, you know I've heard that husbands are supposed to carry their wives over the threshold the first night. I'd like that very much, if you'd do it for me in our house."

"But *Liebchen,* I would love to do it! Oh, my darling Mary, *meine schöne,* you have made me the happiest man in all this world, *wirklich!*" he said, beaming. Very carefully, he lifted her up and managed to carry her across the threshold. Thinking of the words "our house" made his heart pound wildly with delight. When he set her down, she put her hands on his shoulders, leaned forward, and kissed him on the mouth. "You're a sweet man, Julius. I don't think I'll be sorry. I only hope you won't," she murmured.

As for Kenneth Dearing, he was totally enchanted by pretty young Madge. They had spent most of the evening exchanging anecdotes about their earlier lives, and Kenneth found that Madge enjoyed reading. As it happened, he had several books of which he was inordinately proud. "I will get more whenever I can, Madge," he promised. "And newspapers, when they come here from San Antonio or St. Louis, have lots of interesting stories."

She slipped her hand into his and turned to him, trust in her lovely blue eyes. He took her in his arms and kissed her, and he told himself that now truly life was beginning anew in this warm, fertile region of Texas territory. And with so many friends around, life would never be lonely or dreary.

Eighteen

Two days after the group wedding, Stephen Fuller Austin rode into the settlement that his empresario, Eugene Fair, had initiated. He was accompanied by two men, Leland Ferris and Matthias Eberley, from the city of San Antonio, both in their early fifties. They had been friends of Stephen's dead father, Moses, and had urged the Mexican government to grant Moses Austin's request to authorize American families to settle in Texas.

Simon Brown greeted Austin with some awe, for he had heard much of Moses's gifted son, now thirty-three, tall and handsome and possessed of an ingratiating manner, fluent in several languages.

"Mr. Brown! Glad to meet you—I've had wonderful reports about you from Eugene Fair," Austin returned the young scout's greetings. "I'm going to Washington to try to get a ruling on treatment of the Indians in this area. Many settlers have had trouble with them—particularly the Karankawa—and a lot of the settlers believe those Indians to be cannibals. They raid for pleasure and steal for their food. And then we have the Tonkawa, who steal any horses they can find. A few settlers near San Antonio have caught the horse stealers and given them a whipping, but

189

that only leads to bad blood. I'd like the government to allow us to regulate the Indians on a friendly basis.''

"I don't know if you can reason with an Indian, Mr. Austin,'' Simon said, somewhat out of his depth. ''But I know that over at the Double H Ranch, they've had trouble with the Comanche and sometimes the Kiowa Apache.''

"I know,'' Austin said, "and one of these days, the government will have to do something. But before we continue our journey, we'd like to stay here a day or two. I am amazed at the building and development of this community, and in such a short time, Mr. Brown. When I make my report to the authorities in Coahuila, I'm sure that they'll look with favor on this. It proves my point that there are decent people who want to settle and develop the country, people who want no trouble with their neighbors— just a chance to raise their families and live the way God meant us all to live.''

"Amen to that, Mr. Austin,'' Simon said. "I'll have Jim Doring take your horses. He's in charge of our corral. We're going to need another one soon because we expect even more settlers.''

"And I think you'll have them. Eugene tells me that many applications are pouring in,'' Austin declared. He and his friends dismounted, and Jim Doring, a stocky, good-natured man in his late thirties, came forward to lead the horses to the corral.

"My wife and I'd be mighty pleased, Mr. Austin, if you and your friends would have supper with us this evening,'' Simon offered.

"That's very neighborly. We'd enjoy that. You know, I'd like to talk to some of the other men of this community. I want to hear their grievances, if there are any. In every new development where divergent people come together for a communal aim, there are sure to be problems. But these can be ironed out. What really worries me is the attitude of the Mexican government. As of now, Mexico owns and governs this territory. But our Texans feel that they aren't really represented in the government. And then the Mexicans don't believe in trial by jury. That's another stumbling block for the future. These things have me worried, I'll confess. Enough of that, gentlemen. Leland, Matthias, let's walk around. You've a fine new meeting-house there, Mr. Brown."

"Yes, and I'm sorry you and your friends weren't here to see the group wedding we had—eighteen couples, Mr. Austin!"

"Wonderful! The more marriages, the more settlers and families, and the more we show the Mexican government that we have nothing but peaceful designs."

Minnie and Henry Hornsteder, hearing that Stephen Austin was visiting, went to Simon's house about half an hour after the visitors had finished Naomi's plentiful supper. Austin had heard of the redoubtable Minnie—her strength and kindness. "I wish I could take you to Mexico with me, Mrs. Hornsteder," he complimented her. "You are an honest pioneer settler without being a busybody."

"Well now, Mr. Austin, it's very flattering of you to say things like that to an old woman." She could not suppress a self-conscious giggle. "But the fact is, shucks, I'm afraid I am a busybody just the same. I do like folks an awful lot, and when you're nice to them, it brings out the best in them."

"You're a good example for the whole country, Mrs. Hornsteder. Do you have anything you'd like to tell me before my friends and I set out for Washington tomorrow?" he asked.

"Well now, of course we could stand more people here. But I'm just wondering if our people are going to have any say-so when it comes to government."

"Yes, Mrs. Hornsteder, that's a concern to all of us," Austin gravely answered. "I'd like to see if I can get a few more Texan representatives in the Mexican government. And there's another thing we haven't mentioned at all, but it's a serious one.''

"What's that, Mr. Austin?" Minnie wanted to know.

"The matter of slavery. Quite a few of our Texas settlers own slaves, but the Mexicans don't hold with slavery at all. So far, it hasn't become a matter for serious contention, but there's a lot of dissatisfaction over it.''

Minnie Hornsteder spoke her mind, as was her wont. ''I don't hold much with slavery, anyhow. I don't think the Lord meant for anyone to be anybody else's slave.''

Austin nodded his head thoughtfully, then went on to another topic. "How do you feel the community is managing in regard to supplies?" he asked.

"Well, that's another thing, Mr. Austin," Minnie volunteered. "Most often we have to get our supplies from San Antonio. Of course, we can wait for traders to come in from St. Louis and Sedalia and Columbia, but I'm wondering about taxes.''

"The Mexican government is certain to levy taxes on goods brought here, it's true. So far, they've been reasonable. But that's something else I'll have to straighten out. Thank you, Mrs. Hornsteder. My friends and I want to make this a permanent home where you can build for the future. As our country grows, we'll all grow with it.''

It was a little before midnight on the day of Stephen Austin's visit. There were only two guards on hand, for the group wedding festivities had exhausted the settlers, and they had gone to bed early two nights in a row. The two guards, Abner Stillman and Joshua Credenburg, were men in their late thirties, who welcomed the opportunity to be alone with their own thoughts.

Abner and Joshua took their places to the north and south. The community was protected on the east by the Brazos River, and it was the guards' responsibility to alert the settlers to any danger coming from the other directions.

The full, high moon allowed for fine visibility, and if there were any nocturnal attacks against the settlement, both guards would have plenty of time to sound the alarm.

An hour passed, and all that could be heard was the chirping of the cicadas in the thickets well beyond the settlement. A cool breeze had come in from the northeast, which somewhat revived Abner and Joshua, who periodically checked their rifles, sighed, peered out into the distance, and waited stolidly.

From the southwest, at a distance of a quarter mile, fifteen painted, half-naked Tonkawa crawled on their bellies through the mesquite and the bushes. They carried hunting knives and old muskets, and their horses were tethered in a thick clump of live-oak trees west of the Brazos, where they would be out of sight yet close enough to retrieve if immediate flight should become necessary. Mesgarde, the young chief of the Tonkawa, had sent two scouts to come as close to the settlement on the Brazos River as they dared, and they had seen the corral with horses milling in it. Tonight he hoped to steal many horses.

Mesgarde put his hands to his eyes and squinted, then grunted to his chief lieutenant, Nordikay, "All of them sleep. The *wasichu* do not think we would attack them. Send a fast runner to enter the town, and if guards are there, he will kill them swiftly and silently with the knives."

"I hear and obey, O Mesgarde," his lieutenant, a year younger than the chief, eagerly agreed.

At the southern end of the settlement, Joshua now decided that he would have a smoke. He had a pipe, a tinderbox, and an oilskin pouch, which held tobacco. This he tamped into the pipe, ignited a bit of dried wood from the moss in the tinderbox, then lit the tobacco. He sucked it in and exhaled gratefully. It was strong and helped him keep awake. There was nothing doing tonight. Everyone knew that.

Sucking on his pipe until it drew well, he could not

see that the Tonkawa had stealthily approached. Suddenly
he heard a grunt and looked up just in time to see the
half-naked Indian leaping down upon him. He tried to
retrieve his rifle, dropping his pipe, but already the
Tonkawa's knife buried itself in his heart. Joshua moaned
softly, rolled over onto his side, and lay still.

The half-naked brave wiped his knife on the dead
man's breeches, and then, crouching low, he made his way
toward the other guard, to the north of the community.
Abner's back was turned to the Indian, and he died as
silently as his friend had done. Glancing around and making certain that no one was there to intercept him, the
Tonkawa ran to the corral and opened the gate. The horses
jostled their way out, whinnying and nickering at their
unexpected freedom. Then he slapped the horses on their
rumps so they would move toward awaiting braves, who
would intercept the horses and ride them off.

Mesgarde's eyes brightened as he saw the horses
galloping out beyond the commune, and he gestured to his
other braves to follow him. Drawing their knives, holding
their muskets at the ready, the other Indians hurried toward
the settlement.

Simon had not been able to fall asleep at once. What
Austin had said about the settlement's problems had kept
him awake, and he pulled on his breeches and went outside
for a walk. As he closed the door behind him, he saw the
horses from the corral racing through the community and,
startled, cupped his hands to his mouth and shouted,
"The horses are loose! Wake up, everybody! Someone's
taking the horses!"

Mesgarde heard this cry and fiercely gestured to his
warriors to hurry into the community before the sleeping
settlers retaliated. The braves began to pour into the town,
and Simon hurried back into his house to get his rifle.
Hastily priming and loading it, he ran out, crouched down
on one knee, aimed, and fired at a stocky, black-haired

Indian. The Indian uttered a gurgling cry and fell to the ground, lifeless. One of the Tonkawa who had followed Mesgarde broke loose from the others and came running toward Simon, his hunting knife upraised. Unable to reload in time, the young scout reversed the rifle and swung the butt with all his might, smashing the skull of the Indian, who fell dead at his feet. Then he cried out again, "Help! Indians! Wake up! Come out with your guns! Indians!"

From the northwest, a dozen men were riding toward the settlement, headed by Jim Bowie. Spurring his horse to a gallop, he turned to Luke Cocroft, a grizzled man in his late forties who had just recently signed up with the Rangers, and said, "I had a feeling that those damned Tonkawa would try to attack the community!"

Luke's horse—and those of the other eleven Rangers—kept pace. He shouted to Jim, "Look at those devils; they've driven all the horses out of the corral. Let's give them a little taste of good old gunpowder and ball."

Jim Bowie lifted his rifle and fired at the Indian nearest him. The shot Indian sprawled on his belly and lay with arms outstretched. He had just been in the process of seizing the mane of one of the horses to mount it.

The rifle fire and Simon's cries had roused the other settlers. Old Henry Hornsteder hauled on his breeches and came stumbling out of the house, carrying his Lancaster rifle. He was shrilly admonished by his wife, Minnie. "Now you be careful, Henry. Don't expose yourself to danger, you hear me?"

"For God's sake, Minnie, a man has to fight when he's attacked. Don't worry about me! This old Lancaster will work just fine—there's one of those horse-stealing devils—" Henry knelt down, cradled the butt of his Lancaster, squinted along the sights, then pulled the trigger. A young, lean, paint-bedaubed Tonkawa who had just mounted one of the settlers' horses jerked and toppled over to the left, his body striking the ground and rolling over onto his back, dead from a bullet in the heart. The horse went galloping on, whinnying in terror.

The Texas Rangers were circling the community now, and Bowie, drawing his famous knife from its sheath, flung it at Mesgarde, who had just lunged at him and tried to pull him down from his horse. The young chief staggered, stared down at his chest where the sharp knife had entered, then sank to his knees and fell onto his side, his hands feebly trying to draw out the fatal knife as he died.

In the little house he was staying in during his visit, Stephen Austin sprang out of bed, dressed, strapped on his pistol belt, and wakened his two friends. "There's trouble out there, boys. Let's give them a hand!" he called.

Dressing quickly, Austin's two friends seized their pistols and quickly loaded them as they followed him outside.

One of the Tonkawa braves, crouching near the open gate of the corral, saw Leland Ferris and, lifting his old musket to his shoulder, pulled the trigger. Leland stiffened and grabbed at his chest as a red stain spread on his nightshirt. He fell heavily to the ground in death. With an angry cry, Stephen Austin fired his own pistol and killed the brave.

"The damned horse stealers—I never thought they'd bring guns against white settlers!" he groaned as he turned to his friend and crouched down to ascertain the nature of Leland's wound. "Oh, my God, he's dead! His wife and children! What horror—"

Having lost their young chief as well as their war lieutenant, the Indians now frantically tried to leave the settlement, forgetting the settlers' horses and running like scared jackrabbits to find their own mounts. But Jim Bowie directed half of his force to flank them at the left and the others to circle the other end of the community and trap them in a pincers movement. One by one, the Indians were picked off, and only one of the Rangers was slightly wounded by a musket shot, which grazed his right shoulder.

Bowie dismounted and ran toward Stephen Austin, who was still crouching beside his dead friend, tears running down his cheeks. "Mr. Austin, I wish to hell I'd gotten here a mite sooner!" the scout hoarsely exclaimed.

Moses Austin's son looked slowly up at the sturdy scout. "I wish to God he'd stayed home with his wife and children, Jim. I'm the one who has to break the news to her. It's ironic that he and I and Matthias were just about to leave for Washington to try to get a truce or treaty between the Indians and Texans. I wish to hell I hadn't come here!"

"You can't help it, Mr. Austin. I know it's a damned shame. We'll get the horses back for you. Here now, Jesse," Bowie said, gesturing to a tall, lanky black-haired man who had ridden with him, "do what you can to get some of those horses back into the corral. Take some of the boys with you."

"Right away, Mr. Bowie."

Austin slowly rose, then shook his head. "This is bad. We figured the Tonkawa were pesky critters who went for other people's horses. This time they've shed blood. I hope this isn't the start of other uprisings—and I'm thinking about Mexican soldiers just as much as I am about Indians."

"God grant this is just an isolated incident," Bowie solemnly said. "Well, sir, we'll stay around now and get all the horses back where they belong, and then go reassure the settlers."

"Thank you for your assistance. It was lucky you came, Jim," Austin said.

"It wasn't entirely luck—we saw a couple of painted Tonkawa sneaking around way beyond the Brazos and off westward. Knowing how they go after horses whenever there's a chance, we figured that they might try the settlement.''

"Well, God bless you, Jim. We've got a priest here at the settlement, who officiated at the weddings two nights ago. At least Leland will get a proper funeral. He won't be the last to give his life for this land. You can call him a martyr for Texas.''

Nineteen

Antonio López de Santa Anna had made great political and personal strides since the time when, as a nineteen-year-old lieutenant, he had been commended for gallantry by General Joaquín de Arredondo at the Battle of Medina in August of 1813. Santa Anna had risen thanks to cunning strategems and turncoat shifting of his loyalty to whichever faction he believed would be most likely to give him the greatest power. Now he was a brigadier general, in command of a regiment in Veracruz, promoted to that lofty rank for aiding in the revolution that had released Mexico from Spain, whose puppet this vast land had been for so long.

Opportunist that he was, Santa Anna was certain that it would not be too far distant to the day when he would assume the title of *el presidente* and rule all of Mexico.

Since there was no war, Santa Anna schemed how to make his name synonymous with leadership and valor and patriotism. He had read of Stephen Austin's grants to initiate settlements in the territory of Texas and realized that here was a fertile field for his self-aggrandizement. To begin with, the decree by which Austin had been granted land in Texas provided that all the Americans were to become Mexican citizens and Roman Catholics. Santa Anna knew that many settlers had not conformed to this policy. In the three years since Mexico opened Texas's door, thousands of Americans had come legally through the work of Austin and fellow empresarios. Forty years before that, the entire population of Texas had been a mere 2,819. And many newcomers were one-time squatters and fugitives who had, Santa Anna believed, sought refuge in an Austin settlement, where they could plot mischief against the sovereign Republic of Mexico.

With this in mind, Santa Anna rode at the head of his own personal army, some two hundred men in all, outfitted in shakos and the red and green and white uniforms of the dragoons. Each man had his own horse—most of these horses had conveniently been "appropriated" from poor villagers who could offer no resistance in the face of rifles, muskets, pistols, and sabers.

"I am anxious, *hombres,*" he addressed his troops as they set out toward the Rio Grande, "to see if these *americanos* who have been given permission by our great country to settle on Mexican soil fulfill their oath of patriotic loyalty. It would be good to investigate for ourselves, so we shall march to the settlement on the Brazos and see if the men who settle there are as peaceful as they would have us believe—and whether, for all their *americano* birth, they acknowledge that they are citizens of Mexico."

Captain Gilberto Rómez, a handsome, tall, black-haired man in his early thirties, intensely devoted to Santa

Anna, saluted his general and, his eyes glowing with admiration, said, *"Mi general,* you show again the leadership that will one day make you our *presidente.* When we go through these villages on our noble mission, everyone will cheer you!"

"You are a clever man, Rómez," Santa Anna chuckled. "If I am indeed to become *el presidente,* I must show all my countrymen that I am the staunchest of patriots. I shall conceive of something that will make all these *tejanos* prove their loyalty to their adopted country. And, if they do not—" again he chuckled "—there will be retaliatory measures, Rómez, and I know very well how enthusiastically you will carry them out at my orders."

"Su servidor, mi general!" The young captain vigorously saluted, glowing with pride at the privilege of being taken into his beloved general's confidence.

Although ostensibly Santa Anna's purpose in taking his private army through Mexico and on across the Rio Grande was to determine whether the Mexican land grant to Stephen Fuller Austin was being legitimately maintained, his real purpose was to determine the strength of his own popularity. He wanted to create a reputation for himself as a man who put patriotism and love for his country above all else; then, when the time came—and with sufficient military strength to hasten that time to its ultimate fruition—he would be the idol of every downtrodden peasant who hoped vainly for an illusory freedom.

This prolonged march from southeastern Mexico on to the border and into Texas cost him little; he commandeered fresh horses, food, and lodging and, from time to time when his ardors grew intolerable, the companionship of some comely *muchacha.* It was to his mind an honor for any female on whom his roving, lustful eye might fall, for in this she was helping propagate what might well be an immortal dynasty of benevolent rulers of a country that needed a strong hand, a keen mind, and the ability to do whatever was necessary to obtain total power.

Santa Anna beckoned Capitán Rómez, who rode alongside him, and said, "I have in mind, Capitán Rómez, a little scheme whereby the *americanos* will pledge their allegiance to our government. And those who refuse to take such an oath must be punished with the other Texans witnessing so they will learn the lesson. We shall amuse ourselves, Rómez."

By the end of September, Santa Anna and his soldiers had reached Matamoros, where they spent two rest days, their commander's reward to them for meritorious service. To be sure, Santa Anna gave this only as an excuse so that he might amuse himself for two nights with an excitingly lovely *mestiza* who, as he had entered the outskirts of the town, came out of her *jacal* and flung a bouquet of flowers in the path of his prancing stallion. With effusive gallantry, Santa Anna lifted his hand to halt the troop behind him, then dismounted, retrieved the bouquet, and beamingly thanked the *mestiza:* "*Gracias, señorita.* You have made this day memorable! Perhaps you would do me the great pleasure of having supper with me at my headquarters, as soon as I've established them."

"I am too humble—I do not belong in such a place with *su excelencia,*" she replied, but her voice was languorous and her dark-brown eyes sent him a flirtatious look that deepened his smile and heightened his lecherous interest.

"Allow me to be the judge of that, señorita. I shall have one of my men come to your *jacal* this evening and escort you. Do not forget, I, Antonio López de Santa Anna, brigadier general though I may be, am of the people. You must not say that you are too humble, for I, too, am humble, and yet look to what heights I have already attained, and it is only the beginning. Till supper, then, *querida!*''

Giving the signal for the troop to move on, he galloped ahead a few yards, then glanced back to see that she had gone back into the *jacal*.

At Matamoros, Santa Anna and his soldiers took on fresh supplies, commandeering horses and ample food, as well as many flasks of *tequila* and even *pulque,* as gifts from the grateful populace. Thoroughly refreshed by this interlude—as well as by two nights of love with the all-too-complaisant *mestiza*—the self-termed "liberator of Mexico" prepared to cross the Rio Grande. At last, several days later, Santa Anna and his men reined in their horses about a mile away from Eugene Fair's settlement on the Brazos.

"Now then, *mi capitán,*" Santa Anna said, turning to Gilberto Rómez, "we shall ride into this settlement with a strength of force. Issue orders to the men to have their weapons ready for use. We shall require of these *americanos* to demonstrate satisfactorily that they will be loyal subjects of Mexico."

It was a week after the Tonkawa attack on the settlement. Stephen Austin was already on his way to Washington, and Jim Bowie and his scouts were away patrolling far to the south of Eugene Fair's community on the Brazos. Dan Southland, a personable, gawky, twenty-four-year-old scout, was the first to learn of the proximity of Santa Anna and his troops. He rode up to Simon Brown's house and pounded on the door.

"Dan, what's the trouble?" Simon anxiously asked.

"Mexican soldiers approaching, Mr. Brown. They're all decked out in fancy uniforms. Looks like trouble."

"Damnation!" Simon said in disgust. "Haven't we had enough already with the Tonkawa? Well, I don't want any bloodshed, and we don't want these soldiers to find any fault with our community. How far are they from here now?''

"A quarter of a mile. They're in no hurry, almost two hundred of them, Mr. Brown," the scout anxiously declared.

"That's bad." Simon frowned, shaking his head. "Dan, round up all the men you can and tell them to come out unarmed. We're going to welcome the Mexican soldiers and show them that we don't want any trouble with their government, understand me?''

"I sure do, Mr. Brown. I'll go tell everybody, quick as I can.''

"Good boy." Simon shook his head again and went back to Naomi. "Honey, you stay here and take care of the little ones. Don't come out of the house at all.''

"I heard Dan tell you about the soldiers, Simon. I hope there won't be any trouble.''

"There won't be if everybody welcomes them just as if nothing were the matter. I don't like bringing so many soldiers into our settlement. Certainly they must know that we don't have any outlaws here and that we haven't broken any of the terms of the contract," Simon told his wife. "I wish Jim Bowie and his Rangers hadn't left us.''

His handsome face contorted in an anxious frown, Simon hurried toward the clearing that was used as a public square. Meanwhile, Dan Southland had rounded up some fifty men, who poured out into the clearing and waited to receive Santa Anna and his men. Many women came also because the young scout had explained the necessity of showing a peaceful assembly of families.

Meanwhile, Santa Anna turned to the official bugler of the troop. "Sound the formal parade march," he instructed. "I do not think these *americanos* will dare show that they resent us—and, if they do, we shall know how to rebuke them, eh, *mi compañero?*''

"Sí, mi general," the young bugler gulped. He put the bugle to his lips and blew the lively tune that signaled

the formal entrance of Mexican soldiers into a village or town.

Drawing his sword, Santa Anna brandished it in the air and then held it stiffly against his right chest with the point tilting skyward.

From his little house, Henry Hornsteder saw the army approaching. Snorting with indignation, he grumbled to Minnie, "Damned Mexes! They better not try."

"Now you listen, Henry," Minnie tartly interrupted, shaking her finger at him. "Don't you get any ideas of taking on the whole Mexican army. You're a good man, and God knows I love you, but you had to act like a hero when those damned injuns hit us last week, and I'm not going to let you make any fuss now. Injuns is one thing; soldiers is another. The soldiers have guns and lances and swords, and they're just looking for trouble. If you act up, Lord knows what mischief they'll start."

"I know, I know, Minnie, but it galls me something fierce to think I have to smile pretty at them soldiers. We're Americans—"

"I know, and I feel that way, too, Henry honey," Minnie interrupted him again. "Now you just get out there. When you come back, you can tell me everything you've got on your mind, and I'll probably agree with you. Only for once, you're going to keep your flytrap shut, you hear me?"

He glumly nodded, took a longing look at his Lancaster, and then stomped outside to join the other men in the clearing.

By now Santa Anna's troops were riding into the settlement. The uniformed soldiers rode in slowly and impressively, their faces impassive as they scanned the settlers who waited to greet them.

Santa Anna held up his hand to halt the troops behind him and demanded, "Do you have an *alcalde* or someone who will speak for this settlement?"

Simon stepped forward and amiably declared, "I represent this community founded by Stephen Fuller Austin and Eugene Fair with the permission of your government."

"*Es verdad,*" Santa Anna smilingly responded. "Do you speak my language of Spanish?"

"No, I'm afraid I don't, sir, though I know a few words."

"Well then, I shall force myself to speak in a language all of you will understand." The smile vanished from Santa Anna's face. "I have been sent by my government to determine your loyalty to the contract which you, señor, have seen fit to remind me of."

"I think you'll find everything in order," Simon pleasantly responded.

"I shall determine that, señor. Your name?"

"Simon Brown."

"I am General Antonio López de Santa Anna. Perhaps you have heard of me?"

"That I have, General Santa Anna. We're at your disposal, but I wish to remind you that all of us came here to settle down and raise our families and live peacefully."

"I am enchanted to hear such news," Santa Anna said, smirking. "But you see, Señor Brown, as a representative of my government I have been asked to learn just how loyal you are. And so, I am going to give you an order—a peaceful one, to use your own term, to be sure." His voice dripped with honeyed sarcasm. Then, his lips tightening and his eyes hardening, he said for only Simon to hear, "I wish to see all of your men kneel down and kiss this ground, this Mexican soil. By kissing it, Señor Brown, you will prove indisputably that you are, in truth, honest settlers who have come here in peace and wish to foment no rebellion against our beloved country."

"K–kiss the ground, G–General Santa Anna?" Simon echoed, his voice trembling with indignation and apprehension. He had seen Capitán Rómez slowly draw one of his two pistols out of his belted holsters.

"I have given you an order," Santa Anna irritatedly broke in, "and you will see to it that all the men here do as I command."

Simon gasped, unable to believe that this Mexican officer could conceive of so humiliating a ceremony. To make it public, to involve all these men—it was unthinkable! He knew that if Jim Bowie and the Texas Rangers were here, there would be terrible bloodshed, and many innocent lives would be lost. No, they had to capitulate. So while Santa Anna coldly stared at the young scout, Simon advanced to the center of the clearing and called out, "General Santa Anna asks that we prove our acceptance of the terms by which we settled here on the Brazos. He wishes all of our men to kneel down and kiss this Mexican soil. I urge you all to do as he asks. And please, for God's sake"—here his anxiety got the better of him—"let's have no acts of rebellion or refusal. His soldiers are armed."

There was a murmur of dissension among the settlers gathered in the clearing. Several whispered to one another, aghast, indignant, angry. Yet they could see the weapons the two hundred men carried; there was too much strength to dare any resistance.

"Please!" Simon's voice cracked again with stress, as he urged his neighbors to accede to Santa Anna's wishes.

One by one, grumbling, grudgingly, their faces dark with anger and contempt, the men knelt down and bowed their heads to press their lips against the earth. Santa Anna turned in his saddle, observing, his smile deepening, his lips curling sadistically at the show of debasement, this symbolically humiliating act by which the *tejanos* as much as admitted that they were inferior to his men and himself.

"Very good," he purred, looking around. "Very good, indeed."

Old Henry Hornsteder watched with disbelief as men throughout the clearing bowed their heads down to the earth. Fuming all the while, he could bear it no longer and suddenly burst out, "I'll be goddamned if I'll bow to anybody except the Lord God Almighty, and you're sure as hell not Him, Mr. Santa Anna! Mebbe, like you say, we have to be citizens of Mexico, but damn it to hell and gone, I'm not kneeling down and kissing the ground just at your say-so. Now you look here, we've got families here, kids. We're raising crops, not giving you any botheration at all, so why'd you have to come here and raise a ruckus?"

Santa Anna nudged his stallion closer to the defiant old man, then stared at him, a tight-lipped smile on his somber face. "Let me see if I understand you, *señor gringo,*" he drawled in his most insulting tone. "You refuse to do what all your neighbors are doing, am I correct?"

"Kee-rect, Mr. Santa Anna! And you can ride that fancy horse of yours and sit there till hell freezes over, before I'll do any such fool thing! Like I said, I go down on my knees when I'm in church, or when I'm in my house and want to ask God to keep my sweet Minnie by my side—"

He got no further. Swiftly unholstering the pistol at his right hip, transferring the sword to his left hand, Santa Anna leveled the weapon and pulled the trigger. Henry took a step forward, his eyes bulging, and then fell like a lead weight.

The silence of a tomb settled over the entire group. They could not believe their eyes. Simon turned ashen as tears came to his eyes. Others, kneeling opposite him, grimly tightened their jaws, the muscles in their cheeks flexing with savage self-control to keep from denouncing the tyrannical military leader. But no one sought to retaliate, for all of them realized that without weapons, there would be only wholesale slaughter in reprisal.

But Minnie had heard the shot, and she had even heard her husband's angry shouting. She came scurrying out of the house just in time to see Santa Anna wheel his snorting stallion around to head it out of the settlement.

The other men rose now and made way for her, in a horrified silence. She saw her husband dead upon the ground, and she ran to him, knelt down, and gently cradled his head. The ball had pierced his temple; there was only a little blood, but a bluish, deep hole showed the fatal course of that spiteful shot.

"Henry! You've killed my man, you butcher, you— was it you, you there on the stallion?" she cried, her voice hoarse with rage and agony.

Santa Anna shrugged, then wheeled the horse around again to confront Henry's widow. "Señora, no one regrets this incident more than I, but this man dared refuse an act of allegiance to the Mexican government. Perhaps you did not know that, by the terms of such an agreement, all of you *tejanos* must prove your loyalty as Mexican citizens and—"

"And so you shot him down like a dog because he wouldn't do what you wanted? What did you try to make him do, Mr. Fancy Britches?" she cried out, beside herself.

"Minnie, for God's sake!" Simon groaned, dreading a repetition of the needless and ruthless murder.

"Don't you hush me now, sonny! Well now, are you going to answer me, you there on that fine horse? It was you, wasn't it? You were the man who shot him! My Henry, who never hurt a fly—"

"Señora, again I regret this—I had asked that all the settlers kiss the ground, for it is Mexican soil—"

"And he wouldn't do it, is that it? Because I know Henry, and I know that he doesn't kneel to kings or queens or anybody else, only to God. Don't you kneel yourself to

God, or don't you believe in Him, you butcher?'' She
kneeled there by Henry's body, her arms holding his head
in her lap, her bosom heaving and tears running down her
cheeks, but her eyes blazed with a ferocity that made even
Santa Anna quail.

"You are overwrought. Capitán Rómez, give this
woman some money—"

"Oh, now you think you'll buy absolution with *dinero*,
do you? You swine! You murdering pig! May you rot in
hell! One of these days, you'll have your comeuppance!
You think the *tejanos* can eat dirt while you crow, do you?
You mark my words, Mr. Fancy Britches, there'll be a reckoning, and God Himself will judge you for what you've done
this day! You'll regret that you ever crossed the path of a
decent, honest, God-fearing Texan. You mark my words!''

Santa Anna wheeled his horse to leave the village, and
his soldiers followed him, while Minnie, surrounded by her
friends and neighbors, bent her head to Henry's and wept.

Twenty

Diego de Escobar had lain unconscious after that
terrifying, unexpected explosion in the little French restaurant in which he, Doña Inez, Fabien Mallard, and his wife,
Hortense, had been dining after having seen John Cooper

Baines and Dorotéa off on the *Miromar*. Fabien, who had sustained a painful but not serious wound when a sharp piece of wood had pierced the fleshy part of his right arm, had hoped that the old *hidalgo* had not been seriously injured, but it appeared that the latter had received the full force of the blast. Doña Inez had hysterically tried to rouse her husband, but he had not responded. Fabien and the restaurant proprietor had carried Don Diego out to the waiting carriage, with Doña Inez following, wringing her hands and weeping, terrified by her husband's pallor and unconsciousness.

Two men of the civil guard, one with a lantern, had come running into the little alleyway that led to the restaurant and, seeing the proprietor and Fabien carry out Don Diego's body, had anxiously interrogated both men. "Have you any enemies, m'sieu?" the tall, thickly mustachioed French guard demanded.

But the proprietor shook his head and gasped, *"Mon Dieu,* I have no enemies! Can't you see that M'sieu de Escobar is seriously hurt? Please ask your questions after I have done what little I can—what a terrible tragedy—"

Having arrived at the Mallard house, the factor told his coachman to bring Antoine out, and the dignified majordomo and the coachman carefully carried Don Diego's still unconscious body to his comfortable guest suite at the back of the first floor. "Send for Dr. Moreau, Antoine, on the rue de Carondelet. Tell him that it is of the utmost urgency," the Creole ordered.

"At once, M'sieu Mallard."

Hortense Mallard was doing her best to comfort Doña Inez, who had followed her husband into the room and seated herself beside his bed. She put out a trembling hand to touch his forehead and tearfully murmured, "My sweet Diego, may *el Señor Dios* be merciful to you, and to me also, for I should die if you did not recover! Surely *el*

Señor Dios will restore your health so we may have a few more years together, my dearest Diego!''

Twenty minutes later, Dr. Henri Moreau hurried into the house. At once, he made a cursory examination of the old *hidalgo*. He rose and turned to Doña Inez, whose tear-filled eyes besought him for good news. ''Madame, I do not find any broken bones, fractures, or wounds. If as you say, this was an explosion, my belief is that your husband sustained a serious concussion. Otherwise, the vital signs are stable; the breathing is regular. His heartbeat is regular, though not overly strong, and assures me that he will survive with good care. He must be kept very quiet in a darkened room, and I would recommend cold compresses on his forehead. Let him rest all he can, and feed him nourishing broth when he asks for food.''

''And medicine, Dr. Moreau?'' Fabien Mallard anxiously inquired.

The bearded, bespectacled doctor shook his head. ''In such cases as this, M'sieu Mallard, there is no medicine I should prescribe. Now let me take a look at your arm.''

The doctor cleaned and inspected Fabien's arm for any slivers of wood; then the factor's arm was bandaged. ''You are most fortunate, M'sieu Mallard. You could have been seriously injured. I'm surprised you were not.''

''May God be thanked!'' Hortense piously interjected, crossing herself.

''I'm grateful to you, Dr. Moreau,'' Fabien said. ''Will you be kind enough to call on Don Diego tomorrow? And if there is any serious change in his condition, I shall have my coachman go to your offices at once.''

''To be sure! Yes, I shall come at about four tomorrow afternoon.''

Hortense gently put her hand on the middle-aged doctor's shoulder. ''I'll see you to the door. Thank you so much for coming. Your news is certainly welcome to us.''

''I have some other news that may not be so welcome,''

the little doctor said, turning back and eyeing the factor. "I have it from my houseman that there was a robbery at La Banque de la Nouvelle Orléans tonight. The thieves made off with a fortune, I'm told. My houseman met one of the civil guard who had just come from the bank, and you know how people will stop to gossip after an exciting happening. . . ."

"A bank robbery?" Fabien exclaimed, looking blankly at the doctor, then at his wife. *"Mon Dieu,* I have all my capital in that vault. But why in the world should anyone attempt to destroy a charming little restaurant?"

"From what my houseman told me, M'sieu Mallard," Dr. Moreau volunteered, "the civil guard believes that the explosion was made to draw those on patrol away from the bank so the rogues might make off with their ill-gotten gains. There were also several other explosions at various locations."

"A fiendish scheme!" Fabien Mallard shook his head. "I've always thought it to be the very safest bank in all of New Orleans. Tomorrow, I shall see just how safe it was as regards my own deposits."

Fabien Mallard had Antoine order his carriage early after breakfast the next morning and drove down to the bank. He strode directly to the office of the bank's president, Eugene Beaubien.

"Forgive me for disturbing you, M'sieu Beaubien," he earnestly said, "but I heard the disturbing news last night that there was a serious robbery."

"I regret to tell you that's true, M'sieu Mallard." Eugene Beaubien sighed and shook his head. "We are only now determining our losses. The thieves have taken nearly all our holdings—this is privy information, M'sieu Mallard, and it is only because I have known you for so long that I entrust you with it in all confidence."

"Rest assured, I shan't violate your confidence, M'sieu Beaubien."

"Of course. I know that you represent M'sieu John Cooper Baines—he had deposited with us many silver ingots. All of those ingots have been stolen. And I am afraid I have bad news for you personally—"

"Do not spare me," Fabien said, steeling himself.

"If you will come down to the vault, M'sieu Mallard, I shall personally apprise you of your own situation. Believe me, m'sieu, no one in the world would have believed that this bank would suffer such a robbery. And there is something else that is most mystifying: One of our assistant officers, M'sieu Alexander DuPlessis, has not come to work this morning. Most unlike him. I have had no word from him, he is not at his lodging, and no one seems to know what has become of him. Naturally, he would be the first suspect."

With a strong sense of foreboding, Fabien and the affable president went down the stairway to the bank vault. A guard saluted them, then led the way to the back. Fabien uttered a cry, for the contents of his strongbox had been looted. He closed his eyes for a moment, trembling with shock. "These men took all of my capital," Fabien said, putting an arm against the wall to steady himself. "My career as a factor representing important and wealthy men is at this moment in jeopardy."

"I deeply sympathize," Eugene Beaubien said. "We are making every effort to capture the miscreants. I have offered a personal reward of four thousand dollars to anyone who gives information that results in the apprehension and conviction of these wrongdoers." The bank president sighed wearily. "You are not the only depositor who has suffered outrageous losses. I feel ashamed, out of my own personal integrity, that such a thing could happen to this bank."

"M'sieu Baines does not even know that all his silver

has been taken," Fabien Mallard said. "Well, there is no necessity to communicate this news to him until he returns from Argentina. It would be such a shattering blow, and I would fear for the consequences."

The bank president sighed wearily and shook his head. "I have written letters of apology to all the depositors. To you, I tender my most humble regrets that you are deprived of so much capital."

"I shall have to recoup," Fabien slowly declared, "and it will mean a great deal of economizing. Fortunately, I have some faithful clients, notably M'sieu Baines—and, of course, once he is freed from prison, Raoul Maldones will be a man I can count on. There are some others, so I shall not starve—but all the same, this is a bitter blow."

Dr. Moreau again examined Don Diego de Escobar the next afternoon, as promised. Don Diego was awake but extremely weak. The old *hidalgo* could scarcely speak, but his eyes turned constantly to Doña Inez, who had kept an unending vigil at his bedside, holding one of his frail hands between both of hers, willing with all her strength and prayers that he would recover.

The doctor turned to Fabien and said, "I understand that you wish to get him back to his home in Texas, Mr. Mallard, so that he may be among his loved ones. I would wait a few days before such a journey is made, and it must be done very slowly, with many periods of rest. I would recommend that you engage a physician to make the journey with this patient."

"I have thought of that, Dr. Moreau. Would you be kind enough to recommend someone?" Fabien asked.

"Yes. There's an André Malmorain, a very gifted young doctor. He has a small practice, with an independent income from his parents and a beautiful house on the rue de Champêtre. I feel that he would be quite willing to undertake such a consultation and to travel with Don Diego.

Indeed, I shall try to bring him with me tomorrow afternoon, when I come again, so that he may familiarize himself with the patient.''

"That's most kind of you,'' Fabien said. Then after he had ushered the doctor to the front door, he went to his wife's bedroom and knocked at the door. *"Entre, mon amour!"* she called.

"Hortense, I have some very bad news. I beg you not to let it distress you, for it's not permanently harmful, only upsetting and somewhat inconvenient at the present moment.''

She came to him, put her hands on his shoulders, stared deeply into his eyes, then kissed him gently. "I love you so much, Fabien, that so long as I have you and we have our health and the dear God gives us many years together, I am not too distressed by bad news. But what is it, *mon amour?*''

"While we were dining at the restaurant, thieves were entering Eugene Beaubien's bank. The dreadful explosion was purposely planned to keep the night patrols away from the bank. The thieves operated on a grand scale. They took all of M'sieu Baines's silver bars and robbed many of the strongboxes in the vault, including ours. You see, dear Hortense, most of my capital was stolen, and for a few months, at least, we must be very careful about money. I plan to find new clients so that I can build my reserves again, but till then, I cannot do all the things I want for you. Like the necklace I had intended to buy you—''

"You're simply not to think of such a thing! I wouldn't want it at such a time, my darling!'' Hortense assured him. "Do you think I married you for material possessions! Oh, no, dear Fabien, I married you because I loved you and I have complete confidence in you. You're the very soul of honor, and I'm quite sure that before too long you'll have regained your fortune. I'll do whatever economizing you ask, be certain of that.''

"How grateful I am that *le bon Dieu* let you choose me as your husband, *ma chérie!*" Fabien's voice was unsteady as he hugged and kissed his beautiful wife. "I'll work all the harder to restore my fortune so that you need never want for anything. There's so much I want to do for you."

"You mustn't think of me at all in this matter, my darling," Hortense told her husband as she put her head against his chest, closed her eyes, and sighed with pleasure at this communion between them. "We're not exactly destitute, you know. I do have a little money from my family in a different bank on Chartres Street."

"You're a marvel, Hortense. Yet it galls me to have to accept even a *sou*—" he began.

Hortense silenced him by pressing her fingers against his mouth. "Hush, *mon amour!* What is a marriage for, if not for sharing?"

At supper that evening, Fabien Mallard spoke with Doña Inez about Don Diego's travel arrangements. "I esteem your husband as my dear friend and father-in-law of my client, John Cooper Baines. As a gesture of friendship, I shall arrange for Dr. Malmorain's services to accompany you and Don Diego back to Texas. That will be a precaution to make certain that your husband completely recovers from his regrettable accident."

"I heard that you lost a great deal of money in that terrible bank robbery," Doña Inez said. "John Cooper has spoken highly of you, your lovely wife, and of the way you have handled his affairs and his finances from the ranch. Don Diego and I both stand ready to advance you any monies you may need to recuperate from this undeserved loss."

"Oh, no, I couldn't think of it. It's a generous and kind offer, Doña Inez, but really—" the factor protested.

"Please, Señor Mallard, Don Diego and I are comfortable. The ranch has brought us a good deal of profit, and besides, when my husband was *intendente* in Taos, he managed to save quite a lot of money. Let us be realistic. Now we are in our twilight years. What use would we have for wealth that only accumulates and that we may never live to spend? No, if you need any capital for your projects in conducting your business as you are accustomed to, Señor Mallard, you may count on us. I give you my word, and I know I speak for my husband as well."

Dr. André Malmorain visited the Mallard house the next afternoon and made a thorough examination of Don Diego. By now, the old *hidalgo* was able to sit up—propped up by several pillows—and to take some broth for nourishment. Doña Inez remained at his side and had arranged to have bedding brought into her husband's room for the sofa, so she would always be near Don Diego if he called out for her. She took an immediate liking to Dr. Malmorain, as did he to her and Don Diego. The young French physician agreed to arrange his affairs so he could accompany the elderly couple on their return journey to Texas.

"It is very good of you, Dr. Malmorain, and I assure you that you will be well paid for your services," Doña Inez said.

"We need not speak of my fee, dear Madame de Escobar," he answered. "I owe Dr. Moreau a favor, and the experience will be very useful to me. You expect to take more than a month to return?"

"That is right, Dr. Malmorain," Doña Inez answered. "I would assume that Don Diego would be taken back to our ranch in the carriage we drove out in. And, of course, the horses would necessarily keep a slow pace, so as not to jostle my husband."

"And I trust that, with my humble skill, Madame de Escobar," the doctor gently interposed, "you will enjoy many more years together at your ranch. Rest assured I shall be at your service on whatever day you decide to set forth on your journey.'' He took her hand and kissed it, bowing low, and Doña Inez flushed, deeply moved by the graciousness and understanding of the young physician. After he had gone, she went back to the guest room, sat beside her husband's bed, and murmured to him, as she stroked his cheek, "My darling Diego, soon we are going to start out for the *Hacienda del Halcón*. Perhaps by our return we shall have wonderful news from John Cooper and his Dorotéa.''

His eyes brightened, and he nodded. "I pray for that, Inez,'' he murmured.

"Save your strength, *mi corazón*. We shall have a very scenic, comfortable journey, and I shall relieve the tedium by reading to you. You will have a wonderful rest, and when we get back, I will have Tía Margarita cook all the foods you like so much.''

"I adore you, *mi* Inez,'' he said, reaching for her hand and keeping it pressed against his cheek.

She fought back her tears, for she understood that she must present always to him the most optimistic and cheerful of attitudes. When she observed that his eyes were closed and that he had slipped back into beneficial slumber, she let the tears course freely down her cheeks and thanked God for the happiness she and Don Diego shared. Doña Inez had every hope that, with the presence of the gracious and sincere young doctor, Don Diego's convalescence would continue and that by the time they reached the ranch, he would be well again.

Four days later, Fabien drove two strong brown geldings attached to a wagon up to his house and summoned Pierre Durey, his coachman. "Don Diego de Escobar and his wife shall go back to Texas in their own carriage, Pierre, and they will be driven by their own man, Enrique. You will drive Dr. Malmorain in this wagon that Señor Baines left here with me. The wagon is large enough for

the doctor to travel in comfortably, and there is also room
for supplies. I shall have Antoine pack. I wish you to go
with them to Texas, Pierre, leaving tomorrow.''

"But, M'sieu Mallard, won't you need me here?''

"No, Pierre. I'm still quite capable of taking the reins
of my own carriage. You're a good, loyal man, Pierre.
You'll be paid well for this lengthy duty. And I'll see to it
that you have a good rifle, a brace of pistols, and plenty of
ammunition. You're not likely to run into trouble on the
route that you'll be taking, but it's best to be prepared.''

"I'm not afraid of danger, and I can handle a gun
when I have to. I welcome the chance to serve you in any
way I can, M'sieu Mallard. You've been very kind to
me.''

The next day Antoine and the cook packed ample
provisions into the wagon, and it was decided that Don
Diego and Doña Inez, along with Dr. André Malmorain,
would leave New Orleans at about four in the afternoon,
by which time the warm sun would be declining and its
intensity no burden upon the travelers. Fabien drew out a
map, a copy of which he had made for Dr. Malmorain. "It
is a journey of some six hundred miles, *m'sieu le docteur*,"
he explained. "I estimate that the drivers should not try to
make more than twelve to fifteen miles a day. On that
basis, it should take about seven weeks, which would
bring you to the Double H Ranch about the beginning of
December. The heat should not be at all excessive, and
there will be cooling breezes from the Gulf for much of the
way. I shall give you money—the little I have—for
replenishing your supplies in such towns as Lafayette,
Beaumont, and Gonzales before you reach the Frio River.''

Late that afternoon, Enrique carefully led the ailing
old *hidalgo* out to the carriage, where several pillows had
been placed on the seat so that he could sit at ease. Doña
Inez sat beside him, and Enrique mounted the driver's
seat, cracked his whip, and, after farewells to Hortense

and Fabien, the de Escobars began their journey homeward. Meanwhile, Pierre started up the wagon carrying the doctor and the supplies. André had volunteered to take a turn at the reins of the two strong young geldings. "As it happens, Pierre," he had affably told the coachman, "I always drive my own carriage, and I enjoy it. I look forward to seeing the countryside. I've never seen the Southwest beyond New Orleans."

Fabien had procured a cooking pot, utensils, a tinderbox, and a new skillet; Hortense had given Doña Inez several volumes from the Mallards' own collection, which could be read to Don Diego along the journey.

As the Mallards watched the wagon and carriage drive off, Hortense turned to her husband. "The sky is so cloudless and blue," she said, "so beautiful that I think it is a good omen. But I shan't rest until I have news that Don Diego and his wife have returned in all safety to M'sieu Baines's ranch."

While all these events were taking place in New Orleans, the man responsible for the bank robbery and explosion, Christophe Carrière, was enjoying himself immensely. He stood at the rail, looking out over the peaceful dark-blue ocean on a warm night about a week after he had boarded a Dutch ship, the *Rembrandt*. The *Rembrandt* was expected to reach Rotterdam in about three more weeks, but the Creole was in no hurry. He had paid a premium price to have the best cabin—next to the captain's own—and the heavy gunnysack with its contents of jewels and banknotes, gold and silver, had been carefully hidden in a clothes chest.

The moon, high in the sky, lighted the Creole's sardonic smile as he stood contemplating the little rippling waves and the distant horizon. Fortune was really with him, and what pleased him most after his successful robbery of La Banque de la Nouvelle Orléans was the knowledge that he had rendered Madeleine's father virtually penniless. That would pay the swine back for having insulted him when he had asked for Madeleine's hand in marriage!

But that was only the first step of his intended vengeance against that beauty and her haughty father. He would make the girl squirm; he would make her beg for mercy. In his fantasy he envisioned Madeleine in her shift, barefooted, her long hair flowing almost to her hips, weeping, clasping her hands in prayer as she stood upon the paupers' auction block. He would be there with a dozen other men, all lustfully eager to see her stripped and paraded for their sport before they began their bidding. Of course he would outbid everyone else—the contents of the gunnysack assured that! And then, when he had bought her, he would humiliate her. He would make her kneel and acknowledge him as master!

He lit one of his cigars, exhaled the rich Havana aroma, and smiled again. Leaning against the rail, he stared out with a radiant look, and he told himself that he was embarking upon a new and glorious destiny.

Twenty-one

The birth of animals on the Double H Ranch was an important event to the children who dwelt in this huge commune. Young Dolores and Juan de Escobar, the adopted daughter and son of Don Diego de Escobar and his wife, Doña Inez, were thrilled when the wolf-dog Luna gave birth to her puppies, as were Dawn de Escobar, now seven, Ruth and Carmen Baines, eight and four, respectively, and Juan Sandarbal, four and a half. Each of the children secretly determined to implore his or her father for a puppy to keep as a pet.

The ranch's older children, Charles Baines, now eleven; Inez de Escobar, ten; and Tim and Julia Sandarbal, now eleven and nine respectively, considered themselves superior to their younger playmates and were determined to train the puppies just as Yankee, Luna's littermate, had been trained. Charles went to the corral to search for Miguel, and seeing the white-haired *capataz* talking with one of the *vaqueros*, admiring a new colt they were breaking in, he impatiently broke out, "Señor Miguel, will you help train those new puppies of Luna's so they'll be as good as Yankee?"

"Excuse me, Paco." Miguel turned to the impul-

sive boy. "Now then, young master, of course I'll be glad
to help you train the puppies. But they're a little young for
that yet, you know. And you should wait until they're at
least six or seven months old. But I promise you I'll be on
hand to help. And by then, the Señor Carlos will be back
from Taos, and I'm sure he'll want to take a hand in the
training."

Charles nodded, turned on his heel, and hurried back
to his playmates, who were gathered in the large pen
attached to the ranch's kennel, playing with the new puppies.
Yankee, the puppies' sire, was outside the pen, occasionally barking at the children and his pups.

"Miguel says they're too young to be trained. We'll
have to wait until early next year. But we can have some
fun with them now," Charles said, with an air of superior-
ity as he saw Juan de Escobar gingerly pick up one of the
gray-furred little cubs and cradle it in his arms. "Be careful!
Don't hurt him now and don't pull his legs. Look out for
his sharp teeth!"

As if to bear out Charles's statement, the male puppy
turned its head and nipped at the little boy, who promptly
released the pup and backed away, eyes very wide with
apprehension.

"That was silly!" Charles jeered. "If you show you're
afraid, he'll take advantage! You have to show him that he
has to obey—but it's too early yet to do that. You shouldn't
play with them anyway; they're too young!"

With this, he marched off with Inez, Tim, and Julia.
Ruth Baines, in her soft, sweet voice, shook her head and
sighed, "My brother's really getting to be too big for his
britches. He thinks he's a man and can give orders to
everybody. If you want to play with the puppies and if
Luna doesn't mind, go ahead. Be very gentle, pet them,
and let them recognize you so the next time you play with
them, they won't be frightened of you."

Although, of course, Francesca de Escobar, the child

born to Don Diego and Doña Inez in their middle age, was interested in Luna's puppies, she was quite preoccupied with her own pet, the raccoon she had named Chiquitico. Miguel had had one of the *trabajadores* make a little cage for it and had taught her how to train the animal. It was inordinately clean and extremely tame, following her whenever she let it out of its cage.

By now, she had trained it to do tricks, to eat daintily from her fingers, and to roll over and play dead, exactly like a dog. Diego de Escobar, Carlos's son by his first marriage, was Francesca's closest friend, and he often went along when Francesca walked Chiquitico.

By the end of October, only two of Luna's litter had survived: a male and a female. The younger children's hearts were broken. Young Dawn tearfully begged Miguel to bury the dead puppies in a little box and to put a cross to mark the grave, and Miguel solemnly carried out this ceremony, touched by Dawn's fervor and love for helpless animals.

The day after the funeral, wanting to assuage Dawn's grief, Dolores de Escobar thought up a little game. She directed the other youngsters in the making of tiny little *sombreros*, collars, and shoes, in which to dress the male and female puppies and put on a kind of dog show. The dainty little *sombreros* and shoes were made of black cloth; the collars were soft doeskin leather, cut into strips no wider than a half inch, pierced with an awl in the center so that leather thongs could be tied to them as leashes.

Luna, by now, had become used to the children's playing with her puppies. She moved about, wagging her tail, snuffling and prodding the children's legs with her muzzle as they began to dress the little male and female puppies.

Dawn took the leash of the female, while Dolores insisted on leading the male puppy. All the other children had assembled outside the pen to watch the show.

The puppies whined and rolled onto the ground, not at all happy about wearing the shoes and trying to shake off the collars. Luna, with a soft growl, moved up toward her puppies and, without warning, seized the scruff of the neck of the female and carried it away, causing Dawn to drop the leash. Luna deposited the little female cub in a corner of the pen and then returned for her other puppy.

"You'd better give him back," Charles warned.

"It's a shame after our hard work," Dolores sighed. "But I don't want to make Luna angry."

Dolores dropped the leash, and Luna eyed her and then uttered a soft bark, after which she promptly seized the male by the scruff of its neck and deposited him beside his little sister. Then Luna stood there defiantly, the hair bristling around her neck, as if to tell these two-legged companions that she did not permit such mocking liberties taken with her brood.

Carlos de Escobar's absence from Teresa at this middle stage of her pregnancy made her realize just how much she loved her husband. Knowing that it might take two or three months before he returned from Taos, the beautiful young woman became determined to occupy her days purposefully. That was why she, along with Bess Sandarbal, had volunteered to teach and help the nuns, who, under Sister Eufemia, had already begun a special school for the older children.

The *trabajadores* had been working industriously to build a separate little schoolhouse so that the younger children might be grouped in one school, while those reaching puberty could have their classrooms in the other. Now the building was completed, and lessons had begun.

Teresa, being fluent in languages and having read much history, literature, poetry, and drama, had undertaken, along with Sister Eufemia, the supervision of the classroom for children like Francesca de Escobar and Diego de

Escobar. The former was some months past her twelfth birthday, the latter was nearly thirteen, and they found themselves seated beside each other in the classroom.

Teresa taught French, pointing out that it was one of the most expressive of all languages, with a vast literature in poetry and drama. Also, she pointed out that the history of France constituted a particularly fascinating and extended course of study. They would find, Teresa told them, that history has the power to change the life of the individual who adapts to it or who is forced into a different way of life because of its spreading effects.

Both Diego and Francesca were fascinated by the ramifications of history, but Francesca proved so apt and diligent a pupil that one afternoon Teresa and Sister Eufemia both complimented her. The girl flushed with pride, and, at the conclusion of the class, when the children were dismissed, young Diego went up to her and said, "You are very smart, and you know a lot more than I thought. I used to quarrel with you, Francesca, but now I'm very glad you're my friend." Diego admiringly shook his head. "You listen so well and remember so much. I see I will have to work hard to keep up with you." And then, his face brightening, he added, "But I'll bet I can still beat you in a horseback race."

"Oh, you think so, do you, Diego?" Francesca tossed her pretty head until her curls danced in the air. "I'll race you any time you say."

"Well, why not right now? School's over, there's plenty of sunlight, and it's nice and warm."

"All right, let's go to the stable and get our horses. How far do you want to race?" Francesca asked.

"Well, from the gate of the *Hacienda del Halcón* to the Frio River and back."

"All right! My mare can outrace your gelding whenever she wants to."

"Not today, she won't. I know I'm going to beat you." Diego grinned.

"We'll just see about that!" Francesca heatedly replied. She stalked off to the stable, and Diego followed her, half-amused, and yet noticing, as if for the first time, that she was no longer a petulant child who had once called him a loudmouthed boor. She was already beginning to become a woman, and young Diego was experiencing his first awareness of the opposite sex.

Miguel was out in the stable, as it chanced, talking to Antonio Lorcas, and he greeted the two youngsters with a teasing remark. "I'll wager I know what's on both your minds this fine afternoon! You want me to saddle your horses, and you're going to try to see which one of you can beat the other in a race—am I right?"

"Now I know why you're our *capataz*, Miguel," Diego chuckled. "That's exactly it. I've just bet Francesca I can beat her on my gelding."

"Don't be so sure, *mi jóven compañero*," Miguel said with a wink at Francesca. "You say that because you think yourself *muy hombre*. But very often the female of the species can surprise the strongest man."

Francesca had determined to beat Diego, so when Miguel reached for her sidesaddle, she said, "I'm going to ride astride, if you don't mind, Señor Miguel."

"I do not think, with all due respect, señorita, that your mother would approve of it." Miguel tried to look and sound as grave as a benign uncle.

"I suppose not," Francesca admitted, making a delightful moue, "but if you won't tell her, she won't know. Please, Miguel!" She glanced over at Diego, who was smiling. "I want to win, and it's much easier to ride the way a boy does."

"Boy?" Diego belligerently thrust out his chin like a turkey-cock challenged by a rival in the barnyard. "I will have you know, Señorita Francesca, that I am a *man*. And just for that, I shall ride bareback, the way *los indios* do!"

"Then I will ride bareback, too!"

Miguel and Antonio found it hard to keep a straight face. Finally, Miguel said, "Señorita Francesca, if that is your wish, I am, as always, *a sus órdenes*." With this, he held out the reins to their young owners.

Antonio and Miguel looked on, half-amused, half-worried, for it was not seemly for a young girl to emulate a man on horseback. Miguel whispered to Antonio, "She is growing up fast. But we cannot tell her how to ride, for she is the daughter of the *patrón*."

Francesca, tucking up her skirts, had nimbly vaulted astride her mare, revealing sleek, high-set calves and just the hint of lithe, suavely contoured thighs. Her skin was golden from the sun, and her face was unusually animated at the anticipation of fierce rivalry between herself and Carlos's young son. Diego, who had removed his own saddle, now climbed astride his gelding. But he had seen that dazzling if momentary revelation of Francesca's bare legs, and his face was crimson with the awareness of her.

Both held the reins. Miguel volunteered, "If it's a race you're wanting, Señorita Francesca, Señor Diego, allow me to start it for you. I shall count, *'Uno, dos, tres'* and then you will both race, is it agreed?"

"That's fine, dear Miguel," Francesca said. She had always been fond of the white-haired *capataz*.

"Are you ready?" Miguel called. Upon receiving a chorused affirmative, he counted slowly and solemnly. At *"¡Tres!"* both young riders kicked their heels against their mounts' bellies, and the mare at once took the lead, snorting, galloping southward. Diego, for his part, held back a little, admiring the grace and poise that Francesca de Escobar exhibited astride the horse. At the same time, seeing that she was a length and a half ahead of him, he decided it was time to make it a real race. She would not appreciate his letting her win, that he already knew about his lovely young playmate.

In spite of Diego's best efforts—and thanks to Francesca's head start—the swift, eager mare reached the bank of the Frio River about two paces ahead of Diego's gelding. With a joyous laugh, she wheeled the mare around and galloped back, but this time Diego had anticipated her maneuver and, cheating just a little, turned his horse's head before it had reached the same periphery of the bank, some three or four feet ahead of it. Thus he was able to come abreast of her, and now, huddling over the gelding's neck, exhorting it in eager, praising terms, he forced it forward. Francesca angrily clucked her tongue, tightened her lips, and imitated Diego by leaning forward and crooning to her mare, "Come now, Beauty, you're faster than that stupid old gelding. Prove it now. You know that I love you. I'll give you lots of sugar and carrots if you win for me!"

Slowly, the mare caught up to the gelding and even drew a few paces ahead. Meanwhile, Antonio and Miguel watched, hands on their hips, admiring the spirited race between the youngsters: "*¡Hola!* The señorita rides very well, indeed!"

"*Sí, mi capataz,*" Antonio chuckled. "It is a fine show of horsemanship."

"With that, I wholeheartedly agree, *mi compañero,*" Miguel soberly said. "Here we have two young people who begin to see each other as dear friends, and not simply as antagonists."

"They are very handsome, they make a fine couple—"

"That's true, Antonio," Miguel murmured, "but don't forget that they have the same blood in their veins. Francesca is the daughter of Don Diego and Doña Inez, while young Diego is Carlos's son. I only hope—" here he crossed himself and shook his head "—that they do not fall in love with each other, for that would be forbidden, and it would break their hearts. Ah, there they go, and Francesca is doing certainly as well as Diego!''

It was true. With a final burst of speed, Francesca, kicking her heels against the mare's belly, urged it to the last finite excess of energy and finished the race a quarter of a length ahead of Diego's gelding.

"I declare the señorita as the winner!" Miguel solemnly intoned. "Do you not share my opinion, Antonio?''

"I do, indeed. Both of you rode splendidly!" the young *vaquero* said, beaming.

Francesca and Diego swiftly dismounted. The girl's face glowed with delight as she handed the reins to Miguel. "It was a wonderful race, and thank you so much, Miguel, for starting us off and watching how we finished.''

"It was my great pleasure, Señorita de Escobar." Miguel doffed his *sombrero* and gave her a low bow, sweeping the *sombrero* out just over the ground, in the traditional salute to a person of importance. It deepened Francesca's blushes, and she turned to look at Diego, then smilingly held out her hand. "It was such fun! You aren't angry with me that I won this one time?'' she anxiously pleaded.

"Of course not. We'll do it again. I enjoyed it very much, but the next time, I promise you, I'll beat you by two lengths!'' Diego cheerfully boasted.

"Let's go take Yankee for a run,'' Francesca now proposed, linking her arm with his. And the two young people marched off toward the shed where the wolf-dog was kept, while Miguel turned to Antonio and said, "We need a reward for judging the race, don't you think, *mi amigo?* Why don't we go into the kitchen and see if perhaps Tía Margarita or, of course, your Rosa if she's there, can give us a little something to eat before supper.''

Back in the classroom, Teresa was conferring with the elderly Dominican mother superior. "Sister Eufemia,'' she respectfully proffered, "both of us share a love for children and wish to help them achieve a well-founded education. But you must admit there is a limit to what we can teach here."

"Of course, Señora de Escobar," Sister Eufemia courteously responded. "Particularly for our more gifted students."

"I have thought that since Francesca has displayed such outstanding academic promise, it would be best to think of sending her to a fine school for young ladies, such as the Ursuline Convent in New Orleans," Teresa suggested.

"When her parents return," Sister Eufemia said, "it would certainly be worthwhile to suggest it. She has an exceptionally precocious mind and grasps things quickly."

"I'll speak with Don Diego and Doña Inez as soon as they return," Teresa declared.

"My daughter," the white-haired mother superior said, giving Teresa a kindly look, "I have been here now for some time, with my colleagues, and I have observed the great love you bear for your *esposo*, his children, and the other children of the *hacienda*. You are now carrying child of your own, and it is a great thing when a child is born of love between two people who follow our dear Lord's Commandments."

Teresa lowered her head and blushed at this praise, and Sister Eufemia smiled tenderly as she made the sign of the cross over the young woman's head.

Twenty-two

———————————————————◆————————————————————

Some months earlier on the Double H Ranch, the eccentric old prospector Jeremy Gaige had been so enthralled by the stories of Jim Bowie about a lost treasure in the San Saba Valley that he had determined to find it. The old man had spent many years prospecting without ever finding much more than a handful of small nuggets—enough to pay his expenses and to give him a little food.

When Jeremy had decided to go after the secret treasure hidden in a cave in the San Saba Valley, he had outfitted a wagon with supplies, which Miguel had procured for him, and begged his grubstake from plump, genial Tía Margarita. Unbeknown to him, however, young Diego and Francesca had stowed away in his wagon, pulling a tarpaulin over them to evade discovery, until the old man was well out upon the route. When he had found them, they had pleaded so eagerly to stay with him and to help him find the lost gold that he had agreed.

Indeed, he had found the gold on the tenth day of his journey, in a cave near a huge mesa with a series of hills along one side. But just at the moment of his climactic discovery, there had been an avalanche that blocked the entrance to the cave.

Miguel and his *trabajadores* had gone after the old prospector once Don Diego and Doña Inez had discovered that Francesca and young Diego were missing. They had found the cave and rescued the adventurers when the wolf-dog, Yankee, barked in front of the blocked cave mouth. But just as they had gone back to their horses and the wagon, there had been a second avalanche that dislodged the largest of the boulders to crash in front of the treasure cave, and inside, the walls of the cave gave way, so the treasure was buried under tons of stone and rubble.

But Jeremy had not forgotten how close he had been to untold wealth, and he did not believe that the treasure was lost forever. That incredible vein of gold, he was sure, went all the way up the mountain, and if he could blast through the stone and rubble of the rockslide with gunpowder, he was certain to find other caves with gold. True, he was getting on in years, and his stamina was beginning to wane. But if he could summon one last burst of energy, he thought that the Lord God Almighty would surely take pity on him and let him get some gold.

He would go to Miguel again, just as he had done that first time, explain what he had in mind, and beg the *capataz* to spare him the supplies, gunpowder, and three or four *vaqueros* to help him find new treasure.

But there was something else that Jeremy had in mind, a strange new sentiment: He was exceedingly fond of Tía Margarita. She, in turn, had been exceptionally gracious to him. It was clear that she liked the old man, and what was more, Tía Margarita was a widow—had been for some years—and found the old prospector's amiable companionship a blessing. Whenever she set food before him, he was loud and lavish in his praises.

Now that he was thinking of his return to the San Saba Valley, he found himself this October morning struck by a new thought. "Why, shucks," he said to himself, "that nice woman likes me a lot, 'n I like her, too. Now we're both sorta old, 'n she's a widow woman, 'n me, I never got hitched in all my life. Never had the time. But I think we could make each other sorta happy—'n, if I do find gold, then I can give her all the nice things a fine woman like that oughta have. Yessirree, by gum, I'm gonna pop the question to her!''

The only trouble was that neither Don Diego nor Carlos nor even John Cooper Baines, for that matter, was at home. There was no one to give him permission, except, of course, Margarita herself. He was certain that there was nothing to stop her from accepting him as her husband— especially if he could promise that she might be one of the richest women in all of Texas. But if he were to take away the ranch's superb cook, he might make mortal enemies of Don Diego, his son, and his son-in-law.

Accordingly, this brisk October morning, he went in search of Miguel.

"Could I bother you for a minute, Señor Miguel?" Jeremy called out in his piping, reedy voice. He had spruced himself up this morning, plunging his face into the water trough, and even sneaked a bit of homemade lye soap out of the kitchen when Tía Margarita had not been looking. Then he had run his fingers through his straggling white hair and done the same with his beard, so that it would not seem so shaggy. Miguel turned to him and grinned, for the eccentric old prospector was an unforgettable character, and it was quite obvious this morning that he had made a special attempt to look particularly at his best. "But of course, *mi amigo!*" Miguel affably exclaimed. "Tell me what is on your mind!''

"Wal now, Señor Miguel, I'm hankerin' to git hitched up with Tía Margarita. But you see, since Don Diego 'n his son 'n Mr. Baines ain't around now, I don't rightly know how they would take to it if I stole her away from this ranch. She's such a durn good cook—''

"She is certainly that," Miguel said, struggling to keep his expression impassive.

"Do you think they'd be down on me 'n nail my scalp to the stable door if I stole her away from this place?" Jeremy asked.

"Well now, to be honest with you, Antonio's sweet wife, Rosa, could take over all the responsibilities of the kitchen. And personally, I know that Tía Margarita likes you."

"You really think so, Señor Miguel?"

"Seguramente, amigo. The way you praise her cooking, *amigo,* has already won her heart. She would not refuse you."

"I'm much obliged, sure am, Señor Miguel!" Jeremy excitedly said as he held out his hand to the old *capataz* and energetically shook it until Miguel winced. "Now listen, there's somethin' else: Remember some months back when I borrowed a wagon from you 'n some supplies to go off to the San Saba Valley in search of that lode? I think I can still get at some treasure."

"But we saw what the avalanche had done to the caves and how much rubble and stone there are blocking that cave," Miguel protested.

"But there've got to be other caves with gold," Jeremy answered. "I believe gunpowder can blast away rocks 'n boulders. Now, if I could have another wagon 'n you could spare a keg or so of gunpowder, I'll cut you in for a share in the mine—"

"That was a promise you already made me last time, *mi amigo.*"

"Oh, come on, Señor Miguel, this time I got a feeling right in my belly that I'm gonna find it. I'll make Tía Margarita rich, 'n you, too."

The old man's enthusiasm was so contagious that Miguel did not have the heart to refuse him. "All right,

I'll give you the wagon, the supplies, and a keg of gunpowder—maybe two.''

"You're a prince of a feller, Señor Miguel! You won't be sorry!'' Jeremy again reached for Miguel's hand, pumped it energetically, and then hurried off to the kitchen.

He frowned in deep concentration as he tried to formulate a proposal that would be accepted by the plump, good-natured, mature cook. He thought to himself that she had worked all her life, and that if he could find some gold, they could travel or buy a ranch, and she wouldn't have to do any cooking—except, of course, for him, the special dishes he had learned to love here.

"Jeremy Gaige, you old fool you,'' he scolded himself when he hesitated at the kitchen door. "It's high time you showed some guts.''

Suddenly the kitchen door opened, and he found himself face-to-face with Tía Margarita. He had never blushed in all his life, but he came very close to it now. Surely she must have heard him mumbling to himself. Her eyes were very wide, and the ghost of a smile, which she sternly tried to suppress, for she did not want to offend his feelings, began on her full mouth. "¿Qué pasa, Señor Jeremy?''

"I—that is, er—Margarita, can I have a word with you, where nobody else can hear us?'' he gulped, trying to say just the right words and not offend her.

"Pero seguramente, Señor Jeremy. There is no one in the kitchen now. You will be quite alone with me there.''

"Good—I mean, dang it all, Margarita, I got somethin' awful important to ask you,'' he finally burst out, then glanced sheepishly around to see if anyone was eavesdropping.

"Come in, Señor Jeremy.'' She opened the door of the kitchen, stood to one side to let him enter, then closed the door behind him. Then, beaming, she demanded, "And now, what is this *cosa muy importante?*"

"I—now don't go gittin' mad at me, Margarita. Fact is, I wanted to know if you'd hitch up with me." Again he blurted the words out, afraid that if he fumbled for just the right words, he would never finish his proposal.

"Hitched up with you, Señor Jeremy?" she echoed, her face blank. *"No comprendo*—I do not understand what it is you have to say to me."

He took a long breath, exhaled, and then suddenly grabbed one of her hands and held it in both of his as, staring almost frantically at her, he exclaimed, "Doggone it anyhow, Margarita. I mean I want to get married to you. I want to be your *esposo*. There! I finally thought of the right word." He saw her eyes widen. When she remained silent, he added with an even greater anxiety in his voice, "Now look here, I told you I didn't want to make you mad."

"But you have not made me mad, as you say, Señor Jeremy." Now the most wonderful smile curved her lips, and her voice was as soft and gentle as that of a young girl. "You have made me very proud. And the answer is, *sí*, I will be your *esposa*. I know that you like my cooking, and I like the way you are with the children and with everyone. You have so many jokes and stories to tell, and everyone is happy when you are around them. Yes, I will marry you."

"Gosh, you mean you *will?* I'm real happy about that, Margarita. That's jist great! Now look here, Margarita, do you remember that gold mine I found some months back?"

"Oh, yes! Everyone remembers that," she giggled.

"Well, now, Miguel's gonna lend me a wagon 'n supplies 'n some gunpowder to blow away the rocks so's I can git to the gold. You come along with me once we git hitched—I mean married—then, well, we'll both be so rich you can have new dresses 'n a nice ring 'n a watch 'n all that stuff. Does that sound all right to you?''

Margarita Ortiz giggled again and then began to cry, and finally hugged Jeremy, almost crushing him with her exuberant embrace. "*Querido,* I know that you have wanted me, and I have wanted you all this time!" she said between sobs. "I will make you happy. I promise it. And I will fatten you up! You are too skinny, *mi corazón,* but I will change all that!"

Jeremy was a little alarmed at this sudden and over-whelming acceptance of his proposal. "Wait now, woman. I don't figger to git myself too fat, or I won't be able to go prospectin' none, you understand, Margarita honey. No, I'm fine the way I am. 'N you, you're a real hunk of woman, 'n we'll git along jist fine. Now mebbe we better go see the minister, so's he can hitch us up."

"Oh, but no, dear Señor Jeremy," Margarita wailed, looking at him aghast. "We must have a real wedding, in the *iglesia,* and there must be the best man—"

"That will be Señor Miguel," Jeremy agreed. "All right, then, now you stop cryin', woman!"

"*Sí, mi corazón,*" she dulcetly agreed, moving to him and again embracing him until he was almost suffocated. "You will go tell the *padre,* and I, I shall ask some of the *criadas* to be my maids of honor."

"We won't be able to wait for either Don Diego or John Cooper or Carlos, either," Jeremy said. "You see, honey, I want to leave right away on this expedition to make us both rich. With you beside me as my wife, doggone if I don't think this time I'll come back with all the gold!"

And so, on the following Sunday, two days after he had proposed, Jeremy stood stiffly before the altar of the church, with Margarita Ortiz by his side. His beard and hair were neatly combed by none other than the plump cook herself—to whom he had feebly and helplessly protested to no avail. Most of the *trabajadores* were gathered in the church, with their wives and children, to witness the union between the eccentric old prospector and the popular, widowed cook. Miguel was the best man, and his Bess was matron of honor. Margarita's two sons and their wives were in the front pew, proudly watching their mother.

Margarita wept softly as she heard Padre Pastronaz say the words that united her with Jeremy and restored her to the domestic security of marriage with a man who amused her and whom she respected. It was not at all the promise of gold that attracted her but the warm humor and the loneliness of the old prospector.

The problem of finding Jeremy and Margarita a house in which to begin their marriage was one that Miguel had already considered. Until now Margarita had dwelled in her own room in the huge *hacienda,* while Jeremy had bunked with the *vaqueros.* But when the ceremony was over and Miguel had availed himself of the traditional right to kiss the bride, he turned to Jeremy and said, "I've got the supplies in the wagon for you, and I've got two kegs of gunpowder. Now, *amigo,* when you come back, you'll find that the *trabajadores* have built a nice little house for the two of you. Take her to the San Saba Valley on your honeymoon, and this time I truly hope you'll find the gold you've sought all your life, Señor Jeremy."

Three *vaqueros* had volunteered to accompany Jeremy and Margarita to the San Saba Valley in quest of the hidden treasure: Roberto Locada, Manuel Miraflores, and Sebastiano Cardenas. These three experienced *vaqueros* were in their fifties, but they were still vigorous. Moreover, Roberto Locada had worked in a silver mine, where he had used gunpowder in blasting the rich silver veins. He would be, in Miguel's opinion, an ideal aid to have along to help unearth the treasure that had so obsessed the old prospector.

Early Monday afternoon, Jeremy and the blushing

Margarita came out of the *hacienda*—they had spent their wedding night in Margarita's room—and Jeremy Gaige had discovered that marriage, even at so late an age as his, had its untold joys, for the plump cook was ardent and sincere. Miguel and several *vaqueros* had harnessed three geldings to the supply wagon, loaded with supplies, gunpowder, and fuses, all under a tarpaulin. The three *trabajadores* on this expedition had already mounted their horses and were waiting, and Margarita insisted on sitting beside Jeremy as the old prospector took the reins and, after thanking Miguel and the others for all they had done for him, started the horses off on the journey.

As the wagon disappeared in the distance along the well-worn trail leading to the east from the Double H Ranch, Miguel turned to the *vaqueros* and declared, "Let us all pray that Señor Gaige realizes his dream. He is already a happy man, but I wish the best for him. All his life he has sought gold, not to be greedy or possessive of it but to do good things for others. And he will make Margarita happy—which is what all of us want, *¿no es verdad?*"

Jeremy told his three companions that the location he was seeking was near Brownwood, close to the Colorado River, and that it was a journey of about two hundred miles. He estimated that it would take them about two weeks to reach the site, and his cheerfulness was contagious. Plump Margarita, holding his arm, looked lovingly at him as he whistled an old tune that he had learned in the early days of his prospecting, and when he saw the admiration in her soft, dark-brown eyes, he felt inspired enough to burst into song. He was off-key, and his voice was reedy, but Margarita did not mind at all.

His enthusiasm on his quest, intensified by his happiness over his new marital status, led him to shorten the estimated time of the journey to the San Saba Valley. Actually, they came within sight of the mesa and the hills and their caves on the evening of the tenth day after leaving the Double H Ranch. Excitedly, he told Margarita, "Honey gal, we're here! You see all that rock 'n rubble hidin' the base of that hill there? That's where we had the avalanches when young Diego 'n Francesca came along with me. But there's more gold in there, 'n I can reach it, I know it! Miguel gave me two kegs of gunpowder, 'n I'm gonna blow the rubble to Kingdom Come 'n find another cave, 'n then we'll be rich!"

"I have a feeling that *el Señor Dios* is smiling on us, *mi corazón*," Margarita said as she gently squeezed his arm. "But it will make no difference if you are *rico*. I love you for yourself, *querido*."

They made camp, perhaps two hundred yards away from the base of the mountain. The *vaqueros* made their own campfire and took their meal, allowing the newly married couple to have their privacy. Jeremy had brought along two sleeping bags, but the first night on the journey Margarita blushingly whispered, "There is no need for two, since we share our lives together, *querido*."

The next morning, Jeremy was first to rise. Whistling a happy tune, he began to prepare a breakfast of bacon and *frijoles*, and he could even make biscuits, for he had watched Margarita in the kitchen.

Indeed, he startled Margarita by kneeling down beside the bag in which she still slept peacefully, a happy smile on her face and, nudging her shoulder, murmured, "Honey gal, come on 'n get some grub! I made it myself, 'n it's hot. Don't waste it!"

Margarita blushed and giggled. The thought that her husband would prepare breakfast and bring it to her on wakening redoubled her affection. She propped herself up on an elbow, accepted the tin plate on which he had placed bacon, the beans, and some biscuits smeared with honey. " 'N here's coffee, real strong, Margarita. It'll wake you up for sure," he added. Then, seated beside her, he ate his own breakfast, eagerly awaiting her reaction to his culinary efforts.

"It is very good, *muy bueno*," she laughingly protested. "Why do you look at me like that, *querido?* See how I'm eating all of it? Does that not tell you that you have done very well? I am very glad that you asked me to be your *esposa*."

Jeremy grinned like a schoolboy. He had never felt quite so cheerful. And he knew somehow that his efforts this morning would bring treasure within his grasp.

Excitedly, he urged the *vaqueros* out of their sleeping bags and, after breakfast, told them to bring the kegs of gunpowder out. This done, and while Margarita sat watching, wide-eyed and excited, he sought the help of Roberto Locada. "I've used gunpowder, Roberto, 'n I've made some fuses in my time, but I haven't done it for nigh unto ten or more years, so I'm a bit rusty."

"It will be my privilege, Señor Gaige," the genial Mexican smilingly replied. "Show me where you think I should blast."

"Let's just blast right here," Jeremy said, pointing. "Maybe here is where we'll find a new cave of *oro*."

Roberto nodded, satisfied. "The *capataz* sent along enough gunpowder to do the work, of this I have no fear. If we are lucky, perhaps we can find a vein of ore after the very first blast," the *vaquero* assured him.

Jeremy paced back and forth, clenching his fists, breathing heavily, his eyes shining with excitement. Margarita, watching him, sighed to herself and smiled, blushing at the recollection of the tender moments they had already enjoyed as man and wife.

The other two *vaqueros* helped Roberto pack the gunpowder in under the base of most of the rubble, while he cut two fuses and trailed them some twenty-five feet away. Then, with his tinderbox, he gestured to the old prospector that he was ready, struck a light, and lit the fuses.

The three *vaqueros* and Jeremy hurried back to where Margarita was standing, out of harm's way. The old prospector watched the sizzling fuse run its course, until at last it reached the gunpowder. There was an enormous explosion, and rocks and debris flew in all directions.

"By the eternal, you really opened it up, *amigo!*" Jeremy shouted, clapping his hands and dancing with joy.

And it was true; the first charges had been heavily laid, and there was a jagged hole, just deep and wide enough for a crouching man to enter. Jeremy waited a moment to make certain all was stable, then cried out, "I'll go first. Hand me a pickax, *amigo!*"

Roberto at once handed him a pickax, and the old prospector seized it and made his way through the opening. A few minutes later, he cried out in his reedy voice, "It's here! It's all here! I can see a vein, 'n there's lots of nuggets lyin' all over the ground here. You earned a share, *amigo,* you did for certain! We're all of us rich, praise the Eternal!"

The three *vaqueros,* glancing at one another, followed Jeremy into the cave and saw for themselves that it was true: On the ground lay broken shards of dull, glowing yellow metal. Carefully, the old prospector took his pickax and struck several tentative blows along one wall, loosening several other large chunks of ore. "Grab it, *amigos,* take it outta here. I never saw such a vein in all my days of prospectin', 'n that's for certain!" he gleefully cried.

Roberto Locada looked at his two friends and, in a voice touched with awe, declared, "It is like a fairy tale, *mis compañeros!* Go get sacks. We will put the ore into them. I do not know whether this *montaña de oro* will remain secure after the gunpowder, but we must hurry all the same, in case it decides to fall upon us!"

The other two *vaqueros* hurried to the wagon and

brought back sacks, and all three of the men filled them, while Jeremy, talking to himself excitedly, his eyes glittering with delight, struck here and there with his pickax, dislodging more and more pieces of the rich ore.

After about ten minutes, he heard a faint rumbling and cried out, "We got enough! Let's not be greedy. Let's git outta here before it falls on us!"

He and the *vaqueros* hurried out of the opening just as there was another rumbling sound. They stood back and watched, mouths agape, as tons of debris rolled down the mountain and, with a roar, sealed the entrance of this new cave. The four men stood there watching as the dust settled. Jeremy turned to Roberto. "Even if we never git any more, *mi amigo*, we're richer 'n hell—all of us—you, me, 'n Margarita 'n the *capataz!*"

They had six large sacks filled with the precious ore, and everyone helped to load the heavy metal into the wagon. Jeremy could not believe his eyes, and he looked at Margarita and said tenderly, "It's like a miracle, honey gal. It really is! I promised you'd be rich, 'n' I kept my word! Now we'd best go back. We've got somethin' to talk about!" Jeremy hugged his wife. Then, turning to the *vaqueros*, he said, "We'll ride back now. Sure as shootin' we'll have somethin' to show anybody at the ranch that didn't think I could do it!" His face was graced by a wide grin, mirrored in the *vaqueros'* own expressions.

As the wagon headed back toward the Double H Ranch, the old prospector looked back, marking the place. There would be another time to go back and look for more gold. There was certainly plenty of ore here for the taking. It would be a happy life, with what he had now—a wife who loved him and whom he loved in turn.

Twenty-three

Pablo Araiza had brought his band of twenty *bandidos* into the little hamlet of Santa Fuente late in August. His men thought him *loco* for coming here on this mission, for they had been enjoying great success in a series of raids on villages far to the southwest.

Even Ricardo Matsarga, his lieutenant, grumbled to the men as they watched Araiza ride slowly into the virtually deserted little hamlet. "This matter of great importance," he declared with a contemptuous sneer, "we know what that is, *muchachos*. Our *jefe* knew that this *puta* he found in Santa Fuente would bear his child, and now he comes to see her and the baby."

"But, Ricardo, is it not natural for a father to want to see his firstborn?" one of the bandits asked.

"Es verdad," the lieutenant admitted with a shrug, "but to stop us now when we were doing so well in raiding those villages is a foolish thing. We could have continued and made *mucho dinero*. There would always be time for him to see his brat by that girl and to give her a present later, if that is the way he feels. Myself, I have no links or ties with any woman, and it's wiser that way."

"But, Ricardo, we should give Pablo his due. He has

245

led us into many towns where we have taken many *pesos* for ourselves—and all this without losing a single man of our band," the bandit pursued.

The lieutenant shrugged. "*Sí,* but I think this woman and baby have hurt Pablo's judgment. *Amigos,* I have my own thoughts about Pablo's woman. Why, what I think is that this *puta* of his has already found a real father for her brat, and she wouldn't look a second time at Pablo Araiza, no matter what he offered her."

While his men stood well out of sight of the village, the bandit leader advanced to the row of adobe huts. But the village seemed deserted, and when he went to the largest *jacal* and called out "Juana, *querida*, it is your Pablo," there was no answer. Pushing open the door, he found the hut deserted. Pablo scowled as he turned and saw a crippled, gray-haired man come out of a nearby adobe hut. "*Hombre,*" Pablo called to him, "where can I find Juana Consalvez?"

"In heaven, señor," the crippled man responded, crossing himself. "She died having her child, a boy."

"Ten thousand devils!" Pablo swore under his breath. Then, raising his voice, "And her *padre?*"

The crippled man shook his head. "He left a few weeks ago to go to a village in Sonora where his cousin lives. He said this to me."

"But what happened to the child, *hombre?* Tell me!" Pablo angrily demanded.

"Emilio Consalvez said that he did not want it," the crippled man explained. "There were nuns here, and according to what Emilio Consalvez told me, they offered to take it and give it a home, to baptize it and to care for it as if it were their own."

"And where did these nuns go?"

"He told me that they were going across the Rio Grande to find a new home."

"And that is all you know?"

"Sí, es todo."

"I thank you. I shall try to find the child." Pablo thrust his hand into his britches pocket and tossed a silver *peso* to the crippled man. "For your help."

The old man pocketed the *peso*. Grateful for the coin, he tried to be helpful. "The holy sisters, señor, as they traveled north, they would be remembered in the larger villages."

Pablo nodded, strode back to where he had tethered his horse, mounted it, and rode back to his band. "We go north toward the Rio Grande. I must find my child," he explained to his lieutenant. "Juana died giving birth. I shall find my son—I swear this by the horns of the devil himself!"

Pablo Araiza rode with his band on to Frontera, in the province of Coahuila, certain that the group of nuns would assuredly have gone to a large village to rest and acquire supplies. There, in a *posada,* he was told by the amiable proprietor that yes, indeed, nuns had come through the village and yes, they had had an infant with them. Upon seeing a silver *peso* drawn from Pablo's pocket and placed near his cup, the proprietor also offered, "There was an old woman in charge of them all. I think her name was Sister Eufemia. Fine woman, very brave. She told me that they were going into Texas to a certain *hacienda* where the *hacendado* would build a mission for them."

Pablo thanked him, put down another silver *peso* for a bottle of *tequila,* and, after having a glass of it, left the rest of the bottle, saying, "Drink the rest to my health. You have been most helpful, *mi amigo. Gracias.*"

He went back to tell his men that he had almost located his child; it was necessary only to learn the name of the ranch where the nuns were to have their mission. He would doubtless learn that important particular in other towns closer to the Rio Grande.

Some of the men grumbled that this errand had nothing to do with their livelihood, which was robbing and plundering, and so Pablo consented to let them raid a village not far from Nueva Rosita.

The raid was enormously successful, for the little town had had no bandit attacks in over two years, and this restored the band's good humor. Furthermore, Pablo allowed his own share to be divided among his men as an act of good faith.

Flushed with their victory, the bandits rode to an isolated area where there was water and grazing for the horses. They had taken along two pretty young girls from the town and enjoyed an orgy for several days before resuming their quest for Pablo's infant son. The girls were left to go back to the village on their own.

The next step of the search took them to Candela, where, in another *posada*, the bandit leader learned that the nuns were on their way to the *hacienda* of Don Diego de Escobar. Pablo also learned from the proprietor that the nuns had an infant, whom they had named Innocente. The bandit flung down a handful of coins, then galloped back to rejoin his men. "We go to Laredo now," he told them, "and find where this ranch of Don Diego de Escobar is located. There we will find my child, my *hijo*, Innocente! And when I have him, *mis compañeros*, I will return to Mexico and lead you as I have done in the past, and all of you will be *muy ricos!*"

And there were cries of, "*¡Viva el jefe Araiza, viva!*" from his band.

In Laredo, just as he had hoped, Pablo Araiza learned that the *hacienda* of Don Diego de Escobar was in a fertile Texas valley west and southwest from San Antonio.

Now Pablo knew where to find his son. He went back to his men and told them, "I promise that if you help me, I will reward all of you."

And they, already satisfied with the profits of this prolonged trek, wholeheartedly pledged that they would support their *jefe*. Was that not what *compañeros* were for?

And so it was late in October that Pablo Araiza and his band approached the Frio River and saw the outlines of the buildings of the Double H Ranch. He lifted his hand to halt the troop of bandits behind him, turned in his saddle, and exclaimed to his lieutenant, "I'll go in alone, without weapons, in case I am stopped by guards. You have the men wait for me. If I find the child, I'll take him with me. Of course, they'll try to catch me, so it's up to you, my lieutenant, to think of something that will have them turn their attention elsewhere."

"Have no fear, *mi jefe*," the outlaw chuckled. "We've come this far and want you to succeed in your purpose."

"I won't be long—I am certain I can find the child," Pablo said. "Watch for me and do what you have to do!"

"*Comprendo, mi jefe.*"

The bandits crossed the Frio River at the shallowest point, obscured from view by clumps of mesquite and tall live-oak trees. There they waited, while Pablo rode in, flanking the *hacienda* in a semicircular arc toward the northwest, then turning his horse and entering the grazing lands of the sheep and the cattle. He was stopped by a pair of *vaqueros* who were patrolling along the northwest boundary of the ranch, but they let him pass when they determined he had no weapons and was harmless. He had told the *vaqueros* he had wanted to see the *capataz* about finding employment.

He rode slowly, keenly observing what he saw, and came toward the sprawling large ranch house.

Miguel was busy in the corral, helping two of the *vaqueros* break in a pair of wild mustangs, which they had lassoed the night before and brought back to the ranch. It was a sunny afternoon, the weather warm and pleasant.

Pablo's eyes widened, for he saw a little baby on a blanket, with young Julia Sandarbal kneeling on one side and holding a little whittled wooden toy, made by the assistant *capataz* Esteban Morales, to attract the baby's attention. On the other side of the blanket, Concepción Morales, Esteban's wife, smilingly watched the young girl play with the adopted child.

Dismounting, tying the reins of his stallion to a nearby hitching post, doffing his *sombrero*, Pablo approached, affecting his most benevolent smile. "What a lovely little *niño!*" he exclaimed.

Concepción and Julia turned, wide-eyed, at this strange voice and saw the bandit leader. They were not suspicious of him, for each of them thought that he might be one of the new *vaqueros* whom Miguel had engaged.

"*Buenos días, señor,*" Concepción politely greeted the bandit chief.

"And to you, señora. Is this your child?"

"*Sí,* it is little Innocente Morales."

"And she, too," he said, pointing to Julia, "she is yours also?"

"Oh, no, señor, she is the daughter of our *capataz*, Señor Miguel Sandarbal, and his *esposa*, Bess," Esteban's wife explained.

"I see. Yes, a really charming infant. You are his mother, *¿por supuesto?*"

"His foster mother, señor. We adopted little Innocente when the nuns brought the baby here to the *estancia*," she explained.

"That was an act of great kindness. The child, then, had no parents?"

"No, unfortunately, señor. The good nuns helped deliver the child born to a young woman who died giving birth to him. And the young woman's father renounced it, saying that his daughter had run off with a bandit. And so, when Sister Eufemia brought Innocente here, my husband and I took him into our family."

"May I hold him just a moment? I have never known

what it is to have a child, señora,'' Pablo murmured, his
smile deepening.

Concepción hesitated a moment, then nodded. There
could really be no harm in this, and it showed that the new
vaquero had a good heart, she told herself.

Pablo approached the blanket, stooped down, picked
up the child in his arms, his eyes sparkling with triumph.
Then, before Julia and Concepción could comprehend what
was happening, he hurried off to his horse, swiftly untied
the reins, and leaped into the saddle.

"Señor! What are you doing? Our Innocente—"
Concepción cried out, horrified by the unexpected kid-
napping.

"He is my Innocente, the girl was my *novia,* and the
child belongs to me, woman!" Pablo called back, then
galloped off on his stallion.

Julia began to cry, but Concepción's loud shrieks had
drawn some of the *vaqueros* out of the bunkhouse, and
quickly she explained what had happened. They hurried to
the corral and, without bothering to saddle their horses,
leaped astride them and took off in pursuit.

But the lieutenant of the bandit band had already
created a diversion: Two of his men had set fire to one of
the sheds near the sheep grazing field, and billows of
smoke rose from it now as the stored bales of wool went
up in flames. Pablo meanwhile spurred his horse and crossed
the Frio River. His men followed, and by the time the
vaqueros put out the fire in the shed and reached the river
themselves, the bandits were already out of sight.

One of the *vaqueros* rode back to tell Miguel.
"¡Capataz! ¡Capataz! A man stole little Innocente and
rode off with many men, and the shed near the sheep pens
was set on fire. We put it out, but the *bandidos* got away!"

"You'll go after them," Miguel angrily swore. "Sister
Eufemia told me who that child's father is, and I will not

see an innocent child lead the life of an accursed *bandido!*
Take your weapons, *mis compañeros,* and go after them!''

Meanwhile, Pablo Araiza was ecstatic about his success.
Carefully cradling little Innocente in the crook of his left
arm, he held the reins of his black stallion in his right
hand. Pablo's face was radiant. A son, a son of his own
flesh! For a moment he sorrowed for Juana, for she had
been a tender *muchachita.* What a damned shame she'd
had to die. It was a good thing that her father had left for
Sonora, or he'd have had his tripes cut out for renouncing
his daughter and grandson!

As the bandits rode toward the Rio Grande, Pablo
suddenly uttered a startled cry. Two hundred yards behind
them, riding from the northeast, came a troop of mounted
soldiers, and at their head was Colonel Esteban Moravada,
a lean, gloomy-looking man. Knowing that his superior
officer, General Santa Anna, was inspecting the settlements
of the *tejanos,* Moravada, eager to win Santa Anna's praise,
had decided to ride on his own patrol. Santa Anna had intimated that there might be a claim and promotion in rank in
the offing for him.

"The devil take it!" Pablo swore. "We can't run for
it, or they'll know something is up!"

"But what do we do, *mi jefe?*" his lieutenant anxiously demanded.

"We say we're riding back to Coahuila, just peaceful
citizens minding our own business. How can they prove
otherwise? Hide your weapons. Try to look as if you
didn't know the soldiers were coming," Pablo hissed. He
cast an anxious look over his shoulder and slowed his
stallion to an easy trot.

But Colonel Moravada had already led several patrols
against bandits, captured the leaders, and sent them all to
firing squads. The villagers of those towns ravaged by the
bandits had sent off letters to Mexico City praising
Moravada's virtues, and the colonel was determined to win

further approbation. He thus gave an order to his *teniente*, Manuel Cardozo, to bid the bugler blow an alert and to overtake this group of unknown riders. He wished to know their business.

When the first clear notes of the bugle sounded, Pablo swore under his breath again and instinctively kicked his horse's belly with his booted heels to hasten its gait. That was a fatal error, for it convinced Colonel Moravada that these men were up to no good and should be detained for questioning. He gestured to his *teniente*, who took a platoon of riders and galloped off to circle and flank the outlaws at their right. Corporal Jesus Abierto, given a similar order, took another platoon of men and rode off to the left, trapping the outlaws.

"¡*Alto, pronto!*" the *teniente* ordered, drawing his saber while his men leveled their rifles and muskets at the outlaws.

There was no help for it, and the bandits halted, eyeing one another with nervous apprehension.

Colonel Moravada himself rode up to the man on the black stallion who held the wailing little baby in the crook of his left arm. "Your name, *hombre?*"

"It is—it is Pablo Araiza, *su servidor, mi coronel.*"

"Araiza . . . Araiza . . . I seem to remember that name. Wait a bit—you're the *bandido*. Ah yes, now I know who you are! You're out of your territory, aren't you, *hombre?*" The colonel's gloomy face brightened, for now he saw a chance to let his valor be known to Santa Anna. The extermination of a bandit band and its leader would be a glorious entry on his military record.

"I swear that *su excelencia* is mistaken," Pablo began.

Colonel Moravada shook his head. "No, *hombre*, you're the one who made the mistake, coming into our patrol area. You and your men may say your prayers, because you're all to be shot."

One of Pablo's men had drawn his pistol. Colonel

Moravada's lieutenant triggered a snap shot that sent the bandit toppling from his horse.

"A few balls saved that way," Colonel Moravada dryly commented. "All of you *bandidos*, dismount. Abierto, you will take ten of my men to form a firing squad, and you, *teniente*, will command it!"

Pablo Araiza groaned aloud. The colonel sneered at him. "Are you so afraid to die, *hombre?*"

"No, *su excelencia*, it's not that. It's my child here, my *niño*. Please, let me tell you—"

"I am listening."

Pablo advanced toward the insolently sneering colonel who stared at him from his horse. Earnestly, between sobs, he told the story. "You see, *mi coronel*," he concluded, "I did no harm in taking back what was rightfully mine—"

"Your story touches me, but it does not stop your execution, *hombre*. The birth of a child does not excuse crimes such as yours," Colonel Moravada decreed.

"I'm not asking for my life, *señor coronel*. But I beg of you, let the child go back to those kind people, the *monjas* who brought it there, for they can give it a decent home, and make little Innocente a good *hombre*, who will have a better life than mine."

Colonel Moravada stared for a long, silent moment down at the bandit chief. Then he chuckled. The irony of this amused him. "Very well. I tell you what I will do. One of your men will go free, drawn by lot. He will take the child back. But the rest of you will die immediately."

"Thank you. May *el Señor Dios* bless you, *mi coronel*," Pablo said with a dignity he had not before shown in all his life. "I am ready to die."

Colonel Moravada impatiently nodded. "Let's get on with it. Abierto, go find some sticks. Mix them up well with one short stick, and each man in turn will pick his."

Ten minutes later, the bandits chose their fate. It was

the lieutenant of the band, Ricardo Matsarga, who drew the short stick, and he uttered a sigh of relief when he saw it in his hand.

"Give him the *niño* and your horse," Moravada commanded.

Pablo turned to his lieutenant, held out his child. "Go back, tell them the story—tell them that it was my son. Tell them that my last thoughts, my last words, were for little Innocente. *¡Vaya con Dios, mi compañero!*"

The lieutenant nodded, blinked his tear-filled eyes, and took the child. One of the colonel's soldiers handed him the reins of Pablo's horse. He mounted it and rode to the north.

A few moments later, the colonel ordered that the eighteen *bandidos* would face the firing squad in two groups. Pablo would be in the second group. He knelt and prayed aloud, and he begged forgiveness for causing the deaths of his followers. A volley of shots from the firing squad interrupted his prayers. And then, Colonel Moravada, staring with a certain amused curiosity at this bandit chief who had acted like no bandit he had ever met before, ordered, "Your turn now, *mi jefe*. But I salute you—you have courage."

Esteban Morales had hurried out of his cottage when he heard his wife's hysterical shrieking that their baby had been stolen. Miguel told them what had happened, and Esteban, his son Bernardo, and six *vaqueros* had armed themselves and left in pursuit of the outlaws. But the bandit leader and his men had gained a head start because of the fire they had set, and they had also cleverly obscured their trail. Esteban and his party seemed to be riding aimlessly until at last, in the evening, Esteban saw a lone rider coming out of a glade of olive and live-oak trees, carrying a baby in his arms, riding dejectedly, his head bowed. Esteban shouted, "Don't fire, *vaqueros*. The *hombre* is carrying an infant. But have your rifles ready just in case."

He rode forward ahead of the *vaqueros* and his son, holding up his hand and shouting, "*¡Alto, alto, hombre!* I want to talk to you!"

Pablo's lieutenant saw the assistant *capataz* gallop toward him, and he dropped the reins of his horse and lifted Innocente up in both arms so that Esteban could see the child. "I bring him back to you, *hombre*," he called. "Tell your men not to shoot!"

"Explain this, *hombre!*" the assistant *capataz* angrily exclaimed. "We were after you and that man who stole my Innocente—"

"It was not *your* Innocente, señor," Ricardo interrupted. "It was the *hijo* of our *jefe*, Pablo Araiza. He led us across the border to your *estancia* because he wished to claim the child."

"We know this—but you have not told me—" Esteban began.

Ricardo shrugged, uttered a bitter laugh. "You have no vengeance against him or the rest of us, señor. The others are dead. *El Señor Dios* granted me my life that I might bring back your child. Here he is. Now I go my way and ask your pardon. All are dead. And I do not know what I shall do. There is no band left, and it was not a good way to live."

Esteban stared at the man holding Innocente in his arms, tears running down his cheeks as he bent to kiss the child's cheek. Innocente gurgled happily, reaching out his little arms toward Esteban. The assistant *capataz* said in a choking voice, "*Hombre*, if you truly mean this, there is work for you with us. We are all *trabajadores*, and if you act like an honest man and work hard, it will not be remembered that you were once a *bandido*."

"I will go with you willingly to prove that I mean

what I say. I will work for my bread. This I swear.''
Ricardo crossed himself.

Esteban wheeled his horse's head around back from
where he had come. "Ride beside me, then, *amigo*," he
said in a voice that was choked with emotion.

Twenty-four

It was the first week of November, 1826, when Carlos de Escobar and the courier from Taos, Ferdinand de
Lloradier, rode up the winding trail of the stronghold of
the Jicarilla Apache.

During their long ride through the many miles from
Texas on to the Jicarilla stronghold, he and the slim,
mustachioed, black-haired rider, who was about Carlos's
own age, had become fast friends. Carlos saw that Ferdinand had an inner strength, a cheerfulness that made him a
compañero in every sense of the term.

Ferdinand had also made friends with the magnificent
black gelding that Carlos had given to him. This was after
the courier had come from Taos to tell Don Diego that a
nobleman and his party had just arrived from Madrid to
exonerate him of any treason during his career at the court.

"You have never met the Jicarilla," Carlos said as he
and the courier rode up the trail. "They are proud people,

free on their mountain. You will see what strength they have. Already they know we're coming, even though we cannot see them. No enemy, however well armed, could hope to attack them successfully here."

The two men now rode into the village. "I have never seen so many dwellings or such a peaceful village," Ferdinand marveled. "How long shall we stay?"

"Probably the night. There will be a feast in our honor. They might ask you to compete against some young braves in showing your skill with the *pistola* and the rifle, or even the lance or bow and arrow."

"I should enjoy that!" the *caballero* smilingly responded.

Pastanari came out of his wickiup to greet Carlos, whom he had last seen when the latter came to Taos earlier that year. It was shortly after that visit that Kinotatay had died and Pastanari had been made chief. Carlos introduced Ferdinand, and Pastanari put both hands on his chest, the wrists crossed, and inclined his head as he said, "Be welcome to our stronghold, *wasichu*. You are a friend of the *cuñado* of my blood brother, *el Halcón*, and for that alone you are welcome."

"Greetings, Pastanari," Carlos told him. "I have come all this long way first to see you and pay my respects to the new Jicarilla chief. If we may enjoy your hospitality for tonight, we shall make our journey on to Taos in the morning."

"Very well. We shall have a feast to honor you and your friend. And I have something more in mind now—I wish you to become my blood brother, Carlos, as you were the blood brother of the former chief of the Jicarilla, the one whose name we may not speak."

"I am grateful, Pastanari, and I pledge myself to be worthy of the honor you offer me."

"You have no need to pledge it; you have already shown it. But come now, I will take you to a wickiup

where you may rest until the feast!'' Pastanari cheerfully
avowed. ''I am sorry that you were not here to see the
wedding between our young brave Lortaldo and Epanone
of the village of the pueblos.''

''I am sorry that I missed it. I remember Epanone
well.''

''Having come from Taos, she wished to be wed in
the ceremony of her own people. Palvarde, the pueblo's
new spokesman, performed the ceremony. The *alcalde* and
his wife attended and even gave Epanone a lovely gift.''

''He did this to curry favor with you and with the
Indians of the pueblo,'' Carlos sarcastically put in.

''Of course. But let me tell you more about Lortaldo.
He seeks to gain greater education, the *wasichu* education
that will help him tend the sick. He has spoken to me often
of wishing to be a *medíco*.''

''I must meet him. Perhaps I can be of help. My
father and I would gladly send him to a school in New
Orleans where he could learn the skill. In New Orleans,
Pastanari, the *wasichu* do not look down upon the *indio* as
is done in Nuevo México.''

''That is good. Lortaldo and Epanone have remained
in her village. It was her wish that they spend some weeks
there before she came back to live with him here in our
stronghold. If you leave for Taos tomorrow, you will meet
them both,'' Pastanari declared.

Two mountain deer had been brought down by Jicarilla
bowmen shortly before noon, and thus venison was the
palatable center of the feast offered to Carlos and the
caballero from Taos. A young Apache girl, Lonitay, served
hoecakes to Ferdinand and sent a soft, quizzical glance at
his handsome face. He flushed with embarrassment, for
she was exquisite to look upon. Carlos, observing this,
murmured, ''You need not be ashamed of finding an
Apache girl desirable, *mi amigo*. I found my first wife

here, the beautiful Weesayo. An Apache girl is true to her mate, and she will fight and die for him. She has no jealousy, no intrigue, and her life is centered in devoting herself to her man and to the children who come from their union. A girl like this is more steadfast in love than any of the haughty, pampered señoritas you will find in Taos.''

"I know that already, Carlos. As I have told you, I have wearied of the life there. There is smug complacency among those who are the *ricos,* and they live in a world that takes no notice of those less fortunate.''

"I rejoice to hear you say a thing like this, Ferdinand,'' Carlos smilingly answered. ''And I owe you an apology.''

"Why?'' The *caballero* was puzzled.

"Frankly, when you came to the *Hacienda del Halcón,* my first impression of you was that you were yet another *caballero* whose life centered around the *bailes* and the *fiestas,* and that you spent your time devising pretty speeches to the eligible señoritas who would bring you a dowry. I know better now. On this journey, you were as loyal a comrade and as resourceful a one as one could ask for.''

"Believe me, Carlos, this outdoor life has refreshed my spirit, as well as my body. I would very much like to return to Texas and take part in the community that you, your father, and brother-in-law have built.''

"You have my sincerest invitation, then, to join us at the ranch. I would rejoice in having you as my friend and neighbor,'' was Carlos's frank answer.

When the feast was done, Pastanari turned to Carlos and said, ''Perhaps your friend will watch the blood-brother ceremony and understand what it means to both of us.''

"He will, I am sure, welcome this chance to see us bound forever as loyal friends,'' Carlos responded. ''I welcome the chance to exchange my blood with yours, Pastanari.''

And so the shaman came forth out of his wickiup, and

as Carlos and Pastanari stood side by side, he took his hunting knife and nicked their wrists, then pressed them together and bound them with a light leather thong until the blood congealed. And Marsimaya declared, "Thus, you are brothers, and thus, in each of you runs the blood of your brother to remind you unto the death how you are bound, and how your lives are crossed and intertwined. The meaning of the thong is not bondage but commitment; not outward show but deepest friendship and trust. Let it be said tonight that Carlos de Escobar and our *jefe* have exchanged the vows of blood brotherhood because each truly respects the other and is a friend and a counterpart to the other. Thus it has been in our tribe since the very beginning; thus it will be until the end of all life upon this earth."

Ferdinand had listened, spellbound by the mysticism and beauty of the ritual. The night was cool, and the moon was full. As he looked around, he realized that the intent faces of those who watched were not those of savages, but those of friends. He took great comfort in having learned this, and he felt his own inadequacies. Ferdinand was humbled, and thus his own manhood was strengthened.

In the morning, Ferdinand and Carlos went out into the clearing well beyond the wickiups, where the tests of skill were held among the young men. A dozen braves had clamored for the right to compete with the newcomer and with their new blood brother. The first test was the throwing of the hunting knife at a target, and Carlos equaled the casts of a number of braves, while Ferdinand was not quite so accurate. Then each took a turn riding at a target that had to be struck full in the center with a lance. Carlos won this contest handily against ten of the braves, while Ferdinand—although proving that he was an expert horseman—did not have great skill with the lance.

Next was the archery contest, which Pastanari decided to enter. He had a long and supple bow of ash wood, into which he notched the arrow. This he drew back, his face taut with concentration, holding the bowstring motionless for a moment, until he let the arrow fly. A shout from the Jicarilla went up as the feathered arrow flew two hundred feet to the very center of the target.

Carlos smiled at his new blood brother. He took Pastanari's bow, balanced it in his hand, drew the string, and determined the strength needed to draw it to its maximum pull. Then, calculating the wind and its variance, he nocked his arrow in turn and, fixing his narrowed eyes on the target, held his breath as he finally released the arrow. It landed only an inch away from Pastanari's mark, and the cheers from the Jicarilla acclaimed him as a worthy blood brother of their *jefe*.

Ferdinand could hit only the outer rims of the target in three tries, and he was bested by the two braves who wished to compete against him. He confessed rather sheepishly to Carlos when it was over, "*¡Caramba!* I have used muscles today I did not think I had. I see that I am sorely out of practice."

"You need not apologize, *mi compañero,*" Carlos laughed. "The Jicarilla are superb bowmen. It is a matter of survival."

But when it came to the contest of the pistols and the rifle, Carlos and Ferdinand were clearly the victors, with only Pastanari able to match their marksmanship. And thus the competition ended with acclaim for all.

It was shortly after noon when Carlos and Ferdinand mounted their horses and, after bidding farewell to Pastanari, the shaman Marsimaya, and the others, rode back down the trail and on their way to Taos.

Carlos and Ferdinand rode swiftly after leaving the Jicarilla stronghold and reached Taos by early morning of the third day. Above them was the majestic range of the Sangre de Cristo Mountains, white capped with snow; and the cool air, invigorating and thin, reminded Carlos of those innocent days of his boyhood in Taos, the outdoor life, hunting, riding horseback, and making friends with the *trabajadores*—especially Miguel. The friendship and loyalty of such men—humble though they might be as adjudged by the snobbish standards of a royalist Spain—had had a vital and positive influence on the formation of his own character.

"We'll go at once to the house of Doña Elena Pladero," he told his companion, "since the nobleman from Madrid is a guest at her house."

"Not only he, but also two attachés, a valet, and his own personal chef," the *caballero* responded.

"So large a retinue for one man?" Carlos asked, astonished.

"Oh, yes. Don't forget, *mi amigo,* he is a marqués. You will find him a most interesting person, *mi amigo.*"

"I do not care if he is a popinjay or the descendant of a monkey, so long as he brings news that clears my father's good name," Carlos joyously declared.

Half an hour later Carlos and Ferdinand rode into the courtyard of the de Pladero sheep ranch, a vast spread of a thousand acres. A young *trabajador,* recognizing them both, hurried forward with an eager greeting as he took the reins of their horses and led them to the stable. "Is your mistress *en casa, amigo?*" Carlos pleasantly inquired.

"*Pero sí, señor.*"

"*Gracias.* We shall announce ourselves," Carlos said as he and his friend strode toward the large, one-story adobe-and-wood *hacienda.*

"Doña Elena will be very happy to see you, Carlos," Ferdinand said, grinning with anticipation. "And, as I told you, she wishes to go with the marqués to visit your father."

Conchita de Pladero, daughter-in-law of Doña Elena, answered Carlos's knock at the door of the *hacienda* and uttered a cry of joy. "Señor Carlos, what happiness to see you here again in Taos! And Señor Ferdinand, do come in, both of you. My *suegra* is having breakfast with the marqués, as is my husband, Tomás."

As they headed for the dining room, she told them how her mother-in-law's earlier apprehensions about the nature of the nobleman's mission had entirely vanished. "He is a complete gentleman," Conchita explained, "and very interesting company, and we are convinced he has come here for no other reason than to convey the joyous news of Don Diego's exoneration by the Spanish court." Still voluably chatting, beaming with happiness, she led them into the elaborate dining room where Doña Elena sat at the head of the table. At the other end sat a tall, haughty-looking man in his early sixties, with high-arching forehead, heavy-lidded, dark-brown eyes, a patrician nose that was so sharp as to end almost in a point, and a waxed mustache over his thin upper lip. He was dressed in the brilliant, bright blue satin costume of an *hidalgo* of the court, with lace ruffles at his neck and the cuffs at his wrists, and medals of the highest order on his chest.

Doña Elena rose from the table and cried out, "Carlos, how happy I am to see you again! I am glad that Ferdinand has brought you to us. Sit down, do. You, too, Ferdinand. Now then, marqués, may I introduce you to Carlos de Escobar, son of Don Diego, and, of course, you know our faithful courier. Carlos, this is His Excellency, the Marqués Santiago de Viñada, who has come all the way from Madrid to restore your father's name and rank."

"It is my great pleasure to meet you, Marqués de Viñada." Carlos respectfully inclined his head. "As it happens, my father and his wife are presently in New Orleans."

"I trust," the dignitary said in a supercilious tone, "that when I reach your *hacienda*, your father will be there to receive me."

"That's my hope also, Marqués de Viñada."

"You are in time to share this wonderful meal with us, prepared by the marqués's own chef," Doña Elena said. "We have just finished eating, but there is plenty of food. Please join us at the table."

"With the greatest of pleasure," Carlos accepted.

The nobleman clapped his hands and leaned back with a languid expression on his haughty face. Out of the kitchen came a fat little man, wearing an apron and a chef's hat, clasping his hands together and looking anxiously at his master.

"Corbacco," the marqués commanded, "serve Señores de Escobar and Lloradier some of the plovers' eggs with your exquisite Madeira sauce, and a little also of the mushroom pastry." With this the fat little cook nodded and scurried back to the kitchen.

Carlos tried not to smile, but he and Ferdinand quickly exchanged a knowing glance in which he found that the *caballero* shared his secret amusement. All the same, when the marqués's cook emerged from the kitchen with covered dishes, placed them before Carlos and the *caballero*, and, whisking off the tops, proceeded to pile their plates with the plovers' eggs and the mushrooms in warmed pastry, he had to admit that this was delicious, if exotic, fare—a far cry indeed from the jerky and *frijoles* and water on which he and Ferdinand had subsisted for the last ten days of their journey.

"His Excellency has been kind enough to invite me to ride along with him to your *hacienda*," Doña Elena said, trying to initiate conversation. "I look forward to seeing your dear father, Carlos. Everything is running so smoothly here at home, with Conchita raising her children so beautifully and my son so ably handling the shearing of sheep and the sale of their wool. There really is no need for me to be on hand. And besides, I need a change of scenery."

"We shall be honored to have you as our guest at the

Hacienda del Halcón. I will serve as your escort, but just to be sure that all of us will be safe," Carlos proffered, "I have already asked Pastanari to send a dozen of his best young warriors to accompany us. It's always wise to take precautions in uninhabited territory."

"Of a certainty," she agreed. "The Marqués de Viñada and I shall ride together, while his cook, his valet, and his two attachés will ride behind the carriage."

"And I shall carry a case of the finest French champagne, one of Bordeaux, and another of excellent Jerez sherry at the back of the carriage," said the marqués. "We shall lunch and sup in style, even though we may be on this savage frontier. It is important for morale to maintain the highest standards, even in the most primitive surroundings."

Carlos remained silent, for he did not agree with the marqués. But, to Carlos's surprise, the Spanish nobleman proved more sensitive than he had believed. He turned now to regard Don Diego's son, nodded, and with a kindly smile, declared, "Señor de Escobar, the junta did me the honor of appointing me to come across the ocean to bring word that your father has been declared innocent of any charge of treason or disloyalty to the crown."

"That's very heartening news, marqués," Carlos answered. "May I ask how this proof was determined after so long?"

"It will be my pleasure to tell you. The name of the Count Jorge de Murciano should be familiar to you."

"Only too well. He betrayed my father to King Charles."

"Yes, and according to this count, your father believed it to be a blunder of statesmanship for Spain to ally with France. It was actually Prime Minister Godoy to whom the Count de Murciano reported. As you know, Godoy and Queen Maria Louisa were having a clandestine affair. The two of them stripped your father of his honors and had him banished. But the king, knowing your father's loyalty, insisted that Don Diego be placed in a position worthy of his skills and sent him to Taos as *intendente*. You see, Señor de Escobar, the king was your father's ally."

"I understand," Carlos said. He had heard all this before.

"Now, Count Jorge de Murciano made a confession of his wrongdoing to his young mistress. She, being a true daughter of Mother Church, thought over what he had said and could not bear to have the deception uncorrected. She went of her own volition before the junta to give evidence and to tell what her lover had revealed to her. Thus it was that the junta came to the conclusion that it was only malicious and spiteful testimony that resulted in your father's banishment to Taos. The count has since died. *El Señor Dios* has dealt with him, I am sure. The junta has restored all your father's honors. Also, I am empowered to convey a sum of money as compensation for the humiliation that your father suffered. Money does not buy peace or happiness, but it is all that the junta can do by way of showing its good faith and its belief in your father's honor and integrity."

"I am deeply indebted to you, Marqués de Viñada." Carlos's voice was hoarse with emotion. "Don Diego will be overjoyed. The memory of those accusations against his loyalty to Spain is the one shadow in his happy life here."

"I have learned how wonderfully your father carried out the finest traditions of Spanish justice while he was *intendente* here in Taos," the marqués said.

"Again I thank you. I'm at your disposal," Carlos said, warming to the nobleman, "whenever you wish to leave."

"I would be ready to leave as soon as possible."

"So be it. We need only to wait for the arrival of our escort of loyal, strong Jicarilla Apache. I thank God for the news you have brought, marqués. You have my great gratitude for what you and the junta have done to restore my father's reputation and good name."

While Carlos waited for the arrival of the Jicarilla, he rode into Taos and went to visit Padre Salvador Madura. The priest was hearing the confessions of several humble parishioners. Patiently waiting until the last had left, he entered the box and said the ritualistic beginning, "Father, forgive me, for I have sinned."

"In what way, my son?" came the familiar, beloved voice.

"In selfish joy over the happiness that *el Señor Dios* has so kindly granted to me."

"What do you mean, my son?"

"I am Carlos de Escobar, Padre Madura. And, of course, the happiness is that Teresa de Rojado is my wife and is with child."

"How wonderful to hear your voice again, my son! And as I have told you before, your happiness is not selfish but one that is noble and virtuous. I have prayed that our dear Lord would grant you continued happiness, and I am gratified to learn He has seen fit to do so. Take joy also, my son, in the fact that the *alcalde* here in Taos, thanks to your own help as I well know, has modified his outward contempt for the gentle people of the pueblo. And also that the Penitent Brothers and I keep the faith and will see that he does not relapse into his evil ways."

"This indeed gives me the greatest pleasure, Padre Madura. Now, let me make a contribution for your poor."

"Thank you, my son. May you and your wife know every happiness. I would like to baptize your firstborn, but I know it is a very long journey, and I know also that you have a fine young priest at your *hacienda*, Padre Pastronaz. Take my blessing to your noble father, Carlos, and also to his lady. They will never be forgotten by the people of the

pueblo for the love and compassion that they showed
them.'' Padre Madura had emerged from the confessional
box and made the sign of the cross over Carlos's head.
Then, as the priest escorted Carlos out of the church, the
younger man explained how his brother-in-law had been
called back to Argentina to help the father of his new
bride.

"My blessing also to John Cooper when you next see
him,'' the priest said. "May his mission succeed. *Vaya
con Dios, mi hijo.*"

Now Carlos visited the Jicarilla brave Lortaldo and
his pueblo wife, Epanone, who were living in a *jacal*
provided by the spokesman of the village, Palvarde. Carlos
told the Indian brave how he would like to help him with
his education, and it was agreed that Lortaldo and Epanone
would also accompany the group to Texas.

Meanwhile, as these arrangements were being made,
Ferdinand was making a momentous decision of his own,
caused in part by his deepening friendship with Carlos.
While Doña Elena began to say her tearful farewells to her
son, Tomás; his wife, Conchita; and her grandchildren, the
caballero rode back to his villa and there instructed his
majordomo to sell the property and, when that was done,
to send a courier to him at the Double H Ranch in Texas,
where he planned to live, on a trial basis, for the next year
or two.

"I shall write you a note of authorization, Honorio,''
he told the middle-aged servant, "so that no one will
question your right to act in my behalf. I will give you a
third of the proceeds. The money will be enough to provide you with security—you may have your own shop, or
enter trade, or do whatever else appeals to you.''

Honorio, a soft-spoken Spaniard from the province of
Aragon, was deeply moved. "Señor de Lloradier, it is
much too generous—''

"Now, Honorio, we'll have none of that. You have

served me well, and the money is mine to do with as I will. I am tiring of this life here in Taos, with these dreary balls and meetings and eternal suppers with their insipid conversation. I feel myself withering away. If you like, Honorio, after you have sold my villa, you're free to join me. Indeed, I should like to have you there—not as a servant but as a friend and a fellow settler.''

The Marqués de Viñada enjoyed a good night's sleep with no concern for the journey ahead and savored a leisurely breakfast, which his chef, Corbacco, prepared. The marqués permitted his two attachés to sit with him at the table this morning, for he wished to give them special instructions. Carlos, coming into the dining room several minutes after the attachés, greeted the men. One of the attachés was Arturo Mendez, a dapper little man in his late thirties, nearly bald, with a tiny beard and a pair of spectacles; the other was Pasqual Dorada, perhaps five years older, tall and dignified, with a habit of staring pointedly at his toes whenever his master asked him a question, and wanting at all costs not to draw attention to himself. This latter attaché kept a leather case with him at all times, even when he ate, placing it on his lap and the napkin over it.

The Madrid dignitary dryly explained, "In that case, Señor de Escobar, my attaché carries the notice from the junta that clears your father's name, and also a document setting forth a royal pension that will compensate your father for these years of regrettable misunderstanding. I myself have the king's own commission to award your father the Order of St. James of Compostella.''

Carlos was overjoyed at this news. "I must tell you how grateful I am to you, Marqués de Viñada.''

"My own reward will be meeting your father in person, to shake hands with him, and to pin this Order upon his breast. May I say that your love for him stands you in very good stead, Señor Carlos.''

"My feelings are not based on medals, pensions, or recognition, marqués. What delights me is that justice is at last being done after so long that one would have expected the matter to have been forgotten. I wish I could express my profound gratitude to the members of the junta."

"As it chances, Señor Carlos, I am a member of that junta," the marqués drawled. "I will convey your thanks to the other members."

The next day, an escort of twelve Jicarilla braves arrived from the stronghold, and at last it was time to depart on the journey. The marqués helped Doña Elena into the carriage, with the courtesy and florid gestures that he might have made at court to greet a princess. His two attachés mounted their horses, and poor little Corbacco, with a very long face, mounted his, with Carlos and Ferdinand riding at the head of the little processional. The valet, a tall, somber-faced man in his early forties, Francisco Pernari, mounted a piebald mare with a look of trepidation and took his place behind Corbacco.

At the back of the carriage was a huge storage compartment, in which the marqués had obliged Corbacco to load cases of excellent wine, plus marzipan and candied fruits, which he graciously offered to Doña Elena in midafternoon along their way. He had also had his valet hitch a small covered wagon to the back of the carriage, and this contained a fine teakwood table, several chairs, and a complete service of the finest silver, tablecloths and napkins, wine goblets, and a set of exquisite china. And so it was that as they made their way to the Double H Ranch in Texas, the Marqués de Viñada and his party were able to ignore completely the fact that they were in the middle of the wilderness. They lived in high style, for all the world as though they were still at the court in Spain.

Twenty-five

Don Diego and Doña Inez had returned to the Double H Ranch from New Orleans toward the end of November. The doctor who had accompanied them expressed his desire to stay on to look after his ailing patient, who was still feeble and was immediately put to bed after his arrival, his solicitous wife never leaving him for a moment.

The news of what had befallen Don Diego in New Orleans—as well as the bank robbery—spread quickly through the community of the Double H Ranch. Miguel, Teresa, the children—even some of the workers—came to the old *hidalgo*'s room to pay their respects and wish him a speedy recovery. It was hoped by all that Carlos and John Cooper would soon be home to lend their moral support and see to affairs on the ranch.

It was Esteban Morales who was the first to see the carriage, the Indian escort, and the other riders that meant the arrival of Don Diego's son. The assistant *capataz* hurried into the *hacienda* to tell Don Diego and Doña Inez of the approach of Carlos and the other visitors. Don Diego insisted on getting out of bed and dressing, but Doña Inez pleaded with him not to overtax himself by such an effort. Yet he had his way, with a flash of his old forthright independence, and she, with many misgivings, bade him put his arm around her shoulders and walk very slowly out to the courtyard to receive his guests.

Carlos, knowing nothing of the misfortune that had befallen Don Diego in New Orleans, flung himself off his horse and hurried to his father, embracing him. *"Mi padre, how good it is to see you again!"* And then, observing the pallor and listlessness of the old man, he gave his stepmother a quick, searching glance. She swiftly and surreptitiously put her finger to her lips so that he would not comment on Don Diego's wan appearance. Carlos was mystified.

Doña Elena uttered a cry of joy when she saw Don Diego and Doña Inez standing together and came up to the old *hidalgo* and kissed him on the cheek, then embraced Doña Inez while both women began to weep softly in this joyous, moving reunion.

Then Teresa came out of the *hacienda* and ran up to her husband. They embraced for a long time, she murmuring into his ear, "How good it is to see you, *mi esposo.*"

"And how are you—and our unborn child?" Carlos asked, his eyes sparkling as he looked at his wife.

"We are well—very well, now that you are home."

Carlos squeezed her hand, then turned to his father. *"Mi padre,* I now have the honor to present to you the Marqués de Viñada, who, with his attachés, the señores Mendez and Dorada, have come all the way from Madrid to do you honor."

Don Diego summoned all his strength to stand erect and to incline his head in tribute to the dignitary's high rank. "I am deeply honored by your presence, Marqués de Viñada. My daughter-in-law has already given me an idea of the news you bring, and I am stunned, for I cannot imagine that after so many years anyone would still remember the name of Don Diego de Escobar."

"You are far too modest, Don Diego," the marqués

said. By now the *vaqueros* and *criadas* had hurried out
of the bunkhouse and the *hacienda* to learn what was
happening. The news had already been spread among the
trabajadores of the arrival of Doña Elena and the nobleman,
who had come all the way from Taos to visit their *patrón*.

"It warms my heart to hear you say this, marqués."
Don Diego was quite overwhelmed.

"The pleasure is all mine. First of all, Don Diego, an
investigation was made, following the confession of the
Count de Murciano, who acknowledged that out of envy
and hatred for you, he had falsely defamed you to the
king."

"I thank *el Señor Dios* for giving me justice at last,"
Don Diego murmured, and crossed himself.

"Our present ruler is pleased to restore you to your
place of honor. The name of de Escobar now occupies an
exalted rank at the court of Madrid. Your land and
possessions—though, of course, after so many years they
cannot possibly be as they once were—are to be restored
to you. Or, as His Majesty has directed, a restitution will
be offered, which more than equals the value of what you
had to forfeit so unjustly. Further, His Majesty enjoins me
to offer you the most cordial invitation to return to Spain
to visit your homeland."

"How I would like to do that! But alas, marqués, I
have been ill for some weeks now and am only now
beginning to regain my strength. I do not think I could
undertake so long a journey and not at my age—" Don
Diego faltered, fighting the tears that filled his eyes.

Doña Inez quickly kissed him on the cheek.

Marqués de Viñada continued. "You have been
awarded a pension from the Spanish government, which is
equal to one-and-a-half times what you were granted as
intendente of Taos. This will be multiplied by the number
of years since your departure from the Spanish court. It
amounts to one hundred forty-two thousand five-hundred

pesos. His Majesty insists that this pension be bestowed upon you, belatedly though it undoubtedly must seem, so that you will realize that the throne will never forget the valiant service you have offered to Spain. Mendez, bring that other case to me at once!''

''Sí, excelencia,'' the attaché eagerly nodded. Hurrying to the compartment of the carriage, he opened it and slid back a little bolt at the very side, which revealed a narrow compartment in which reposed a leather valise. He tried to lift it out, but found that it was necessary to have aid, and Pasqual Dorada assisted him. The two men hauled the valise over to the marqués.

''Don Diego de Escobar,'' the nobleman said, turning back to the old *hidalgo,* ''this is a down payment on your pension. The rest will be dispatched in time to reach you by the Christmas holiday. It will come in a Spanish ship that will anchor in New Orleans in mid-December. But I have the pleasure of presenting to you now twenty thousand silver *pesos.''*

Don Diego gasped and reached for his kerchief to blow his nose, for by now he was very close to breaking down with tears. It was as if by magic the years had been rolled back, and he was once again an *hidalgo* upon whom the king relied and who was respected by everyone at the royal court.

Doña Inez whispered to him, *''Mi corazón,* I have a suggestion for you. What is coming on the ship is a fortune that will give us comfort for the rest of our days. Let this down payment be, therefore, a loan to that gracious gentleman Señor Fabien Mallard. With this money he can begin to rebuild the capital lost in the bank robbery.''

''Yes—by all means—you think of everything, my sweet Inez! I shall have one of our most trusted men with an escort ride to New Orleans and take this money directly to him,'' Don Diego murmured. Then, turning back to the nobleman, forcing his voice to remain level, he responded,

"When you return to Spain, Marqués de Viñada, I beg of you to take with you the most sincere expression of my deepest gratitude to His Majesty. Tell him that my loyalty to my native Spain never wavered, even in the black hour when I stood accused. And say to the members of the junta that I shall go down on my knees in chapel tonight to thank *el Señor Dios* for such good, honorable men who bothered to look back into the past and to examine out of their own conscience the true facts of my unwavering loyalty to Spain!"

"Rest assured I shall convey your messages, Don Diego. And I tell you, sir, that this is as happy a day for me as it must be for you," the Marqués de Viñada declared. "And now, I am to bestow a decoration upon you."

With this, the marqués took out his case, opened it, attached the Order of St. James of Compostella to Don Diego's chest, and embraced him. "I hereby bestow upon you the Order of St. James of Compostella," he solemnly pronounced. The *trabajadores* and *criadas* cheered, and tears ran down Don Diego's cheeks.

It was a long moment before he could regain his self-control to declare, in a choking voice, "This is indeed the happiest day of my life. How grateful I am to *el Señor Dios* in His infinite mercy to let my *trabajadores,* my beloved wife, and my son know that I have been found guiltless and a true patriot to my native country. I insist that you and your companions be our guests here at the *hacienda,* until such time as you must resume your journey, marqués."

"It will be my pleasure," the autocratic dignitary said.

Doña Inez kissed her husband, and she wept softly in her own joy to see him. Later she would tell Carlos about his father's state of health. At the moment, however, her maternal and protective instinct took over, and she whispered into her husband's ear, "Diego, please, if not for your sake, then for mine, welcome your guests; then go directly back to bed.''

"Very well, *querida*," he whispered back. And then aloud, "Marqués, you shall have the most comfortable rooms in our *hacienda*. After you have rested, we can meet at dinner and talk of our homeland."

"Of a certainty," the dignitary replied.

As the marqués and his two attachés entered the *hacienda*, the former turned and said disdainfully to little Corbacco, "You will continue to serve me while I am here, Corbacco. Introduce yourself into Don Diego's kitchen, and explain how I wish my food served to me." He added, for the benefit of Doña Inez, "You will forgive me, señora, and I have no wish to disrupt your household, but Corbacco has been with me for years and knows all my preferences. It would be far too difficult to explain them to any hostess, nor should I wish to importune her. So I ask you only to allow my chef to visit your kitchen and to prepare such meals as I may require, for in this way you will not give your household additional work just because I am your guest.''

"I shall be happy to grant you that request, Marqués de Viñada," Doña Inez answered. "As it happens, our most experienced cook is no longer with us.''

"Tía Margarita is not here? What happened?" Carlos asked.

"Well, Carlos," Doña Inez smilingly told him, "I only just learned myself when we got back that Señor Gaige proposed to Tía Margarita and married her. They went away together, prospecting—''

"Prospecting—" Carlos echoed.

"Oh, yes! Don't you remember the gold mine that Señor Gaige found, the time that Francesca and your son, Diego, hid away in the old man's wagon?"

"Oh, yes, only too well," Carlos admitted.

"Well, this time, they went with a few of the older

trabajadores," Doña Inez replied. "Señor Gaige says that he is going to find a new mine and make Tía Margarita rich. And now, I think we have stood outside talking long enough. Carlos, after you have had a chance to greet your wife and children, I should be grateful for the opportunity to talk with you. Marqués, if you will allow me, I will show you to your room."

Meanwhile, Corbacco, the plump little chef, had hesitantly and somewhat fearfully gone out into the kitchen and exclaimed over its spacious size and conveniences. He clasped his hands and shook his head, admiring what he saw, while Rosa Lorcas, Tía Margarita's replacement, whom Corbacco had not seen because she had been busy at the cupboard and far to his right when he had entered, finally and timidly proffered, "May I help you, señor?"

Corbacco whirled, with a startled cry, and then, seeing the lovely young woman, managed a courtly bow. "I am Maximiliano Corbacco, *su servidor, señorita.*"

"Señora," Rosa automatically corrected, blushing deeply. "Señora Lorcas, *por favor.* I am delighted to meet you."

"Let me explain. My master and I have come to visit Don Diego de Escobar, and I am his *cocinero.*"

"But here, Señor Corbacco, we have a cook, and it is I."

"A thousand pardons, Señora Lorcas, I am sure you are very good at it. It is just that, wherever we go, my master insists that I prepare his meals for him specially. It is not that he does not trust you or anyone else, Señora Lorcas; it is just that this is why he engaged me." Corbacco heaved a weary sigh and shook his head. "It is not always easy to devise something new to his palate, which, I hasten to add, is most discriminating."

"I see." Rosa giggled, for the situation in which this amusing, little man found himself was, at least to her, highly diverting. "Well then, there is no reason why, while your master is here, you cannot go on with your duties."

"You are most kind, señora. Perhaps we can collaborate, you and I. Do you cook with wine?"

"Not very often, Señor Corbacco. But I have herbs and spices that, if we do not get them from New Orleans or grow them ourselves, the *trabajadores* find for me near the creek and in the woods beyond the river. They add flavor to ordinary dishes. Have you ever cooked, perhaps, chicken *mole?*"

Maximiliano Corbacco shook his head, completely mystified.

"Or again, *mole de guajolote*," Rosa Lorcas went on. "This is a Mexican dish of turkey, which I serve with a chili gravy."

"That sounds most interesting! Could you show me how to do it?" he eagerly asked.

And so, for the next hour, the plump little cook and Rosa collaborated, and he was effusive in his praise of the deft and knowing way she went about preparing Mexican dishes, which, until now, his master had never tasted. That was why, for luncheon, the Marqués de Viñada was served a *mole de guajolote* and exclaimed loudly in his praise of it. When he called Corbacco out from the kitchen, the latter insisted on bringing the highly embarrassed, blushing young wife of Antonio Lorcas and declared to his master, "It is she who gave me the recipe, master. She deserves the compliment, not I. But, in return, I have learned much, and I will teach her several things."

There was a ripple of laughter around the table, and Doña Inez smilingly interposed, "We shall be sorrowed not to have Tía Margarita in the kitchen, but I foresee that with Rosa here and with the help of this very talented chef of yours, Marqués de Viñada, we shall have found ourselves a veritable treasure among *cocineros!*"

* * *

Shortly after the arrival of the Marqués de Viñada, the three *trabajadores* who had accompanied Jeremy Gaige and Tía Margarita to the San Saba Valley returned, each carrying a sack with ore nuggets, which they excitedly showed to Miguel Sandarbal. And Jeremy had kept his word: Roberto Locada had brought back an even larger sack for the *capataz*. "The Señor Gaige bade me tell you, *señor capataz*," he explained as he handed Miguel the little sack, "that because you have given him two grubstakes, this is a down payment on your investment."

"*¡Caramba!*" Miguel gasped, and then he burst into laughter. "It is like a fairy story, and it has a happy ending. But tell me, Roberto, did the Señor Gaige and Tía Margarita remain there in that lonely place after they got the gold?"

"Oh, no, *señor capataz*," Manuel Miraflores interrupted. "On the way back to they ranch, they decided to go to San Antonio, there to spend their honeymoon. The Señor Gaige said that he wished to buy his sweet *esposa* many pretty dresses and some jewels to wear, so that she would be the most elegant lady when she returns. They will come back, but they are in no hurry. And they seemed most happy when they rode away in the wagon."

"Perhaps we shall see them at Christmastime, then," Miguel chuckled. "This is indeed good news. Such good fortune is well deserved by that hardworking old *gringo*, and surely by our beloved Tía Margarita. Tonight, *mis amigos*, we shall drink *tequila* to their health, long life, and happiness!"

Twenty-six

John Cooper, Dorotéa, Felipe, Oudobras, and the tall Texan's two surviving *vaqueros,* Bartoloméo and Jaime, had ridden to Buenos Aires after the death of Porfirio Ramos and the crushing defeat of his henchmen. The three surviving *gauchos* had decided to return to the *pampas* and their families, with the heartfelt thanks of John Cooper and Dorotéa. The men would not be needed in Buenos Aires, John Cooper explained, but when things were finally set to rights and the Maldones property was restored to the family, the *gauchos* could look forward to the renewed patronage of the Maldoneses.

Thanks to the fact that he had kept a sufficient amount of Argentinian currency from his first visit to the land of the *pampas,* John Cooper was able to rent a little house some three blocks from the huge city square, conveniently near the *calabozo* in which Raoul Maldones was incarcerated. The lodging was uncomfortable at best, but it sufficed their needs, for John Cooper had decided to reconnoiter to see what plan could be made for freeing Dorotéa's father.

Oudobras, who had been to Buenos Aires several times purchasing supplies and running other errands for his former *patrón*, had volunteered to buy what food they would need during their stay. Its duration would, to be sure, depend on what luck they had in devising a plan of escape for Raoul Maldones.

The blond Texan decided first that an open declaration of his intentions might serve to disarm those government officials who were suspicious of him because he was a *gringo americano*. And so, two days after they had moved into the little house, he went to the *cabildo*, the municipal town hall that housed the governmental authorities of the Port of Buenos Aires. It was his hope that he could convince the *porteño* officials to grant freedom for Dorotéa's father if the old man would go to live in Texas.

Indeed, the night, before, he had discussed this with Dorotéa. *"Mi corazón,"* he had told her, "so long as this government is in power here, there is no guarantee that, even if your father should be freed temporarily, they would not attempt some reprisal against him once we went back home."

"I think my father might be happy in Texas," Dorotéa mused.

"I think you're right, my dearest," John Cooper had enthusiastically agreed. "As to his holdings and the *hacienda*, I'm sure that his good friend Heitor Duvaldo would look after them."

"Well, as you say, dear John Cooper, it's worth a try," Dorotéa had assented. "What a pity, though, after all his years of hard work, my father should have to think of giving up his home and all that he's worked for."

"Whatever the cost, we must get him out of prison. Even the strongest of men are weakened and their health injured by long stays in prison. And Porfirio Ramos intimated that the threat of execution hangs over your father's head. One of the other *porteño* officials might suddenly decide to send your father before a firing squad. If the officials will not release your father, I shall try something else.''

And so he had gone this morning, observing the regularity of the streets, the appearance of the public buildings and churches, the cheerful look of the white stuccoed houses. It seemed also that the people had an independent air to them, as if they were their own masters. That spoke well, at least outwardly, for the politics of this huge port.

John Cooper made his way into the spacious public antechamber at the entrance of the *cabildo* and approached a colorfully dressed guard who stood stiffly at attention, holding a halberd. In his best Spanish, the tall Texan inquired where he might find an official in authority who represented the justice department of the *porteño* government.

"At the end of the hall and to your left, señor,'' the guard said.

John Cooper followed the guard's directions and saw a huge double door made of Paraguayan wood, as hard as teak, smooth and glossy, that was painted in gilt lettering with the words *Gregorio Pordoña. Oficina del Interior* was written underneath the name. John Cooper now remembered the three government men who had also been passengers on the *Miromar* during his first voyage to Argentina, and Gregorio Pordoña was among them. It was Pordoña who had spoken to him, had warned him not to do business with Maldones, that Raoul Maldones was not looked upon favorably in Buenos Aires.

But then, John Cooper thought to himself, he had faced many dangers, and the only way to overcome them was exactly that, to face them.

As he paused before the huge door, John Cooper frowned, speculating on whether this insolent and powerful man might not have already learned of the death of his influential aide, Porfirio Ramos. Now he drew a deep breath, turned the knob of the double door, and entered.

Two guards at once halted him, one of them demanding in Spanish, "What is your business, *gringo?*"

"I wish to see His Excellency, Señor Gregorio Pordoña," John Cooper boldly declared.

The two guards conferred, glancing suspiciously at the tall Texan, and then the one who had accosted John Cooper made his way through a doorway. He came out a moment later, with a sneering smile on his bearded face, saying, "His Excellency will see you, but only for a moment."

"Thank you, *amigo,*" John Cooper pleasantly replied. He walked calmly, without the least haste, a smile on his face, wanting to show these two men that in no way did he fear their insolence. He found himself inside a lavishly furnished office, with the skins of ocelots flung casually upon the floor. The fat *porteño* official, with his thick, drooping mustache, was seated behind a huge teakwood desk. He was smoking a cigar and blowing wreaths into the air, the progress of which he watched with lazy eyes.

He blew several more before he deigned to recognize John Cooper's presence, and then finally drawled, "I am surprised to see you in our country again, señor. I remember you aboard the *Miromar,* the *americano* from Texas."

"Your memory is flawless, Señor Pordoña."

"I have no need of your *gringo* flattery," Gregorio Pordoña sneered as he took another puff of his cigar and then, again lifting his face toward the ceiling, watched the rings slowly waft above him. "Now, if *your* memory serves you as well, you will remember, *señor gringo,* that I had told you it would be wise not to become too friendly with the *estanciero,* Raoul Maldones. Perhaps you are not aware that he has been given a fair trial, convicted of treason to the nation, and imprisoned. It is fortunate for him that some leniency was shown, or else he would assuredly have been before a firing squad long before this."

"I know that he is in prison, and I have come here, Señor Pordoña, to ask you to release him in my custody."

"What are you saying, *gringo?*" The fat man straightened, his cigar in a corner of his mouth, a scowl on his face.

"It's very simple. If you release him and he goes back with me to Texas, with the promise that he will not return, you will have achieved the same thing as imprisoning him here."

"Your argument has no bearing upon the situation here. Your request is denied." The official stood behind his desk. "Now, if you will leave me, I have much to do. We have nothing more to say to each other, *señor gringo.*"

"Then I have the honor of bidding you a pleasant day, Señor Pordoña." John Cooper masked his irritation with a bland smile, turned on his heel, and left the office of the *porteño* official.

For the next several days, John Cooper made the effort to see other officials, to plead the case of Raoul Maldones. Everywhere, he met with deaf ears, and finally a minor official took him by the elbow and led him down the long hallway, until both were out of hearing of any other visitors to the *cabildo*. "I should advise you, señor, not to come again. Your visit and purpose are known throughout the government. For your own safety, and that of your loved ones, I'd advise you seriously to consider returning to your country. Raoul Maldones will never be released."

Before his visits to the government, John Cooper had instructed both Felipe and Oudobras, dressed like poor city dwellers, to spend their days keeping watch on the *calabozo*. It was not far from the calle de la Reconquista and the imposing Church of San Francisco. The church had a great arch, and above it a tower with three spires, with a statue below of the *Cristo*. Halfway up the arch on each side, there were miniature arches in each of the façades, and atop these, statues of the saints. On the tenth day, Felipe Mintras came back to the little house and excitedly reported, "I saw a priest going into the *calabozo* this afternoon, and I thought at first it was the one who married you and the Señora Dorotéa. Then I told myself, it could not be, for I saw that good man die with a Charrúa arrow in his heart, another example of the treachery of Porfirio Ramos, who put the Indians up to that heinous deed. . . . But I forget myself. And so, astonished as I was and not thinking of the risk in talking to him, I asked, '*Mi padre,* excuse me, but you resemble a *padre* I knew on the *pampas;* his name was Padre Emilcar Rancorda.' And then the priest said, 'My son, I am his brother, Augustín Rancorda.' "

"It's like a miracle, Felipe," John Cooper gasped, grasping the *gaucho*'s shoulder. "Did you ask him if he had seen Raoul Maldones?"

"*Sí, Halcón,* and he said that he has visited him often since he entered the *calabozo.* He said, too, that the Señor Maldones spoke of you and the message that was to be sent to you. He prayed you might find a way to free him."

"Yes, truly a miracle—and you're sure there's no mistake?"

"As sure as my name is Felipe Mintras, *sí, Halcón!* This brother priest is a few years younger, it's true, yet he looks so much like the one at your wedding that, as I told you, I thought at first I had seen a ghost." Felipe composed himself, then went on, "Well, he went into the *calabozo,* and then I bought a jug of water from a water carrier near the church and talked to him about what was happening in Buenos Aires these days. He is very poor, the water is of poor quality, being taken from the—"

"Yes, yes, of course, Felipe. But what about Padre Rancorda?" John Cooper anxiously pursued.

"Well then, about half an hour later, Padre Rancorda came out of the *calabozo* and made his way to the Church

of San Francisco, which is not far from it. It is possible
that he is attached to that church."

"He could be a tremendous help to us since the
guards are allowing him to see Raoul Maldones," John
Cooper excitedly said. "Tonight, I shall go to the church
to say prayers. Perhaps I can contrive to meet him."

"You had best say prayers for all of us, *Halcón*,"
Felipe Mintras wryly said, "that the authorities don't find
out you are still in Argentina."

"I promise you that if Padre Rancorda is able to help
us, we'll leave Argentina immediately," John Cooper said.

He spoke with determination in his voice, but inwardly he had misgivings. A prayer was surely the next
step, for with the help of God, everything was possible.

Dorotéa put her hand on John Cooper's shoulder as he
was about to leave the little house on his way to the
church. *"Mi corazón,* would it not be wiser for Felipe or
me to visit Padre Rancorda? Surely it would be wise for
you to stay out of sight in order to make the authorities
believe you have left the country."

Felipe nodded in agreement. "Although I would be
glad to go, I think it is more in keeping that a woman goes
to the church to pray. I do not think the authorities know
you by sight, Señora Dorotéa, and it seems to be much
safer for all of us."

"Of course. You're both right!" John Cooper exclaimed. "Very well, then, Dorotéa. Go to the Church of
San Francisco, and ask for Padre Rancorda. Find out in
what way he might be willing to help us. We must arrange
an escape that will not arouse suspicion." He pondered this
for a moment, then went on, "If we are able to rescue
your father, how shall we find a ship to take us back to
Texas?"

"I would suggest, *Halcón*," Felipe said, "that we
cross the Río de la Plata to the port city of Montevideo in

Uruguay. There are many fishermen from Buenos Aires who ply the waters of the great Río de la Plata between Argentina and Uruguay. Perhaps Oudobras or I can arrange with someone in a dinghy to take us all across to Montevideo at night."

"That's an excellent idea, Felipe! But I can make the arrangements myself while Dorotéa goes to the church," John Cooper said.

"But," the *gaucho* persisted, "do not forget that you are a *rubio,* assuredly a *gringo,* and even the simple folk will wonder why you seek passage to Montevideo. Oudobras and I can arrange for such a journey without arousing curiosity."

"How long do you think it would take a small boat to reach Montevideo, Oudobras?" John Cooper said, turning to the former *capataz.*

"It is well over two hundred miles, *Halcón,* and it would take nearly an entire day and night. It would be best to leave at night, as Felipe says."

"Are you familiar with the country of Uruguay?" John Cooper asked.

"Yes, I have a cousin there."

"Very well, then, Oudobras," John Cooper decided, "I shall wait here while you learn about finding us a dinghy that can take us all to Montevideo." He turned to his lovely young wife. "Tell Padre Rancorda, *mi corazón,* that we shall never forget how his brother united us, and now, as proof of the strength of the union that he blessed, we are both here to try to save your father."

Dorotéa nodded, gave her blond husband a quick kiss, and then left the house. Oudobras waited a few moments, and then, with a casual air, he sauntered down toward the port that faced the mighty La Plata River.

After Dorotéa left the little house, she slowly made her way to the Church of San Francisco. She knocked on the door of the rectory and was admitted by a severe-faced, gray-haired woman in nun's habit. "May I see Padre Rancorda, *por favor?*" Dorotéa asked.

"I will tell him you are here. Do you wish to give your name, my daughter?"

"Tell him it is Dorotéa. He will know who it is, *gracias,*" John Cooper's wife softly replied.

A few minutes later, a plump, nearly bald priest, wearing the white robe of a Dominican friar, entered the rectory. His eyes were aglow with delighted surprise, and he held out his arms to Dorotéa. To the nun, he murmured, "Sister Feliz, I should be grateful if you would leave me alone with this daughter of Mother Church."

"Of course, *mi padre.*" The nun inclined her head and left the rectory.

"I did not think to see you here, Señora Baines!" the priest exclaimed as he came forward and, taking Dorotéa's hands, kissed her on the forehead, then made the sign of the cross over her. "I can guess why you have come."

"*Sí, mi padre,* to help my father out of his wretched imprisonment."

"It is very bad. I saw him only today, a few hours ago."

"I know that. Padre Rancorda, I have come to ask your help in trying to save my father. We wish to take him back with us to our *estancia* in Texas."

"It will be difficult, there's no doubt of it. Let me think a minute." The old priest put his hands to his forehead and closed his eyes. Then his expression brightened, and he opened them. "I think I have a way to help. I know a younger priest who administers the last rites to those convicts who are sentenced to die and conducts masses for them on Sundays and on Tuesdays. I will talk to him, and if you will return to this church tomorrow afternoon, I will tell you if he will aid us."

"I am grateful to you, Padre Rancorda." She put out her hands to touch his, and there were tears in her eyes. "I wish to tell you that the marriage your brother sanctified on my father's estate has been all and more than I prayed it would be. My *esposo* is a brave, good man. And one thing more, Padre Rancorda—I am with child.''

"And you made this long journey knowing that?'' the priest said.

"It is still early, *mi padre,* and *el Señor Dios* has given me good health and inner strength. There will be no danger with the child.''

"I will pray tonight in chapel for your continued strength, *mi hija.* And now you must go.''

"Just one more minute. Tell me, how is my father, Padre Rancorda?''

"He is treated like the commonest of criminals, my daughter.'' The old priest sadly shook his head. "He is given very little food. One of the guards said to me that it would not be long before the last rites of Mother Church would have to be administered to this traitor from the *pampas.* I do not wish to alarm you, but I should not be surprised if they plan to execute him. And this is all the more reason we must act quickly.''

"Oh, *Dios,* grant that my father will live long enough for us to take him from that dreadful prison and bring him to a place of safety.'' Dorotéa's voice choked with sobs. "I shall never forget your kindness, Padre Rancorda,'' she said tremulously as she rose.

He made the sign of the cross over her head and murmured, "*Vaya con Dios, mi hija,* and have faith in Him Who will not permit an innocent man to die as a lowly criminal.''

When Dorotéa returned, she related her conversation to her husband. Both were downcast at the news of her father's treatment, and, in an attempt to raise their spirits, Felipe made a joke. "Do you know, *Halcón,* you might think of dyeing your hair black. With that crop of wheat that grows so abundantly on your chin and head, every *porteño* will know that you are not one of the people.''

"He's quite right there, *mi corazón*,'' Dorotéa said, giggling. John Cooper glanced at them and then his two *vaqueros,* who had effaced themselves at the back of the large room that served as both bedroom and living room. Then the Texan chuckled in his turn. ''You may have been making a joke, Felipe, but it's not a bad idea. I don't give my blondness a second thought. But I see what you mean—there are only sun-bronzed, dark-haired people in Buenos Aires.''

And so John Cooper sent Jaime Portola out to an apothecary shop to purchase some black dye, and after all of them had had a simple supper, he proceeded to shave his beard to a point and to tint both it and the blond hair of his head. Dorotéa helped him, while Felipe and Oudobras made quips as to how he looked truly like a *gaucho*.

On his visit to the harbor earlier, the former *capataz* had found an old white-haired fisherman who had proved to be most sympathetic and was willing to rent his sailing boat for an extremely modest sum. Oudobras had given him five *pesos* and told him that he would come to the shore the day before he would require the use of this boat.

The next afternoon, Dorotéa went back to the rectory. When Padre Rancorda entered, he was accompanied by a tall, slim priest not yet forty, with gentle features and soft voice, whom he introduced as Padre Benito Diaz, whose duties included visiting the *calabozo* and giving what spiritual comfort he could to the prisoners.

Dorotéa earnestly detailed what had happened to her father, and, to be sure, Padre Rancorda had already told Padre Diaz of the happenings on the *pampas* since John Cooper had made his first visit to Argentina.

"Señora,'' the younger priest gently declared, ''I have seen with my own eyes how inhumanly and unjustly the enemies of the *porteños* are treated. My spiritual duty is to *el Señor Dios,* to do what I can to right what wrongs I can perceive. Thus, though I am willing to help you, I will not violate the law of man, nor, of course, that of *el Señor Dios* Himself.''

"Whatever you can do, Padre Diaz, will give us great hope. You have seen my father?''

"Yes, I have met him. He is a kindly, intelligent man, naturally greatly depressed by his stay in that gloomy cell. But he is a true son of the Church.''

Padre Rancorda turned to the younger priest. "Benito, I have thought of a way to free Raoul Maldones. For now, let me tell you nothing more except that I will require you to accompany me to the prisoner's cell.''

The younger priest stroked his chin and thought for a moment. "I see no harm in that, Augustín.''

"*¡Bueno!*" Padre Rancorda exclaimed, grinning. Then, turning to Dorotéa, he added, "Once your father is out of his cell, you must take him far from Buenos Aires. Have you thought of a plan?''

"Yes, *mi padre.* We will go to Montevideo, which is a port to which foreign ships come. From there, we should be able to return to los Estados Unidos in all safety.''

"Good. When you have all in readiness,'' Padre Rancorda said, "come see me again. We will effect the escape then.'' He turned to Padre Diaz. "I shall communicate with you, *mi hermano en Cristo,* as soon as I have had word from the Señora Baines.''

"I shall wait for it.'' The younger priest rose and made the sign of the cross over Dorotéa. "You are indeed a loyal wife and daughter.''

"My eternal thanks, *mi padre,*" Dorotéa said, reaching for the young priest's hand and kissing it. "You may be sure that when we return to Texas, we will pray for your long and happy life in service to those who need the blessings of *nuestro Señor Dios.*"

"I shall hold you to that," the younger priest responded with a smile as he took his leave.

Padre Rancorda turned back to Dorotéa. "I trust him implicitly. He would never betray us. I will not tell you yet what I have in mind, because you might not agree with it. But when a man grows old, he thinks of what he might have done with his life to have been more worthy in the eyes of his Creator. I have had my faults, and the dear God has pardoned me. I do not pardon myself, however, which is why I must carry out my plan. I have thought this over carefully, and I am certain that my scheme is the only way to get your father out of the *calabozo*."

She did not know what the *padre* had in mind, but it clearly meant great danger and sacrifice. Nor did she press him for an explanation—she was not sure she wanted to know.

Twenty-seven

When Dorotéa returned to the little house, she at once told John Cooper of her meeting with Padre Rancorda and his younger colleague and how the latter had promised to help. John Cooper nodded and then turned to one of his *vaqueros*. "Jaime, I've a mission for you. You've stabled our horses down the street, I believe?"

"Yes, *patrón*. Where do you wish me to go?" the *vaquero* asked.

"To the *estancia* of Heitor Duvaldo," John Cooper gravely declared. "You are to tell the Señor Duvaldo that Adriana has inherited her father's ranch because Rodrigo Baltenar is dead, dead by the hand of Porfirio Ramos, who himself is no longer alive."

"Yes, Señor Baines."

"Then you will tell the Señora Josefa, who is the *dueña* to the Maldones daughters, that she is to bring the two younger ones here to Buenos Aires and to board a ship bound for los Estados Unidos. Tell her that we plan to rescue Señor Maldones and make our own way to that country, but in the meantime, she is to go directly to New Orleans, to the house of the Señor Fabien Mallard."

"A fine idea, Señor Baines!" Jaime Portola said.

"Tell Señora Josefa that she and the girls should wait in New Orleans for three weeks in case we are delayed."

"I understand it all."

"Finally, you will tell my son Andrew and Señorita Adriana to ride back with you. They will go to the rectory of the Church of San Francisco and ask for Padre Rancorda. He will give them sanctuary. They will wait until we are all ready to leave on the sailboat for Montevideo. It is better that they travel with us than with Señora Josefa, for if she travels with too large a group, it is certain to draw unwanted attention."

The *vaquero* repeated the instructions to John Cooper and proved he had memorized them.

"Very good, Jaime. You and Bartoloméo are good men. I regret only that your two companions had to give up their lives here in our mission. I do not want any unnecessary risk-taking on your part, so take great care when you ride toward Lobos. Be off, now, and make good time," John Cooper told the *vaquero*.

Jaime shook the hand of the tall Texan before departing.

John Cooper had one last piece of advice to give him. "Regrettably, my Argentinian money is almost gone. I will be grateful if you would ask Señor Duvaldo to lend Señora Josefa the ship-passage money for the girls and herself. When I reach home, it will be paid back to him with considerable interest."

"Yes, *patrón*. I will forget nothing," Jaime told him. Then the *vaquero* left the house.

John Cooper sighed, turning to Oudobras, Felipe, his other *vaquero*, Bartoloméo, and Dorotéa. His eyes shone with excitement. "So far, so good. With any luck, they should all be back within five days."

"I thank God for you, *mi esposo*," Dorotéa whispered, beginning to weep.

Felipe, Oudobras, and Bartoloméo discreetly absented themselves, and Dorotea linked her arms around her husband's neck and kissed him passionately.

John Cooper held Dorotéa in his arms. "Dorotéa, if you shed any more tears, the dye on my beard will run off!"

She laughed at this and gave him a quick kiss. "I do love you so!" she told him, and held him tightly.

At John Cooper's suggestion, Felipe went to the customhouse the next day to inquire if there would be any ships bound for New Orleans within the next several weeks. This information would be for Señora Josefa's use. An officious clerk, sneering at Felipe's costume of a poor city dwellers, replied, "A week from now, the *americano* ship *Bedford Maid* will dock out beyond the end of the La Plata. To be sure, you will need to take the ferry boat out to reach it, and that will cost you two *pesos*."

"I have that amount and more, *hombre*. I thank you for your information."

"Be off with you, vagabond!" the clerk haughtily declared with a wave of his hand. "I would lay a week's wages that you do not have enough *dinero* to take that long voyage. But, if it pleases you to dream of it, be amused. Go on; get away! I have much work to do, and there are others waiting for information of far more importance!''

Meanwhile, John Cooper was determined to learn more about Uruguay, for that would be their refuge after the escape of Raoul Maldones. He asked Dorotéa to procure a map. She was able to find only a crude one, but there was enough data for John Cooper to determine the route they would take to reach Montevideo.

John Cooper scowled as he studied the map. As Oudobras had said, the distance from Buenos Aires to Montevideo appeared to be about two hundred miles, sailing out to sea on the great Rio de la Plata and north to Uruguay. The trip would take an entire day and night, but it was a good plan, and John Cooper explained to Dorotéa, ''Once your father's with us, there's no way the civil guard or the soldiers here can get word to the authorities in Montevideo before we land. As an extra precaution, we'll steer away from the city itself and see if we can't land near the outskirts.''

''I just hope that Jaime brings back Señora Josefa and the girls in time to board the *Bedford Maid* a week from now,'' Dorotéa said. ''If they miss its sailing, and with us in Montevideo, I don't know what they'll do.''

Jaime had spared neither his horse nor himself in riding to the estate of Heitor Duvaldo. By dawn of the third day, he had reached the *estancia* and, reining in his foaming horse, dismounted and hurried to the entrance. There he banged on the door with his fist until a scandalized *criada,* wakened by the noise, abruptly opened the door and demanded to know if he was a lunatic and how dared he wake the household. ''Tell the *patrón* I'm from *el Halcón. Pronto, querida!''* he gasped.

''But everyone sleeps at this hour, señor!'' the maid protested.

"This is of the greatest importance! Please, or I myself shall waken your master!"

"Oh, no, señor, no, never! I will go waken him. You stay outside. Do not dare come in!" With several frantic glances over her shoulder, the *criada* hastened toward the bedroom of Heitor Duvaldo.

A few minutes later, the *hacendado* emerged, in dressing gown and slippers, his face still swollen with sleep, but his eyes were alert. "You bring news from *el Halcón*, you say? What is it?"

"He is about to rescue the señor Maldones, and I am to tell you that Porfirio Ramos is dead and with him the señor Baltenar, also. And so the señorita Adriana inherits her father's *estancia* and the house. And there is more—"

"Wait a bit, *hombre*," Heitor interrupted. "I can see that you've ridden like the devil himself—where did you come from?"

"From Buenos Aires, Señor Duvaldo."

"Go into the kitchen and tell Isabella to give you some breakfast. I will waken Adriana, Paquita, María, and the señora Josefa."

"Gracias, Señor Duvaldo. The señor Baines, he tells me that they must leave with me to go back to Buenos Aires and to prepare—" Jaime began.

"Hold your news until they are awake and can talk to you, *hombre*," the genial *hacendado* retorted. "Fill your stomach and rest a little, especially if you plan to ride back. I'll go waken the others!"

Twenty minutes later, lovely young Adriana Maldones, her two younger sisters, and Señora Josefa, all dressed in their robes, hastened into the kitchen where Jaime was gratefully downing a breakfast of warmed-over stew and some *tortillas* with strong coffee. The little *criada* who had let him into the house had gone into the kitchen to prepare his meal for him and cast him covert glances in which admiration and not a little apprehension were mingled.

Heitor observed this with a chuckle and said, "Thank you, Isabella, for giving this man *la comida*. You've done exactly what I wanted. *Gracias.*"

"And to you, *señor patrón*," the little maid said, as she hastened off.

Adriana now came forward and seated herself opposite the *vaquero* at the table. "Is it true that Baltenar is dead and Ramos, too?"

"*Sí*, Señorita Adriana," Jaime nodded, hastily gulping down a mouthful of *tortilla*. "Señor Ramos shot Señor Baltenar when he drew a *pistola* on your sister Dorotéa. Later Ramos's men ambushed us, and when Ramos was left alone, he came down pretending to surrender but instead drew a knife and put it to the throat of Dorotéa—"

"*¡Gran Dios!*" Adriana gasped, paling.

"But your sister was most resourceful, Señorita Adriana," the *vaquero* continued. "She fell to the ground, and it was a *bola* that broke the neck of that incarnate fiend. And Señor Baines says that I am to tell you that you have inherited the house and the land of your father."

Adriana seemed to grasp the enormity of the responsibility that had suddenly fallen to her. She turned to Heitor and said in a decisive tone, "Señor Duvaldo, I ask you, as my father's friend, to send your two sons to the *estancia* of my father and to administer the estate until I can decide what is to be done with the property."

Heitor bowed, suppressing a smile at Adriana's grown-up manner. "Your wish is my command, Señorita Adriana."

"And now," Jaime went on, "Señor Baines wishes me to tell you this: Señora Josefa is to take María and Paquita into Buenos Aires and board a ship that will go to New Orleans, where you will wait for him. I do not know when the ship will leave exactly, so all of you must prepare to ride back with me at once to Buenos Aires."

"I shall see to the preparations," Heitor put in.

Señora Josefa uttered a startled cry. "I am to travel all that long way?"

"Yes, Señora Josefa. You must continue to be the *dueña* for the younger girls," Heitor gently told her. "Do not alarm yourself—there is no danger to you and the girls." Then, turning back to Jaime, he demanded, "Is it known in Buenos Aires that Ramos and Baltenar are dead?"

"Señor Baines does not think so. I know myself that he went to the *cabildo* to ask for the release of the señor Maldones, and he was told it was not possible. But he has a plan to rescue him. And now, Señorita Adriana—" he turned to look at the girl with whom Andrew Baines was by this time madly in love "—Señorita Adriana, you and the *hijo* of the señor Baines are to go with us. You will stay in the church, where Padre Augustín Rancorda will hide you until everything is ready for you to go back to los Estados Unidos."

Heitor's eyes glowed with joy at the news that his friend would be released. "There's no time to lose. Unfortunately, neither Señora Josefa, Paquita, nor María can ride horseback such a long way. I have a carriage, and I shall have two of my swiftest horses harnessed to it. Señora Josefa, you and the younger girls will ride in it."

"I can ride long distances, Señor Duvaldo," Adriana proudly broke in, tossing her lovely head and staring at the *vaquero*. "Tell me, *hombre*, is my sister well?"

Jaime Portola grinned sheepishly. "*Pero sí*, Señorita Adriana. Your sister Dorotéa is beginning to grow large with child."

At this breech of propriety, Señora Josefa gasped and turned crimson, hiding her face in her hands, but Heitor indulgently laughed. "Now, Adriana, you'd best go waken your friend, the young señor Baines."

"*Sí*, Señor Duvaldo." Quickly, she ran out of the

kitchen, while Paquita and María giggled, only to be rebuked by Señora Josefa's sibilant, "Hush, *niñas.*"

Andrew, having been wakened by all the tumult, had drawn on his breeches and shirt, thrust his feet into his shoes, and was coming toward the kitchen, having heard voices there. He and Adriana collided in the hallway, and her face turned scarlet as their eyes met. "What's happened, *querida?*" he demanded.

"The very best news, Andrew!" Adriana said. "Everything is in readiness now to free my father. You are going to ride with me back to Buenos Aires, at all speed."

Andrew grasped her hand, but before he could speak, Jaime came out of the kitchen. The man belched, and as the two sweethearts stared at him, he stammered, "Forgive me, señor, señorita. I ate too fast. There is no time to delay, though. If you wish to eat something, you'd best do it now. I shall go see to my horse—I may have to exchange the poor beast. I've ridden like the very devil all the way from Buenos Aires." So saying, he put his hand to his forehead to salute them both, then hurried back through the kitchen to the stable.

Meanwhile, Heitor had given several of his *trabajadores* orders to harness his brown carriage to two of his best horses, and Señora Josefa hastened the little girls back to their room. "Very soon, you will be with your *padre* and your sister Dorotéa," she assured them.

Once dressed, she hurried back to the kitchen to heat herself a cup of coffee and to bring the little girls some corn cakes and *leche*.

Adriana and Andrew had chosen their moment of privacy in the kitchen, holding hands and staring deeply into each other's eyes. "Adriana, you know how I feel about you," Andrew hoarsely said.

She nodded silently, her eyes searching his face. He felt the squeezing pressure of her fingers and trembled at the intimation of her feelings for him. "We're going to ride back," he continued, "and save your father. When we go back home, you'll have a mare of your own, a real palomino. You'll like it in Texas. In a few years, maybe you and I can get married. I want that very much."

"Do you really, Andrew?" Her voice was the loveliest he had ever heard. He was undone by her bashful, blushing confusion in his presence.

"More than I can ever say, Adriana. Even your name—I love to say it."

"You are very sweet, and I do love you, too. And I will marry you when it is time. But first, we must save my father," Adriana murmured. Then she flung her arms around him, pressed herself against him, and gave him the longest, most passionate kiss he had ever known. It left him shaken, but then, just to let him know that he was not to take advantage of her, she drew away and saucily teased, "And now, Señor Baines, let us see if you can ride faster than I do on a horse because, as you say, we have a very long way to go!"

As Jaime Portola prepared to take a fresh horse from Heitor Duvaldo's stable, he clapped his hand to his head and said aloud, "¡Estúpido! You have forgotten one of the most important things!" Leaving the horse, he ran toward the *hacendado* and, his face red, explained, "Forgive me, Señor Duvaldo, but I had forgotten one of the things *el Halcón* told me to ask you. I—you see, señor, *el Halcón* asks if you can give Señora Josefa the money it will take for her and the little *niñas* to board the ship for los Estados Unidos. He promises he will pay you back, and he will give you interest on it. I beg your pardon for not having remembered earlier."

"Have no fear, *amigo*, you have done all of us a service." Heitor smiled. "I shall give enough *dinero* to Señora Josefa to have a fine passage to their new home."

"*Gracias*, Señor Duvaldo. And now we must ride

swiftly,'' the *vaquero* said. He nodded courteously to the *hacendado* and hurried back to the stable, finished saddling his horse, and rode out into the courtyard. The carriage already waited, and Heitor had assigned one of his young *trabajadores*, Gil Perez, to drive it. The *hacendado* helped Señora Josefa and then the little girls into the carriage. Then he turned to his coachman. "Gil, you are a fine young man, courageous and loyal. If you can be of any help to Raoul Maldones, do not worry how long it takes for you to return."

"Comprendo, patrón."

Andrew and Adriana mounted their horses and rode alongside each other, just ahead of Jaime. Heitor and his two sons stood on the porch of his villa, waving farewell. Then he turned to his sons and told them what Adriana had requested. "Now is the chance for you to show that you are men. You will live at Adriana's *estancia*. I will send some of my best *trabajadores* with you. When word spreads through the *pampas* of Baltenar's and Ramos's deaths, some of the *gauchos* will certainly return and help to defend that estate. You need not fear the rest of the *porteños* in their fine homes in Buenos Aires, so far from the *pampas*."

His sturdy teenage sons, Benito and Enrique, looked at each other with pride. They were already expert horsemen and marksmen and had proved themselves many a time. Enrique said to his father, *"Mi padre,* no one will trespass on the estate of your good friend unless he kills me first."

"Now then, Enrique," his father laughed, easing the tension and emotion between them, "there is no need to be so melodramatic. Pretend it is your own estate. You will put the *trabajadores* to work at the tasks that you know are done here, for Raoul's *estancia* is not unlike mine. And I will send a courier for the *gauchos* on the *pampas* to come and pledge their loyalty again. They will be ready to defend you. My blessings go with you, for you are both fine young men."

Twenty-eight

Felipe had learned that the *Bedford Maid* would arrive at the port of Buenos Aires almost forty-eight hours before its scheduled sailing back to the United States. When he communicated this news to John Cooper, the latter enthusiastically declared, "So much the better! It's quite possible to board ship ahead of sailing, as soon as one has one's tickets, and to remain in the cabin until sailing time. Therefore, as soon as Señora Josefa, María, and Paquita arrive here, they will be taken to purchase their tickets and will be put safely on board. Once they're aboard the ship, there'll be no connection between ourselves here and them, and I doubt very much that even the *porteño* soldiers would connect two little girls and a *dueña* with Raoul Maldones."

Dorotéa spoke up, standing beside her husband, a hand on his shoulder. "Do I understand, *mi corazón*, that you plan to rescue my father on the very day the ship sails for the United States?"

"The night before, Dorotéa." Seeing that she looked agitated, he took her elbow and guided her to a chair. "They will sail out on the *Bedford Maid*, and we will go

303

directly to Montevideo. We'll all meet in New Orleans. It will be just fine, *mi esposa*. Try not to worry."

"I know, John Cooper. But I have so many misgivings, now that we're so close to success." Dorotéa sighed.

"Let's just rest and be with each other and think that soon all of us will be back on Texas soil, beginning a new and happy life." Then John Cooper said, in a gentler voice, as he kissed her on the lips, "And we'll have time to think of the wonderful child you're going to give me, my dearest one."

Then he frowned and bit his lip, and Dorotéa, seeing this, anxiously demanded, "But what's wrong, sweetheart?"

"I just remembered that I won't have enough for passage money for our own party back to the United States. I guess I'll just have to convince the captain of whatever ship we take that I'm good for the money. Never mind," he said, turning back to her with a warm smile, "I've a feeling that everything's going to be all right."

The next afternoon, Oudobras returned from visiting the fisherman who had agreed to let them have the sailboat. "I've learned something, *Halcón*," he excitedly told John Cooper, "that may help in planning our escape. He says that instead of Montevideo, we should sail to Colonia, also in Uruguay. He has taken the trip himself and says it is only about forty miles, directly across the Rio de la Plata. What's more, my cousin lives near Colonia, and he can help us go overland to a large port, where no soldiers or authorities will bother us."

"That might be better—it would be a much closer destination. But from what port can we be sure to find a ship that can take us home?"

"The old man said that many large, foreign-bound ships stop at Maldonado. From Colonia to Maldonado, he thinks, would be about two hundred miles, traveling overland."

"I'm grateful to you, Oudobras," the Texan said.

"These plans make great sense. You've been a faithful friend to both your master and myself, Oudobras, and if you want to come with him to my *estancia,* I can find a good job for you there."

"You are kind to think of it, Señor Baines." The former *capataz* proudly drew himself up. "But this is my home."

"If you ever change your mind . . ."

"You are very kind, and I will not forget that. And now, let us hope that soon the others will come from the señor Duvaldo's place!"

Jaime Portola led the way, Adriana and Andrew Baines riding behind him, and the carriage with Paquita, María, and Señora Josefa following. The young coachman, Gil, cracked his whip, his face earnestly contorted in his desire to keep up with the forerunners. Adriana, the hot breeze tossing her curls, glanced back at Andrew with a merry insouciance, as she leaned forward over the neck of her horse and urged it on to greater speed. Andrew, living in a kind of fantasy world, saw only Adriana, and his body throbbed with vigor and delight.

As for the *dueña,* she crossed herself and prayed to be kept alive after so jostling a journey. "*¡Santísima Virgen!* It is too much—I cannot bear this—oh, María, oh, Paquita, how can you sleep so soundly when we are being driven as if the end of the world were in sight!" she groaned to herself.

In the darkness, under the hazy light of the December moon, they neared Buenos Aires. Lather foamed from the horses' mouths, and their flanks were sleek with sweat. It was shortly after midnight on the fifth day since he had left Buenos Aires that Jaime slackened his horse's gait and signaled the slowing down of this little band of hopefuls.

"Señora Josefa," he panted, as he wheeled his horse back to the carriage and leaned forward to talk to her, "we are coming into Buenos Aires. I will take you to the house where Señor Baines and his *esposa* await you. And you," he said, turning to Adriana and Andrew, "I will then show you the church where you are to go, *¿comprenden?*"

The two young people nodded and exchanged a glance of steadfast loyalty.

They rode now toward the northeast, for the *vaquero* wished to enter the city without attracting attention, at a point where there would be few passersby or *soldados*.

Luck was with them. On this sultry night, the city was silent, and the carriage entered by a side street not far from the little house where John Cooper, Dorotéa, Felipe, Oudobras, and the *vaquero* Bartoloméo Mendoza awaited them.

About a block away from the house, Jaime held up his hand, and Gil obediently halted the carriage. The *vaquero* said, "We will walk from here, leading our horses. Señor Andrew, Señorita Adriana, you'll both follow. The church isn't far from the house."

"Comprendo, gran vaquero," Adriana said to the young *vaquero,* who grinned and touched his forehead with his forefinger in acknowledgment of the tribute the young girl had just paid him.

Señora Josefa, again crossing herself and praying, opened the carriage door and slowly stepped down, then wakened the two little girls. *"Mis niñas,* we are home with your sister, and everything will be fine, and your father will soon be with us, you'll see! Don't make a sound now, my darlings, and we'll walk to the house where you'll see your sister."

Her exhortations prevailed, and Paquita and María each took one of her hands as she hurried down the side street, following the *vaquero* and Adriana and Andrew toward the house.

There was no light, no sign of life in the streets. The hot wind off the river, with the smells of decay and fetidness, wafted to them, and Señora Josefa wrinkled her nose and shrugged. "No wonder my *patrón* preferred to live on the *pampas! ¡Gran Dios!*"

Jaime tied his horse in a shadowy alleyway, patted it, and whispered, "Now be silent. You have done very well thus far." Then, moving quickly to the frightened *dueña* and the two little girls who looked up anxiously, he whispered, "Turn right, go down two houses, and it is the white stuccoed house at the edge of this next street. Wait for me there."

Then, to Adriana and Andrew, who held the reins of their horses and looked questioningly at him, "Come this way to the rectory, and there you will be safe."

Adriana and Andrew nodded, and Jaime whispered, "Tie your horses here. Come quickly!"

He led them into the courtyard of the rectory and pointed to the door. "Knock softly, but keep knocking until Padre Rancorda takes you in. I must go help the Señora Josefa and the two little *niñas. Adiós, hasta mañana.*"

Adriana and Andrew, holding hands, hastened toward the rectory door, and Andrew knocked, glancing around anxiously. The moon's rays touched him and touched Adriana's hair, and in the darkness of her eyes he saw the glow of love.

The door was suddenly opened, and it was the old sister who acted as housekeeper. She crossly scolded them, "At what hour do you young sinners come? The church is closed!"

"Pardon, Sister," Andrew spoke in Spanish. "We are Andrew Baines and Adriana Maldones. We have come a long way to see Padre Rancorda. Please, *por favor,* let him know that we are here."

"This is unheard of! I tell you, *señor joven,* you must come in the morning," the nun persisted.

But Andrew shook his head. Tightening his grip on

Adriana's hand, he stalwartly declared, "Please, Sister, this is very important. He will know why we are here."

"Well, you speak like a nice young man, but mind you, it is very bad to come so late. All right, if he is up, I will tell him. Otherwise, you must come back tomorrow," the old nun grumbled.

She closed the door of the rectory, and Adriana looked blankly at Andrew. "I pray nothing goes wrong." Acutely aware that he was alone with his love, Andrew huskily answered, "Do not worry, *querida;* it will be all right. We must have faith. I love you, Adriana."

Suddenly she was tender and soft and embarrassed. "You say such sweet things that you frighten me sometimes. I love you, too. But now we must do whatever is necessary to help my father. Believe me, Andrew, I will not act so frightened again, *mi amorcito!"*

Andrew felt as if a sudden wind had swept throughout his being, igniting a flame of desire and love. He turned to her, lips trembling, but suddenly the door opened, and the plump old priest, a finger to his smiling lips, beckoned them inside.

"Señorita Adriana, Señor Andrew, how good it is to see you! Come now, quickly!"

He led the way, closing the door behind them, into the obscure darkness inside. He lit a candle and lifted it up so they might see. They were in a bare, narrow cubicle hidden behind the nave, but it would suffice. There were blankets and pillows on the floor, and Andrew took Adriana by the hand and led her in. "Let's go to sleep. Here, I'll make your bed for you."

She nodded, bemused by his attentiveness. He knelt down and put one pillow atop another, smoothed out the blankets, and then gestured to her to take her place and sleep.

Adriana sighed, then snuggled under the blanket, turned her face to the right, and was soon asleep.

He knelt there a long moment watching her, his heart trembling with a joy and torment that mixed within his very being. Then he crawled into his blanket and, pillowing his head in his arms, he, too, was claimed by sleep.

Jaime put the horses away in the stable with as little noise as he could and then hastened to knock at the door of the house, where Josefa and the two girls were waiting for him. John Cooper, who had been drowsing, sprang up and hurried to open the door. Señora Josefa, not recognizing the Texan because of his dyed hair and trimmed beard, uttered a cry, but he clapped his hand over her mouth, apologizing, "Señora, we mustn't waken anyone, please! Come in. Ah, here are María and Paquita. Dorotéa, your sisters are here!"

He closed the door quickly and led the two sleepy little girls and the scandalized *dueña* into the house. Dorotéa had wakened and, donning her robe, came out to greet her sisters. They uttered cries of joy, thoroughly wakened now, and ran to her. She knelt down, enfolded them in her arms, and kissed them both. The *dueña* watched this with tear-filled eyes.

John Cooper ushered her to a chair. "Tomorrow morning, Señora Josefa," he said, "you and the girls will board the *Bedford Maid*. Did Señor Duvaldo lend you the money for passage?"

"Oh, *sí, sí*, Señor Baines," the *dueña* said. "Do you mean to say that you have already taken the *patrón* out of the *calabozo*?"

"No. Tomorrow night. Did my son and Adriana come with you?" the tall Texan asked.

"Oh, yes, *Señor Halcón*," Jaime spoke up, eagerly nodding. "I saw them go into the rectory. All is well with them."

"Very good! Jaime, when we get back to Texas, I'll see that you're rewarded for a job well done. Now the first thing to do is to find a place for Señora Josefa and the little girls to sleep. You will have a busy day tomorrow. Your ship will be in port all day and will sail the day after tomorrow. If everything goes well, and with God's help, all of us will meet in New Orleans and then go on to Texas!''

"I do not know if I can bear such anxiety, Señor Baines!'' the *dueña* fussed.

"Well, you needn't worry anymore about that. We're all the same family now, Señora Josefa, and I'll take care of you,'' John Cooper said. "Come now, I think we can find blankets for the girls to sleep on. I'm afraid we have no other bed; you'll just have to make do until the morning.''

Suddenly, Señora Josefa uttered a cry and, rolling her eyes, clapped both hands to her forehead. *"Ayúdame,* I have forgotten our luggage is with the young driver who brought us here!''

"We left the driver about a block from the house,'' Jaime explained.

"I will go find him and get the luggage,'' John Cooper replied. With this, carefully opening the door, he went out into the night. Turning to the left, down the little side street, he observed the fine coach standing beside the stone statue of a Spanish conquistador. Gil, the young coachman, sat on the driver's seat, his figure slumped in sleep, his hands still holding the reins of the two magnificent horses.

A sudden inspiration struck John Cooper as he walked up to the carriage and, cupping his hands to his mouth, whispered, "Wake up, *hombre!*''

Young Gil straightened with a start, gasped, then stared down at John Cooper, whom he had once met at Heitor Duvaldo's house but did not now recognize. "And who are you to tell me to wake up, *hombre?*''

"Shh, lower your voice! I'm Señor Baines.''

"A thousand pardons—your hair and beard—''

"Keep your voice down!'' John Cooper hissed. "Do

you know the location of the church where Adriana and Andrew went?''

"¡Sí, seguramente!"

"Then here is what you will do, *hombre*. Drive the carriage into the courtyard near the rectory. We may have need of it tomorrow night to transport Señor Maldones and the rest of us to the sailboat that will take us to Colonia.''

"My master, the Señor Duvaldo, bade me remain in Buenos Aires to help you as long as necessary," young Gil began.

"Thank you. I won't endanger you, and Señor Duvaldo has done quite enough already. If there is a stable at the rectory, unharness the horses, feed and water them, give them a good rubdown, and let the poor beasts get some rest.''

Gil nodded and, after John Cooper took the luggage, drove the carriage through the arch and into the courtyard near the rectory. Finding a stable, he unharnessed the horses and took care of their needs, then led them into stalls. Then he went back to the carriage and stretched himself out on the padded bench where the *dueña*, María, and Paquita had sat. He was soon fast asleep.

Twenty-nine

John Cooper had had little sleep, thinking all night long about Raoul Maldones. Dorotéa had not slept either, and soon after John Cooper dressed, she began to prepare breakfast for Señora Josefa and her little sisters.

The Texan embraced his wife. "When you've finished, it would be a good idea to go over to the church to find Padre Rancorda and learn exactly what his plan is."

"Yo sé, querido." Dorotéa clung to him for a moment, looking up at him with her lovely eyes as intently as she could, as if to memorize his features. "After the little ones and Señora Josefa have finished breakfast, I'll send them to the customhouse."

"Yes, of course, *mi corazón*. And they should board the ship just as quickly as they can," John Cooper said. "We must think of a name for Señora Josefa to use. She obviously cannot use Maldones."

Felipe, Oudobras, Bartoloméo, and Jaime now came in and sat down at the long, rickety wooden table that acted as their dining table. Dorotéa served them. She had made a porridge out of cornmeal, molasses, and milk, stirring it into a thick gruel that was delicious and filling.

312

There was also chocolate to drink, which the *dueña*, María, and Paquita particularly loved.

John Cooper paced back and forth, thinking out the plan for that night, speculating on what might go wrong and how to avoid any traps that the *porteño* authorities might possibly lay for him. Until he found out what Padre Rancorda had in mind, however, no specific plans could be made.

Finally, he turned to Bartoloméo and, putting his hand on the *vaquero*'s shoulder, declared, *"Hombre,* I want to ask a favor of you."

"You don't have to ask, Señor Baines."

"That's good of you, Bartoloméo. I want you to take Señora Josefa and the two girls to the customhouse and see that she has her passage and that she and the girls board the *Bedford Maid.*" At this, the *vaquero* nodded, continuing to look intently at the tall Texan, awaiting further instructions. "If she uses the name of Maldones, there's a chance she will be connected with the escape. Would you pretend to be her brother and let her give the name of Mendoza?"

"Of course, Señor Baines. There is nothing I would not do for any member of your *esposa*'s family."

"All right, then. Enjoy your breakfast. There is ample time."

About half an hour later, the children and Señora Josefa emerged, the *dueña* yawning and then blushing as she saw the four men at the table. She mumbled a greeting to them and then herded Paquita and María to the table while the *vaqueros* swiftly rose to cede their places to the trio. Dorotéa served up the porridge and chocolate, and the two girls ate heartily. Señora Josefa sniffed disapprovingly at first, but after she had tried a few spoonfuls of the porridge, she began to eat ravenously and even asked for a second cup of chocolate.

"I congratulate you, Señora Josefa," John Cooper

said, a smile curling the corners of his mouth, for the moment called for a little levity to ease the growing tension of this momentous day. "You have acquired a fine, reliable *hermano!*"

Señora Josefa almost dropped her cup of chocolate and stared at John Cooper as if she could not believe her ears. "What are you saying, Señor Baines?" she finally said.

"The thought occurred to me that if you say the name of Maldones when you buy your passage—"

"*¡Gran Dios!*" the *dueña* interrupted, immediately grasping the situation. "I must give a different name."

"Yes, and Bartoloméo Mendoza here, very obligingly, has offered to lend you his. You may claim him as your brother. The name of Mendoza will not be suspect."

Señora Josefa coyly looked at the sturdy *vaquero*, then blushed. "He could be my brother. That would be most agreeable."

Bartoloméo grinned, swept off his *sombrero*, and made her a long bow. "*¡ Bienvenida, mi hermana!*"

The *dueña* bridled, covered her face with her hands, and then timidly, but showing that she had a modicum of humor, responded, "After all these years, it is good to know that I have so fine and polite a brother."

"I'm indebted to you, Señora Josefa," John Cooper chuckled. And then, to add to her complete confusion, he leaned over and kissed her heartily on the cheek, at which Dorotéa could not help giggling.

The *dueña* rose from the table, suddenly as officious and dictatorial as she had always been with her charges. "Now then, *mis niñas*, we are going to leave on a great ship, to sail a long way over the blue ocean to a wonderful new land. Be good now, and if you do not talk at all when I get our passage, I will give you a reward once we are on the ship."

Some twenty minutes later, Señora Josefa took each

little girl by the hand and then, fervently looking at Dorotéa, murmured in a voice choked with emotion, "I will say prayers for you. *Adiós,* Dorotéa, Señor Baines. I see now what a brave, good man you are. I can pay you no higher compliment."

John Cooper smiled and gently came forward to the *dueña,* kissed her on both cheeks, and whispered into her ear, "You are really a very fine woman. Remember to wait three weeks in New Orleans at the home of the Señor Fabien Mallard. If we do not come then, he will send you on to our ranch in Texas to wait for us. Go with God, Señora Josefa!"

She was weeping as she nodded, and then turned, stifling her tears, and once again was peremptory with the little girls. "Come now, pay attention! We are going!"

Bartoloméo shook hands with John Cooper, bowed before Dorotéa, and held open the door for the *dueña* and the little girls. Then picking up their luggage, he glanced back at Felipe, Oudobras, and Jaime, and was gone.

Now it was Dorotéa's turn to leave the house, to learn what it was Padre Rancorda had in mind for them to do. She walked slowly to the Church of San Francisco and knelt and prayed in one of the rear pews before the mass began. She saw that Padre Rancorda was in the pulpit to deliver the sermon. He swung the censer, evoking the presence of the Trinity, and then turned to the participants to bless them as they prayed.

And when at last the church had cleared, she went to the confessional booths, for the *padre* had caught her eye and surreptitiously nodded as the service ended.

In the confessional booth, she knelt to pray and said aloud, "Forgive me, Father, for I have sinned."

A moment later, his comforting, voice came, "In Him Who made us all, there is eternal forgiveness, my daughter."

"I ask of you to tell me what it is I must do, *mi padre,*" she murmured.

There was a rustle in the opposite booth as Padre Rancorda made certain that there were no eavesdroppers. Then, leaning forward toward the grille, he murmured, "You must dress as a nun, *mi hija,* and your husband as a monk. I have a bundle in a sack, and you will take it with you when you leave here. It has the garments you and your *esposo* will wear. Padre Diaz will accompany us. Thus, there will be four of us, and I will feel more assured of the success of our mission with you and your husband along. We shall go past the guards, and I will tell them that we are to give comfort to Raoul Maldones. And I have heard some most distressing news in the *calabozo* before I came here to mass, *mi hija.*"

"Oh, *Dios,* what now?" Dorotéa groaned.

"Hush, Dorotéa! Do not let anyone hear you. The guards said that I may as well convert this *traidor* before his last moment on earth comes, tomorrow at dawn."

"Oh, no—tomorrow morning!" Dorotéa groaned again.

"Please, please, lower your voice, *mi hija!*" There was anxiety in the old priest's voice. "My feeling is that the *porteño* authorities decided that the best way to rid themselves of possible interference was to have your father dead. No one would question their motives. Our rescue must be tonight!"

"Yes! Señora Josefa has taken Paquita and María to the ship that lies out in the harbor. By now they may be aboard it. Oudobras has found an old fisherman who will let us have a sailboat to take us into Uruguay."

"Good. Now I must swear you to secrecy. Once we enter the cell of your father, I intend to change places with him. Thus, he will wear the habit of a *padre.*"

Dorotéa was speechless, for the ruse was indeed ingenious, and yet it required the *padre* placing himself in great jeopardy. Finally, she murmured, "But, *padre,* what will happen when the guards discover what you have done?''

"Do not concern yourself. No harm will come to me. I'm a priest, *mi hija*. I am happy to do this for your father, a dear friend, a faithful man, a man whom *el Señor Dios* touched with His goodness. The authorities may scold me, but they will not kill me. They are *católico*. And if they should execute me, I do not fear death—to give a life for one that is worthier, this is the best of all ways to die. Finally, I wish to do this in memory of my brother Emilcar. Now, Father Diaz and I are expected at the prison a little after nine this evening, my daughter. Come to the court-yard of this rectory and do not be late.''

"How are Adriana and Andrew?'' Dorotéa anxiously inquired.

"Have no fear. They are both safe. You shall come back here when it is all done, and they can leave on your sailboat with you.''

"Oh, Padre Rancorda, I don't know how to thank you—''

"Hush, *mi hija*. You must be brave, play your role well, and tell your *esposo* to do the same.''

"We shall do everything you wish. Nothing will go wrong now that you and Padre Diaz are helping us. Forgive me my sins, and say a prayer for my husband and me, and one, too, for the child within me. May it be born to a happier world in which there is no injustice or tyranny.''

That night, after Dorotéa had explained the elderly priest's plan, John Cooper donned the monk's garments and his wife donned the robes of a nun, and they left the little house to meet Padre Rancorda and Padre Diaz at the church. Oudobras—who had gone earlier that day to let the fisherman know when the boat would be needed— Felipe, and the two *vaqueros* waited behind, ready to leave as soon as John Cooper returned for them.

The tall Texan drew the collar of his heavy-hooded cloak about him. With his hair dyed and his beard cropped, he indeed resembled an Argentinian.

The night was sultry; the heat, intense. Dorotéa opened the rectory door and quickly entered, with John Cooper following her. The old nun who had accosted her on her first visit to Padre Rancorda did not recognize her in the nun's garb and merely nodded with a smile, then inclined her head in reverence toward John Cooper, thinking him a priest. "Padre Rancorda awaits us, Sister," Dorotéa said in a soft voice.

"I will bring him directly."

A few moments later, Padre Rancorda and Padre Diaz emerged, and the former smiled and nodded. "Sister Feliz told me that a priest and a nun awaited me. Let us hope that your disguises will have the same effect on the guards. Adriana and Andrew will be waiting for us here until we return from the *calabozo*."

"I'd like to see my son, and Dorotéa wants to see Adriana," John Cooper replied.

Padre Rancorda nodded, then left the rectory room, to return a few moments later with both Andrew and Adriana. Dorotéa uttered a cry of joy, Adriana flung herself into her older sister's arms, and they exchanged a long and tender embrace. Then Adriana began to chat volubly while John Cooper put his arm around his son, the boy's eyes never leaving Adriana.

"Well, son," John Cooper muttered, "this is what we came for. With any luck, we'll all leave tomorrow for the United States and the Double H Ranch."

Padre Rancorda turned to John Cooper. "It's time we went to the prison, Señor Baines. Padre Diaz knows exactly what I am going to do."

"Padre Rancorda has made his decision," the young priest said, "and I will pray for the success of it."

Adriana hugged Dorotéa and whispered, "Tell our *padre* that I am longing to see him."

"Of course I'll do that, *querida.*"

John Cooper went to the carriage and told Gil to ready himself for the moment when they would bring Raoul Maldones back. The coachman harnessed the horses while Padre Rancorda, Padre Diaz, Dorotéa, and John Cooper moved stealthily into the still night, making their way to the *calabozo.*

At the gate, a bearded sergeant recognized Padre Rancorda and Padre Diaz. He saw the other two figures dressed in clerical robes, their heads lowered, but he was not suspicious. He gruffly bade them go forward into the office of the *comandante,* who would give them a pass to see the prisoner.

"Is it Maldones whose soul you're trying to save, *padre?*" the *comandante* demanded. Then, with a sarcastic laugh, he added, "You'd best give him all the help you can. The order is the firing squad at dawn tomorrow in the courtyard."

"My son," Padre Rancorda gently responded, "every man, even the worst murderer in creation, deserves the chance to make atonement to his God. You will not deny this poor soul that."

"Not I, *mi padre,* I'm a good *católico.* You can only have half an hour with him," the *comandante* remonstrated, making the sign of the cross. "Now give me your blessing before you give it to the *traidor.*"

"Willingly, my son." Padre Rancorda made the sign of the cross.

Then the small group left the *comandante*'s office, Padre Diaz fingering his rosary and praying. They passed several cells, and Dorotéa shuddered when she looked through the bars and saw emaciated men, dirty, unshaven, lying on straw pallets, hardly moving. In one cell, there was an old man, nearly bald, with a long white beard, whose mind had given way. He uttered peals of cackling laughter, then brandished his fists and hammered them against the iron bars of his cell.

At the very last cell to the right, Padre Rancorda paused, and a guard who had followed the four down the row of cells came forward with a surly expression on his face, jangling a bunch of keys. "Half an hour now, Father," he said. "I'll be back to take you out of here." He stood back as the four entered Raoul Maldones's dungeon cell, and then, with a mocking laugh, walked slowly down the hall.

Raoul Maldones had been sitting on his rough, lumpy cot, his face buried in his hands, utterly despondent. He had been told of his sentence and had hardly eaten what would be his last meal.

"My son, we have come to hear your confession," Padre Rancorda softly murmured.

Dorotéa tried to control the sudden impulse to burst into tears. When her father raised his head, his face was abject, contorted with anguish, and his beard was unkempt and his eyes bloodshot. John Cooper squeezed her hand to give her courage, but he, too, was moved by the sight of his father-in-law, a broken man, awaiting death.

"Yes. They have told me. In the morning. *Padre*, I want to pray, I want to—" He glanced up and was startled by the sight of four in the black habits of priests and nun. Dorotéa drew aside her hood. "Oh, *Dios!*" Raoul gasped, his eyes glazed and wide as they stared at his daughter's lovely face.

"Hush, my son!" Padre Rancorda bent to the weakened *hacendado*. "Yes, it's your Dorotéa and your son-in-law. They have come to rescue you. I am going to take off my priest's garb, and you, Señor Maldones, will put it on. Then you and the others will leave, and I shall take your place."

"Am I dreaming? Is it you, *mi* Dorotéa?" Raoul

whispered in a trembling voice. He turned to look with tear-filled eyes at John Cooper, who bent toward him and whispered, "Yes, it's Dorotéa and John Cooper, Raoul. Do what Padre Rancorda says, and please be quick!"

"It is like a dream! I've been trying to get myself ready for—for—tomorrow. And now this! I have prayed, but I did not know whether the message got to you, John Cooper."

"Keep watch, my son," Padre Rancorda whispered to John Cooper. "Let us know if you hear footsteps. Hurry, Señor Maldones; you must put on my priest's robe. I must wear your clothes." Padre Rancorda chuckled. "I fear that my girth is more than yours."

"I shall never forget what you have done for me, Padre Rancorda." Raoul's voice had now become stronger as hope rose in him. He undressed swiftly, and the old priest handed over his robe and sandals, then moved over to the cot and began to tug on the prisoner's clothes, in his turn.

"But my father's beard!" Dorotéa groaned. "It will be seen."

"Wait!" John Cooper whispered. He had brought with him his Spanish dagger, hidden its sheath in the wide sleeve of his hooded cloak, and now drew it out, free of the sheath. "I do not mean to hurt you, but I must pull your beard taut, to cut it as close as I can to your chin."

"I can stand a little pain." Raoul closed his eyes and stood erect, arms at his sides, as John Cooper carefully slashed at the beard. The *hacendado* winced but did not move, and at last it was over.

"There. That'll do," John Cooper breathed. He tossed the handful of beard under the cot. Dorotéa was listening intently for approaching footsteps. "Do you hear anything, *mi corazón?*" he asked.

She shook her head, her eyes wide and brimming with tears. Meanwhile, Padre Rancorda had, with a great effort, managed to draw on the torn shirt and the trousers, until they were strained to the utmost and threatened to burst.

After the priest had finished exchanging clothes, John Cooper whispered, "Padre Rancorda, I plan to tie your wrists and ankles with leather thongs that I brought. When the guards discover what has happened, you can say that you were overpowered and forced to give up your clothing."

"As you like, my son."

John Cooper told Padre Rancorda to put his hands behind his back, then bound his wrists and ankles as well, whereupon the priest sat on the cot with his back to the wall, hiding his hands and his feet.

Padre Rancorda then said, "Now, Padre Diaz, when you hear the guard's footsteps, give me absolution as if I were Raoul Maldones. And then you, Señor Maldones, let Padre Diaz speak, for I fear that your voice would give your identity away to the guard."

"I hear footsteps!" Dorotéa hissed, putting a finger to her lips.

"Padre Rancorda, let me put this gag on you," John Cooper suddenly spoke up. "Then they won't wonder why you didn't cry out." The priest nodded, and John Cooper gagged him, telling him to keep his head down.

Now the young priest chanted the ritual of absolution after confession, concluding with the words, "You have been forgiven your sins, thanks to Him Who died upon the cross to save all mankind. I will pray for you tomorrow, my son."

The key turned in the lock, and the guard entered. "Time's up. I'm to take you out right away. Well now, *traidor*," he called out to the figure on the cot, whose gag and bonds he didn't see, "I hope it's made you feel a little better so we won't have to drag you out there tomorrow morning. All right, then, *padres*, come out with me!"

Raoul took his place behind Padre Diaz, with John Cooper behind him and Dorotéa just behind her husband. John Cooper was ready at a second's notice to support the weakened Raoul if he should stumble. Hearts pounding, they followed the guard down the long hall, past the *comandante*'s office, and into the street. The first step of their risky undertaking had been successfully accomplished, but there were many more steps before Dorotéa's father could enjoy his freedom.

John Cooper whispered to his father-in-law, "Raoul, keep your head down, and walk slowly. There's a guard at the corner, and if we get past him, we can go back to the church to get Adriana and Andrew, then get the others at the house. Then Gil will drive the carriage to the sailboat!"

"Comprendo, mi yerno," Raoul Maldones whispered back.

The guard at the corner of the building greeted Padre Diaz, "A good night to you, *mi padre*. The heat is stifling; let's hope *el Señor Dios* sends us some cool rain."

"It is truly to be wished. And a good night to you, also, *mi hijo,*" the priest answered.

John Cooper covertly glanced back into the huge open square of the port, and far beyond he saw the tiny pinpoints of light that came from the *Bedford Maid.*

Once out of sight of the guard, they walked to the church. John Cooper saw that Gil sat in the driver's seat of the carriage, holding the reins, ready to be off when ordered. "Go ahead and get Adriana and Andrew, Padre Diaz. May God bless you for what you've done," he said.

"My son, I wrestled with my conscience, but I could not live knowing that an innocent man had gone to his death without my trying to help him. I will take penances for my lawlessness and hope that our dear Lord will forgive me," Padre Diaz solemnly responded. He turned to them now, made the sign of the cross over their heads, and said finally, "They will question me for my role in this, that I know, and I will have to say I was coerced at knife point. But I swear that I shall not betray you."

"I could ask no more than that, *mi padre*," John Cooper said as he held out his hand.

The priest grasped it, then went into the rectory, saying as he opened the door, "I will send the young ones out to you."

The door closed behind the priest, and the tall Texan turned to his father-in-law. He now explained how Señora Josefa and the younger girls were on board the *Bedford Maid*, headed for the United States. John Cooper added, "You should know something about your daughter Adriana before she comes out. To keep your *estancia* in the family, she bravely agreed to marry Rodrigo Baltenar on the condition that if anything should happen to him, your estates would revert to her. Now Baltenar is dead—by Porfirio Ramos's hand—and Ramos himself is dead. Señor Duvaldo sent his two sons to your *estancia* to administer it until something can be done with the property that will benefit you and your daughters."

"So many dear friends and relatives! I am truly a lucky man, *mi yerno*." Raoul's voice throbbed with emotion.

Adriana and Andrew hurried out of the rectory. *"Mi padre, mi padre!"* Adriana burst into tears as she embraced her father. "You're safe, I was so afraid—"

"There's no time for reunions, I'm afraid," John Cooper said as he again glanced around with an uneasy look. He shepherded them to the carriage and called out, "To the house!" and gave Gil directions.

"At once, Señor Baines!"

Once inside the carriage, Adriana sat beside her father and put her arms around his neck, tears running down her cheeks. He patted her head and wonderingly said to John Cooper, "It is amazing how mature Adriana has become!"

"My son is smitten with her," John Cooper chuckled,

"and I thoroughly approve. I could ask nothing better than that there be another match between our families."

"Pa, oh, gosh!" Andrew blurted, turning red in the face.

But Raoul Maldones laughed and reached out to grip Andrew's wrist as he said, "I liked you from the first day I met you. You will make Adriana a good husband. And I pray I live to see our families grow and leave descendants who will carry on in honor the names of Maldones and of Baines."

Now it was Adriana's turn to blush at the reference to children, and she gave Andrew a shy yet passionate look that made his pulse race.

As the carriage headed for the house, both Jaime and Bartoloméo came rushing down the street, gesturing frantically. John Cooper leaned out the window of the carriage. "What's the matter, *hombres?*"

"*Patrón,* Bartoloméo was watching outside in the street while I waited here on the lookout for the carriage," Jaime hastily explained. "Bartoloméo said that soldiers came pouring out from the *calabozo,* calling 'The *traidor* has escaped! Close the port!' *Patrón,* we must get to that fisherman's boat and across the river! Quickly!"

"Get in!" John Cooper threw open the door, and the two *vaqueros* climbed inside. Then Gil quickly drove the carriage the rest of the way to the house, where Felipe and Oudobras emerged, threw sacks containing weapons and supplies in the storage compartment, and climbed onto the carriage roof. Then John Cooper called to Gil, "Go to the outskirts of the city, about half a mile southward. Then head for the bank of the river. Quickly, now!"

"*¡Comprendo, comprendo!*" Gil called, as he whipped at the horses. The carriage clattered down the street, heading away from the city square that was suddenly teeming with soldiers and guards.

Inside the carriage, Raoul asked, "Señora Josefa and the girls will be all right?"

"Indeed they will, Raoul," John Cooper quickly answered. "Your *dueña* used Mendoza as her last name as a precaution. She and the girls will not be suspected of any connection with you. No, the *Bedford Maid* will lift anchor and proceed tomorrow."

"I cannot believe all that you have done in so short a time, *mi yerno,*" Raoul said. Then, overcome by the stress of the last few weeks, he covered his face with his hands and silently wept while Adriana and Dorotéa, on either side of their father, did their best to comfort him.

Gil called from the driver's seat, "Señor Baines, we're coming to the riverbank."

"Good!" Leaning out the carriage window, John Cooper called up, "Oudobras, you'll go on ahead and find your fisherman. We'll all get out of the carriage but stay in the shadows in case any soldiers come out as far as this from the port itself."

The coachman drew the carriage to a halt. John Cooper opened the door and leaped down, helped out Dorotéa, her father, and Adriana, while Andrew and the two *vaqueros* got out from the other side and Felipe and Oudobras jumped down, retrieving the bags of weapons and supplies from the storage compartment. John Cooper and his wife threw off their clerical disguises, then the Texan called to Gil, "And now, *mi amigo,* go back to your master and tell him that we'll communicate with him when we've safely returned to los Estados Unidos!"

"¡Vaya con Dios!" Gil waved his hand in farewell, started up the horses at a gallop, and disappeared in the night.

Thirty

John Cooper turned to watch the carriage disappear in the distance, swallowed up by the murky night, for there was only a sickly moon casting eerie reflections on the muddy water of the wide La Plata River and on the coarse loam of the bank. It was the impoverished side of the city, and a few dark hovels stood off to one side. The die was cast. From now on the success of their venture would depend entirely upon his resourcefulness and that of his companions. What lay ahead in Uruguay, he could not tell. But imprisonment and death awaited them in Buenos Aires, and to go back to Heitor Duvaldo's villa would be foolhardy.

Oudobras had gone ahead, turning back to beckon to them to follow. One by one, they hastened down the uneven and high-perched bank of the La Plata River, where a dinghy with oars and a sail in the middle floated in a cove. The dinghy had been secured by a stout hemp rope tied to a metal ring at the prow and the other end to a wooden piling. There was little movement in the shallow water, but once they had put distance between themselves and the bank, the current would flow swiftly toward the ocean—in the opposite direction from their immediate destination, Colonia. Thus the need for oars and a sail.

An old man, wizened and emaciated, his skin as brown as that of an *indio*, waited for them beside his boat, lifting his hand to Oudobras and calling out in a soft gutteral voice, "*¡Hola, mi compañero!* I am here, as promised!"

"*Gracias,* Batuque," Oudobras told him. "There are nine of us, Batuque. Will your boat hold us all?"

"*Pero sí, mi compañero.* I have gone out many times, as far as the ocean itself in this boat and come back with heavy catches of tuna. Oh, yes, you will be safe in it."

John Cooper warmed to the old man and took hold of his hand, lifting him onto the bank. "God bless you, Batuque. Now it may be we'll be better off buying the boat from you. That way when we get to our destination, we can just let it drift out to sea, never to be implicated with you." He reached into his leather purse for a handful of *pesos,* which they had obtained by selling their horses back in the city. "Here are twenty *pesos,* in addition to the five Oudobras already gave you. They should be enough to buy you a fine new boat." He now turned to his companions. "Jaime, Bartoloméo, Felipe, Oudobras, you four will take the first turn at rowing. Andrew, you and I will sit in the stern with Dorotéa. Raoul, you and Adriana will be in the prow. Oarsmen, get in first and steady the boat. I'll get in last and cast off."

The old man waved to them from high on the bank, then disappeared into the night. The sacks containing their weapons and supplies were handed on board; then everyone climbed into the dinghy, with the exception of John Cooper, who went to one of the nearby huts and asked a kindly peasant to fill his leather flasks with water from a little well. Then the Texan returned to the dinghy, untied the rope from the piling, and carefully stepped into the boat as it began to drift toward the east and the open water.

Felipe, Oudobras, Jaime, and Bartoloméo dipped their oars into the murky water and began the energetic work of turning the dinghy toward the northeast and to Uruguay—to escape and ultimate freedom!

The dinghy was well built and heavy, but it responded well as Jaime and Bartoloméo, Felipe and Oudobras dipped their oars and propelled the craft toward Colonia.

"Old Batuque told me that there are whirlpools in the middle of the river," the former *capataz* volunteered. "We must be careful."

"After what I have endured in that prison cell, Oudobras," his former *patrón* spoke up, "I shall be cheerful over the worst hardships. At least," he added, chuckling softly, "if we should be overtaken by a whirlpool, I would have a chance to live with my own strength and prayers. In the *calabozo*, all I could expect was death." He sighed and turned to stare at John Cooper, who now had his arm around Dorotéa as they huddled together. *"Mi yerno,* I have never been more happy. To see you, Dorotéa, held by your husband, so trustingly resting against his heart, and knowing that you bear his child within you— this is why my life has been spared, and I pledge to make something of it."

"You can be of great help to me on the Double H Ranch, Raoul," John Cooper earnestly responded. "Your knowledge of ranching is invaluable, and our *vaqueros* and *trabajadores* can learn much from you. You'll be very welcome."

"I will do whatever I can to be of use, *mi yerno*. And now, if you will excuse me, I will try to get a little sleep. It has been—" Raoul chuckled—"a somewhat exhausting day."

By dawn, they had come close to one of the small whirlpools, and with all their strength the four oarsmen directed the dinghy out of danger. At this point, John

Cooper and Andrew, who had dozed a few hours, insisted on replacing two of the men. The two *vaqueros* argued with the two *gauchos* to convince the latter that it was really the *gauchos,* and not the *vaqueros,* who were showing the first signs of fatigue. The good-natured bantering made everyone laugh, and it was decided that, to be fair, one *vaquero* and one *gaucho* should rest.

Even Raoul Maldones was inclined to make a joke, indicating that his spirits had soared. "You cut my beard very close to the skin, *mi yerno,*" he chuckled as he felt his chin. "It will take me quite some time to grow it back. I must have looked like the hermit who lived in a cave not far from my villa."

"If it were possible, do you think you might go back to regain your estate, Raoul?" John Cooper asked.

"Knowing the political situation in my country, it will be a long time before I could even think of going back. There will be a growing struggle between the *porteños* and the *hacendados* of the *pampas.* No, *mi yerno,* I can content myself knowing that my *estancia* could not be in better hands than in those of Heitor Duvaldo's two fine sons and the *gauchos* who will come to their side."

John Cooper and Andrew toiled at the oars from dawn onwards. Jaime and Oudobras took their *siesta* while the two *gringos* replaced them. Felipe had also put down his oar and was sparingly doling out food from a sack he had brought. Then he passed around a leather flask of water, warning all to be content with a swallow or two since it must last until they reached shore. And still, even in the bright sunlight, they could not see the opposite bank.

There was scarcely any protection from the sun, although John Cooper discovered a tarpaulin in the bottom of the dinghy toward the stern and told Adriana to drape it over her father so that he would not be badly burned.

Adriana lay with her head pillowed against her father's chest while he supported her shoulders with his left arm

and gazed tenderly down at her. He glanced back at Dorotéa
and smiled, and she blew him a kiss. They were in a
happy mood. By noon, Felipe and Bartoloméo slept while
Oudobras and Jaime returned to the oars. Even though
Raoul several times offered to do his share, his proposal
was vetoed by all the others.

John Cooper looked at the crude map and sighed.
"From what I can tell here, I'd say we probably won't
reach Colonia for another few hours."

"I think you are right, *Halcón*." Felipe had wakened
from his drowsing and sat up alertly. Then he suddenly
cried out and pointed directly north. "*¡Cuidado, el
remolino!*"

Roused by this cry, Bartoloméo wakened, too, and
uttered a cry of terror. Two hundred feet to their right
swirled whitecaps from a whirlpool with a narrow but
powerful vortex.

"Row with all your might!" John Cooper ordered,
and dipped his own oar deep, pulling with all his strength
to draw the dinghy away from the dangerous current. The
grasp of the whirlpool became stronger, the water moving
swiftly toward its dangerous center. If the dinghy fell
victim to its power, surely they would all drown. There
was no hope of swimming to shore.

The four oarsmen strained with all their might, but
the dinghy seemed to make no progress for a moment, and
then suddenly it lurched slightly forward. John Cooper did
not stop, though he was dripping with sweat, until Oudobras
called out, "We're safe now, praise be to *el Señor Dios!*"

Andrew showed signs of exhaustion, so Felipe and
Bartoloméo resumed the oars with John Cooper and Andrew
lying back to rest.

They had seen no other ships or boats on the river,
and now they could believe that Raoul's escape had been
realized. Yet there remained the grave problem of traveling overland a hundred and eighty miles, from Colonia to

Maldonado, where they hoped to find a ship that would take them to the United States.

It was midafternoon when they saw the pleasant beach of Colonia. With new vigor the oarsmen headed the dinghy toward a narrow cove where they could wade onto the beach. Setting in motion the next part of their plan, they allowed the small sailboat to drift away, to move slowly eastward, ultimately to be lost in the vast Atlantic.

Oudobras sighed and shook his head. "It served us well, that little boat! And now, *Halcón,* we must find my cousin. That is our only hope of getting horses, since we have so little *dinero.* That reminds me—if we find a ship at Maldonado, how can we pay for your passage?"

John Cooper shrugged and chuckled. "So far, we've had the best of luck, and I think our prayers have helped a lot. My mother used to tell me to put my faith in the Lord and that He would provide. And I think that's as good an answer as any, *mi compañero!"*

As they waded to the shore, weary and thirsty—for by now the leather flasks of water had been emptied—they were conscious of the intense heat. Ahead of them lay miles of the hilly meadows of Uruguay, with a strand of sandy beaches along the coast. It was a small country first discovered by the Spanish explorer Juan Diaz de Solís in the year of 1516, but he and his band of *conquistadores* were almost instantly attacked after their landing and all put to death by the fierce Charrúa *indios.*

"Let's hope we can find your cousin, Oudobras," John Cooper declared. "You've been here before?"

"Sí, Halcón. My cousin lives not far from here. He is *capataz* for his *patrón,* just as I was for Señor Raoul. I'm certain we can find him."

"Let us hope it is done swiftly, Oudobras. All of us could use some food, sleep, and a bath."

"But *I'm* fine, Pa, honest I am!" Andrew Baines hastened to reassure his father.

John Cooper surveyed his disheveled son. There were dark rings under his eyes. He nodded grimly, then said to Oudobras, "I hope your cousin will be willing to spare horses for all of us," the Texan declared. "Even though I don't have the money to pay for them."

They began to walk. Their limbs were numbed and cramped, but they knew that the exercise would restore the circulation. John Cooper put his arm around Dorotéa's waist, and the two of them moved forward, and Andrew emulated his father by escorting Adriana. Raoul, though still a little weak, kept up with Oudobras while Felipe flanked him on the other side. Jaime and Bartoloméo, bringing up the rear and looking around warily, wanted to take two of the pistols from the sack of weapons.

Oudobras, however, called back, "They are friendly in Colonia, *vaqueros*. Do not show your weapons. If the villagers nod to you, nod back to show that you are *amigos*."

"It occurs to me," John Cooper thoughtfully mused, "that once we get to Maldonado, we can leave our horses at the port and Oudobras can bring them back to his cousin. In that way, we'll only be borrowing them."

"I am sure my cousin will agree, *Halcón*, but first we must find him. This way," Oudobras gestured, and they passed through a little village with many huts.

Then they came to a rolling, grassy plain, with barns and a few houses, the estate of the *hacendado* for whom Oudobras's cousin worked. They came into the countryside, past a tall eucalyptus tree in which a pair of green parakeets was nesting. A covey of partridges crossed in front of the group, and far beyond, there was what looked like a small ostrich racing across the field. "That is a *nandú*, perhaps a cousin to the *rhea*," Oudobras explained. "And here you will find many *apearás*, which are like the *capybara* of the *pampas*." He turned and pointed. "Look, *Halcón!*" as a small armadillo scurried into a thick flowery bush well beyond the road. "They call this the *cachicamo*. There is much to hunt here."

John Cooper enjoyed the countryside, which seemed more verdant here. Doubtless his sojourn in Buenos Aires had made him forget the wild beauty of the countryside and its junglelike fertility.

Suddenly, Oudobras saw a rider on horseback and cried out, *"¡Hola! ¡Aquí, hombre!"* and then, excitedly turning to John Cooper, he said, grinning, "That is my cousin, Manco Corinchaca!"

The distant rider galloped his horse toward them, and John Cooper saw a stocky, genial-faced man in his midforties, wearing a wide-brimmed hat, a poncho, wide *bombachas*—pantaloon-type trousers gathered at the ankles— and shining leather boots, with his *facón* thrust through his belt and his spurs jangling. He reined in his pinto before Oudobras and called out in a deep voice, *"¿Hombre, qué pasa?* I did not expect you here in my country."

"I did not expect to be here, Manco. This is my *patrón,* Señor Raoul Maldones, for whom I have the greatest respect. He believes in the freedom of those who ride the *pampas* and herd the *ganado*."

"Then he is my friend, too, my cousin," Manco laughingly declared. He tipped his wide-brimmed hat to Raoul, eyeing with some curiosity the two young women. "And who are your other friends?"

"This man here," Oudobras said, pointing to John Cooper, "is the *yerno* of my *patrón,* and this *mujer linda"* —here he gestured toward Dorotéa—"is his *esposa, comprendes?* This is her *hermana,* Adriana, and this is my *patrón's hijo,* Andrew, or Andy. And these two men" —now Oudobras pointed to Jaime and Bartoloméo—"are *gran vaqueros* who have come all the way from *Norte America* to help take the señor Maldones out of the *calabozo,* and this"—pointing to Felipe—"is a noble *gaucho* like myself. And now we must talk business, Manco."

"Ask what you wish of me. We have the same blood. I will help all I can."

"We need horses for all these people, Manco. We must reach Maldonado before any *soldados* find us."

The older *gaucho* tilted back his head and laughed, hugely amused. Finally, he said, "Do not concern yourselves with *soldados*. All you need fear are the *indios*, the Charrúa. I can get you nine horses, if that is what you want."

"We have only a little money to pay you for them, Manco," Oudobras declared in an apologetic tone.

His older cousin shrugged. "Am I ever to get the horses back?"

"Of course, and I will bring them back to you from Maldonado," Oudobras said.

"I shall give you the best horses I can spare, my cousin. As it happens, my *patrón* is not here, so he will not miss them. And besides, we have more than we need. But I would advise you that I cannot give you saddles because there are not that many to go around for all our *gauchos*."

Adriana drew herself up. "I can ride bareback. It is no problem whatsoever," she announced to all.

Manco led the way to a large rectangular wooden barn with open doors. John Cooper could see many stalls for horses. At first glance, these mounts seemed small yet wiry, and most of them were pintos, spotted, with strong withers and hocks. Manco gestured at the stalls. "Help yourselves. They're all good. Not easily tired, get along on very little to eat and drink. In some ways, I think they are as durable as llamas."

"And now how many *pesos* do we owe you, *mi primo?*" Oudobras asked as he reached for the money that John Cooper had just given him. "Remember, I will return them from Maldonado. Give me a week to reach there and a week to return. And also, if you could spare a little dried beef, some water, and cornmeal to tide us over until we can find another village, we will try to pay you what we can for that, too.''

"But I will not take any money, not for the food or for borrowing the horses. My *patrón* will not even know the horses have been taken, and he certainly does not need *dinero*.'' He strode off toward the sprawling house, which in some ways resembled that of Heitor Duvaldo, while John Cooper and the others selected horses. They took mares for Adriana and Dorotéa, geldings for the men.

Manco returned with three sacks of provisions, also having filled the leather flasks with water. "If you head northeast, you should come to another village before nightfall, although it is not far from a camp of the Charrúa.''

"I thought they were farther inland," John Cooper said, puzzled.

"There are several tribes—a few are reasonably friendly—some even come to Uruguay from Argentina in order to barter," Manco explained. "But there are others who like neither *gringos* nor *gauchos*. These tribes move around, hunting and bartering, so be careful." He nodded to Oudobras. "*Vaya con Dios, mi primo,* and to all of you, good fortune!"

Thirty-one

❖━━━━━━━━━━━━━━━━━━━━━━━━━━━❖

They rode until nearly sunset, stopping a few times for Dorotéa and Adriana to rest and freshen themselves. At dusk they made a little camp where they ate part of their provisions. The beef was well dried and salted, and there were handfuls of raisins and even a few corncakes that Manco had thoughtfully provided. The water satisfied their thirst, and the intense heat lessened in the latter part of the day. There was now a cooling breeze from the not-too-distant river.

The scenery was verdant, and the soft, rolling hills created a restful panorama.

"We might well sleep here for the night," John Cooper suggested.

Oudobras and Felipe eyed each other, then shrugged. The former said, "I would suggest pushing on. Not far from here there may be Charrúa."

He had hardly finished speaking when suddenly there was the sound of footsteps, and a dozen painted *indios* surrounded them. They carried lances, bows, and arrows, and one scowling man carried an old Spanish musket.

Each member of the party was armed now with the weapons they had brought in the sack, but when Jaime and

Bartoloméo raised their rifles, John Cooper gestured at them to put the guns down. Then he rose slowly, his palms extended upward on either side of him, the sign of peace. Suddenly he uttered a cry of recognition: The man with the musket was none other than Micidata, the Charrúa whom the Texan had met during his first visit to Argentina. *"Soy* John Cooper Baines, *americano,* Micidata! You know me from that time when Potormingay brought me to you, after your braves had attacked the *estancia.* And here," he said, pointing to Dorotéa, "is the *mujer* I wed that day of the attack. We come in peace."

The suspicious look on the Charrúa leader's face vanished, and he grinned, nodding energetically; then he spoke a language that was part Spanish, part Portuguese, and the rest Charrúa dialect. John Cooper could make out only a few words. But he could recognize one phrase: "Yes, you are friend to Charrúa."

John Cooper attempted to communicate with Micidata by gesturing and speaking slowly in Spanish. "We go to Maldonado, to take an American ship back to our country."

Micidata listened intently to the tall Texan's words, paid careful attention to the gestures, and then grinned again and nodded. "Yes, I know you. You go in peace. It is good. Other Charrúa are farther down and near this coast," Micidata informed him. "And one of them is the *traidor,* Potormingay. Him, I sent from our tribe. He has sworn with others who do not trust any *gringo.* Beware! Potormingay hates all *gringos.* I give you something you will show if they capture you. Perhaps it will help you. I tell you this with a straight tongue."

With this, he gestured to one of the warriors, who untied from his belt a sack made of the skin of a puma, with drawstrings made from the sinews of an antelope. Micidata took the sack, drew open the drawstrings, and, grinning cruelly, lifted out a skull. John Cooper tried to keep his face impassive. But Micidata dropped the skull back into the sack and then lifted out an amulet. It was crudely shaped, like a rough cameo, and Dorotéa gasped, for the central stone was a giant emerald. It was scarcely polished, yet its magnificent green luster caught the glint of the campfire. Its setting was a hollowed nest made of tiny dried bones of birds, cemented by a powerful gumlike substance tapped from a tree in the forests near the jungle. There was a thong, thin but strong, made of the sinews of the small deer, which threaded through the sides of this amulet so it could be worn about the neck. Micidata lifted it up, turned it, grinning and nodding as he saw the firelight play upon the green emerald, and then put it around John Cooper's neck. "It is the amulet of the sun god. It should protect you, *gringo valeroso*, even from the worst of the Charrúa, who hunt for heads."

"It is a great gift, and it is too much to give me," John Cooper said as he touched the green stone with his hand and glanced wonderingly at Dorotéa.

"You promised when first we met to give me a gift of cattle, one for each warrior I had lost in a raid. That you did for me, and this I do for you. This is a sacred stone, and I know where there are others. I have one even larger, so that when I go among the other tribes, they will know that I am *jefe* and that I come as one of them, that the gods protect me with the magic of the stone and the light upon it," Micidata said in his deep, guttural voice.

"We had thought of staying here for the night and going on our journey to Maldonado when the sun rises in the sky," John Cooper said slowly.

"*Sí*, it is safe here. In the morning, you go quickly. My braves and I must be on our way or we would go with you. I do not know if Potormingay and the other tribe are near. Beware of him." With this, he made a gesture to his fellows, and they moved off into the darkness.

The tall Texan turned to Dorotéa. "It will be safe to sleep now, and we can all do with a rest."

*   *   *

At dawn the next morning, they divided up what food was left and drank the rest of the water, then mounted their horses and rode on. Jaime and Bartoloméo were sent ahead to scout for the village that Manco had told them about. They rode back to say that they had found it, but that there was only a handful of *mestizos* there, none too friendly, and the *jefe* said that he would sell them water and food if they could pay in guns, not *dinero*.

"I don't like the idea of trading our weapons. We have a lot of territory yet to cover, and we might need every gun we have." John Cooper disconsolately shook his head. "Jaime and Bartoloméo, you have your rifles. Of course, I've got 'Long Girl,' but nothing in the world would make me trade or sell her. We have some pistols and I guess an extra rifle or two. We can't go without food and water in the hope that maybe a few hours away from that village, we'll find one that will be more hospitable. Against my better judgment we'll have to barter with them."

John Cooper rode ahead with the two *vaqueros* while the others took a more leisurely pace behind him, and when he entered the small village, the elderly *jefe mestizo* of this tiny hamlet haggled long and loudly in a broken Spanish-and-Indian dialect that John Cooper could hardly understand, until at last, after about an hour, the *jefe* grudgingly agreed to trade some cornmeal, a few corncakes, and a few strips of dried meat for a brace of pistols. The old man refused the few *pesos* that the Texan repeatedly offered as payment.

There was a well nearby, and John Cooper bade the *vaqueros* fill the leather flasks. When the old *mestizo* glowered at them and began to complain, John Cooper took the Spanish dagger from around his neck in its sheath, and handed it to the *mestizo*, saying, "I will give you this for the water. But, if you came to my country, I would

charge you nothing for water, because it is the gift of God
to all men.''

This speech seemed to shame the *jefe*. Two of the
younger men had come out and were listening and gravely
nodded when they understood John Cooper's words, and
so at last the *jefe* curtly declared, ''Take it then. Keep your
dagger. But leave here now. I do not like *gringos* any
more than I do *soldados*.''

Three days later, they rode into the little town of
Canelones, having traversed some ninety miles. Manco's
horses had boundless energy, it seemed, and they grazed
contentedly on the rich grass along their path. Between
Canelones and Maldonado, there were another ninety miles,
as John Cooper estimated from the rough map. Bartoloméo
had bartered his brace of pistols for food in two little
villages some eighteen hours earlier. The villagers in those
hamlets were much more generous than the first man had
been, and thus their food lasted through this fourth morning.

They found a small tributary of a river where John
Cooper and his party drank their fill and filled their canteens for the days ahead.

The day after leaving Canelones, the weather turned
scorchingly hot, and they slowed the horses and made
many stops along the way. In the evening they made camp
near a deserted village, where jungle foliage had crept in at
the outskirts. John Cooper saw a wild deer burst out of a
thicket of colorful wild flowers. He quickly drew out
''Long Girl'' and fired, bringing down the deer. Felipe
galloped up to the fallen animal and, dismounting, began
at once to skin it and to cut strips of meat. At the last village,
he had traded his second *facón* for a bag of salt, so that he
could cure any meat that fell to just such fortuitous hunting
as John Cooper's.

As night fell they could hear the chittering of birds
and monkeys, and the occasional, though distant, roars of a

jaguar. John Cooper primed "Long Girl" and bade Andrew see to his own Lancaster rifle.

"Those cats are swift, Andy," he told his son, "so you'd best stand your ground and be sure your first shot counts—a jaguar won't give you time to reload."

Just before they made camp on the fifth day after leaving Colonia, Andrew saw a small antelope and, swiftly drawing his Lancaster out of its saddle sheath and aiming it, pulled the trigger, stopping the antelope in midflight. His father applauded, as did the *gauchos*. As for Adriana, he read in her eyes an accolade that, if truth be known, was sweeter to him than his own father's praise.

Thus they had meat aplenty, and there was no further need to haggle with villagers along the way. This was most fortunate, for they had little left to trade. In all, they had six rifles and enough ammunition and powder, but only two pistols, which had been given to Dorotéa and Adriana so they could defend themselves.

John Cooper stood guard and bade the others to get what rest they could before continuing the journey. The night was sultry, and tiny gnats, attracted by the dying embers of the campfire, buzzed about. John Cooper put his hand to his throat, where the emerald amulet rested. The Spanish dagger in its sheath was hung around his neck also, and he lifted his Lancaster rifle, examining it to make certain that it was primed and loaded. Micidata's warning had been uppermost in his mind, and he thought about Potormingay and how the exiled Indian had joined a rival tribe that was known for its savagery against all strangers.

The Texan glanced down at Dorotéa, who lay with her head pillowed in her arms, already fast asleep. He moved on a few paces, then looked down at Andrew and Adriana, who were not far from each other.

John Cooper suddenly heard the squeal of a peccary and its rush into a thicket of bushes. Then there were the hoot of an owl and the chattering of monkeys in the distant trees. At the sound of footsteps behind him, John Cooper whirled, to find a hideously grinning Charrúa, painted with red and yellow, facing him. Two others tore his rifle from his hands. One of them struck him a glancing blow on the back of the head with a club. John Cooper cried out, trying to wake the others, but blackness claimed him.

He regained consciousness slowly and found himself bound against an *ombú* tree with his wrists painfully tied behind his back against the harsh wood. A fire had been lighted, and there were dancing flames, and he saw a dozen Charrúa Indians brandishing their lances, clubs, and long knives. All of them were painted in red and yellow, the colors of war. Slowly, he turned his head, wincing from the throbbing pain that shot through him. As his head pressed against the hard wood, he could feel the lump from the blow that had knocked him unconscious. His two *vaqueros,* plus Felipe, Oudobras, and Raoul were each tied to a smaller tree in a semicircle, and all of them faced the flickering fire.

His eyes widened with horror as he recognized a kind of ritualistic altar, and then saw Adriana and Dorotéa kneeling, a Charrúa behind each, hands gripping each captive's shoulders, and each with her own wrists tied behind her back. Dorotéa's riding dress had been brutally ripped to the waist, while Adriana's *camisa* had been torn off entirely and her riding breeches tattered so that he could see her white muslin drawers through the rents. The stone slab altar was set upon a pile of small flat stones, and on the stone slab itself lay a knife larger than Jim Bowie's famous weapon. This was a sacrificial knife, and John Cooper's gorge rose at the realization that his own beautiful wife and her younger sister were to become victims on that Charrúa altar.

He heard a whisper just behind him. Andrew, bound to a small tree just at his left and a little behind him, said, "Oh, Christ, Pa, look what they've done! We couldn't fight—they took us by surprise. I tried to get my rifle, but they clubbed me, too!''

"Keep your voice down, Andy. We'll see if the amulet Micidata gave me does any good. And I've still got my Spanish knife around my neck. Wait a minute! I recognize that Indian! It's Potormingay!''

The renegade who had been banished from Micidata's tribe stepped forward and began to harangue his fellows. John Cooper could not understand all of the dialect, but there were enough Spanish words to give him a clue to what was intended. The Charrúa intended to sacrifice these two young women to their mighty sun god, then kill the male captives and use their skulls as drinking cups.

Potormingay made a sign, and one of the Indians who wore a ceremonial mask—made of bark and daubed with cabalistic signs of grinning skulls and spears and arrows— and with feathers stuck through his hair, came forward and bent to Adriana. He plunged his fingers into her thick tresses and dragged her to her feet. Adriana cried out in pain and tried to twist away. But the man, evidently the shaman or witch doctor of this band of fierce Charrúa, forced her down, half-naked as she was, on her back upon the altar and twisted the fingers of both his hands into her luxuriant hair to hold her captive, while Potormingay lifted the knife toward the sky.

John Cooper called out in Spanish, "Is this how the noble Charrúa treat friends who have the sacred amulet of your sun god? Are you such fierce warriors you must kill women? I demand to speak! I demand to show you the amulet that shows that I come in peace!''

Potormingay turned, his eyes narrowing as he studied the tall Texan's face. He did not recognize John Cooper Texan, not with the closely trimmed little beard and the dyed hair.

"You lie when you say you have an amulet! I do not

believe you. The *mujeres* will be sacrificed to the sun god, as Itanzu, our medicine man, has decreed!"

"Tell your medicine man to open my shirt at the throat, and he will find the amulet," John Cooper ordered.

"When we will see that you speak with a forked tongue, you will die by fire." Potormingay hesitated a moment and then turned back to the masked Indian who held Adriana. He released her and came slowly toward John Cooper but barked out an order so that two other Indians forced Adriana to remain where she was by holding her at the thighs and the chest just above her heaving naked bosom.

Slowly, Itanzu walked up to John Cooper and then, with a mocking laugh, put his hand to the collar of the Texan's shirt and ripped it down. There was a simultaneous cry as the Charrúa braves, watching this intently, saw the green emerald glow and transmit the darting flames of their sacrificial fire. And to a man, they prostrated themselves, with a cry of awe.

Itanzu turned to Potormingay and said in his deep, guttural voice, "He speaks truth. We must let him go."

"But he would kill us all—"

Itanzu hesitated again, then scolded Potormingay. At last, with an angry mutter, Potormingay took the sacrificial knife and cut the bonds at John Cooper's wrists and, in turn, those of all the others.

"Itanzu says you are to go free. If I were the shaman I would kill you all," he angrily complained.

But Itanzu rebuked Potormingay in an angry tone, and the renegade, glowering at John Cooper, turned his back and walked back to the altar. Adriana had flung herself off the altar and stood with her arms crossed, hiding her nakedness, while Dorotéa still stared coldly and defiantly at the Indians.

John Cooper flexed his hands, trying to restore the circulation, for they had been bound tightly against the harsh wood of the *ombú* tree. And then suddenly, Potormingay shrieked with maddened rage, raised the sacrificial knife, and lunged at John Cooper.

There was just time for the tall Texan to leap to one side and, in the same movement, draw out the Spanish dagger from its sheath. The other Indians called out, excited by this fight to the death. Potormingay again lunged at John Cooper, crying out, "You have disgraced me, but you will die for it, *gringo* dog!"

Potormingay's narrowed eyes glittered. He panted hoarsely, cursing ferociously while he lunged and struck, leaping this way and that. Dorotéa bit her lip and prayed silently while Andrew clenched his fists, yearning to come to his father's aid but knowing that he must not.

Potormingay leaped backwards and plunged his left hand into the sacrificial fire, heedless of the agony, lifting a burning stick and flinging it in John Cooper's face.

The tall Texan had the presence of mind to ward off the blow with his right arm, and the flaming wood struck his arm, then dropped harmlessly to the ground. Potormingay unleashed an unearthly yell and leaped at his foe. John Cooper crouched, and Potormingay was thrown over his shoulder, the frustrated Charrúa stabbing vainly at the air.

John Cooper drew back, gripping the Spanish dagger, warily moving on the balls of his feet. Once again, Potormingay charged, slashing upwards, wanting to gut his *gringo* enemy. With a savage swipe, Potormingay made John Cooper jump back, but the latter lashed out with the slim, strong Spanish dagger. With a clash of metal, John Cooper forced Potormingay's weapon back, and then squatting again, he drove the Spanish dagger with all his strength into the pit of the Charrúa's belly and ripped upward.

Potormingay bellowed like an animal and stared down at his gushing wound. He lunged weakly at his *gringo* adversary and then toppled to the ground, rolled over, and

lay sprawled on his back, his sightless eyes staring up at
the moon that shone upon this savage scene.

John Cooper stood panting while the shaman, in his
hideous mask, stared silently at the *gringo* who could fight
as fiercely as any Charrúa. Then he said, staring at the
amulet and reaching out to touch it with a tentative finger,
"Go. You have won freedom for all of you."

"I thank the shaman of the Charrúa. I did not wish
this fight," John Cooper told him.

The masked shaman nodded, then turned and gestured
to the watching braves. With a piercing cry they ran off
now and deserted this place that was to have been a
sacrificial site. Only Potormingay's corpse attested to the
violence that had beset John Cooper and his party on their
way to safety.

Dorotéa, overwhelmed by terror, clung to her husband.
She trembled, stifling her sobs after what had appeared to
be imminent death by sacrifice to a pagan god.

Young Adriana put back on her tattered clothes as
best she could, turning away from Andrew, who, scarlet-
faced, averted his eyes, lest he embarrass her. But that
glimpse of her beautiful body, nubile and satiny, had
reinforced his desire, chaste and idealistic as it might be.

No one spoke, for their experience had been too
shattering. They lost no time in collecting their weapons
from where the Charrúa had dropped them. Then they
mounted their horses and rode off toward Maldonado. By
midafternoon of the next day, they found another little
village where the very sight of the amulet glistening on
John Cooper's chest secured them a gift of food and water
from a *jefe* who was half-Indian. He wished only to touch
the sacred amulet.

By nightfall of the third day, they rode their exhausted horses into the port of Maldonado. Rain had fallen
heavily most of the day, but it had been refreshing after
the intense summer heat.

On the outskirts of the little port, they saw a huge stable and a sprawling, rickety house built of clay and wood, from which there emerged an elderly, portly man dressed in *gaucho* costume. John Cooper hailed him and explained that they were friends of Manco, who came from the vicinity of Colonia.

The man chuckled and patted his belly, "I know him well, señor. If you are a friend of his, you are welcome."

"*Gracias*. We are seeking a ship to take us to los Estados Unidos. Can you help us find one?" John Cooper asked.

The old man nodded. "*Pero sí*. I have heard that a tall ship with sails will come here in two or three days. It is bound for Nueva Orleáns in los Estados Unidos. It has gone on to Buenos Aires to unload cargo, but it will return."

"It will do very nicely. *Muchas gracias*," the tall Texan thanked the portly *gaucho*. "We have come a long way. Can you give us shelter? Even if in a barn, we should be most grateful."

"*Seguramente, hombre*. You may come to the *hacienda* of my *patrón*, and your horses will be looked after by the other *gauchos* here. I, Roberto Durando, offer you this because you know Manco and because I can see that you are a good, honest man."

The next day, there was a sad farewell as Oudobras rounded up the horses and prepared to return them to his cousin, assisted in this by some of the other *gauchos* who worked for Roberto Durando's *patrón*. They would be paid with some of the remaining *pesos*.

"I am almost sorry I am not going off with you after all," Oudobras told John Cooper and the others. "You are like family to me. But as I told you before, this is my home. This is the land I love."

"We will miss you, Oudobras," John Cooper said.

"And I will miss all of you." His eyes were brimming with tears. "Well, now we must be off. *¡Gauchos, adelante, pronto!*" he called, and the men on their horses galloped off to the west.

The next day, John Cooper, Andrew, Dorotéa, Adriana, Raoul, the two *vaqueros,* and Felipe walked down to the shore. There at the dock they saw a tall, three-masted frigate moving toward them from the south, the ship that would take them home after their perilous adventure.

Most of their clothing was in shreds, and it was imperative that Adriana and Dorotéa, at least, be properly clothed. John Cooper traded their last pistols for two hand-woven dresses for Adriana and Dorotéa and antelope-hide breeches for the men.

A dinghy had been put out from the frigate to pick up goods piled up on shore. John Cooper's party boarded the dinghy and went out to meet the captain. John Cooper himself was greatly relieved to hear the New England accents of the ship's crew.

The ship was named *The Narragansett,* and as John Cooper nimbly climbed the rope ladder to the quartermaster's deck in search of the captain, he uttered a sigh of happiness. The rescue mission had been completed. Soon they would be on their way home.

John Cooper spotted the captain, a short, stocky man with a thick black beard and heavy sideburns, chatting with a tall, solemn-faced first mate, and approached the two men. The captain turned to him and asked, "Can I be of service, sir?"

"Captain, I'd be obliged if you could take my party to New Orleans—"

"By the Eternal," the captain interrupted. "I hadn't expected to find a Yankee here in Maldonado!"

"That's what I am. My wife, her sister, my son, my father-in-law, two of my *vaqueros* from my Texas ranch, plus a *gaucho* comprise our party."

"Well, we've room enough. What's your name, mister?"

"John Cooper Baines."

"Glad to meet you, Mr. Baines." The captain thrust out his hand. "I'm Captain Henry Boswell, out of Boston. We're sailing in two hours—"

"I couldn't be happier. But there's just one matter that I have to talk to you about, Captain. I'm embarrassed for want of money, but I have something that you could hold in trust until I can redeem it in New Orleans." John Cooper lofted the amulet from his neck and held it out to Captain Boswell. "It was given to me by some local Indians. Unless I'm very much mistaken, that green stone's an emerald, which certainly ought to be worth passage for all of us."

"Damn my liver and eyes if that isn't an emerald, I'm not one to turn down good collateral. So long as I can show my owners a profit, I'll take anything that's salable, Mr. Baines," the captain chuckled. "I'll put it under lock and key in my strongbox in my cabin, I promise you that."

"Thank you, Captain. When we dock in New Orleans, I'll have my factor redeem it."

"Who's your factor, Mr. Baines?" the captain asked.

"A gentleman named Fabien Mallard, Captain Boswell."

"It's a small world! I've handled business for Mr. Mallard. If he's your factor, I don't even have to keep the amulet. Bring the rest of your party aboard, and we'll find comfortable quarters for them." The captain shook hands again with John Cooper. Then he gestured to his first mate. "Larson, see that Mr. Baines's people get aboard and settled into our available cabins. It really isn't a passenger ship, Mr. Baines, you see," he said as he turned back to John Cooper, "because mostly we handle cargo."

John Cooper hurried back to the rail, and he and

several sailors helped Dorotéa and Adriana climb onto the deck. He held his young wife in his arms and kissed her, murmuring, "It's all over now, *mi corazón.*"

"Yes, *mi esposo!*" Dorotéa breathed as she happily nestled against his chest, sighing with pleasure.

"You were a true *compañera,*" John Cooper murmured, "and no man could have surpassed you in loyalty and courage, in not complaining over the hardships we faced."

"That's sweet of you to say, my dearest one," Dorotéa whispered as she stroked his beard, which was growing out, the dye fading. "I think I like a full beard much better than that dreadful pointed thing, which reminds me of that detestable Rodrigo Baltenar. And for what you've done for my father, I shall never be able to repay you, except to do my best to make you happy."

"Your father is a fine man, and I was happy to do anything I could to help him. And now I think you and Adriana should get some rest. I just want to be sure that when we get back to Texas, you'll be in the best of health."

"Very well, my husband," she said docilely with a feigned meekness. And then, with a flash of her delicious sarcasm, she tugged at his beard as she freed herself from his embrace and whispered, "Don't forget that I'm not fragile, and if I had to, I could come right back here and save my father all over again and still bear you a good, healthy son, John Cooper Baines!"

He burst into a roar of delighted laughter, and Captain Boswell and the first mate turned, startled by the unexpected boisterousness. But when both saw the loving look beautiful Dorotéa gave him, they eyed each other knowingly, then chuckled and went about their duties preparing for departure.

* * *

A day after *The Narragansett* had raised anchor, buffeting rain slashed down upon the frigate. The ship bucked and pitched, but the sturdy keel and the ability of the helmsman kept it well on course into the blue-gray waters of the Atlantic Ocean.

The *vaqueros* and Felipe, though they would not admit it, were seasick. Each stiffly and proudly isolated himself in his quarters and did not come out on deck for two days, until at last the sailing no longer made them queasy. John Cooper and Raoul tactfully refrained from noticing the absence of these three stalwart men.

Andrew managed to overcome the *mal de mer*. There was good reason for this, for when the storm was at its height and he could no longer bear the turning and tossing and pitching and rolling, he closed his eyelids tightly, clenched his fists, and summoned up the image of smiling, laughing, Adriana, with her dark eyes and her infectious smile. The permeation of delight swept through him and kept him from being overcome by mortal pangs of seasickness.

Within two days, the sky and the sea were again serene. John Cooper stood on the deck with Dorotéa, his arm around her waist, his right hand holding both of hers as they contentedly watched the blue-green ocean waters cut by the prow. And Raoul Maldones recovered his full strength and healthy color, the sun having bronzed his features. He stood at the rail, looking forward to the new life and home that he was determined to embrace with all his heart and soul. It mattered nothing to give up his Argentinian possessions, for even now that Porfirio Ramos was dead and his tool, Rodrigo Baltenar, along with him, there would be other greedy materialists to replace them. Having lived long in Argentina, he knew only too well that the years ahead would be filled with turmoil and war.

Meanwhile, Felipe and Jaime and Bartoloméo, at the other end of the frigate, commented on the spectacular dawns and sunsets on the ocean, on the gulls flying, on the dolphins' friendly manner, as if escorting *The Narragansett* on her homeward journey. And Felipe thought that he was a most fortunate man, for he would soon see his Luz and his boys. He dwelled upon the happy knowledge that he had done all he could to free the man who had been like a kindly foster parent to him when he had lived in Argentina and had been a *gaucho* of the *pampas*.

Thirty-two

The personable young French doctor, André Malmorain, had remained all these weeks on the Double H Ranch, attending the ailing Don Diego. André had entered into a dedicated friendship with the old *hidalgo* and the valiant Doña Inez. Moreover, the life on an isolated frontier commune had been a refreshing contrast to his New Orleans practice. Everyone liked the young doctor for his friendly manner and genuine interest in ranch life. Consequently, after he had visited Don Diego each day, he went outside to talk to the *trabajadores* and the *vaqueros*. On several occasions, he had been called to treat injuries in the absence of the ranch's doctor, Dr. Pablo Aguirrez, who was away visiting Mexico City with his family.

When one of the *vaqueros* had fallen off a wild

mustang while trying to break it in and suffered a badly
sprained ankle, Dr. Malmorain had utilized a splint.
The *vaquero* was able to ride again and round up the stray
calves and steers within two weeks.

Dr. Malmorain had also attended the birth of a baby
girl of one of the *criadas* who had married a *vaquero*, and
he treated the community's children for their various
ailments.

As December went by, the young doctor became
gravely concerned over Don Diego's lagging vitality. It
was not that the elderly patient did not have the will to
live—far from it, for each day he hoped that a courier
would ride into the ranch with word that John Cooper and
Dorotéa were safely home. But the shock to the old *hidalgo*'s
nervous system that the concussion had caused, compli-
cated by his advanced age, hampered his total convalescence.

Two nights before Christmas, Doña Inez voiced her
concern that Don Diego might not recover. "I am really
worried, Dr. Malmorain, because Don Diego seems to
have no strength left. He eats enough, he sleeps well, but
his eyes are dull and his skin seems paler than before. Tell
me honestly, Dr. Malmorain, will my husband recover
from all this?"

The physician chose his words carefully so as not to
cause her anguish or give her false hope. "Doña Inez,
your husband has not made the progress I had hoped for.
Still, it is difficult for an old man to regain his strength
after so taxing an experience. He is doing everything he
should; he is eating well, sleeping, not getting excited, and
heaven knows how thoughtfully you've cared for him."

"Because I love him so, Dr. Malmorain," Doña Inez
said in a voice choking with tears.

"I understand. Doña Inez, God has been kind to your
husband in giving you to him as his wife."

Such unexpected gentleness, such heartwarming words,
broke down her reserve. She turned away, covering her

face with her hands, and her shoulders shook with stifled
sobs until at last she regained control. Then, turning back
to him, she said, "I am the one who is fortunate, whose
life was dreary and alone until he showed that he needed
me. In the years we have had together I have been blessed
among women. Can you wonder, then, that I am so deeply
concerned over his lack of progress? Tell me the truth, Dr.
Malmorain." Doña Inez put a hand on the French physician's wrist, her beautiful eyes intently staring into his
handsome face.

"I do not think he will recover, but he may live for
many months. I am being frank with you, Doña Inez,
because you have demanded it. It is best that you prepare
in the event that he is taken from us."

"Oh, *Señor Dios*, be merciful!" Doña Inez cried out
hysterically, clasping her hands as if in prayer and lifting
them toward the sky.

The young physician turned away so as not to intrude
upon her private anguish. But then suddenly she collected
herself and said in an almost level voice, "I respect you
for your honesty, *señor médico*. One must be realistic. It
will break my heart if he dies, but he has lived long
enough to see his name cleared and to have honor from his
native country. I think he waits now for his *yerno*, John
Cooper, and for John Cooper's sweet new wife."

"Yes," he said sympathetically. "I have learned that
on this ranch there are love and a strength that ally all
members of a family into a compassionate whole. And I
promise you that I will give your husband every care
within my power, because he is such a fine, honorable
man, and I value him as a friend."

There were tears in Doña Inez's eyes as she took his
hands, kissed them, and murmured, "I am grateful to *el
Señor Dios* that He saw fit to send you to care for my
husband. I could ask for no one to whom I would entrust
his life as I do to you. I know that if he has any hope of

escaping death, it will be because of your caring and skill.
I shall go to the chapel and pray that *el Señor Dios* will
grant him time enough until his *yerno* returns.''

Margarita Gaige and the old prospector Jeremy returned to the Double H Ranch just before Christmas with
gifts for everyone, and there was a warm welcome for
them both. Miguel and his Bess arranged a *fiesta* in their
honor, and there were musicians who played in the
courtyard, as the plump, radiant woman whom everyone
had known as Tía Margarita sat beside her white-haired
husband, holding his hand under the table, as if they had
just fallen in love.

She wore a red silk dress, and there was a pearl
necklace around her throat, while Jeremy, quite self-
conscious about his appearance, sat in a handsomely tai-
lored waistcoat with a flowery cravat, and new shoes,
which, he complained to his genial wife, hurt his feet; he
squirmed when he saw Miguel and some of the *vaqueros*
grin and wink at him.

They had had their honeymoon in San Antonio, and
he had opened a bank account there, putting into the vault
hundreds of pounds of pure gold ore, a fortune. He and
Tía Margarita would never want for anything. And yet,
when he was asked to make a toast, he cleared his throat
several times, gazed fondly down at his wife, and then in
his reedy voice declared, ''Folks, whatever luck I've had, it
don't make me any different. I like it here. That's why we
both came back. Oh sure, we could live stylish as all
get-out, but if you'll have us around, we'd like to stay
where we have our friends 'n where I found my sweet
wife.'' And then, amid cheers, he leaned down and re-
soundingly kissed Margarita on the cheek. Overcome with
emotion at this speech, she hugged him to her, covering
his face with kisses. The feasters burst into merry laughter

that did not poke fun but warmly paid tribute to these two lovable people who, in their twilight years, had merged their lives to find companionship and happiness.

The *Bedford Maid* docked in the harbor of New Orleans on December 16, 1826, and its affable captain arranged for a stevedore to take Señora Josefa, Paquita, and María to a carriage and thence to the house of Fabien Mallard. His gracious wife, Hortense, received them with a warm welcome. The *dueña* explained that John Cooper had instructed her to bring the children to the Mallards' house and to wait there for him for three weeks.

"I'm sure they'll be here soon," Hortense told the worried *dueña*. "Meanwhile, you'll be our guests of honor. You're just in time for Christmas. Since we have no children, Fabien and I will enjoy having these sweet girls here for the holidays. We'll have a Christmas tree and many presents for them—and for you, as well, Madame Josefa."

"You are too kind. Forgive me, but I am so worried about my Dorotéa and Adriana—" the *dueña* anxiously began.

Hortense nodded knowingly as she touched the *dueña*'s shoulder in a reassuring gesture. "God looks after those who are just and courageous. Have no fear, Madame Josefa. And now, let me have our majordomo show you to your rooms, and you will have a long *siesta*—you see, I know a word of Spanish already! Later we shall have a wonderful supper, and there will be special treats for these delightful little girls." She bent down, took María and Paquita in turn into her arms, and kissed them. Señora Josefa beamed proudly as the tired little ones hugged and kissed Fabien Mallard's handsome wife.

The *Narragansett* dropped anchor at the port of New Orleans seventeen days after Señora Josefa had arrived at the Mallard residence.

John Cooper and his party had enjoyed their holidays aboard the three-masted frigate, for its captain had done his best to provide a warm, familylike atmosphere. The ship's cook had made plum duff pudding and baked a cake with spices and raisins, and since the frigate had made a stop just beyond the Brazilian coast at a small port where he was on friendly terms with the authorities, he had been able to procure a dozen suckling pigs for the holiday feast.

As the frigate's gangplank was lowered at the port of New Orleans, John Cooper hooted with joy to see Fabien and Hortense standing at the dock, while Raoul almost simultaneously exclaimed, "Señora Josefa, *y mis niñas*, Paquita and María!" for the *dueña* and the two youngest Maldones daughters, dressed in their very best, stood there, straining for a sight of the *hacendado*.

María and Paquita hurried up first to their father, then to Adriana and Dorotéa, crying for joy and embracing them while John Cooper shook hands with his factor and the latter's handsome wife and thanked him. "I can't imagine how you knew we would be on this ship, M'sieu Mallard," John Cooper chuckled.

"The fact is, M'sieu Baines, we've been meeting every ship from South America since Madame Josefa and the girls came. Hortense and I were certain that you'd make it safely back. And you've also brought back M'sieu Maldones! It will be a great pleasure for me to meet him in person, for we've been faithful correspondents for some years, as you know. That's how all this began, isn't it?"

"Yes," John Cooper gravely answered, nodding almost reminiscently. "That letter you sent me, telling me he was in the market for some good Texas longhorns and some of my palominos, changed my life. We're friends, m'sieu, always will be, even if we never did any further business together. I can't tell you how much you've helped me. But now I'm afraid I'm going to have to ask you a favor."

"Ask away!"

"I used up what cash I had on hand in Argentina, and I persuaded Henry Boswell, the ship's captain, to give us passage by saying that you were my factor and would lend me enough to pay the passage."

"Of course. I have some news for you, too, in connection with money, M'sieu Baines. But first, let me settle with the captain. I know Boswell; there'll be no problem." The factor made his way toward the gangplank and stood talking with the captain of *The Narragansett*.

Presently, he returned to the dock and said to John Cooper, "I've arranged to give Boswell a draft tomorrow. However, if you'd asked me this the day after you sailed, I don't think I could have done it."

"What do you mean by that, M'sieu Mallard?" John Cooper was mystified.

"Step over here. I want to speak with you privately," Fabien murmured.

They walked down the dock about a hundred feet away, and then Fabien turned to John Cooper. "As you know, Don Diego and Doña Inez were our guests, and we took them to a restaurant the evening you sailed."

"What happened, M'sieu Mallard?"

"Well, to make a long story short, someone had planted some gunpowder just outside the restaurant, and just as we were ready to return to my house, the powder exploded. Don Diego was affected very badly and had to stay at our place under a doctor's care until he was fit for travel back to your ranch."

"My father-in-law is seriously ill, then?"

"He was not very well when he left here, though he is under the excellent care of a young doctor, André Malmorain. I cannot guess what his condition is now, but let me get to the other part of this, which ties in with the explosion. It was part of a diversion, you see, to draw the civil guard away from M'sieu Beaubien's bank, where you had your silver bars and I my working capital. The back door was forced, all the silver bars were taken, plus an incredible amount of cash and jewelry. I was left virtually penniless—at least, so far as immediate capital was concerned.''

"My God! Do you mean—? All the ingots?''

Fabien nodded solemnly. "There's no doubt that quite a few people took part in the robbery, but the only one that we can assume was involved for certain was a man by the name of DuPlessis, a minor officer who was bypassed for promotion. The remains of his body were found a few weeks ago, fished out of the river. He was identified by some papers found in his coat. M'sieu Beaubien thinks that either he was forced to aid the thieves or joined them to get revenge for not obtaining the post he wanted. In any event, it is believed he had been killed with a knife and thrown into the river after the robbery.''

"But this is incredible!'' John Cooper gasped. "Thank God my ranch is thriving and my family and my workers will not be in want. But that silver was meant for the poor of Taos and the Jicarilla Apache. Some of it I intended as a legacy for my children and for improvements on the Double H Ranch, money for the families of the loyal *vaqueros* and *trabajadores*. Is there any clue yet as to who besides DuPlessis could have planned this theft?''

"No. But whoever the conspirator was, he's become extraordinarily wealthy in a short period of time.'' Fabien shook his head and sighed. "Somewhere there's bound to be a slip, some random bit of information haphazardly come by or boastfully dropped, perhaps in a tavern or the like—so naturally I'm hopeful that our money will be restored along with your silver. I may tell you, the one piece of good news I can give you about Don Diego is this, for it concerns me. A courier came to me recently from the Double H Ranch to say that a nobleman had come in search of Don Diego, all the way from Madrid.

Don Diego's name was cleared by the junta, and he has been awarded the Order of St. James of Compostella. He also will receive monetary compensation for his confiscated property and the years of his banishment. Indeed, the first installment of this money has already arrived from Spain, and Doña Inez has given it to me so I could continue my business."

"Well, that's wonderful news about Don Diego. I knew he was never guilty of treason." John Cooper drew closer to Fabien and, glancing around to make sure that no one overheard, declared, "I'm going to find the robbers. I swear it. One day, with your help, M'sieu Mallard, I mean to recover that silver so that it may be shared with those who deserve it. And, in the process, God willing, I'll recover what you've lost, as well."

"I could not ask for a better friend than you, M'sieu Baines," Fabien earnestly said. "I pledge to give you every assistance in tracking down the cunning thief." He offered his hand, John Cooper shook it, and the two men exchanged a look of steadfast friendship and purposeful dedication.

That night, the Texans and Argentinians were the guests of Hortense and Fabien Mallard. The supper was served with the utmost thoughtfulness and elegance. María and Paquita were more talkative than was their wont, overjoyed at the reunion with their father, Adriana, and Dorotéa. And Señora Josefa relaxed her vigilance and permitted herself an indulgent smile when either of them became too noisy at the table. No one seemed to mind. The Mallards laughed joyously, and John Cooper felt a warm deepening of affection for the factor and his wife.

"Do you know, M'sieu Maldones," Hortense suddenly said as she sipped her coffee, "I think it would be wonderful if you and your daughters remained in New Orleans with us for a few weeks, until you regain your full strength."

"I was about to suggest that myself," Fabien said. "We've corresponded for some years and done business together, but now that we have you here at our table, we're enchanted."

"Your sincerity is greatly appreciated," Raoul said.

"Not a bit of it!" Hortense gaily went on. "M'sieu Maldones, you might consider sending Adriana, María, and Paquita to one of our fine schools. The girls are so wonderfully bright, and the Ursuline Convent School is the very best of schools. M'sieu Baines's mother-in-law, Doña Inez, wrote me to say they will be sending young Francesca there next year. Since we are all of the Catholic faith, it would be highly appropriate if your girls attend, too."

"Do you know, Señora Mallard," Raoul said, "I've had that notion myself. On the *pampas,* there are no schools. I acknowledge here and now before everyone my indebtedness to Señora Josefa for what she has done with my girls. They are ladies, courageous and yet proper and good. But now, I should like to visit this convent school and see whether it would be advantageous for my daughters. They will need that final polish, which will make them poised and charming and eligible for marriage to the right men."

At this, Adriana glanced at Andrew, who tried not to look at her, but could not help stealing a glance. Adriana's father saw this interplay and, hugely pleased with the nuances, remarked, "Of course, in Adriana's case, I think she has already chosen her *novio!* And let me say again in the presence of all these gracious witnesses that I, as a father, totally approve. Mind you, the young Señor Baines and my daughter are still too young to effect a marriage, but in a few years let us see what transpires. But I shall give my blessing in advance."

There was applause from everyone at the table, and both Andrew and Adriana, finding themselves the center of all this attention, turned a furious red and preoccupied themselves with the remnants of a superb dessert that Antoine himself had prepared in the kitchen, a *bombe surprise*.

On this last Sunday of December, Christophe Carrière was enjoying a quiet supper for two in the elegant four-story house on the rue de Carondelet, at the center of the fashionable quarter of New Orleans. He was in high spirits, as well he might be. He had purchased the house only the past Thursday, paying cash for it, as part of a draft he had brought from the leading Amsterdam bank. He had returned to New Orleans on Monday, having made substantial deposits in banks in Paris, Amsterdam, and London, monies that he had exchanged for the bank notes stolen from the vaults of La Banque de la Nouvelle Orléans. As for the jewels, he had converted these into usable funds by selling them at half their value to an unscrupulous Parisian jeweler. Disposing of the loot quickly, he reasoned, and returning to New Orleans wealthier than he had dreamed more than made up for not taking a longer time to sell the jewels at their real value. There were also all those silver ingots buried in front of his abandoned, isolated plantation house. And, upon his return to New Orleans, he had deposited some thirty thousand dollars in two sizable, flourishing banks whose officers did not know him personally.

He had spent the previous morning most profitably in hiring a factor, a certain Étienne Remontrier, a Creole like himself, who had made a fortune for his clients through land speculation. Remontrier had bought up many plots of property that had been either abandoned or fallen to the city through delinquent taxes, had kept them for a year while New Orleans began to attract increasing numbers of settlers, and then sold them at enormous profits.

He had learned that Joseph de Courvent, Madeleine's father and the man who successfully had squelched any hopes Carrière had of marrying the lovely girl, had suf-

fered great financial difficulties after the bank robbery—
which was no wonder, since Carrière had stolen the contents
of de Courvent's bank deposit box. Carrière had instructed
Remontrier to purchase the fine house in which Madeleine
and her father lived with their retinue of servants.

Late the previous afternoon, his new factor had
reported, "I have learned from the city tax records that
Joseph de Courvent is in arrears by some eight thousand
dollars. He does not have the money, and his note to the
bank falls due within two weeks."

To this, Carrière had retorted, "Follow the situation
and strike when the time is right. I wish to own that
property and to turn M'sieu de Courvent out into the
street. This will be my revenge for his slighting me in the
past." And, to ensure the factor's interest in the project,
the handsome Creole had added, "If you accomplish this,
Remontrier, I will pay you a bonus of two thousand dollars.
But let this be strictly *entre nous, compris?*"

Now that he was rich and all-powerful, Christophe
Carrière would soon settle accounts with that condescend-
ing bitch Madeleine. He had already taken the first step
toward revenge, in the form of a spectacular young woman,
Amy Daroudier, who was twenty-five, the illegitimate
daughter of a count and his seamstress mistress. Carrière
had met her the very first day out of Le Havre, standing at
the rail watching the receding shore of the French port,
with a soulful expression on her piquantly lovely face. She
was nearly five feet eight inches in height, with the most
ravishingly sleek figure and a most exotic face that roused
his carnal ardour. Black-haired, green-eyed, with a small
but lasciviously ripe mouth, she had comported herself
with a regal air, and he had observed all this, to his
delectation.

Two nights later, after he had invited her to his table
to share supper with him and ordered lavish wines and
cordials, they had become lovers. And since it suited his

fancy to have a *petite maîtresse,* he had suavely proposed
to her that she come live with him. Finding him virile and
amusing, and sensing that he was enormously wealthy,
Amy had quickly consented to this arrangement.

He stood now in his robe and sandals, in the bedroom
of the large house he had just purchased, puffing at a fine
Havana cigar, while in his left hand he held a beaker of
aged brandy. He studied Amy as she lay upon the four-
postered, canopied bed, naked except for long, white-silk
stockings held up on her sleek long legs with red rosettes,
and a purple silk blouse whose hem descended to her
navel. Pillowing her head in her arms, she enticingly
arched up one knee, a languidly sensual smile curving her
moist, red mouth.

But as he stared at her, it was not Amy that he saw,
despite her enticing and flamboyant near-nudity. Instead, it
was Madeleine de Courvent. It was Madeleine who plagued
his imagination, clad in only her shift, her wrists bound
with a leather thong behind her back, her long, dark-brown
hair streaming almost down to her hips, her face tear
stained, and her dark-brown eyes poignantly entreating him
for mercy. He grinned sardonically, and Amy petulantly
called to him, *"Mon amour,* why do you look at me like
that?"

"I am not thinking about you, *ma belle,* be sure of
that," Carrière retorted. He unbelted his robe and let it fall
to the floor. He stood naked, wiry, muscular, a patch of
gray at the center above his forehead standing out from the
jet-black gloss of his hair, and the trim little Vandyke
beard making him look like a satanic satyr. He finished his
brandy, tossed the beaker into the fireplace, took a last
puff at his cigar, and crushed it out in a silver ashtray. He
glanced down at his right hand, observing the gold ring
with its enormous onyx placed upon his long, artistically
tapering right forefinger. Then at last he drawled, "Amy,
ma belle poule, I was only thinking that one day you may

help me pay back a certain mademoiselle who gives herself airs, like a princess, but to my mind and my taste, *ma chérie,* you are far more satisfying.''

He reveled in his anticipation of the future. Now it did not matter one whit what the rest of New Orleans thought of him, not with such a fortune at his command. He would see to it that all his enemies were paid back, and he would save Madeleine de Courvent for the very last.

Thirty-three

Two days after their arrival in New Orleans, John Cooper, Dorotéa, Andrew, the two *vaqueros,* and Felipe said farewell to the Mallards, Raoul, Adriana, her sisters, and Señora Josefa. Fabien provided them with horses, and John Cooper handed him the amulet. ''I wish you to sell the emerald for as high a price as you can and take out of it the money you advanced for passage, the cost of these horses, and your commission. If there is a balance, let it be put into the bank in my name, and we shall continue to do business as we've done before.''

''I will do exactly as you wish,'' the factor said. ''An emerald like this, raw and uncut, should bring at least eight to ten thousand dollars. I have a friend who occasionally travels to Amsterdam, where, as you know, there are many jewelers and diamond merchants, and I am sure that I can sell it there for perhaps even more on the exchange.''

"Fine. It is a lucky omen, a talisman, and it saved our lives. And now, good friend, I want to get back to Don Diego and tell him that all is well. God bless you and your wife, Fabien!''

Some two weeks later, riding hard and with great anticipation, John Cooper and his beautiful Dorotéa, leading the little troop of riders, came within sight of the Double H Ranch. John Cooper reined in his horse and turned to beckon to Felipe. *"Amigo,"* he said, "as I promised, you're back to see your Luz and the boys.'' Then he called to his two faithful *vaqueros,* "Jaime, Bartoloméo, we're home! Now let's ride so that we can get there the sooner!''

It was Miguel who first saw the horseback riders approaching. He squinted and, waving his *sombrero,* let out a joyous cry, *"El Halcón* returns to us, *amigos!* Let us go meet him! To your horses, *hombres!''*

Carlos, who was near the corral with young Charles Baines, stopped dead in his tracks as he heard Miguel's cry and, his eyes brightening, exclaimed to Charles, "Your father's here. They've all come back safely! He's done it, *por Dios!* Let's go meet him!''

Young Charles quickly mounted a gelding that Miguel had in reserve for him while Carlos mounted the palomino that John Cooper had presented him the previous Christmas. And both of them rode out to greet the six riders, with Yankee following, barking furiously.

Carlos raced ahead of young Charles and then wheeled his horse to ride alongside John Cooper. He could see from his brother-in-law's beaming face that his mission had been a success, and he leaned across to slap John Cooper soundly on the back. "I've prayed every day that you'd come back safely to us, John Cooper. And there's wonderful news: Not only has my father's honor been restored, but I've a daughter by Teresa!''

"Congratulations! And Don Diego?"

Carlos's face shadowed, and he shook his head. "My father is dying, John Cooper."

"Oh, no!"

"Alas, it's the truth. I think he's forced himself to live by will alone until you returned. Every day, he keeps asking for you, asking when you and your sweet Dorotéa will come back.'' Carlos sighed and looked away. Then, drawing a deep breath, he added, "Let us go to my father as quickly as we can. I'll have Miguel see to the comfort of those with you. Dorotéa, I'm so happy to see you back! You rescued your father?"

"He's in New Orleans, Carlos, with my three sisters until he establishes the girls in school. May I congratulate you on the wonderful news of the birth of your daughter!''

"You have a kindness in your heart that shines like the light in your eyes, Dorotéa," Carlos said in a choked voice. "Come, John Cooper, now let's go right to my father. It's been a trying time, and yet there's been happiness too, knowing that at last he's had justice in Spain."

"I know. My factor in New Orleans told me how this nobleman had come all the way from Madrid to Taos in search of Don Diego," John Cooper interjected.

"Yes, and you shall meet him, for he is still here as our guest, as is Doña Elena, who came with us from Taos. She and this Marqués de Viñada seem to have taken to each other, John Cooper. I wouldn't be surprised if the marqués decides to court her. And, oh, yes, the courier from Taos who rode with me back there, he is also our guest, and he wants to remain here. And there's something else I want to talk to you about—very quickly. When I went to Taos to escort the nobleman, I met with Epanone and Lortaldo, who had been married in both a Jicarilla and a Pueblo ceremony. I found that Epanone's fine young *esposo* wants to be a doctor. And he has come here to the *Hacienda del Halcón,* perhaps to go back to New Orleans with Dr. Malmorain and study under him. And there is other news, which I learned from Miguel. Jim Bowie was here, and he and Miguel arranged for some of our *vaqueros* to go to work as Texas Rangers. Our Texans who live on the ranch will go, too, though they have been waiting for you to return, until everything here has quieted down and returned to normal. In the place of our men, new settlers will come to the ranch to live. . . . But I talk too much, and here's Charles. . . .''

John Cooper halted his horse long enough to embrace his younger son, who cried out of sheer joy to see his father, forgetting that he wished to be quite as mature as Andrew. But this time, his older brother, having learned compassion from his arduous adventure in another land, did not mock him.

Miguel and a dozen *vaqueros* by now had ridden up to the six arrivals, and Miguel snorted and blew his nose and pretended that there was dust in his nostrils as he vigorously shook John Cooper's hand and effusively welcomed Dorotéa back to her home.

"Dorotéa, *mi corazón,* come with me to Don Diego," John Cooper said to his lovely wife, and she nodded, her eyes blurred with tears at the thought that the kind, good, old man was soon to die and yet had wished to remain alive to see her.

John Cooper turned to his older son. "Andy, come in with us. Don Diego is dying, son. You've been courageous throughout our journey, and I know I don't have to sermonize you. It's going to be real sad to see your grandfather, but you're adult enough to go in there with Dorotéa and me."

Andrew could not speak, for such a compliment from his father, whom he revered, touched at the very core of his being.

Doña Inez was waiting at the door of the bedroom where Don Diego lay, and she held out her arms to Dorotéa, hugged her, weeping softly, and then turned to John Cooper. "You do not know how I have prayed that you would come back safely. You have heard that Spain has cleared the de Escobar name?"

"I heard that in New Orleans, my dearest Doña Inez," John Cooper said softly. "And I heard, too, of your generosity in sending that first payment from the junta to Fabien to relieve his financial stress. That was a beautiful gesture. I only wish that Don Diego had still many years ahead to see the birth and childhood of Dorotéa's child."

"He will know it in heaven, my sweet John Cooper." Doña Inez tried to stifle her sobs but could not. "Go to him. Every day, he asks me, 'Is *mi yerno* back yet? Is that rascal back from all his adventures? And I wish to see Dorotéa again, and you must pray doubly hard to bring them all back safely, my sweet Inez.' Yes, John Cooper, can you conceive of what grief I feel in my heart? He has given me all these wonderful years as a husband, the most considerate and tender companionship, love, and devotion— and the deepest sorrow to know that our days together are soon to end. Go to him, before I turn into a fountain of tears."

Overcome with emotion, Doña Inez went into the chapel, closed the door behind her, and sank down on her knees.

Don Diego lay back on his pillows, emaciated, but his eyes were burning in their sunken hollows. They widened now at the sight of John Cooper with his arm around Dorotéa, and Andrew just behind them. *"Mi yerno—mi yerno*—God has answered my prayers. Ah, *mi nieto* Andrew! I praise give unto Him Who has given me such wonderful friends and such a wonderful wife and you, *mi yerno*— And you, sweet Dorotéa, in whom I see my Catarina, and yet, you are you, and you will have a child by this good man who has done so much for my life—''

"Hush, *mi padre.*" Dorotéa sank down on her knees and stroked his cheek as she adjusted the blanket over him. "Yes, we have come back, and your prayers have helped us all. My father is safe in New Orleans, and he will come to us soon, after arranging for my sisters' schooling. And your *yerno,* my wonderful *esposo,* is the man who saved my father's life. I thank you for letting me be part of your family, Don Diego. I will never forget it, and in my prayers I have already sworn to the *Virgen Santísima* that I will give him love and tenderness and kindness all the days of his life.''

"God is good. Now at the end of my life He gives me joy such as I could not dream of having, even in my own home of Madrid. I am ready to die now, without grief or sorrow—no, do not cry for me, *mi hija*—'' for Dorotéa had put her hands over her face and turned away her head and was trying to stifle her sobs.

Andrew gulped and, remembering what his father had said about courage, tried to control his own tears as his father approached the other side of the bed and sank down on his knees. John Cooper took one of Don Diego's emaciated hands and said, "I will never forget you, your spirit will live in me and in the child that Dorotéa and I will have, and we will name him after you. And, when we see our child grow—for I know that *el Señor Dios* will give us a son—he will be you, valiant and honorable in all his days.''

"*Mi yerno, mi hijo,* how I love you. You do not know what it meant to me to learn that my king redeemed the honor of my family and of my father and of my father's father, but it is nothing when compared with this moment when we are all together. Please, call Inez to me. I do not wish to make her weep, for I have had a full, rich life, and I have had twice the joy that most men know in a lifetime. Call her, for I wish her to be with me when I tell all of you how proud I am to have had you come into my life and sustain me in my darkest hours—''

John Cooper wept like a child as he turned to the door and went in search of Doña Inez.

As he stepped into the hallway, she emerged from the chapel, her eyes swollen with weeping, and John Cooper went to her and put his arms around her shoulders and murmured, "He calls for you, sweet Doña Inez. Come, there is no sorrow in this death. It is blessed and beautiful. And he bequeaths to us his courage and his honor, which will sustain us all the days of our lives."

"That thought comforts me, John Cooper. How kind you are."

Don Diego tried to raise himself from his pillows as he saw Doña Inez come toward him.

"Oh, no, sweetheart. No, Diego, rest there. I come to you, my heart, my life!" she murmured in a constricted voice as she hurried to him. She eased him back upon the pillows, then knelt beside him, a hand on his shoulder, staring into his pale, contorted face. But his eyes burned brightly as if, with a supreme effort, he was summoning up the last iota of energy to be alive and to encompass all of them here within this room, whose four walls contained the very essence of his being and of his death and of his immortality of soul.

"Inez, Inez, I cannot die without telling you what you have meant to me, what joy you have brought to my life. And all these people who have come into our lives, sweet Inez, it was through you—for I know now that it was you who urged my *yerno* to take my willful Catarina and make a woman of her—and to give me such happiness in their lives together—and it was you, too, who kept me from brooding upon what I had lost in Spain—and now, thanks to your prayers, you see that *el Señor Dios* has wrought a miracle and given me back my honor and my good name. I cannot bear to see all of you weeping, no. I die happily, for I have achieved everything, more than any man has a right to expect. Your sister Dolores gave me Carlos and Catarina. You taught me love after I had thought there could be no more—all of you—oh, *Dios*, hear me now as I give my soul to Thee—look down upon all these people here with me and bless their lives, oh, glorious *Dios* of our fathers—I thank Thee for such kindness and such joy in summoning me to Thee—I thank—''

His breath stopped short, he tried again to raise himself from the pillows, and then he sank back, his eyes glazing, with a smile upon his lips, as if he had seen the angels beckon to him at that final moment.

They who had known the passing of the soul of a great man were silent in this room, and they turned to one another and wept. They knew that his spirit would be implanted within them all in the days to come, no matter what joys or tribulations would visit the *Hacienda del Halcón*.

Coming in Spring 1985 . . .

A SAGA OF THE SOUTHWEST: BOOK VII

QUEST OF THE HAWK

By Leigh Franklin James

The thrilling saga continues . . . with John Cooper Baines summoned to an eerie mountaintop meeting with the mystical shaman of the Jicarilla Apache. The legendary Texan is told of another fortune in silver in a lost New Mexican silver mine, and with his Indian blood brothers, John Cooper embarks on a daring quest for treasure. But there are others who covet the silver, including the infamous Mexican general Santa Anna, and John Cooper must fight bands of savage Indians and rescue his beautiful Argentinian wife before the silver is safe and peace returns to the great Double H Ranch.

Meanwhile in New Orleans, the suave Creole bank robber, Christophe Carrière, lives a life of luxury, taking his revenge on the lovely young woman who once spurned him by making her his prisoner. Carrière, too, will have to confront the intrepid John Cooper Baines, in a ferocious hand-to-hand fight in the swampy, snake-infested bayous of Louisiana.

Read QUEST OF THE HAWK, coming in Spring 1985, from Bantam Books.

★ WAGONS WEST ★

A series of unforgettable books that trace the lives of a dauntless band of pioneering men, women, and children as they brave the hazards of an untamed land in their trek across America. This legendary caravan of people forge a new link in the wilderness. They are Americans from the North and the South, alongside immigrants, Blacks, and Indians, who wage fierce daily battles for survival on this uncompromising journey—each to their private destinies as they fulfill their greatest dreams.

☐	24408	**INDEPENDENCE!**	$3.95
☐	24651	**NEBRASKA!**	$3.95
☐	24229	**WYOMING!**	$3.95
☐	24088	**OREGON!**	$3.95
☐	23168	**TEXAS!**	$3.50
☐	24655	**CALIFORNIA!**	$3.95
☐	24694	**COLORADO!**	$3.95
☐	20174	**NEVADA!**	$3.50
☐	20919	**WASHINGTON!**	$3.50
☐	22925	**MONTANA!**	$3.95
☐	23572	**DAKOTA!**	$3.95
☐	23921	**UTAH!**	$3.95
☐	24256	**IDAHO!**	$3.95

Prices and availability subject to change without notice.

Buy them at your local bookstore or use this handy coupon:

Bantam Books, Inc., Dept. LE, 414 East Golf Road, Des Plaines, Ill. 60016

Please send me the books I have checked above. I am enclosing $_____ (please add $1.25 to cover postage and handling). Send check or money order—no cash or C.O.D.'s please.

Mr/Mrs/Miss _____

Address _____

City _____ State/Zip _____

LE—8/84

Please allow four to six weeks for delivery. This offer expires 2/85.